# IMMUNITY
# INDEX

# ALSO BY SUE BURKE

*Semiosis*
*Interference*

# SUE BURKE

# IMMUNITY INDEX

**TOR**

A TOM DOHERTY ASSOCIATES BOOK
NEW YORK

This is a work of fiction. All of the characters, organizations, and events portrayed in this novel are either products of the author's imagination or are used fictitiously.

IMMUNITY INDEX

A Tor Book
Published by Tom Doherty Associates
120 Broadway
New York, NY 10271

www.tor-forge.com

Tor® is a registered trademark of Macmillan Publishing Group, LLC.

The Library of Congress Cataloging-in-Publication Data is available upon request.

ISBN 978-1-250-31787-2 (hardcover)
ISBN 978-1-250-31786-5 (ebook)

Our books may be purchased in bulk for promotional, educational, or business use. Please contact your local bookseller or the Macmillan Corporate and Premium Sales Department at 1-800-221-7945, extension 5442, or by email at MacmillanSpecialMarkets@macmillan.com.

First Edition: May 2021

Printed in the United States of America

0  9  8  7  6  5  4  3  2  1

*To Mike.*
*You're in here.*

Yo soy yo y mi circunstancia, y si no la salvo a ella no me salvo yo.

*I am myself and my circumstance, and if I do not save it, I do not save myself.*

—José Ortega y Gasset

# IMMUNITY
# INDEX

CHAPTER
1

Avril heard chanting ahead, coming from around the corner.

"All equal—equal all!" voices chorused to a drumbeat and echoed off the skyscrapers in downtown Chicago.

She hesitated, turned, and began walking the other way. Chanting meant a protest, and she couldn't risk it, even though she knew exactly what they meant. For a moment—just a moment—she considered joining them. American citizens had been reclassified: some first-class, some second-class, and some people stripped of their citizenship entirely. She believed in equality, she argued for it with her friends, the protesters were right . . . but protests got violent too often. She'd come downtown to meet a friend on a sunny August morning, to visit an art museum and have a nice lunch before they went their separate ways to start college, nothing more.

She kept walking and she hated herself. Any violence wouldn't be the protesters' fault. That was what made protests dangerous. Still, it sounded like only a couple of dozen voices. Few people would dare to protest at all. Maybe such a small number wouldn't attract a counterprotest. Now a half block from the corner, she looked back. She could watch as they passed on the cross street and give a thumbs-up from a safe distance.

They came into view, a lot of them elderly. Who else would have free time to protest on a workday? Some carried signs displaying five words in script from the Declaration of Independence, and she knew which ones. A man dressed like a Revolutionary soldier played a snare drum: an old-fashioned protest for old-fashioned freedom. As she raised her hand to signal support, everyone started running in all directions. Without waiting to find out why, she turned and ran, too.

A buzz zoomed down the street behind her: a drone. Oh, no. She stopped and threw herself flat against a building, took a deep breath, and held it. Up and down the street, everyone froze. The drone hovered in the middle of the street, oversize blades whirling. Sometimes a counterprotest drone would be attracted to movement and attack, and the blades would slash like razors.

It spun slowly around as if observing, searching; then it banked and dove in her direction. She tried not to blink, tried to will her heart to stop pounding, her clothing to stop stirring in the breeze, her body to stop trembling. The drone slowed and hovered over the sidewalk in front of her at the same height as her throat, and after too many infinite seconds, it flew slowly up the block past protesters and passersby pressed against the walls like wide-eyed statues.

She heard a dog bark and didn't dare turn her head to look. The drone's buzz dropped in pitch as it swooped . . . and the dog's bark was cut short—a yelp, a howl, and people screamed. She squeezed her eyes tight and shuddered. Another howl, a small crash, more screams, but now no buzz. The drone must have been damaged, maybe destroyed. She let out her breath, finally, inhaled deeply . . . exhaled and inhaled again, listening to her breath instead of street sounds. One more breath to be sure she was steady, and she turned away from the uproar, opened her eyes, and did not look back as she walked.

Avril sent her friend a message canceling their day together. She needed to think—alone and hard.

A week later, she'd made a decision. She was about to join the mutiny. Would it be risky? Of course, but . . . that dog. She had arrived at the university only a few days earlier, a mere incoming freshman, but she could fight back in a lot of ways. Any minute now, the mutiny would begin—she felt sure. So she'd made a few comments at her dormitory's traditional welcoming party around the old firepit, and she'd met people who said they might have a connection. Now someone was going to join her for breakfast to talk specifics.

She left her dorm room and waited for an elevator, aware that people like her should be content with the state of the nation. Her parents could pay for a good education and an upper-end dorm. But unlike almost all of her smug, self-satisfied classmates back in high school, she knew better. And here at the university, did the other people in the hallways or on the elevators know better, too?

The dormitory's food court proved the need to mutiny all by itself. She walked up to the door, held her hand in front of a scanner for admission, and gritted her teeth.

*The Prez keeps me safe. Liberty must have limits. Hard times require hard choices.* Sure. Freedom was old-fashioned, and the world had changed. She'd heard that mantra too many times. But things just kept getting worse. Now only first-class citizens could attend universities or vote. Vote!

She joined the long line for the one food-service area open. The other vendors had lost their licenses, their shelves now bare, their counters unattended. The windows of the big ground-floor room still offered a view of the pretty little lake next to that edge of the campus. Bright artwork graced the walls. But gone was any sense, which must have once existed, of community, of the excitement of learning, of intellectual freedom. Even the decades-old once-stylish sleek hallways and architecture reminded her of something the past did better than the present.

"This food is punishment," she murmured to the young man ahead of her.

He glanced back at her and shrugged. "There's shortages."

"Not really, not this," she said. "There's plenty of food available all over. It's just not being served here anymore."

He shrugged again and turned away, unwilling to risk talking, but he knew—everyone had to know—a new chancellor had been forced on the University of Wisconsin to destroy it, especially the Madison campus. Step one involved needless, niggling austerity. Breakfast had become a choice of greasy overprocessed pastries, gritty cereal, some sort of fake milk, equally fake juice, and something that didn't even smell like coffee. And it was so easy to engineer quality synthesized coffee!

Step two, she imagined, aimed at closing down the campus with its forty-five thousand students and thus destroying the city of Madison, long a beacon of liberty. The Prez and his supporters couldn't even muster subtlety. They didn't have to anymore.

She selected an unnaturally bright yellow muffin and a lukewarm cup of brown liquid, and took her tray to an empty table. There were a lot of empty tables. Anyone with spending money ate off-campus, where good meals could easily be found—and which meant more money for the chancellor's fast-food cronies. Machine-generated pop music blared throughout the food court, another way to make eating unpleasant. The muffin tasted like artificially sweetened sand.

Where was her contact? She tried not to look around. *Be discreet, that's the first thing. Someone is always watching.* She took another bite of the dry, awful muffin. She stared at her phone display as if she were studying. Finally, someone approached. He seemed old enough to be a graduate student and wore a blue T-shirt with a logo for a game company. He carried a cup of the bilge coffee.

"Avril Stenmark? Hi, I'm Cal, a longtime resident here, and I want to be sure you're getting along all right. May I join you?"

She studied his face: brown, smiling, and innocent. Fake innocent. "Yes, please. Thanks. I'm doing pretty well, all things considered." She gestured at the remains of the food on her tray with disdain.

He nodded as he sat down. He wore a visor-screen, which would be telling him things as they spoke. "Yeah, it's not like it used to be. So, you're from near Chicago, your profile says."

"Kenilworth. It's a suburb."

"A nice one."

She caught his reproach: a wealthy suburb, so she'd never struggled. She was a white girl, very white—blond, in fact—who'd led a sheltered life. "I know what's going on," she said.

"Yeah?" He leaned forward, but he looked doubtful.

"Can we talk here?"

"That's why the music's so loud."

The dormitory management was part of the conspiracy, then. *Well, they could choose better songs.* No matter. She had decided exactly what to say, one example of outrage out of so many, this one especially relevant because she'd heard the mutiny would have a nationwide protest soon. He would know that she understood what she was getting into. She spoke quietly so the music would hide her words. "I know why protests are banned in a lot of places. They didn't do that to protect protesters, or I mean, that wasn't the first step."

He nodded, staring at her face. His visor might pick up signs of lying. Fine. She wasn't about to lie.

"A while back, protesters went to the Supreme Court to ask for protection from the police because they had the right to protest, they said. The right to free speech. And the court said that they had the right to protest, but so did antiprotesters, and if the two sides clashed, that was the price of freedom."

He nodded. He had to know this, even if most people had no idea about the history behind the bans.

"So if antiprotesters did something, like fire guns over the heads of crowds to scare people—which was the test case—and that made protesters panic and run, and if someone got hurt running away, that was the protesters' fault. The court said free speech doesn't guarantee the right to speak safely. But the ruling effectively abrogates that right. The dissenting opinion made the need for physical safety clear. If you can't speak safely, you can't speak. And the attacks got even worse after that."

She'd read the dissent. She'd learned a lot, including the meaning of the word *abrogate*. Cal seemed to be listening patiently.

She leaned forward, tapping the table for emphasis: "That's why some cities, even whole states, banned protests—to protect protesters.

That's just one of the cases that got us here, into the mess we have now where none of us are safe."

He showed no reaction. "Have you ever been to a protest?"

"Well, no, not exactly." But now she wanted to do that more than anything else. "I saw one just a week ago in Chicago, it went past in the street while I was there." She lowered her voice to a murmur, afraid she might shout. "Maybe you heard about it. A drone killed a dog."

He shifted in his chair. "Tell me about your family."

Why did that matter? "Um, my mother is a property manager, and my father is a lawyer."

"Mick Stenmark."

She nodded—and then she understood.

"Michael Stenmark," Cal said, reading something on his visor. "Assistant United States attorney for the Northern District of Illinois."

She could explain. Yes, he worked for the Justice Department, and she never understood why, since it made him so angry. "He's the one who told me about how wrong the Supreme Court was. He . . ." Her father hated the Prez and his constant theatrics, he hated everything the Prez and his cronies did in Washington, but that wasn't something she should say to just anyone—in fact, to hardly anyone. Maybe not even to this Cal guy. Who exactly was he? Could she trust him?

"You talk to him often?"

Even without a visor of her own, she read the suspicion in his face and suddenly knew how this conversation would end. She wasn't going to get to join the mutiny. She swallowed. *Be discreet.* She took a deep breath. She wouldn't throw a fit and attract attention.

It wouldn't matter that she didn't talk to her dad much because he was always busy. Her mom had been in touch every single day since she'd arrived on campus, and Mom talked to Dad, so it was like talking to him. He might tip off the authorities—anyway, that was what the mutiny would think.

But he wouldn't tip them off! It wasn't fair to reject her for her father's job. In fact, her father would help the mutiny if he could. Wouldn't he?

Probably. Or maybe not. No one could trust anyone anymore. Not even family.

She said quietly, firmly, hoping to save face, "We have to fight back." Her father had once told her to always act undefeated, no matter how badly things go—because you might see those people again, and you want them to think you never get handed a defeat, only a setback.

"I can't help you," Cal said.

*I'll show how strong I am. They'll see that I can help them.* But she said nothing, not trusting herself to remain discreet.

He stood up. "I'm glad we got to talk."

"Yeah." She tried to smile. Although she'd eaten a meager breakfast, she felt like she might throw up anyway. The music throbbed in her ears and on her temples.

"Hey," he said, "I know it's tough being new on campus. If I can help you out some other way, I'll be around. This is Dejope Hall, and we have our traditions, and one of them is watching out for each other." He was speaking loudly now. "I'm glad we had a chance to talk."

"Thanks." She wondered if he meant that or if he was just saying it for eavesdroppers.

He walked away. She stared at the sickly yellow crumbs on her tray. This was only a setback.

*      *      *

Berenike was about to break the law. She passed a man sitting on the downtown sidewalk who was obviously homeless, maybe even a noncitizen. As she did, she caught his eye—just briefly. That would be enough to tip him off. No one looked at the scruffy people sitting on the curb, their faces lined by living outdoors, with a worn, stuffed backpack that probably contained everything they owned.

Berenike took a couple more steps and dropped a piece of trash, a candy bar wrapper, and inside it was a little cash. Federal law outlawed donations to noncitizens, but the City of Milwaukee government objected to that and a lot of other federal and state actions, so it refused to enforce all the new laws. Still, cameras watched everyone everywhere, and even though the private companies hired for surveillance had lowballed their contracts and provided substandard service, they did carry out random, minimal spot checks. She didn't look back to see if he retrieved it, but most hungry people understood the ruse.

She wished she could give him more than a measly dollar. She wished she could also give to the other homeless people she passed as she walked through downtown. *Four more days of this nonsense.* That thought didn't improve her mood.

Her papa wanted to meet her for a late lunch after her shift was done at work. Fine. Late lunch for her was breakfast for him, and he'd suggested meeting at a pizza franchise he often mocked as "pizza putz." Fine, too, and convenient, just a few blocks away from her job. The food was okay. It would be even better if he paid, at least for his own meal. She had faint hope for that.

Instead, she tried to look forward to fake pepperoni and a few laughs. Papa was a funny guy. She turned at the corner around an old brick building and saw him, a skinny man who had taken to wearing a violet-colored tie at all times, sort of a trademark. He opened his arms to hug her.

"I've got great news," he said. "I'll be going to Iowa tomorrow for some live shows."

*This isn't great news.* "For how long?"

"Weekend shows. I'll be back Sunday night. You'll miss me?"

"Just come home safe." *That's not guaranteed, not the way you are.*

"I've got a title," he said. "'Finding the Food Line.' How's that?" His ongoing comedy series was called *Finding the Line.* Crossing the line meant charges of disorderly conduct, if not sedition or libel, and he tended to get much too close. That was what made him popular.

And if the mutiny won—a big *if*—and the government collapsed, his comedy series would collapse, too, because what would he make fun of? Actually, no, it might not. He still could make fun of the old government or even the new government—old-fashioned free speech would be reinstated—but without the danger of arrest. With unfettered hindsight, he might find even more to make fun of.

Instead of all that, she said, "They're letting you into Iowa?" Its farmland was isolated against crop contamination.

"As long as I don't step on anything green, what could go wrong? Maybe I can start a food fight."

"Maybe you can get beat up. Or go to jail." He might be in custody when things started to happen.

She was hungry and began walking toward the restaurant, not hiding her frown, as if he would notice.

"Yeah," he said, "I better not ask why rationing is for certain people. Imagine, two people come to a restaurant, but only the classier American gets to eat. Happens all the time. Why should the truth hurt?"

She knew why, and so did he. His grin said he would ask too much about it anyway.

She pushed open the restaurant's glass door. The air smelled of oregano, toasting cheese, and yeasty bread. NEVER FROZEN! a sign boasted, but the food wasn't made on-site, either. The decor in the green, white, and red of Italy's flag looked equally prefabricated.

"So, um, Nike, with everything I have to do for the trip," he murmured, as if it were an important secret, "I can't pick up this lunch."

She nodded and smiled thinly, expectations confirmed, and held up her hand to the scanner to pay. The prices weren't too bad, at least. Some corporations got price-controlled supplies, and besides, only the crust was what it seemed to be, wheat flour and yeast. The rest was artificially flavored . . . stuff. She chose tap water as her beverage to trim the bill further. He chose coffee with his meal—synthetic but still not cheap.

She knew she'd be eating bags of chips for dinner for the next two days, and she'd never lose weight unless she could afford good food. She collected her tray and ignored the lone human staffer tidying up after the robots. If she made eye contact, they'd have to smile at her per company policy, and she knew how that felt. Would the feeling propel them to mutiny, too?

As they ate, Papa recited a monologue for his show: "What if politics was like football? One team always has the home advantage because all the games are played at that team's home field. One team gets two balls and an anointed quarterback. Only one team has cleats. The referees wear the home-team colors. If the wrong team somehow wins, the game gets replayed. And one side always loses, even though it has lots more fans in the stands. Why can't football be played the old-fashioned way?"

That word, *old-fashioned*, might cross the line. Or maybe he knew, too, what was about to happen. He might know that its color would be purple, and that could explain the violet-colored ties. But she couldn't say that and breach the secret of the mutiny, although it probably wasn't a very well-kept secret. She found herself fidgeting, aware of what he wasn't saying, not that she wanted to hear it, wondering if he was in more danger than she'd thought.

"It's going to take some work, maybe 3D graphics," he admitted, briefly dropping his on-screen persona, who was unwary and slightly bewildered. "And I wanna find out if it's sedition to make fun of the losing side because then it shows that there are winners and losers and what the winners are like. The losers are only angry because they can't afford rising prices, right? So I could ask, how poor are they, in actual fact, compared to the winners?"

He thought out loud for a while about that, especially about the scarcity of actual facts, then about how even getting the real score for the game might cross the line, and why anyone bothered to play the game anyway. "We try and even if we win, we wind up losing bigger."

*Yeah, that's what I'm afraid of. If we fail at the mutiny, it's like a death sentence. How much will we have to do to at least earn a capital M from history, the Mutiny? We could be dead but not forgotten.*

She was eating the pizza crust, not wasting a precious crumb, when he finally said:

"I need you to know something, Berenike."

He was about to get serious. He'd used her full first name, all four syllables, *bear-eh-NEE-kay,* the ancient Greek form of Berenice, instead of the two-syllable nickname *NIGH-key.*

"I really loved your mother, I did. I love you, too. I love being with you. Her, it was just—we were two peas in a pod. You know that old saying? We were just like each other, like peas. We got on each other's nerves. And then we fought. But hey, you know that."

She nodded, although her parents had never seemed very much alike to her. "It's okay, Papa."

"I know you blame me."

"No, I don't." She blamed him for a lot, but not that. "I was glad when you said you wanted a divorce." Predictably, that announcement had triggered a vicious drama that ended with Momma's death. An accidental overdose? Momma did use drugs. But was it a bid for attention or a deliberate suicide? Berenike and Papa would never know, and uncertainty would weigh heavier than the truth. Momma would have liked that.

And besides all the drama, if Momma had been insured—if she'd had really good insurance—she would have gotten better care and might have survived.

"Look," he said, "I know this was hard on you, and she dragged you into this. She probably told you it was all my fault, that she gave birth to you and so you owed her. Stuff like that."

Berenike had been subjected to a lot of stuff, so much that she had recently splurged on an online counseling AI to learn some coping techniques. It told her to question and verify everything her parents had ever said or would say. Papa was wrong about one thing, though. "She didn't forget I was adopted." She had never let Berenike forget that for a minute, another thing, like being overweight or having a job "any cretin could do," that Momma thought she should feel guilty about.

He leaned back and stared at the menu on the restaurant wall. "You're . . . honey, that's . . . I know we always said that, but no, not exactly."

"Not exactly?" She set down the remaining bite of crust.

"No, and I never liked that she made me lie about it."

*What kind of lie?* She looked at him and waited as she tried to ratchet up her new coping techniques. This wasn't going to be good news.

He drummed his fingers on the tabletop's fake red wood. "Here's what happened. We couldn't have kids, so your mother's parents, because they really, really wanted to be grandparents, they decided to give us a child as a gift. They bought a fertilized egg from a clinic and paid for everything, and then they wanted to claim you as their child instead of ours, and there was this big fight. You've heard about the fight, just not the real reason why."

She'd assumed the fight was over her parents' drug use and poverty and their neglect of her. She tried to relax her shoulders.

After a long gulp of expensive fake coffee, he continued. "That's when we cut off all communications, and your momma was so mad that she didn't want to remember what they did, not one thing. So she began to say you were adopted, and I didn't want to argue because she was right about what shits her parents were. You gotta admit, adoption was a pretty believable story. You don't look like us at all."

No, she didn't, blond next to their dark hair, for starters. She took a slow breath. The air smelled of pizza, but the scent wasn't real, not at this putzy chain. It was just food-scented air freshener. Fake, the smell. Fake, her birth story. She'd never been able to trust her parents. This was a big—betrayal? Yes, yet another one. How surprised should she be, really?

*Stay calm. Drink some water.* That was what the AI counselor would have said.

"You can check your birth certificate," he said. "I know, it sounds stupid now."

"So . . . it was one of those donor eggs?"

"I don't know," Papa said. "Her parents set up everything."

"So maybe it was like, when a couple has leftover eggs after a fertility treatment, they donate them." *I might be a leftover.*

"Yeah, maybe. Hey, then there'd be someone exactly like you. You'd be like sisters, secret sisters." His tone of voice shifted: free-associating for a monologue. "You gotta find her. We can make a video. Two sisters meet for the first time. And you get into a fight, not really, it would be in the script, but it would be right up to the line. People would love it."

Berenike didn't think she'd love it. She wasn't loving much about this lunch, either.

As he chattered on about squabbling families, she tried to breathe slow and deep and to examine her feelings like the AI had taught her. This news wouldn't change things much. In fact, her parents had told her a lot that hadn't turned out to be true. And she had never known exactly why they were estranged from Momma's parents, only how viciously. Now she did. Maybe.

Perhaps Momma hadn't picked her up at an adoption agency, she'd given birth to her. But Momma hadn't provided the genetic material. Neither had Papa.

Maybe she did have an in vitro sister, and that girl had parents who were very different from her own. Momma and Papa's girl? No. When she'd believed she'd been adopted, she had long ago surrendered her heart to the mysterious man and woman who, she'd imagined, had given her up as a newborn to what they hoped was a better home and more loving arms. They hadn't known those arms would spend a lot of time waving around in senseless anger and ugly arguments.

But if Papa was telling the truth, those loving birth parents were a total fantasy. Instead, perhaps, they'd given away a bit of themselves to anyone who wanted it, carelessly, keeping one beloved girl for themselves. Maybe she had no wonderful parents, real or imaginary.

The pizza wasn't sitting well.

"Life is full of surprises, you know?" Papa was saying—the man known as Papa. "Families grow and change, right? It's just you and me now, Nike. Better for me, better for you."

She was going to need some time to process this. "Yes, it is."

She needed to find those wannabe grandparents and hear their story as soon as she could. Maybe they'd be what she'd hoped for. Maybe. Question and verify.

*    *    *

Irene stood and watched the woolly mammoth shuffle aimlessly. His yard-long shaggy hair gleamed rust brown in the afternoon light. For all his huge magnificence, Nimkii looked desolate, pitiful, even out of place, although ten thousand years ago his kind had dominated North America's grasslands. He stopped dead in his bare pen and rocked back and forth, a sign of forlorn boredom if not an aching mental health crisis.

He looked at Irene and rumbled. He recognized her—as a source of food but perhaps not as the person who cherished him more than anyone else did. She got back to work and shoved a bale of grassy hay into the chains that hung from the sling of the crane alongside the pen. The bale weighed half of what she did. Every day, he'd eat seven bales along with fruit, fresh-cut long grass and alfalfa, a pail of elephant chow pellets, vegetables, and more.

A quarter ton of fodder in all, every day. Irene's armpits dripped with sweat. Summer heat and humidity wouldn't end until late October.

She switched on the motorized winch to lift up the bale, and directed the crane's arm to swing over the outer fence, marshy moat, and interior fence, then drop the hay. She reversed the motor immediately to reel up the chains as Nimkii rushed for them, jerking his trunk in the air, grabbing at them. He could move gracefully when he wanted, but now he was unhappy. He had reason to be unhappy. So did Irene.

Alan, head of the family that owned the farm, was leaving the house. *Is he coming to help me? Not likely.* Nimkii gave up on the chains, roared, and ripped apart the hay bale. A crow cawed on a fence post next to the pen, oblivious to the grassy funk of mammoth droppings. The pen desperately needed to be cleaned.

Alan approached, grinning in a way she didn't like. He stood tall, a middle-aged man, his weather-creased face always flushed. Next to him, Irene felt small and fragile and pale, her hair bleached blonder in the sunshine and held in place by a University of Wisconsin baseball cap.

"We're getting sort of a tour group today," Alan announced. "A shelter home for dupes is coming to visit." He laughed.

Irene had long ago learned to hide her cringe at the word *dupe* and at laughter more mocking than joyous. He seemed to expect her to say something. "That'll be nice," she said without enthusiasm.

"Dupes like him." He pointed to Nimkii, still grinning. That grin added to Irene's deepening certainty that Alan and his family had no love for Nimkii. And to her certainty that she had come to a very wrong place.

"I'll take any visitors we can get," Alan added defensively, perhaps because she hadn't laughed. "The tourism board doesn't do crap for us anyway. We thought this was going to be a great idea, our own little zoo with a big star animal to show off. It's just not working out."

*Maybe no one wants to visit a sad, stinky animal.* Irene began to load some apples into a box for him, rejects from a nearby orchard that were small, misshapen, or blotched—and fragrant in the heat. Her mouth watered.

"I was thinking," Alan said, "about getting some passenger pigeons.

Maybe that would bring more people. They could visit central Wisconsin the way it used to be."

*They'd never guess by the way it is now.* Visitors saw endless industrial farms covering sweltering land that only a half century earlier had held cool, beautiful forests. Worse, the farm corporations were pushing for travel restrictions like the ones in Iowa, which would mean no visitors at all.

"You know," Alan said, "I thought I'd feel connected to him. I'm a little Ojibwe. My ancestors knew mammoths firsthand. That's why we called him Nimkii."

The name meant *Thunderbird* in Ojibwe. A Missouri exotic-animal breeding farm had raised him with an elephant surrogate mother and had called him Big Babar. Irene knew a little about the breeding operation and liked none of it, including the thoughtless names. Nimkii had suffered a cheerless childhood in a pen even smaller than the one where he lived now.

"There's always so much to do," Alan said. "And the cost just for alfalfa keeps rising. He eats too much." He waited for her to answer.

Fruit was expensive, even bad fruit. "Yeah," she said, faking a little enthusiasm. "We'd better get ready for visitors."

Alan shrugged and returned to the farmhouse. She picked out a good apple and slipped it into her pocket before she fitted the box into the chains. A twittering flock of sparrows was scavenging inside the pen for bugs in the mammoth scat. Nimkii rumbled, glaring at them, as if they were stealing his dinner.

In July, when she'd arrived as an unpaid intern, Irene's heart had broken the moment she'd seen the woolly mammoth. Or rather, it had broken when she saw his pen. Six acres had looked bigger in the photos. They showed him standing in a lush tallgrass prairie under wide oak trees, wildflowers brushing his belly.

But in real life, the pen resembled an inadequate prison exercise yard. The grass and flowers had been eaten or trampled to bare sandy soil, and the savanna oaks ripped apart. Six acres, just over four football fields, was nowhere near enough for a creature who in the wild might range more than thirty miles in a single day.

Irene had not expected love at first sight, and now she dreamed of somehow petting him as he towered over her. But if he behaved like a wild fourteen-year-old adult male elephant, and it seemed he did, no one could come close. He would assert dominance, and with a casual swipe he could kill.

She hadn't expected love, but she had arrived with a secret kinship with Nimkii. Like him, she'd been genetically engineered. No one seemed to remember that artificially engineered, cloned humans used to be sort of legal.

On graduation day, when she received her bachelor's degree in environmental ecology, graffiti had been scribbled on her dorm room door. *Dupe.* Duplicate, clone. Then she got threatening messages, one showing her at a restaurant with friends the evening before. It was time to get out of town fast and cover her electronic tracks. A mammoth farm in Wausau might be far enough from Madison, only one hundred fifty miles due north, since she'd told no one besides her mother where she was going—and Mamá hadn't wanted her to go but had no better ideas, either. Now she was cut off from almost everything that mattered.

*Second-class now, too, if anyone finds out.* Well, things might change soon, from what her mother had told her. Irene found it hard to hope for changes that big.

She hadn't faced much competition for the internship. Nimkii was legal, but was his existence ethical? With only twelve other mammoths alive in North America, he might be alone his whole life, condemned to solitary confinement. Male elephants seemed like loners but actually led social lives at least as complex as a human's. Humans in solitary confinement went mad.

He lived in a little pen at a failing farm where the house had fading siding, the barn had a leaking roof, the shed sat on a cracked foundation, and the driveway needed a fresh layer of gravel.

On some days, no visitors came to help pay for his fodder. So when the little bus arrived carrying three residents from the sheltered home, Alan and his gruff wife, Ruby, came out to meet them. Irene busied herself on the far side of the pen, watching surreptitiously. One of the residents wore leg braces, but the other two seemed normal—like Irene. She knew for a fact she was normal. Some clones had been badly designed, physically or mentally, and needed special care. Others could live just fine on their own like anyone else, but they were often pressured into surrendering to protective custody.

Irene didn't want to think about it. She took the tractor to cut some alfalfa for Nimkii, hoping to distract herself, but she thought of nothing else the whole time. *That could be me.*

When she came back, the visitors were gone, and Alan and Ruby were in high spirits.

"Hey, Irene, they were nice!" Alan said.

"No one snapped," Ruby said. They both laughed. Dupes were supposedly mentally unstable.

"That's good," Irene said, lifting a bundle of grass from the tractor, her hands trembling with mental rather than physical exertion. *How long before I snap?* If she hadn't fallen in love with Nimkii, if things didn't change soon for the better—much better—she'd pack her suitcase and go. Anywhere would be an improvement.

*       *       *

I, Peng, designer of life and master of its language, began my day tasked with the unsealing of a package of dead chickens. Three chickens, to be precise, sent express from a farm in Iowa to the lab in Chicago where I labored. My life had come to that, and I hoped it would not grow worse. I still had much to lose. Every day I looked death in the eye and quaked.

To stave off impending disaster, I activated the armatures inside a biosafety cabinet to slit open the seals of the package. I sat on the safe side of the glass window. A coworker stood next to me, as was protocol, and offered encouragement; we took turns doing the physical donkey work, a small act of mutual kindness to share the burden. We were about to perform a crucial task. Together we would discover exactly what had ravaged a distant flock of chickens to determine whether it would also ravage the Earth and all of its biota.

"Wanna bet what it is this time?" my fellow donkey asked.

The armatures eased out the half-grown chickens, their feathers soaked in blood. I shuddered. Life offered splendor, death only repulsion.

"You okay?" the donkey asked.

"I feel better when they send vials of fluids."

"Me, too. Someday this job is going to make me puke."

A minimum of two people worked in the lab at any given time, but the exact staff varied by the day, as did the shift, depending on who was available and how much work there was. We were contract donkeys, all pretty much alike. Efficient. Skilled. Reasonably friendly and often enjoyably snide. Willing to take turns on the most disagreeable jobs, like handling bedraggled blood-soaked chickens. Bored out of our minds despite the urgency and terror, but we needed to earn a buck, so we were doing this until we could find something better. Although I might never find a better way to hide.

I said, "Given all the blood and detached heads, I conclude that they died of knife wounds."

She laughed. Today's fellow donkey was a middle-aged woman, a refugee from flooded New Orleans, one of the few from that disaster who had been allowed to relocate while the rest languished in ghastly camps. She was wasting enormous talents in this job—and she had just asked me the most worthwhile of questions: What was it this time? The specific answer—the specific cause—meant life or death. If a flock of fowl (or some other assemblage of livestock) fell ill, farm managers would slaughter and incinerate the animals. Or they would douse them with some kind of treatment that might be worse than the affliction but would cut their losses.

If we had reason to believe that the answer we found could endanger more than just that flock or species, we could try to trigger a national or even worldwide emergency, for all that shamefully underfunded public health services could do. Meanwhile, we would all pray, stiff with fear, asking our various gods to keep us safe from everything being created by nature or fools with gene-splicing labs in their garages. Major havoc was being wreaked in too many places. Inevitably, and no doubt soon, it would reach us. (You might think that all this responsibility would be reflected in our paychecks. No.)

"I'll collect some of the blood for analysis," I said for the record.

She made a note. "We'll get external material in the blood, too. Feces might add special flavor notes to the final dish."

"A full autopsy would be wise," I added. That was the running joke. It was always true that we ought to be performing a more in-depth analysis, especially given our usual findings.

"Not in the budget." That was the cynical punch line, although obsolete. Budgets had increased lately, but it was soothing to think that closer scrutiny hadn't become our anxious routine.

"A safe bet," I said, "would be avian infectious bronchitis."

"Yeah, a safe bet for big operations." She hated big farming operations, although we owed our jobs and dinners to them and the flabby lumps that chickens had been overbred into.

I gave the machine a few commands, then checked the electronic label. "These were free-range chickens. Outdoors. Maybe they got it from wild birds."

"I heard that chickens outnumber wild birds in Iowa."

"That's the most disastrous thing I've ever heard. We took all of nature and overran it with chickens."

"I can top that disaster. The Sino cold." After a moment, she added, "Sorry. I hope that isn't a problem for you."

Yet another epidemic had befallen China, and anyone who looked

Chinese might be shunned. Or murdered—apparently some misguided patriots considered homicide an effective vaccine. Unfairly, too, since that coronavirus had been traced down to a wild boar carcass revealed by thawing permafrost in Siberia, nothing Chinese about it, and China had responded fast and well. Borders had slammed shut like guillotines, the population frozen in place by quarantine, medical procedures applied with rigor and success. But everyone was jittery about epidemics, China was an enemy, and slander was a potent weapon. She knew me by my official name, Huning Li, not my artistic name, Peng, but both were unequivocally Chinese.

And she saw my broad, elderly man's face and heard a slight accent I tried but could never erase. With my wispy white beard, I could pass for Confucius rather than Peng, and as Peng, I had once been known as a lovely woman. Gender presentation ought not to serve as concealment, it ought instead to serve as one's genuine identity, but a bullet in a lung can lead to desperate measures. I, founder and CEO of SongLab, designer of life and master of its language, was protected from death by that glass wall and from my creditors by bankruptcy, but little stood between me and fools.

"We face death in many ways," I said.

"A new one every day." She then entertained herself, but not me, by reciting some of the known pathogens threatening our health or food supplies. Her tasks during that shift included a sample of feces from sick pigs, and she would soon set about examining it.

Then three soil samples arrived by certified courier and were dropped off in the airlock to our clean room. Did the soil contain the fungus that was blighting bean crops in Mexico? Urgent question. I took some cultures. Common cloned strains of beans offered no resistance to this fungus. Evil genetic engineering and the evil nature of cloned crops (not irresponsible practices by profit-hungry corporate farms) had endangered the world's food supply, and by extension, me and the children I had once genetically designed and cloned.

Rancor, thy name is Peng.

(Or the fungus could have been a targeted biological attack, but at what target? The answer was beyond my means to know, but recent turmoil had made me believe in its possibility. Rancor was always epidemic.)

As I was finishing the cultures, the cameras in the automated reception area showed a hazmat-clad courier dropping off a container marked with top-level biohazard warnings.

That was unusual.

"Received," I said over the speakers. The courier waved and hurried out. The container cycled through the airlock into the clean room. I dropped what I was doing and opened it. Inside were ten vials of human blood. We were tasked to determine whether the bloods' previous owners were infected with the Sino cold (a variety of delta-CoV, to be properly more technical—or better yet, Stone Age boar coronavirus).

I checked the instructions again, hoping I was mistaken.

"Who sent this?" my coworker demanded. Another very good question.

"The label gives randomized ID. Corporate knows exactly who. We're not supposed to know."

"I'll let you handle those samples." She noticed my eyes wrinkle from a wry smile behind my face mask. "Hey, I got kids."

"Retirement can't come soon enough for me." I began the search for viral RNA in the blood, and if I didn't find that cold, what would I find? Presumably the patients were ill from something awful.

By then, three hours had passed, and the chickens' death had a cause. She looked at the report on the screen. "Avian infectious bronchitis, like you said."

Another gammacoronavirus, a familiar foe. "Ah, but what variety? Databases want to know."

I studied the output, then the raw data from the RNA bases. The program had compared strains and highlighted unexpected differences. "Oh, now this could be bad," I said, master of the grammar of base pairs, seeing a potential death sentence in the wording. "Look right here." A hologram screen created a three-dimensional representation of a protein. I rotated it. "Coronaviruses have a proofreading function, which is expressed here, and this variation isn't in the databases. I don't know how this segment would function. And I should."

She gave me a side-eye. Perhaps I had said too much if I wished to remain incognito. Few people shared Peng's skill in predicting genetic changes. Or perhaps she hadn't wished to imagine that chickens or, worse, wild birds were coughing up mutant viruses all over Iowa.

"Then it's a good thing those chickens are dead," she said. "But take a look at this for bad. Parasites in the pig shit."

I came to look. Her screen displayed an unmagnified sample that contained smooth, pale worms several centimeters long. They were twitching. I shuddered and looked at her other screen, which displayed a genetic breakdown of the contents.

"Nematodes," I said.

"You sure?"

"I've seen them before."

"I wish I had your memory."

"I mean the worms, not the DNA." But I lied.

"What kind?"

"The world has far too many nematodes. Perhaps *Ascaris,* given the size and location."

And so they were, as she was able to confirm: big disgusting round-worms, living in pigs no less, not quite *Ascaris suum* or *lumbricoides* or anything else, so either we had a new species (for which we wouldn't get naming rights), or a mutation (which was becoming far too common across all species for a long list of reasons), or some careless fool had been tinkering with the language of life (also distressingly common). Both pigs and humans, and perhaps other animals, could be at risk.

"How dangerous is this?" she asked.

"Veterinarians could tell us."

After a moment, she said, "I wish they treated pig shit more responsibly on farms."

Whatever this worm was, its propagation was only one easy mistake or minor disaster away from our drinking water.

"If a stable has burned down," I murmured, remembering a quote attributed to Confucius, "do not ask about horses, ask about men."

She looked at me.

"Worry about people, not animals," I said.

"You got that right."

By then the soil sample was ready. No fungus. (Yet. Sooner or later it would blow in on the wind.) We joyfully reported that.

She looked over my shoulder at the initial results from the blood samples. Delta-CoV had been isolated from six of the ten.

"Oh, no!" she said. "Not here!"

"They could have come from anywhere," I said, knowing the samples were more than likely local. "And it matters which virus."

"It's delta," she said like an accusation. Sino was a delta, and the only one of that genus that affected humans—so far as we knew.

"We can compare it to the Sino virus," I offered.

She backed away, as if the virus could propagate through the screen. I worked rapt, finally able to see this monster up close. Yes, it was Sino—but no, it wasn't. Not quite. My fingers grew cold from fear. I called up a model, then twisted and turned it and slowly grew both more and less frightened.

"Look," I called out to her. "The neuraminidase is different. I don't think it would be effective." I pointed to a section of the enzyme.

"Effective at what?"

"I think the virions couldn't get out of the cell to infect someone else."

She gave me that side-eye again, uncertain of my competence.

"I have two Ph.D.s," I admitted. Actually three, but one had been merely honorary and subsequently withdrawn.

"How did the enzyme change?"

"Good question." I quickly thought of an answer. "If I wanted to make a vaccine, this could be one avenue, a sort of attenuated virus." Rumors said China had begun development, although rumors eventually asserted everything.

Her eyes got wide. "Yeah, that would work. Shaky ethics, though." She had a Ph.D., too. As I said, she deserved a better job than the one we had. "Who's doing this?"

I read her the serial number of the client. "I hope they have high ethics." We often had doubts about our clients—and in this case, I had grave doubts. Or hopes.

We filed our reports marked by the categories *Urgent* and *Alert,* and destroyed our samples (terror prodding us to noble thoroughness), and thus our workday ended with the discoveries of a mutant virus proofreader that might devastate Iowa fowl at any moment; unfamiliar and dangerous worms on a digestive tour of pigs; safe soil (for now); and damning evidence of tinkering with an enemy epidemic. When I stood up, I felt dizzy from fear.

We left the lab, housed in what resembled a dreary warehouse in a part of Chicago notable for its dreary warehouses, and we went our separate ways. I enjoyed the warm evening air on my fear-chilled fingers. I wanted to go to the elevated train stop because I liked human company and got too little of it, aware more than ever that we could all die far too soon for no good reason. Sharing a train car with other passengers would bring me comfort. But as I waited for the train that evening, I heard a child's voice.

"Look! Is he sick?"

I didn't hear the response and instead decided to travel by other means and in safety, alone except for wraiths of fear and a never-vague memory of the feeling of a bullet piercing my chest. I left the platform, descended the station's quaint old steps, and outside on the sidewalk, I raised my phone to call an autocar.

A man wearing military fatigues approached. "Dr. Li?"

This wasn't going to be good, and lying wouldn't help. "Yes," I said. "Could you please come with me?"

Fighting wouldn't help, either. I canceled the call. "Of course."

"Thank you," he said. "I want you to know you aren't in any trouble."

I didn't trust his words. Confucius and I both believed in benevolence. In his long life, he had suffered exile, arrest, and attempted assassination. I was already too much like him.

Irene heard voices from downstairs as she was getting dressed before dawn. She couldn't make out all the words, but she recognized the anger. The farm family quarreled a lot, especially Alan and Ruby, sometimes right in front of Irene.

What was it this time? Her curiosity wrestled with her desire to respect their privacy, and curiosity won. She tiptoed to listen at the stairwell. She knew that Ruby, a stout and acid-tongued woman, did all the housework, begrudged rural life, and worried about money, since she kept the books and worked part-time at another farm or someplace. Alan did all the heavy farmwork and resented what he thought was an unfair physical burden. Their teenage son, Will, gardened, fished, and gathered food for the table—and he would slip away with his dog when the arguments got heated, too emotionally fragile for conflict. Irene suspected he'd been abused in his childhood, maybe by his parents, maybe by someone else.

They seemed to love each other, but the stress of the farm was testing that. She suspected that each one unconsciously believed that if they ignored Nimkii long enough, the problems he posed would somehow go away.

"It isn't just a flag," Alan said.

A flag? Probably to display in support of another government policy that Irene hated.

Ruby said something in return.

"I need your help to put it up," Alan continued. "That's all I'm asking for. They're already bought and paid for."

Ruby had a long response.

"The point isn't more visitors," Alan said. "It's to show where we stand. That's not going to drive people away."

Will said loud and clear: "People aren't coming because they don't like clones." Irene had never heard him raise his voice before.

"Cloning's okay for animals," Alan said.

Ruby said something about "too far away."

"Okay, we'll do it, Will and me," Alan said. "You can stay here and stew." Soon the back door opened and closed.

Irene returned to her attic room, finished dressing, brushed her hair, put on her college hat, and as a way to avoid going downstairs for a few more minutes, checked to see what her friends were saying online. More channels had gone missing. Again. *But no, it's not censorship, it's holding people responsible for promulgating misinformation.* The friends she could find were complaining about possible new travel restrictions. And her mother had created an illustrated polemic against rationing. That was so much like Mamá, but if she kept that up, pretty soon she'd be censored, too, or arrested for standing up for old-fashioned freedom.

How soon before the mutiny started? Because it would come soon, now just a matter of days—as far as Irene knew. *Not soon enough.* What could she do up in Wausau when it did? What would happen to the farm? She knew for sure what side Alan and Ruby would be on.

She also found out what displaying the flag was about: The United States had accused China of trying to infect Americans with the Sino cold. Flying the flag would show solidarity with the Prez in his effort to keep the country safe. *Safe from the cold!* The debate had already turned ugly, even though no one in America or even outside of China had been infected, at least according to official reports. Was the Prez really threatening quarantines? War? Direct reprisals for dissenters? *Don't worry,* online chatter assured everyone, *he'll protect us!* Others asked if the virus was already really here because they knew about people who were coughing, or if it was just another common cold circulating. She had no way to know for sure anymore about much of anything.

She got a message from Mamá to call her—why was she awake so early?

"Hija, eso del catarro es mentira total," she said when Irene called back. *My girl, this stuff about the cold is a total lie.* She always spoke Spanish with Irene.

"¿Banderas? ¿Cómo? No nos miente el Prez nunca." *Flags? How? The Prez never ever lies to us.* Irene could be snide in both languages.

*It's one way to get rid of people. A cold. Fake colds,* Mamá said.

Irene was pretty sure the Sino cold was real, even if it ought to be called something nonracist, like maybe the delta cold. Fake colds? She believed that, too. The Prez might do anything and get away with it. She knew his attractive persona was fake. Mamá had demonstrated in an underground art piece how his face had been sculpted over time to look handsome and his body to look vigorous. Not much could be done about his mind, though. Before Irene could answer, Mamá asked:

*How far are you from the city of Wausau?*

*Close. Only a few miles.* Was Mamá coming to visit? Oh, no. She'd wind up in a screaming battle with Alan and Ruby for sure, and Irene would be fired, and Nimkii . . .

*Just asking. I want to send you some information.*

About what? It could only be one thing, one exciting thing, the mutiny. *Yes, Mamá.*

*I'll send it to you with a secure courier.*

*Okay.* Lately life had been one long series of frustrations, and now something would change—for the better, Mamá was sure, and Irene wanted to believe that. They chatted a little more.

Mamá asked, *How is the pedazo?* The piece—the piece of her heart and soul, a nickname for Nimkii in the language that meant family and affection for Irene. No one besides Mamá knew how thoroughly she loved him, and while her mother might never forgive her for failing to become an artist like herself, she seemed to accept Irene's love of nature and its wonders. Then Mamá, who had gotten up ridiculously early to set up an art show, had to go.

Mamá, the artist. Irene was a work of art, of genetic art, unique—Mamá always said that. Irene had talked about that once with Peng. He was an old friend of Mamá's, both of them with similar artistic aspirations. His answer was a little cagey, as usual, and said his art was all about making people who could be their best, and every single person was unique by genetics and environment. For Irene, being that close to art all the time hadn't made her feel good about becoming an artist. Irene had seen how her mother struggled, and hardship hadn't turned her into a better person.

Irene also didn't look at all like Mamá, who had invented the story of a brief love affair to explain the difference. A lot needed to be unpacked in that, and someday the right day might arrive when they could talk about it.

She guessed it was finally was safe to go downstairs. Ruby was at her desk in the living room and never liked to talk to her much anyway, so Irene had the kitchen to herself. Still, the silence felt edgy. She ate some toast and drank a little cheap synthetic coffee, the best the family could afford, as she checked the official news on her phone. Yes, new restrictions had been proposed, but only for resettlement of refugees, not routine travel. And yes, a minor cold was circulating, but not another killer epidemic, so don't worry about it. *Finding the Line* didn't have a new video. Too bad. It would have skewered the flag-versus-cold thing hilariously.

By the time she slipped on her fluorescent orange staff vest and left the farmhouse, the sun had just risen over the horizon and the sky was clear.

Alan and Will had been busy. A big American flag, creased from long storage, hung tacked to the window frame on the barn's second story. A smaller flag flew from a staff in front of the farmhouse, and two little flags, the kind handed out for rallies or parades, were taped to the outer gate on Nimkii's pen. The bright colors of the flags contrasted with the worn, faded paint on the barn and house.

She hoped good weather would attract visitors. If none came today, Alan's aggrieved prayers at dinner would be especially hard to listen to, asking not for blessings but curses. *If there is a god, he/she/they/it is not petty and vengeful.*

Meanwhile, without help as usual, she had to feed Nimkii breakfast, and as she did, she thought about ways to attract visitors and money. Maybe an observation tower would provide a better view of Nimkii, but even a simple construction project would cost a few thousand dollars. A robot to help with chores would never happen.

Would passenger pigeons really help? What attracted a lot of visitors was the zoos for mythical creatures like engineered unicorns, dragons, and bigfoots, no matter how poorly made and sickly they were. Nimkii was different, real. Peng had found a research paper that included Nimkii's DNA and called it extraordinarily well thought through.

An hour later, she heard horse hooves on the driveway. The staff at a stable a mile away urged riders to visit the farm and the mammoth, and every time mounted visitors came, Nimkii would stop what he was doing to watch the horses.

But the visitors would come from the south and observe the worn graffiti on the pavement—predating Irene's arrival—of the word *cloNE* surrounded by a circle and cut through with a slash. *Ban clone.* Irene felt dismayed by the graffiti and by its poor execution, upper- and lowercase letters mixed for no reason and a rather squarish circle—like it or not, she would always be the daughter of an artist. More important, it threatened Nimkii. She'd asked Alan about spray-painting over it.

"It's not the best way to greet visitors," Irene had said.

"It's almost faded away anyway," Alan had answered. Neglect was his specialty.

The visitors were an elderly couple. They hitched their horses on the outer fence around Nimkii's pen before Irene could warn them that he might lumber too close and spook the horses. Well, she'd have to hope he would behave for a while, although he was already staring at the animals.

"Hi! Welcome to Prairie Orchid Farm," she said as she approached, smiling. Maybe one of them was the secure courier.

"Good morning," the woman said without warmth. The man just stared at Nimkii, who was reaching his trunk toward the horses, sniffing. If they were couriers, of course they would be discreet about it.

"This is Nimkii," Irene said, trying to act receptive.

"We know," she said.

The man took out a camera drone from a backpack. "Is he really dangerous?"

"Only if he sees you as a rival, and he might," Irene said. "This is his territory."

The man tinkered with his drone and launched it. The woman began to walk around the pen, silent, eyes narrowed. Usually visitors liked to chat, and she had to give a potential courier a chance, so she remained near him as he directed the camera to record Nimkii from various angles.

"Why all the flags?" he said with a frown.

"The owners put them up." He still frowned. "I'm an intern. I recently got a degree in environmental ecology at UW–Madison." She hoped her meaning would seep through—and confirm her identity.

"Then you know."

*Know what?* About rationing? About Nimkii's substandard living conditions? About an imminent mutiny?

Nimkii approached, rumbling.

"I hope he doesn't scare the horses," she said. That was very possible, although they seemed more interested in nibbling the timothy grass that grew alongside the fence.

"What does he eat?"

Irene went through the list. Visitor or courier, she wanted to be friendly. "It's based on elephant needs, with more calories for a colder climate." She didn't add that it was all guesswork.

And because the farm had so little money, they were feeding him trimmings from Christmas tree farms, oat straw, soybean husks, and even sawdust pellets. Despite that, Nimkii seemed healthy.

"He should be roaming free and feeding himself," the man said. "You should just open the pen and let him out."

She wasn't sure if he was kidding. *Nimkii ought to range freely.* The thought burned every time she had it, which was often. "Well, there are farms around here, so it would cause problems."

"So you're saying there's no way he can lead a natural life."

She didn't have a good answer. "I'm hoping to enrich his environment. Toys, more space, different foods."

The man grunted, called his camera back, and fiddled with it for a bit. Then he said, "Look what I did." He used his phone projector to show her not a secret message, but a video with Nimkii apparently wandering through nearby meadows—a breathtaking and heartrending vision.

He added, "That's how he ought to live. He'd live longer."

"I know." *I know that better than you do. And you're not Mamá's courier.*

Nimkii trumpeted at the horses and arched his trunk. They backed off as far as their reins would let them, flashes of white around their eyes. The man rushed to untie them from the fence posts and lead them away.

"The mammoth could take care of himself in the wild," he called to her.

Irene doubted that and wished she were wrong, but Nimkii had no experience with foraging or defending himself. Maybe she could teach him that somehow—in case things went wrong, like an epidemic delta cold or a mutiny with bad consequences. She ought to start lessons soon, somehow.

The woman joined him, and they chatted a bit between themselves, then mounted the horses and left without saying goodbye, but at least they paid the suggested visitor fee. She tried to forget about them but couldn't.

Later, Will came home, carrying a fishing pole and three little trout in a net, set the tackle in the barn, and tied up his dog, a typically friendly chocolate-brown Labrador who deserved to be free and treated like a member of the family. Instead it was usually leashed and ignored like a piece of equipment. Will disappeared into the house with the fish. Irene had her doubts about the cleanliness of the local rivers. When Irene entered the house to get a cheese sandwich for lunch, Will and Ruby were out on the front porch, and she heard them talking about how Alan had volunteered to deliver flags. Ruby thought he had better things to do.

Irene had just finished eating when a family pulled up in the gravel driveway, two adults and a teenage son who looked glum and utterly bored. Was one of them the courier?

The parents hurried to the far side of the pen, where Nimkii was. The boy seemed far too handsome and husky for his own good, as if he'd been tweaked, even cloned. If so, did he know? How did he feel about it? Irene knew how she felt, and all Peng's well-intentioned words about how ordinary and normal she was had left her with different conflicts, not fewer.

But if that boy was secretly a clone, too, then maybe his family was going to mutiny since he was now a second-class citizen. Maybe they'd carry a message.

Rather than follow his parents, he approached her. He wore a visor-screen, and she wondered how much attention he was paying to his surroundings.

"That's the mammoth no one else wanted, right?" It sounded like an accusation.

She tried to blame his hostility on boredom. "The herd in the Canada mammoth range is too closely related genetically, so he needed a different home."

"And the United States needs all our land to grow food."

"Yes. We hardly have room for wildlife of any kind anymore. It's sad."

He squinted, perhaps not expecting agreement. "Is he really completely imprinted on humans?"

"You've done your research." Maybe the boy wasn't so hostile, or maybe the conversation was a cover for a handoff. "We don't know. And it would be hard to find out, at least here. These aren't the ideal facilities."

"Is he smart, like elephants?"

"Oh, yes. He recognizes different people, and when he hears a car, he comes to see if there are visitors."

"So he likes to see us?"

"Yes. Look at how he went over to watch your parents. And sometimes when a bird calls, he answers it. He pays a lot of attention to his surroundings." He also sometimes hiked around the perimeter of his little world in restless circles, and if he came upon a bird or small animal, he tried to kill it.

"He's never going to get to live a normal life," the boy said.

*Why does everyone have to keep reminding me?* "We're trying to do the best we can for him."

"And this won't really work for deextinction. There aren't enough mammoths for genetic diversity. Or saber-toothed tigers, either. People should be really working harder to protect the wildlife we have. Hundreds of species go extinct every day."

*Well, yes.* He'd done his homework, and now he was delivering his report to a captive audience.

"He's not a real woolly mammoth anyway," the boy said like a coup de grace and walked away to join his parents. She watched him leave, thankful he'd left just before she ran out of self-control. *Definitely not the courier.*

The family said hardly anything more to her, which was fine. Her phone chirped. The father sent the fees, at least.

"Thanks for the visit," she said with all the fake cheer she could manage. Maybe more visitors wasn't such a good idea if they only came to criticize. Nimkii watched them go, then paced around the perimeter of his pen, growling.

"Pedazo," she called to him, and he stopped to listen, "people understand you. I'm not sure if that's a good thing, though. You didn't ask to be what you are and where you are." He couldn't do anything about it, either. "I really need to get you a toy. How about an old tractor tire? You'd enjoy destroying that. One of them has to be easy to find, and free."

A tiger-striped squirrel raced past, someone's genetic tinkering that now threatened to outcompete the native gray squirrel. What was real or normal anymore?

She thumbed her screen for a distraction. The new resettlement proposal, it turned out, had looser limitations for people with a certain level of net worth, the ones who could afford private rescue services from disasters like hurricanes or sea rise. The poor were left to sink or swim in neglected refugee camps.

Maybe the lack of visitors was due to worries about food and colds, and maybe those worries were making visitors peevish. Maybe. Would she ever know what was really going on?

In the late afternoon, she took out her phone and checked on her friends. They said that even though no cases of the cold had been discovered, the Prez's flag-waving ploy had created a backlash. People had interpreted it to mean that he knew the cold was coming soon, so stores and warehouses were being cleaned out as people stocked up on food and supplies. The official news, of course, remained upbeat. Patriotism would cure the cold. *Sure.* Everything about the day had been disappointing or bad.

Meanwhile, it was going to rain, and she had to make sure that Nimkii's food was securely stored.

*    *    *

Avril had a new plan. The mutiny was going to hold a protest, she was positive about that. She'd find out about it and show up, and then the mutiny people, the ones besides Cal, were sure to welcome her. Protest dates and times were secret so antiprotesters couldn't break them up, but she'd find out, somehow.

A friend from high school—no, not a friend, just an acquaintance, Avril didn't want friends like that—who attended a university in California had confirmed the protest rumor. "People keep whispering about it. It's going to be huge. I hope they all get trampled and die," he'd said on their high school alumni forum. A couple of other ex-classmates said they'd heard rumors, too, and likewise hoped the protesters suffered. Something big and nationwide—and Avril would be part of it.

She thrilled with excitement and, she admitted to herself, fear. *That dog.* But she wouldn't back down. She looked out of her dorm room window. She'd always loved being near Lake Michigan back home, and she tried to calm herself with the view of Lake Mendota. The dorm management had notified her that her roommate was about to arrive—the joy of having a room all to herself was ending—and she wanted to make a good first impression.

The door opened. A young woman walked in tugging a cart piled with suitcases and boxes. She was tall and tan with long black hair and big dark eyes, and she looked at Avril and around the room, judging everything she saw.

This moment would decide whether the school year would be heaven or hell. Avril decided to set the tone. She lowered her phone, smiled, and said, friendly but not too perky, "Hi, I'm Avril."

"Shinta." No reciprocal smile.

"I haven't done much to the room. I was waiting for you."

"Good."

First impressions could be misleading, but Shinta didn't seem friendly. "Can I help you with anything?"

"No, I'll take care of it. Go back to what you were doing. By the way, I'm Indonesian, not Chinese. I grew up in Dallas." She had hints of both Indonesian and Texas accents in her speech. "I just want everyone to know. In case they decide to round up the Chinese. Which they should."

If Shinta believed that, she might also want protesters to be trampled to death. Still, they'd have to live together. Avril tried to think of something compatible to say. Shinta beat her to it.

"We should set some ground rules. I assume the right side of the closet is for me."

"Yes."

"Pffft. That's all? This is ridiculous."

Avril's heart stopped. She'd scrupulously left half the space empty.

Shinta's voice grew louder. "Who thinks that's all the space we need?" She turned. "But we'll split it, fifty-fifty. Half of not-enough."

"Yeah." Avril breathed again.

"The ground rules. Number one. We can't be lovers. Not ever. That will only backfire sooner or later."

"Agreed." The thought hadn't crossed Avril's mind.

"And food: No sharing food. Or clothing. We keep things picked up and clean."

Avril nodded. The idea seemed amenable. Not the tone, though.

"Music on earphones. We can decide later how to decorate. Now we should set up the furniture."

"You've thought this through."

"I want everything ready as fast as possible. I got here late, and I'm going to work hard and learn all I can, and that's all I care about."

"Me too." *Not really.*

They quickly stacked the beds into bunks, agreeing—or rather, Avril conceding—that the lower one was for Shinta. They arranged the desks and other storage on either side of the window, with the left side for Avril. She excused herself as Shinta continued to unpack.

She wondered about her new roommate as she walked out. Was she just a random student, or was she sent to spy on Avril? And if so, by which side? *You can never trust anyone.*

She had contacts in the mutiny besides Cal. She'd spoken to a senior at Dejope Hall's start-of-the-semester welcome party, a short, energetic woman named Hetta, the one who promised to get her in touch with someone else, who turned out to be Cal, but he was just a setback.

She was going to find Hetta.

\* \* \*

Berenike knew her grandparents were named Linda and Christopher Swoboda. They had lived in the Milwaukee area, and perhaps they still did, so she hurried to rummage through the customer database of the autocar franchise where she worked. The momentarily empty reception area had a counter on one end that held a screen and equipment, all of it emblazoned with the teal corporate logo for AutoKar. A pair of teal plastic benches waited for customers in front of a wall-sized window, where that morning she'd hung a small American flag on corporate orders, grumbling during every minute that it took her. Electronic panels on the opposite wall depicted cars slightly more lovely and spacious than the real thing.

Assistant managers had mid-level access to the database, and the franchise was popular, so if the Swobodas existed, she could find them—and in the process violate at least two big rules against accessing the database for personal use. No one could tell why she was looking them up, though. And she was hardly the first to search for personal reasons.

There they were: in a well-heeled suburb and about the right age. He was a retired doctor who had worked in oncology at a large hospital. She was also a medical doctor and had retired from teaching at a medical college. They frequented garden supply and athletic equipment stores, as well as specialized grocery stores and local parks. Lately only Christopher had called for a car. Linda had been deactivated, which probably meant death—with divorce, she'd be in the database at a different street address. Judging by the times he called for an autocar, he had a lot of free time. His photo showed a smiling man with features a lot like his dark-haired, round-faced daughter, Momma, who had hated him for decades.

Momma had always said that when Berenike was adopted, both she and Papa had been unemployed—which wasn't unusual—and they had no insurance, so Momma's parents thought they shouldn't try to raise a child. She said her parents were horrified by the idea that she and Papa possessed so few resources and yet had dared to start a family.

"Think of what's best for the baby," Grandmother Linda had said, according to Momma, who had apparently made it all up. "We can take her for a while, just until you get your lives in order again."

"My life is in order!" Momma said she answered, still shrill with rage years later. She would add as Berenike got older, "They got a court order. Child welfare inspectors! Private detectives! That's how much they wanted to snatch you. We couldn't take our eyes off you for a moment. You were so unbelievably precious to us."

She added when Berenike got even older, "They were always trying to control my life. They hated your father. Called him totally fucking useless. They did everything they could to undermine our marriage."

Berenike would be bombarded by these pronouncements around the holidays, when families were supposed to gather and bond. Once, on the day before Thanksgiving, she was shoveling dry cereal into her mouth to get to school on time when she dared to ask a question.

"When was the last time you talked to them?"

"You were two, so thirteen years. Lucky thirteen!" Scorn sparkled in the words.

"Then why are you still so angry about it?"

Momma leaned in close. "You don't know how much they tried to hurt me. The things they said about me. Slander! They tried to ruin our credit rating by getting a court order. We had just enough money to raise you but not to pay a lawyer, too. They bad-mouthed us on every network they could. You'd have led a better life when you were little except for all the harm they did to us, to our family."

The next day, during the holiday dinner, Momma continued the tale. "They got obsessed about you, Nike. They couldn't leave us in peace."

Berenike remembered that dinner's processed turkey and stuffing from a cheap takeout, spiced with well-aged resentment, and even at the time she'd felt sure she wasn't hearing an especially accurate story. She'd already realized that if she knew more, she might feel differently about her grandparents and her parents. There were never completely innocent parties in any battle.

Bearing that in mind, she stepped outside the AutoKar franchise office during her lunch break and took the first step, steeling herself for the likely consequences. She dictated a formal electronic mail message, very polite and proper. ". . . and I believe you may be my grandparents . . . I know there are disagreements between you and my parents, but if you would be interested in a meeting . . ." She included her contact information and a photo as proof of sincerity.

*Stay calm, whatever happens.* There were so many ways this might go wrong. She might never learn the truth. Or she might learn the truth and prefer the old fake story about herself.

Less than an hour later, her phone rang: Christopher Swoboda. She stepped outside again.

"I would love to meet you." He was sobbing, tears dripping past his smiling lips. "Oh, Berenike, Berenike, for years we wondered about you, about what kind of woman you've become. Look at you!" She heard echoes of her mother in that voice and that emotion. "We have to meet! Today, tomorrow? I can't wait."

*I,* not *we.* Apparently, Linda really had died.

"Tonight?" he said. "Dinner! Let me take you to dinner. Linda would have loved to meet you, but she died only two months ago. She almost got to meet you! Where do you live? I can go anywhere you want."

They agreed to a downtown restaurant. Berenike tried to sound as happy as he was, but he sounded a lot like Momma, and Momma had been dangerous, willing to do anything to get her way.

Berenike got out of work in time to go to her shared studio apartment on the Near North Side and change out of her uniform. She took a rental bike to her neighborhood because she could earn a little money repositioning it, and arrived sweaty at her building, a brick-faced box that had absolutely no architectural interest. She tiptoed into her unit to avoid waking a roommate, and after a shower, she took a bus back. AutoKar, which also owned the buses as well as the bicycles, let her ride for free, although in the event of a problem, she had to respond as an employee, on-call for no pay, so it wasn't really free.

She hoped that her grandfather—was that the right word for him?—would pay for the meal. He seemed to have money.

What else did she hope for? She tried to keep her expectations low so her disappointments would be few. Truth was always in short supply, so that might be too much to want. Maybe she could learn just a little more than she already did—but she needed to brace for possible bad news.

She looked at all the American flags suddenly on display. Even some homeless people were holding little flags to show their love of country— the country that was deliberately starving them—as they conspicuously did not beg on the sidewalk. People and businesses were being pressured into sheeplike patriotism, although her employer might have put up the flags willingly. *That'll stop a virus. The Prez has everything under control. Sure. Three more days of his preening idiocy.*

She found the restaurant in one of the old two-story brick buildings near the river. The elaborate arched windows clashed with the faux Tudor English decor inside, and she tried to ponder the aesthetic mismatch and the American flag at the door to distract herself. For some people, family meant comfort, but familial comfort would be a new experience for her, and she couldn't expect it.

The reception robot, another period misfit made worse by the Beefeater tunic and ruff draped over it, told her that Christopher Swoboda had arrived, and it led her to his table. At the sight of her, he leaped up, smiling so wide that his eyes became slits. He wrapped his arms around her tight and held her for a long time, rubbing his gray-flecked beard on her cheek. For a little too long. She pulled back.

"Grandfather." That seemed like a polite, conflict-avoiding title. He didn't feel like family, despite how much he reminded her of Momma. Maybe some sort of biological link was missing, a connecting family scent she'd heard about but never experienced. He smelled of a piney cologne, pleasant but meaningless.

He gripped her hands. "You're a full-grown woman now. I haven't seen you since you were a baby. You look so beautiful!" He stepped back to study her from head to toe.

She felt more uncomfortable. "You look a lot like Momma."

"How is she? You'll have to tell me. First, I want to know about you. What have you been doing, Berenike? All these years. . . ."

They sat down. The table screen lit up, sensing that everyone had settled, and asked for their orders. She considered a glass of wine, which she could never afford for herself, and decided on iced coffee instead—maybe real coffee at a place like this. It would pay to be sharp. She chose simple-to-eat, healthy dishes. She wanted good food for a change, and knew she'd likely be talking a lot.

"How is your life?" he asked again.

"Fine." She talked about schooling in general terms and how she was working in management at a busy franchise, not mentioning exactly how humble the job was, what humiliating steps had brought her there, or how her work left her disappointed with her life. "Momma died just a month ago, though. Papa is well, still living here in Milwaukee."

"I'm retired. I used to be a doctor, an oncologist."

News of Momma's death didn't bother him at all, or maybe he already knew. He kept right on talking about other things. Momma would have put on a show of sorrow and concern, even if it had been fake, and a false show would have been more comforting than indifference.

"I knew you'd be smart." He beamed, gazing at her intensely. "That was what we asked for, a pretty, healthy, smart little girl." A robot cart, painted in Beefeater red and gold, rolled up carrying the drinks. He handed her a tall glass of iced coffee, then picked up his glass of red wine and took a contented sip.

She had been troubled about his indifference, but what he had just said, if he had meant those exact words literally, seemed like a bigger worry. "What you asked for?"

"Yes, what we asked for." He set down the glass and looked at her with an odd kind of expectation. "How much do you know? I mean, what did Olivia and Jackson tell you?"

"They always told me I was adopted."

As she expected, he stiffened at that.

"At least," she said, "that's what they said my whole life, until yesterday. Then Papa told me you bought them in vitro fertilization with a donor egg because you wanted to be grandparents." She was going to take this step by step, so she wouldn't mention the supposed battle yet.

He nodded. "They wanted children, and we were happy to be grandparents, so we paid for it. We thought it would help them settle down, and we were wrong. Stupidly wrong. That never works. Children aren't therapy. They asked . . . begged for our help to have a child when it turned out Jackson had a . . . fertility issue." He shook his head as if to dismiss Papa as worthless in everything. "And we caved. We agreed, your grandmother and I, to get them the best. We learned about a lab from China, I think, offering not donor eggs but engineered zygotes, more expensive, but they came with guarantees."

Engineered zygotes. That meant . . . *Stay calm, breathe deeply. Slow and deliberate. Sip some coffee, dark-roasted, genuine, and strong. Go step by step.* This was worse than she'd expected, much worse. "Guarantees?" she said.

"Healthy, most of all."

"You said you knew I'd be smart." She left out the *pretty* part.

"Oh, that was just a grandfather talking. You're the smartest young woman in the universe. The most talented. The prettiest, by far. We knew you'd be intelligent, blond, healthy. That's what you get when you buy an engineered zygote. It's all there, sort of like a catalog. We picked out one that was tweaked to be perfect."

"Tweaked." From a catalog.

"Yes. I worked in cancer treatment, so I know about cells."

*Engineered. Duped.*

The cart arrived carrying her soup, his salad. She swallowed a few spoonfuls, not tasting the broth and vegetables. She knew the laws about clones and how they were now second-class citizens. She knew what people thought about dupes—the same things that she herself thought.

He speared a wedge of tomato in his salad, thinking. He looked up and his expression changed. Maybe he'd noticed her shock. "It's okay. Here's how it works, simply put. The lab takes apart DNA, combines various bits, makes some changes, picks some mitochondria, too, puts it all in an empty ovum, and lets it divide like an ordinary fertilized egg. Those new cells get separated and then divided some more. In the end, they had ten viable zygotes."

"There are ten of me?" Ten dupes. This was getting even worse.

"No, only one. This is where things started going wrong. We would have been happy with twins, and you would have been identical twins, just like identical twins the . . . traditional way when a zygote splits in the womb."

He had shied away from the word *natural,* the politicized word in *natural law.* He knew what he was saying and what it really meant. But he wasn't offering any empathy. Something was dangerously wrong.

"In this case, Olivia was implanted with two embryos, and usually only one takes, but this time two did, and she only wanted one, so the other one was injected with a drug and killed. We were heartbroken, but to her it was a triumph."

Berenike almost had a twin. She waited for him to say more, meanwhile trying to think and not feel. She had always desperately wanted a sister, but not this way. No one would want one from cloning. *Stay calm. Breathe.* He was lying, he had to be.

"That's when we first thought she wasn't ready to become a mother." He looked down, as if it hurt to remember. "She'd gotten clean, stopped using drugs for almost a year. We thought she was ready. . . ." He looked up, again with that odd expectation. "Are you all right?" He took her hand and held it tight. His was warm and moist. And if his concern had been sincere, he would have offered it earlier.

"I . . . well . . ."

"She got rehab, and she seemed better. She wanted to begin a new life. Be a normal person, that's what she said, normal. And Jackson, we thought he was going to be okay, too. All I ever cared about is you."

She gently tried to pull her hand back. He wouldn't let go. She worked very hard to keep breathing.

"And," he said, "it turned into a big fight. They went to court. And we weren't allowed contact. We tried to keep an eye on you through third parties until we were sure they'd settled down and you'd be safe."

"They told me I was adopted." A normal child, not a dupe.

He squeezed her hand. "I'm sorry you had to find out this way. Don't worry, your secret is safe with me."

Safe? Even her hand wasn't safe with him. He was worse than Momma. *Stay calm. Protect yourself.*

"Are you all right?" he asked.

"Yes. Well . . . this is a lot to take in." She was a dupe—if he was telling the truth.

"I don't want to hurt you."

*Too late.*

"You should come and live with me."

*What?*

"I know you have a miserable job. I can give you a much better life."

*No you can't.* "I'm doing okay."

"Does AutoKar employ second-class citizens? Does anyone?"

She tugged to free her hand, groping for words. How did he know where she worked?

His grip squeezed painfully tighter, and he leaned forward with a smile, a horrible smile. "I'm not lying. I'll send you the contract from the lab. You'll see. You're not a natural human."

"Let me go."

"Go where? Go home? You're not going to have a home much longer." But he loosened his grip on her hand.

She stood up. "We're done here."

She walked out as self-controlled as she could, and soon she was panting and trembling, but at least she'd restrained herself until she was out of his sight. AutoKar wouldn't just fire her, it would demand repayment of all her wages and training on the grounds of misrepresentation of identity, and she'd wind up homeless and in the gutter, unless . . .

Unless he was lying, and she knew he was. She felt like a normal human being, and dupes always had something wrong with them. She hurried around a corner and stepped into an alley so she wouldn't be seen by Swoboda if he came out. She leaned against a wall, the bricks still warm from the setting sun. She worked downtown, and its streets and alleys had always felt familiar and safe, but now . . . She had to talk to Papa.

She sent him a message. "Urgent. We need to talk. Right away."

And she wanted to get home, to calm down. A bike—yes, she could find a bike, work off some energy, and get away.

Papa hadn't answered by the time she stashed the bike and walked through the humid twilight to her apartment building.

Two of her three roommates were home when she arrived, eating as they stared at their phone displays. One looked up from her rice and beans.

"Oh, hi, B." Her expression changed. "Rough day? Still hurting about your mom?"

"Yeah." That seemed like the easiest explanation. She had good roommates—but would they want to live with a dupe? If clones weren't physically handicapped, they were morally deficient, unnatural, and soulless. It would be like living with a known thief, and if the mutiny changed the law, it wouldn't change minds about the things that everyone knew.

She hadn't eaten, but she wasn't hungry, just exhausted, or something that felt like exhaustion. "I'm going to bed." She put on pajamas and climbed into her bunk, but she didn't sleep. She watched a stupid movie for a long time.

Papa didn't answer. Maybe he was busy putting on a show. Or distracted. Or off on some drug trip, or sleeping it off. Maybe Papa would help her, but she couldn't count on that. What else could she do to prove that she wasn't a dupe?

*    *    *

I had no choice, either as Dr. Li or secretly as Peng, no access to that easily pronounced word of one simple syllable: *no.* If I had refused, uttering that word would have been more irresponsible than any other error in my life, and I'd made more than enough already.

The soldier who had been waiting for me when I left the train station on my way home from work escorted me (with exquisite politeness) into the back of a windowless white van. It was driven to someplace near an airport, judging by the sounds—but not O'Hare, far too few flights. I disembarked in an underground parking area of a building, probably smallish, since there were a limited number of parking spots. Once inside, a colonel named Wilkinson sat across from me at a table in a meeting room, greeted me (also with exquisite politeness), and explained:

I would be working for the United States Army Medical Research Institute of Infectious Diseases. "I've heard of it," I said. It researched countermeasures against biological warfare, and it had a reputation for responsibility and rigor. I could only hope that it was true.

"Our concern, Dr. Li," he said, "is a vaccine."

I remembered the blood delivered to the lab that day. "Against the deltacoronavirus cold?"

"Yes. You spotted that."

"It would be a common approach to create an attenuated virus as a vaccine."

"We're thinking of something slightly different. Something self-administering."

For a moment I was confused. Then I was appalled. He meant to create an attenuated virus that would not be administered as a normal vaccine—by injection, for example. Instead, this one would be set loose to spread from person to person through direct contagion. No one had ever tried that before successfully.

He noticed my reaction. "We need to act quickly because we can be certain the virus will be here in the United States within a week, maybe a lot sooner. In all honesty, China has done its best with containment and has done well, and it's destined to fail. We're aiming for a version of the virus that's highly contagious but causes no harm to the host."

That was exactly what had appalled me. "It will be hard to do. The does-no-harm part, especially." The virus in the blood samples I'd seen back in the lab hadn't seemed contagious but would have made the hosts very ill, as I'd reported. (What had happened to the people infected by that virus?)

"We don't have time for test subjects."

I felt a little light-headed, and not without cause. Fainting would be one way to flee a looming disaster. "That causes more difficulties." That was unspeakably unethical, even in times of emergency, as he was well aware.

He nodded. "We know you can read, so to speak, genetic material, especially for human beings." He paused, then added, "We'll inform your employer that you'll be working for us for a little while. By law, there can be no effect on your employment. You'll be paid through them for your time. I needn't mention that this project is of the highest secrecy. You have special clearance."

Declining was not an option, and I understood the government's need to commandeer expertise. A mistake in the design could be even worse than the disaster of the actual delta cold, but a perfect design would save billions of lives. Here I was, Peng, creator of life, cornered and trapped. Here was my chance to be an unsung hero. They must have been desperate to want to hire me, but they obviously knew of my extraordinary work.

"I agree." Hubris, thy name is Peng. I had to sign a lengthy contract that held the United States government and all its agencies harmless from liability for every imaginable unfortunate occurrence. It held me responsible for everything but inclement weather. They allowed me to contact a friend to ask him to care for my pet bird in my absence, which I described to him as a sudden work-related trip.

I was led down the hall to my new office. I had a comfortable chair, a big L-shaped desk, five screens, a keyboard, a graphics pad, and two dictation microphones, but no windows to outdoors—no surprise, among other reasons, because I suspected I was in a basement. In a short briefing, I learned that I had the latest DNA analysis programs: newer, more powerful versions of the ones I used in the lab where I worked.

I also had access to a small, well-stocked kitchen and a bedroom provisioned with my preferred brands of soap and deodorant (that was disturbing), and some lab scrubs in my size to wear in the coming days. They had been expecting me.

I worked late into the night and returned to my desk after minimal sleep, exhilarated intellectually—and terrified in every other respect. I worked with colleagues off-site somewhere, and we knew each other only by designations we hadn't chosen for ourselves. We had voice as well as text communication, but the voices were clearly altered. We discussed the expression of a carefully engineered section in a strain of the virus with one essential question to answer: Would it remain human-to-human contagious in its pulmonary form but not cause deadly symptoms?

The virus by its nature damaged and killed infected cells. The host's body could react, possibly too strongly, to the damage and inflammation, which by itself could lead to death. As was sometimes the case with cold or flu infections, especially with the delta cold, people developed rapid respiratory failure—very rapid—and if they survived that, they could still fall prey to secondary infections, including pneumonia, which could be equally fatal, or they could die from worsened chronic conditions like congestive heart failure.

We wanted a virus that would irritate the lungs enough to cause coughing to spread the illness, but that would cause no serious symptoms. To accomplish that would require big changes, too many changes to create in one day, maybe in a week, but we had to try.

During our discussions, I insisted on using the terms *people* and *human beings* rather than *hosts* or *subjects*. Confucius would have been proud. Some of my colleagues clearly lacked his compassion.

The survival of any species involved a constant struggle against death from enemies of all kinds. Releasing the perfected virus (if we ever got it close enough to perfect) would be humanity's greatest risk ever. We had no margin of error. I, Peng, designer of life and master of its language . . . I should have expected something like this eventually.

Only ten years ago, I'd had a lot to say about medical ethics. No one listened, in the end. Few even remembered my testimony at a United States Senate Select Committee on Health and Technology. As time went on (but not soon enough), fanatics found unfaded and far more worthy targets.

I arrived for the hearing in a nondescript car that pulled up to a rear loading dock. Meanwhile, at the front of the Hart Senate Office

Building with its quaint white rectilinear styling from the twentieth century, hundreds of protesters screamed through bullhorns and shared the event live through video. They feared that I and DNA designers like me could make them second-class humans. Indeed, second-class humans eventually came to pass, but the people capable of creating them thrived in legislative halls, not in laboratories. As everyone learned through hard experience, all it took was a few legally binding words, not a few carefully selected genes.

No matter. Police feared violence and escorted me through back halls. I arrived in my finest pearl-gray suit made of top-quality synthetic spiderweb fiber, incidentally and conveniently bulletproof. I looked female then, walking confidently in formal spike heels, but I didn't get to cross the building's beautiful atrium. Too risky, the building security officers said, and I had received enough threats to accept their warning.

I arrived on time according to the summons, only to discover to no surprise that the hearing was running two hours late.

I waited in the greenroom. On the other side of the wall lay the Central Hearing Facility, a boring, functional name for a grand hall with handsome age-darkened wood paneling and, behind the committee-member dais, a gleaming white marble backdrop. The waiting room on the other side of the marble-clad wall offered standard-issue beige sofas, a coffee and tea maker, a watercooler, an adjoining toilet, and walls painted pale green out of tradition. A screen on the wall showed what was happening in the hearing room.

What was happening was a parade of failed genetic engineering.

Senators were gently grilling a ten-foot-tall young man in a motorized wheelchair. Rather, they fulminated against what would have been called in Roman times a monster, an unnatural creature, and these days what we politely called modified, a kinder term. Or some called him a dupe, which was both rude and inaccurate.

"Although my bones grew, my nervous system couldn't keep up," he said. "I have little or no feeling or control below my knees or elbows. Even if I did, I could hardly walk very far." He joked about it, true to his famously stalwart personality. "I can never play basketball."

I watched as angry as those senators. That poor young man was a botched job. Anyone who knew physiology would have known that bones and nerves were separate systems and both needed tweaks to grow in tandem. Beyond that, hearts could beat only so strong, digestions work only so hard, and lungs breathe only so fast. Humans had limits.

The DNA-modifying engineer responsible for that disaster sat near me in the greenroom, hauled out of his suicide-watch prison cell, waiting to testify, still manacled, and if he had not sat hunched over and weeping, I would have given him something to wail about. Spike heels could make good weapons. He never looked at me, although his police handlers did and seemed to equate us.

Meanwhile, the young man testified to other modified failures who hadn't survived infancy. Gills that didn't work even for children born underwater. Tails that involved unviable architectural changes to the spine. Some attempts to improve vision hadn't killed the thoughtlessly modified children but had left them blind because their brains couldn't process what their unnatural eyes saw.

"Would you agree with the majority, perhaps the unanimity of this committee," a senator asked the young man, "that human genetic engineering ought to be banned?"

"I support natural humanity," he said—what was he supposed to say? And he used that magic word: *natural.*

He wheeled himself out, and the abject designer of that failure was called in for a tongue-lashing with a cat-o'-nine-tails. I watched astonished at the senators' verbal skills and aghast at their ignorance.

My lawyer sipped a cup of minty tea and glanced at the screen. "Five minutes. Any last questions?"

"Any last words?" I answered. "That's all this is, words." But I knew that if Congress passed the wrong law (or other countries did, for that matter), my fate was prison.

"Yes. The most polite words are likely to win." She looked stern. She knew me.

"I've spent all last night studying the playbook."

"Good," she said. But she blinked for too long, as if she were hoping not to witness what she saw coming.

"These senators have no gist of what they're even saying," I complained. "The staff wrote the questions."

"And if the senators are smart," she said, "they'll stick to the questions so they don't prove that they're showboating idiots. Remember, the real audience is far away, the people who can still be convinced."

Good woman, that lawyer in her nice, fashionable haircut. Smart and efficient. If I were going to make a human being, and I had, I might have made her, a pinnacle of humanity. That was all I had ever wanted to do.

So, sworn in, I sat at that table twelve feet from the frowning committee chair, with bright lights overhead, a microphone ready to capture my wisdom, and, as that excellent lawyer had bargained for, I got to read a two-minute opening statement.

"Consider the definition of *medically necessary:* to prevent or treat an illness, condition, or disease or its symptoms that meet the accepted standards of medicine. Prevention. We do that all the time. Would you outlaw DNA vaccine production, especially after the cholera outbreaks five years ago? Treatment. Would you outlaw gene therapy and tell cancer patients they can't be cured? Then why not provide medically necessary prevention and treatment before the moment of conception?"

Such blank stares! Obviously, some form of sudden deafness had infected the senators.

"I've been accused of attempting to engineer perfection, and it's true. Perfect human beings are merely ordinary human beings brought to their optimal level: perfectly, optimally typical. Responsible genetic engineering can bring people to their best, but not one step beyond that—because as you have seen, to step beyond normality is to fall into the abyss."

No one believed me, a humble technician of the language of life. Behind me, an audience watched and tables of reporters placed context and commentary around my words. I might be reasonable, but what about the others? What about the ones who tried to make feathers and wings? What about the ones who would trick grieving parents into thinking they could resurrect their dead child? What about the ax blade of suspicion that fell unfairly on naturally conceived children with some disability or difference and who were tainted by this hysteria?

What about all that? Senators now glowered at me as if I were the ignorant one.

"It's true," I explained oh so patiently, "strawberries can be made purple, cows can produce insulin-filled milk, wheat can be perennial, woolly mammoths can be resurrected. Each of these amounts to a parlor trick, not playing god, and we need to be aware that these kinds of tricks are not applicable to the human genome."

My attorney was right. I was speaking to showboating idiots and beyond them to a panic-stricken world.

"People are like—think of a triangle," I testified, an explanation designed for nonscientific minds. "An equilateral triangle. You know, all three sides are the same length? The perfect person is like that, balanced on all sides. None of us are perfect. We're all a little more or less lopsided: taller, shorter, stronger, weaker, smarter, stupider.

With a lot of work, we can draw an almost perfect triangle. We must be balanced to be perfect, and the perfectly ordinary human being is the one best adapted to their environment in the many ways that evolution has shaped us."

I could have gone on, but I was asked instead about deextinction, which I felt passionately in favor of, yet I wanted to say more about the real issue, and eventually someone asked a question I could use to tangent into the facts.

"No, Senator. No one can successfully make a superman. That person would be disproportionate on one or even two sides of the triangle and ultimately fail. People can be made too tall for their nervous system, as you've seen. A superbrain would demand so much energy from the body that circulatory and digestive systems would falter. Perfect is balanced, like the scales of justice."

I didn't add that perfection was impossible to achieve, like all worthy artistic goals, but I could get close.

And finally I was dismissed. Yes, maybe I believed in limits, but others did not, which the senators knew for certain, and to be fair, they were right. Thus human "designer babies" were outlawed without exception. Justice was skewed by legislation designed to please crowds with loopy definitions that left us in the field not entirely certain of what was and wasn't legal.

No matter. I had crossed that wavering line with SongLab. By then all I had left from my business were creditors nipping at my knees. And babies, dozens of babies, now toddlers and teens (all of their DNA containing a tiny, inconsequential sequence of me as a signature of my artistry). A few of them were as perfect as humans could be, with occasional parlor tricks like red hair or the ever-popular above-average IQ to enchant choosy parents.

Red hair was easy. Humans could breed for it by their choice of sexual partner if they wanted to. Above-average IQ was harder, actually more likely to be produced by parental expectations and early childhood interventions than by anything I could do. Humans tend toward the norm in IQ, the most human of all characteristics. But I could make promises, and lo, if they were believed, they would come true. Placebos were effective medicine.

But that was all behind me, and a court order now banned me from initiating contact with my children. The past, tucked into the back of my mind, gave me frequent nightmares about fine people who became pariahs through no fault of my own besides ambition.

Two days after the testimony, in a hotel room in New York City, a tiny robot gun waited for me to return. How it got there was somehow never determined. It had two bullets. One lodged in the woodwork, the other in my left lung close to my heart, where it exploded. A fragment sliced open my pericardium. I never knew if the emergency-room staff approved of my work, but I was most grateful for theirs.

Now that lay in a past that felt much more distant than it was, and before me lay the immediate chance to save or murder billions.

# CHAPTER
# 3

Irene woke up a little before dawn—time to get to work, and she'd never get used to getting up so early. But just like elephants, mammoths didn't sleep much. Nimkii would be waiting for her. She listened for rain. It had stopped. Good. She listened for quarrels. Silence. Good. She got up, dressed, decided to skip breakfast, and was out as sunshine crept over the horizon. Raindrops clung to everything, sparkling like a magical landscape. . . .

He wasn't there.

That was impossible. She climbed on the truck bed for a better look at the far side of the pen. Maybe he'd lain down to sleep.

Instead she saw that the water trough had been torn up and out, its pipes broken and spouting water, and she could figure out what had happened next. The flowing water had eroded the soil around a fence post, and he'd pulled down a whole section of fencing. He'd charged through the opening, waded across the moat, dug a ramp through the soft dirt on the other side, and torn through the wire fence meant to keep out humans. It would have been like cobwebs to him. His big prints marked a path through the mud.

"Nimkii!" She didn't expect him to answer. She heard only a distant crow. Nimkii was out, free, wandering somewhere. Maybe even stolen. Or hunted, slaughtered. Gone.

Her breath trembled. No. *Stay calm.* Step by step. First, tell the owners. Then search. What would she need for a search?

"Nimkii!" she called again. "Pedazo!," as if he would answer—well, maybe he would, maybe with a roar or a trumpet. . . . But he didn't. She jumped down from the truck bed and ran into the house.

"Nimkii's out! He got out!" she shouted as she opened the door.

Ruby was stirring oatmeal. Alan was sitting at the kitchen table. Their wide eyes asked the same question.

"He tore up the watering trough, and the water wore down a way for him to get out. I can't find him."

Alan was on his feet, scowling, before Irene had finished. "He has a radio tag around an ankle. We can track him."

Irene followed him to the little office nook in the living room. "Open IDSleuth," he told the screen. "This will tell us where he went."

A message said: "Subscription expired."

"Hey, Ruby!" he shouted toward the kitchen. "Did you renew the tracking subscription?"

"You mean IDSleuth?" she shouted back.

"Yes. For Nimkii."

"They raised the rates a lot."

"You didn't talk to me about that."

Irene knew where this discussion was going. "I'll go look outside. Tell me if you learn something." She didn't wait for an answer. She wasn't even sure if Alan had been listening.

She ran up to her room, put on heavy boots, slipped on her phone, grabbed a whistle—and what else would she need? Her wallet with an ID because the authorities might get involved. She ran down two flights of stairs and out.

"Nimkii!" she shouted, running to the moat. "Pedazo!" He knew that name, too. Maybe he hadn't gone far.

Grass was trampled in a wide area around the pen, as if he'd hesitated over where to go. It would have been dark. He'd never been outside a pen in his life. He would have probably been frightened and would seek someplace that felt safe. What would that be? She walked in half circles, head down, looking for more trampled grass.

He'd headed west, then come back. East? Yes, around to the gate of the pen. He'd looked at it for a while, then kept going . . . to the area where they unloaded food. A bale of hay had been ripped up and some of it had been eaten. Then?

No clues. She shinnied up the winch's scaffold and saw an obvious path trampled through the alfalfa field alongside the pen. The tracks led straight to a line of aspens to the north that served as a windbreak. She slid down and ran toward it.

On the other side of the aspens was a creek, then a bit of scrub lowland, and beyond that a cornfield. He'd passed through the aspens—white-barked, tall, slim, straight, leaves rattling in the wind and a few already turning yellow. He'd shoved down some of them. On an impulse, she tried pushing on a tree. It didn't move. She pushed harder, and her feet slipped on the wet ground. Yet Nimkii had felled an identical tree. A big, strong, frightened animal was roaming loose.

Her phone rang: Alan. "Irene, where are you?"

"East. I'm at the north creek. He's come through here, I think. I'll keep following him."

"We're about to get the tracking up. Then we'll call the sheriff. They have tranquilizing darts for the rifles."

*No!*

Alan was right, though. Nimkii needed to be captured. But where would they take him?

"Just find Nimkii," he said. "We'll take it from there."

"All right." That wasn't what she wanted to say, but that was what she had to say.

*All right. Keep going.* She ran out of the aspens and splashed through the stream. His path through the scrub was easy to follow. Far downstream, a buck stood outside a clump of dogwood large enough to hide a herd of deer. He turned from the cornfield to look at her, then turned back to stare at the field. He was standing guard and knew where there was danger: in the corn. Maybe he feared a mammoth.

She sprinted to the edge of the field. The corn grew more than two feet above her head. If he was in there, he'd tower over it, but she'd never see far enough to spot him.

But there up ahead: mammoth scat. She knelt to look. Not dry at all, but cold, so it was at most an hour old. Trampled weeds led east along the edge of the field. She would follow the trail. How far could he go in an hour? How far would the buttery scent of his fur travel? Would he trumpet or grumble? Answer her call? Or would he run from her?

The wind rustled the corn behind her. Another breeze sounded deep, resonant, yet no leaves rustled. It sounded again. It carried a hint of buttery scent. Then an inhalation lasted longer than the breath any other wild animal would draw.

She turned, knowing what she would see.

Nimkii. Looking at her, very close, only half hidden by cornstalks.

How much did he hate her? How frightened was he? Could she outrun him through the brush? He was close enough to touch her with his trunk.

"Nimkii." If she stayed calm, he'd be more likely to stay calm.

He blinked.

"Nimkii, are you lost, pedazo?"

He roared. In a cat throat the sound would have been a mew.

Running would be a provocation. Especially if it made him feel deserted.

"Nimkii, would you like to follow me? I know the way to go home."

She took a step toward the creek, then turned back and gestured, long sweeping movements with her arm as if it were a trunk. He was smart. He would understand—she desperately hoped.

"Come with me, follow me." She held her breath and waited for him to turn and flee, to attack, or to hesitate, still undecided.

Instead, he reached out! He wrapped his trunk around her wrist—and didn't yank.

She needed to stay calm. She stifled an unbearable urge to shout with joy.

"Come with me." She took another step, pulling on his trunk. He took a small step.

"Keep going, we've got it." His trunk felt warm, its long hair rough like a dog's. She turned to lead and slid her hand down to the end of his trunk to clasp the thumblike extension at its end.

He followed, each of his steps as long as three of hers.

She heard faint sirens even before they had reached the creek. Of course. A mammoth couldn't be allowed to roam free, especially not if he was frightened. He had no survival skills. He was going to be shot full of tranquilizers and hauled away. How would he react? The best she could do was lead him to someplace to make the capture easy on him. *I'm sorry, Nimkii.* If he was frightened now, he'd be terrified then. And he'd blame her. Hate her forever.

But what else could she do? "Let's go to the road and then head home."

They walked downhill, then splashed through the water. He stayed docilely beside her. She let go of his trunk and reached up to gently gather a handful of the hair hanging from his flank, yard-long hair reaching to his knee, and his knee was at the height of her elbow.

They passed a bare, dead oak snag next to the line of aspens, and suddenly she had an idea of how to get him home safely, a crazy idea but better than what was likely to come. He'd seen people on horseback. Had he understood it?

She tugged on his hair. "Nimkii, stop for a minute. Come over here. Yes, here. Like that. Okay, now hold still."

She climbed up the tree trunk, out onto a branch, and pulled herself onto his back.

Nimkii took a few steps and shuddered. Irene already regretted the idea. He curled his trunk to reach over his shoulder and touch her leg splayed across his back. The tendons in her groin hurt, pulled too wide. But his hair and underfur were soft, and a thick layer of fat cushioned his shoulders, like sitting on a hairy pillow. She put her arms around his shoulder hump and held on.

"Forward, mighty steed!" If she was going to die of stupidity, at least she could have fun doing it. She rocked back and forth to urge him to move. He took a hesitant step and shuddered again. "There you go. Another step. Keep going. I'll steer when you need to turn."

He began walking through the alfalfa field. Good. She tugged the hair on the left side of his head. He turned his head, and she rocked, and he turned his body. He kept walking, slow and uncertain.

They were spotted even before they reached the road. A car came racing toward them and stopped a hundred feet away.

She smiled and waved. "We're going back to the farm!"

If this worked, it would make a great video. And everyone would know where to find Irene Ruiz the dupe. Well, it was now too late to do anything but cope.

She urged Nimkii onto the road's old worn asphalt to continue toward the farm. Ahead red lights were flashing. Two sheriff's cars. Would they spook Nimkii? Maybe the tracker was on again. She ought to call ahead and warn them. She lifted up her wrist and told her phone to place a call.

"Alan. I have Nimkii."

"We've spotted him. On the road."

"I know. I'm riding him."

"You shouldn't be doing that!"

"He wants to come back home. It's scary out here. So we're on our way!"

"She's riding Nimkii!" Alan shouted to people around him. "They're coming here. . . . Irene, listen, we can come and tranquilize him. We'll be right there."

"But he's coming home. You don't need to do that."

"We'll come to meet you!"

"I'm fine. Be careful. Don't spook him."

"We're coming."

Irene knew she should be afraid. She should be worried about a long list of things. Or . . . this could be performance art. Sure. Girl rides mammoth. She ought to be dressed in prehistoric furs and leather. Her T-shirt would have to do. At least it was brown.

"Ahead, mighty steed! Now, stay calm, Nimkii. This is where things get tricky. I'll try to get you to your pen. How about extra elephant chow today? And apples. A watermelon or two. Think about the watermelon, not about all the annoying people and cars."

They passed a man on the shoulder of the road recording a video. He backed away. She waved and smiled—a big smile—regardless of the consequences. Nimkii turned his head and stopped, but she rocked to keep him going. The driveway was coming up. She tugged on his fur. "Okay, now turn down here. Pedazo, can you smell it? It smells like home, doesn't it?"

Apparently it did. He rumbled, turned willingly, and walked a little faster. The rumble might have been a purr. Another sheriff's car was approaching with its lights flashing. Then the car steered onto the gravel shoulder, still far away, and stopped. A man in uniform got out.

"Are you all right?" he called.

"Yes. The mammoth took a little walk, but now he wants to come home. I don't think there'll be trouble if we all just stay calm." She patted the hump. "Nimkii, you're calm, aren't you?" He was still purring.

"Irene!" Alan shouted from far up the drive. "Is he coming back?"

Irene didn't want to shout too loud for fear of spooking Nimkii, but she waved and tried to act relaxed.

Relaxed? She was riding a full-grown male woolly mammoth. No one had ever done that before—maybe in all of human history.

Nimkii knew where he was going and seemed focused. Alan and Ruby ran toward them, followed by Will's barking dog. What if the dog attacked Nimkii?

"Hold the dog!" Irene said.

Alan grabbed it by the collar and held tight, looking stunned. Ruby looked angry, but she always looked angry.

"Open the gates!" Irene called.

Alan jumped. "Ruby, take the dog!" He ran ahead to the pen.

Nimkii seemed to have no interest in anything besides the open outer and inner gates. He rushed toward them. Irene held on tight.

The slipper-soft feet made no noise on the bridge, but the wood creaked. Once inside, he finally stopped, turned around as if to reassure himself, and trumpeted as loud as he could, deafening. The vibration traveled up Irene's legs to her fingers and the top of her head. He was home.

Behind them, Alan closed the gates. Irene leaned forward and hugged Nimkee's shoulder hump tight. The sheriff, a deputy, and the man from the side of the road, still recording, had come to the outer fence. She waved at them.

Now she needed to get down. A snag of a tree stood close enough. She tugged on his fur.

"Nimkii, take me to the tree." She rocked toward it.

He took a few steps, uncertain. She rocked again. He started walking. With a little more coaxing, he stood close enough for her to grab the trunk and shinny down. He stepped back and watched, shifting his weight.

When her feet were on the ground, she turned to face him, her hand out.

"We had a great trip, didn't we? Now it's time to get back to work. You entertain the visitors while I get you some yummy food. We can play again sometime soon."

He twined his trunk around her arm, and when he seemed ready, she lowered her arm and began walking away. She could slip through the inner gate, now closed, and then she'd have a lot of explaining to do.

In fact, all sorts of things might happen, a lot of them bad, maybe catastrophic, but whatever came next, it had been worth it for now. Nimkii was safe, and he trusted her.

\* \* \*

Berenike had almost finished her work shift, managing the morning rush hour with no special problems other than the usual cranky customers because there were never enough cars, a boring job at best, demeaning in every other way. Worse, her job and its drudgery gave her too much time to think.

Being fired wouldn't ruin her life. What came after it would, since no one would want to have anything to do with her. A sheltered home? That would be like jail, and it would last only as long as the funding for those homes did, and then—maybe one of those reeducation camps? She'd heard rumors about them, none of them good, and she believed the rumors.

Swoboda would be a worse fate, though . . . if he was telling the truth. He'd sent her a message, and she'd ignored it. She had nothing to say to him.

But according to her phone, Papa hadn't even received her message to him from yesterday. Maybe he had been arrested. *Maybe the next time I see him we'll both be in a camp.* But she was catastrophizing. On the other-hand, catastrophes happened.

Or they might not happen. *Two more days.* And then, everything might change, if everyone was lucky and everything went right. If she could last for two more days . . .

Her replacement, Jalil, arrived with only a few minutes to spare before his shift started, not eager to come early to a job he hated and couldn't escape. They'd gone through training together, selected by AutoKar at high school graduation. Supposedly they could say no to the training, which had a guaranteed job at the end, but then they'd have nothing, no other scholarships or offers, because they'd turned down an opportunity. And once hired, they couldn't even switch to another company, because a court case had ruled that AutoKar deserved to recoup its investment. Shared anger had turned them into friends.

She trusted him enough to have told him about the coming mutiny. He was all in. Their role was simple: they'd merely ignore corporate rules that ran counter to old-fashioned freedom, like no cars for people who weren't citizens in good standing. Every customer would be equal. No revenge, only justice. And an important part of the infrastructure would remain up and running. Then . . .

In two days, they'd be free—if everything went right. It couldn't possibly be that simple, but she'd do her part, and she was going to try to enjoy it while it lasted.

As he walked in, Jalil looked around for customers, then waved his phone.

"Hey, you gotta see this. She looks just like you." He wasn't smiling.

His display showed a video of a young woman up in Wausau riding what looked like a woolly mammoth.

"It escaped from a farm where it was, where she works, and she brought it back. It's a real woolly mammoth."

She looked exactly like Berenike, only skinny. *Fuck. Swoboda wasn't lying.* Berenike gripped the edge of the counter, a little dizzy and a lot angry.

"Well," she said when she could speak, "her ride's better than anything we've got."

Jalil nodded, complicit. "Some coincidence, hey? I thought you'd like to know. I'll go clean some cars for a while." He'd give her some space to process. He knew what he'd seen and what it meant, and he sympathized. He knew how close to second-class a young black man could be, too, if one or two tiny things went wrong for him through no fault of his own.

*I'm a dupe. Really.*

*Breathe deep. One step at a time.* Had Swoboda seen that video? It had been posted a few hours ago. She checked his message. He had seen it, and he'd somehow identified the woman in it: Irene Ruiz. "Everyone's going to see this," he said, joy lilting in his recorded voice.

*Fuck.*

Using Irene's name and location, Berenike looked her up in the corporate database: age twenty-two, mother Celia Ruiz, an artist—Berenike knew about her, an author of kids' books—from Madison, Wisconsin. Irene had used AutoKar until early summer for trips in

Madison, where she'd been living in a University of Wisconsin dorm. At the end of May she'd received a bachelor of science in environmental ecology.

The database had several photos of her, and every one of them confirmed that they were look-alikes: dupes.

Berenike paused, breathing deep. *Fuck. Fuck Swoboda, fuck everything. But stay calm.*

There were likely more dupes, too, everyone knew that. She would need to look for them. She ought to learn everything she could as fast as she could.

Using Irene's face and her own face as parameters, she ran the database's facial recognition. Three potentials came up, but two were only 75 percent matches. A 98 percent match was Avril Stenmark, who had just graduated from high school and was now at the University of Wisconsin–Madison campus, living in a different hall from the one where Irene had lived. Her father was Michael "Mick" Stenmark, assistant United States attorney; mother Emily, real estate manager. . . .

Company policy forbade personal searches, and sending data to her own phone would be monitored, so she used the work-around she'd learned from a friend: she wrote the information down with the paper and pencil she always carried in case she needed to do something subversive. It was easy to find herself doing something subversive. Her hand shook, though, and she had to struggle to write legibly.

There was a lot she needed to do. "Hey, Jalil," she called over the intercom, "I'm going!"

"I'll come down, then." He took his place behind the counter as she left, and he gave her a sympathetic look. "You be careful."

"Thanks." No amount of carefulness might be enough.

She biked home, stopping to buy something for dinner, crappy food, and there wasn't much else on the shelves anyway because the people who had put out the flags also panicked and bought all the food and toilet paper that they could. Some cricket protein chips were left— those were sort of healthy, and the sriracha flavor wasn't bad.

The apartment was empty. Good. She wanted to learn more about her potential . . . sisters. Triplets. Much nicer words than *dupes*. University education spoke of privilege, but no child could pick their parents. *For a while, though, parents could pick their children.*

Avril's family lived in a rich suburb of Chicago. Beauty was only skin deep, but privilege seeped down to the bone. Avril had a negligible public footprint because she had only recently turned eighteen years old, but her high school math and computer team had won some big awards.

Irene hadn't been doing anything online since she'd arrived in Wausau. Berenike watched the video of her ride three times. If Berenike got to Wausau, would Irene let her ride Nimkii? Or pet him? Or at least treat Berenike as an equal?

Swoboda had found Irene. Would he find Avril? And if Avril was studying at Irene's old campus, how long before she got found out by other people there?

Berenike had their contact information. She ought to do something. But was she the one to tell them they were dupes?

The apartment door opened. Another roommate had come home, Deedee. She gave Berenike a hard, steady look and closed the door.

"We need to talk." She put a finger to her lips, gestured to the door, and took the phone off her wrist. Berenike took hers off, too. By law, everyone was required to have their phone with them at all times. But now and then a person could leave it someplace where they might logically remain for a while and sneak away.

They left the studio apartment and walked down the musty hallway and stairs. As familiar as it was to Berenike, she felt as if she had no idea where the walk would lead. No, she knew exactly where: she was about to be kicked out. She followed Deedee outside to the old parking lot behind the building. No one living there could afford a private car, so the cracked pavement now hosted an abandoned, decaying picnic table and a scattering of trash and broken toys.

"Let's sit down," Deedee said. She didn't seem angry. Was that good?

Berenike sat across from her, picking out a spot on the bench without splinters. *Take some deep breaths. Be calm, centered*—not angry, which she would be if she thought about the situation for a moment.

Deedee owed her, and she was about to kick her out. Deedee's employer had placed limits on her paycard—every employer had the right to limit their employees' purchases based on the deeply held religious and personal values of the owners/corporation and other sorts of other I-own-my-workers-night-and-day bullshit. Berenike couldn't use hers to buy alcohol, among other things, but she could buy over-the-counter birth control, and Deedee couldn't. So she bought it for Deedee, who ought to be, well, maybe not grateful but at least have some sense of solidarity—although everyone had stopped trusting everyone else a long time ago. Denouncing paycard cheats was a common trope in crappy movies.

Finally, Deedee spoke. "I saw a video with someone who looked just like you in it."

Berenike tried to match her matter-of-fact tone. "I saw it, too."

"You know what that means." Her tone said that she knew exactly what.

"Yeah."

"Do you? Because really, it doesn't mean much. Not to me. I know, there's laws and stuff, and what people say, but that's not true. You know that, right? You know that you're okay?" Deedee actually seemed worried about her. Solidarity? Maybe.

*I'm okay? In what way?* "The laws and stuff matter."

"For now. Maybe not for much longer."

*What? Does she know?*

"I mean," Deedee said, "there's a lot wrong, too much, and . . ." She shrugged. "It can change to . . . the way it used to be."

*To old-fashioned freedom. Yes, she knows.* And she was one of the least political people Berenike knew. She'd once said in complete seriousness that a fast-food chain called Food Fed must be run by the federal government because it had the word *fed* in its name. Apparently, someone had recruited her. Berenike hadn't. That was one of the rules. Try to keep a low profile so that the size and scope of the mutiny will come as a shock to the system, especially if your role will be crucial.

"I hope things can change," Berenike said, "because I'll be in a lot of trouble otherwise."

"You're not in trouble with me. And I think, not with the rest of us, the other roommates. There's facts, Berenike, I know that, even if I don't always know what they are. I don't know a lot of things, and I think I ought to be able to find them out."

"Yeah. It's hard to know what's true."

"Did you hear about the cold?" Deedee said. "The Prez says there's a cold going around, a common cold? Not the Sino cold. Don't worry, he said. Do you believe that?"

Berenike felt safe enough to let sarcasm drip into her voice. "I thought he said the flags would stop the cold."

"Exactly. That's bilge. Hey, do you know what's his real name, the Prez?"

*Interesting question, and not one he likes people to ask.* "The Prez is his real name. You mean what did his name used to be? I heard—well, I heard a couple of things, but what I think is true is that he used to be . . ." She thought for a moment. "Nicholas Tyre, yeah, that's it, and then when he was twelve years old his parents said they knew he was destined to become president, and they changed his name."

"He was twelve," Deedee repeated. She counted something on her fingers, maybe how many years had passed between the time he got the name and got the job. Maybe she had heard the details of the path he had taken to power, and how it all started when he had made himself seem smart. In his teens, he'd had a show where he answered people's life questions, such as career choices or even whether to get a pet. The questions were screened or invented, the advice produced by a team of professionals rather than him, but he had seemed wise beyond his years if no one listened closely. He had shown that he could help people lead better lives, which turned into proof—supposedly— that he could lead the country to better times.

Berenike watched her and felt a tiny ember of hope glow in her chest. If Deedee was a mutineer, then anything was possible, even a successful mutiny.

"I hope things change soon," Berenike said. "Or else we're all in trouble."

Deedee smiled, and she had a beautiful smile. "Be ready. It's going to be big. So now we better get back before our phones miss us."

\* \* \*

Avril came back to her room after morning classes and an off-campus lunch, having learned that Hetta was in Minnesota with a crew doing some sort of bird-migration study. But she'd be back tomorrow. That wouldn't be too late, Avril hoped. She didn't want the protest to start without her.

Shinta was sitting on her bunk bed and looked up when Avril entered.

"We need to talk." She didn't look happy.

"What about?" She'd kept the room clean and been a model roommate. As she set down her backpack and sat at her desk to face her, she tried to steel herself for whatever accusation was coming. Maybe she'd somehow heard about Avril's mutiny ambitions.

"You're a clone, aren't you?"

*What?* That—that didn't even make sense. "I am not."

"Then what about that video?"

"What video?"

"I'll show you." Shinta held up her wrist and turned on the phone's display. Avril leaned forward. A woman was riding a woolly mammoth, and when she turned to wave at whoever was recording the video, her face looked exactly like Avril's.

Exactly.

"It happened today," Shinta said, "up in Wausau. A hundred miles north of here. My classmates told me she used to attend college here, and they used to see her." She lowered the phone. "Two people can't look that much alike by accident."

*I'm not a clone. How could I be?* Avril said, "I don't know anything about that. Maybe it's a fake. It's easy to fake a video."

"Maybe, but people knew her." She sat down at her own desk, closer to Avril. "If it's not a fake, if you're really a clone, I want you to know that it doesn't matter. I know better. I'm in bioscience. I know what cloning really is, DNA engineering, and it's nothing. You're as human as anyone. All the rest is just lies and horror movies."

"Really?"

"Yeah, really."

"But I'm not a clone. I'd know if I was."

"Yeah." She looked down at her phone. "Look, I didn't do this to hurt you. I'm sorry. I thought you should see this before . . . Hey, maybe you should talk to your parents. I can leave you alone, if you want. Will you be okay? Or I can stay with you if you'd rather. I mean, clones, there's lots of kinds of things that are clones. Like bananas. People don't understand that. They don't understand biology."

Avril's thoughts were swarming like bees. "I'll be okay," she said automatically. "Yeah, I should call my parents." *And say what? Is this true?* They would know. And if it was true . . . "Where did you find that video?"

"Here, I'll send it to your phone. I can go now for as long as you want. But if you need anything, call me. If anyone tries to hurt you, I'll hurt them."

"You don't have to do that."

"I want to. I know what kind of person I want to be."

"It isn't your problem."

"That you're a clone, no. That you're safe, yes." She flexed her arm. She was on the swim team and had enough muscle to hurt someone permanently. "And if you want to keep this a secret, I'm good with that, too. It's like in a writing class yesterday, we were supposed to write about our biggest secret."

"Oh. One of those assignments."

"Yeah, you know. I mean, I went through all this before in high school. It's like if you tell a story, then everyone expects you to keep living that story. You're always that thing. Like, and this is for example, it's not true, if you told how your father raped you as a child, you'd always be the raped little incest girl."

Avril nodded. Maybe Shinta's secret had to do with the death camps China had set up in Indonesia. Maybe that was why she hated China so much. Or maybe something else. It didn't matter. Maybe it could be even worse than being a dupe.

"Some secrets I want to keep," Shinta said. "You understand. Like this with you, if there wasn't a way that anyone could find out."

"Yeah. If I got that assignment, I'd make up something." She would pretend that she'd never seen that video.

"Telling the truth is overrated. Truth needs to be optional. You can give people it like a gift. You choose to give it if it makes you happy."

"Yeah."

They sat for a while thinking. Avril had once heard an idea sort of like that debated: confession equaled authenticity. That worked only if your authentic self was your public self, fully transparent, no secrets. But instead, you might actually want to keep your different selves separate. Because if you confessed, you'd always be that thing, and you couldn't grow and change. Everyone who really wanted to could figure out what Avril was now, if that video went viral, and people on campus had already seen it—and maybe she really was a dupe. Somehow. And maybe that was different than her real self, whatever that was now.

"So do what you have to do," Shinta said, "and tell me what you want me to do and I'll do it. Stay safe. I'll be back when you tell me it's okay. Or when it's necessary." She stood up, patted Avril on the shoulder, picked up her backpack, and left.

Stay safe? As soon as the administration found out, she'd be thrown off campus, and Shinta couldn't do a thing about it. Unless the video was a sham, or maybe it was real and Shinta was going to turn her in, because everyone knew dupes weren't fully human and now they weren't first-class citizens. Her father had been furious in June when the law changed, and he never got furious . . .

Because he knew.

He knew. Her parents had lied. And that meant they weren't really her parents, not her biological parents.

She sent the video to them. No words. They could do the talking.

There was a family rule: no lying and no secrets, which were a form of lying. Even if the truth hurt, it had to be told. Lies were what got Avril in trouble. But that worked both ways. If she asked a question, her parents answered honestly, no matter what. If she had a problem, they listened. She'd tell the truth, and her parents would keep their part of the bargain.

They'd have to tell her the truth now, not as a gift but as a duty.

And that woman in the video? Shinta said she used to attend Madison. Avril could ask around and get her name—if she left her room, which she wasn't going to do, not anytime soon.

What if Avril really was a dupe? Everyone said that dupes were unnatural, so they had no innate moral compass. Nothing stopped them from turning evil. The spark of divine burned inside people because God made them in His image, and if people were made in an unnatural way that God hadn't intended, the spark wasn't there. Dupes were cold inside. None of her building blocks of DNA was labeled "soul."

But not for a moment had she ever believed it, not at all—and for that matter, neither had her parents. It was just superstitious mumbo jumbo: natural law doctrine. Her father hated that doctrine.

Of course he did. He'd bought a clone for a daughter.

Worse—and this was for real—sometimes the DNA engineering left dupes crippled or superpowered. Like extra smart, and they went insane. Extra ambitious, and they became serial killers. Did she have a superpower?

Her parents had never let her make dupe jokes, but she knew them: *If you cloned Henry IV, would he be Henry V, Henry IV, Jr., or Henry IV, Part II? Is it true that if you clone yourself four times, one will be Chinese? What do you call a pessimistic clone? A double negative. What do you call a female clone? A clunt.*

In high school some kids began to say a boy named Hassan had a twin brother who was sent to live with an uncle so no one would think he was a dupe. Others said he really was a dupe. Then they found out he used a hearing aid, so he must have been a failed design. People started mocking him—and Avril had been one of them. He went home early that day and never came back.

She looked at the video again, pausing it to study the woman's face. It could be a fake. Her father made enemies in his job, and criminals would try to hurt him by hurting his family.

Her mother called. "Your father and I are coming to see you."

"So I'm a dupe."

"We'll talk." She was using a video call, obviously at work, judging from her surroundings. "We care about you more than anything else."

Avril hadn't turned on her video, so Mom was staring at a blank screen. "Some things have to be said in person. We'll be there in an hour, two at most."

"Okay." Mom would have denied it over the phone. Having to talk in person meant that it was true. Arriving that soon meant they'd pay extra to have their car travel in the express lane.

"We love you, Avy." When Avril didn't answer, her mother ended the call.

Avril considered the equation of love. DNA plus technicians plus womb equals family. Would the equation survive peer review? Her peers. The whole world.

An hour. She tried to do some homework to distract herself, differential equations. She planned—had planned, it wasn't going to happen now—to specialize in bioinformatics. To fight back against the mumbo jumbo, to fight for freedom.

Studying made no sense anymore. She slammed the button to power off her screen. She turned on some music. That didn't make her feel better, either.

Eventually, a knock sounded at her door—and there were her parents, looking as somber as if someone had died. Well, yes, their daughter was as good as dead.

Her mom reached out to hug her. Avril stood stiffly.

Her father took a few steps in. "We should leave our electronics here and go talk outside."

Avril shrugged. It didn't matter anymore.

Silently, they rode the elevator to the first floor. Her father sniffled a few times. He seemed to have that cold that was going around. She led them to a couple of benches facing each other along the lake, shadowed by trees. The afternoon sun was shining a little too warm even through the leaves. She sat facing them. For a long moment, the only sounds were the distant voices of students on their way to and from classes.

"You deserve the whole truth," Dad said, as if under courtroom oath and looking as uncomfortable as a witness facing hostile examination. "We really wanted a child."

"We did," Mom said, "more than anything else. We were going to get in vitro fertilization, but we both carry recessive genes, we found out, for cystic fibrosis, and some cancer genes, and it would have been complex to edit out. So we decided to get a third-party embryo."

"So I've seen. I'm a dupe."

"You're completely ordinary," Dad said quickly.

"But I have engineered DNA."

"It was legal then," he said. "Or not illegal, at least. All we wanted was a healthy child. And that's what we got. The natural law doctrine came later, and it's based on irrational fear."

"I'm healthy and ordinary." Her tone of voice said she didn't believe it.

He said, "You've lived long enough to know that's true."

"So you just, what, went to a lab and told them what you wanted?"

"Actually," her mother said, "they had a catalog. We took one pretty much at random because we . . . as he said, all we wanted was a healthy child. We thought of some letters, SD because I grew up in South Dakota, and took one that included SD in the serial number."

"I was a serial number. You bought me and that was that." She looked at them, both sitting still with their musty tattoos and piercings, as if the slightest movement would unleash a torrent of emotion. "Why lie about it? You always say, don't lie."

"At the time, it wasn't illegal." He paused to sneeze. "Sort of a gray area. That changed, and . . . I come under a lot of scrutiny for my job."

Avril wasn't going to cry, wasn't going to rage. Wasn't going to forgive. "You always said I looked a lot like Grandma."

Her mother glanced at him. "Small children don't understand family secrets, and we needed to tell you something you could repeat because we knew you would repeat it." Her sentence sounded rehearsed. "But now you're old enough to understand, and you need to. We're your parents, not your biological parents, but still your real parents. We love you, Avy, we always did and we always will."

"They're going to kick me out of college."

"First they have to prove your legal status," he said.

"They can tell just by looking."

"It will take more than that." He sniffled again. "They'd need conclusive evidence, and in the meantime there's a case that should overturn the entire executive order declaring classes of citizens. It's clearly unconstitutional. There should be an injunction within a month."

"In the meantime," Avril said, "dupes get beat up and stuff."

"You're entitled to legal protection regardless of your status."

*Yeah, that'll work.* "We know what the Supreme Court will do. Maybe I should come home."

Her mother sighed. "If you want to. If you'd feel safer."

"By the time it gets to the Supreme Court," he said, "a lot might change. Do what you feel you need to do in order to protect yourself, and we'll support whatever you decide, but this isn't the end of the world."

It was up to her. Avril stared at the lake, its water ruffled by the wind. She could go back home, but . . . the mutiny couldn't say no to her now if she was one of the kinds of people it was fighting for. Old-fashioned equality, including for all second-class and disbarred citizens. *Nothing about us without us.* That was an old doctrine and a good one. She could stay and fight back. Her dad was right about one thing, too. If she was anything weird, if she had some failed super-power, she'd know by now.

But staying on campus was dangerous. The thought jolted her with a realization: She wanted danger. Injustice coalesced around her now. She could be part of the mutiny, a big part.

"I think I'll try to stay."

"I'm proud of you," her father said. He seemed to be thinking. "In the meantime, I recommend against contacting that woman with the mammoth. That would only make it easier for you two to be connected and your status to be confirmed. Besides, she might not know." He thought again, and his hand with the swirls inked into the skin on his fingers clenched in a white-knuckled fist. He was angry, very angry, but not with her. "I'm glad you want to go on with your life, but there might be a fight, and it will likely be long and hard."

Her mother added, "You're being very brave and understanding about this. We want you to know we love you."

"We brought some information for you," he said. "It's printed on paper so it will be hard to trace, and it will tell you more about yourself. Now that you know, you should know everything."

This was as much of an apology as she was going to get, even though she deserved a lot more. They weren't even really her parents. She didn't have real parents.

"The whole truth." She stood up.

They both stood up, too.

"We'll be here for you," her mother said.

Avril couldn't think of a way to refuse to walk them up to the room to collect their electronics and then back to their car, so she did, and after hugs and murmurs of "I love you" that she couldn't avoid without making things worse, her mother took an envelope from her purse and handed it to her, and they left.

She sent Shinta an all-clear message and went to the room, clutching the envelope. There seemed to be only one sheet of paper inside.

She opened the envelope the moment the door to the dorm room was closed behind her. The sheet looked to be a copy from an official

document with parts of it erased—everything that would have identified it as hers.

*Baby girl, 8.22 pounds, 21.2 inches, vaginal delivery, no complications,
inconsequential scalp bruising. Full-term SongLab zygote AP 5Y08SD71x6.*

That was all. That was enough.

She searched for information about SongLab. It had been based
in Shanghai, China, and went out of business eleven years ago. Its
owner, a woman named Peng, had been accused of creating designer
babies, built piece by piece, a human being created from scratch, not
just a modified real person, although Peng sold modifications, too.
SongLab had promised hair and eye and skin color, body build, traits
like intelligence, creativity, general personality such as extroversion
or curiosity, and of course perfect health. Mix and match or choose
from a catalog, get implanted, deliver nine months later, and give that
beloved little bundle of joy a name.

She'd been engineered. Blond hair, dark eyes, a bit taller than average, slim, smart enough to pick her university since her parents
could pay for anything, good at math, and very healthy.

Her parents were also white but not blond, not dark-eyed, and their
faces were more angular than hers. Her mom was slim only because
she got monthly microbiotic therapy. They used to tell her that she took
after a grandmother who'd died before she was born, that she had her
hair color and her personality. Her eyes stung. She took a deep breath.

A quick search for "mammoth" and "Wausau" yielded the video
and eventually the information that the woman was Irene Ruiz, and
she could be traced through the university to her recent degree in
environmental ecology. Her hometown was Madison, her mother
Celia Ruiz, an artist famous for her children's picture books. Avril
had brought one of those books with her to campus from home, that
was how much she'd treasured it. For a while when she was little, she
had read it every day.

Shinta arrived with a question on her face. Avril nodded—nothing
more to say.

They now shared a secret like shiny new knives. What were they
going to do with it? Avril was going to carve a new persona for herself: the mutinous dupe.

*       *       *

I hadn't seen the sun or talked to anyone for more than a day (I felt
confident the clocks in my underground cell were correct) other than
my distant coworkers and occasional laconic military staff who tidied

and resupplied my quarters. Those conversations were limited and transactional.

And yet, I felt uneasy, as if I'd unconsciously noted a foreshock to an earthquake. The delta cold was coming—perhaps arriving extremely soon rather than very soon. Because of that, I wanted to work at all deliberate speed, but my coworkers, perhaps even more spooked by that ineffable tremor than I was, wanted to work faster, even recklessly.

We had found a way to suppress some of the attenuated virus's virulence, but the people infected could still contract secondary infections because the virus could overwhelm alveolar macrophages, at least by my analysis, and the ultimate death toll would be too high.

"This is worrisome," I told my far-off coworkers.

"It could be prevented by antibiotics," said someone identified as Node 6, whose voice was static-strewn. I was Node 3. (Node 1 listened but never spoke.)

"I don't think that it would be practical," Node 2 said. The voice, despite distortions, sounded female, at least to me. I thought of her as Grrl because her falsified voice growled. "We'd face a lot of problems, and a big one is quantity. We have barely enough antibiotics for normal times. We couldn't even double the amount in a month, and we'd need a whole lot more a whole lot sooner than that."

"And they would only work for bacterial infections," Node 5 said.

"Is there a way we could make the virus cause less lung damage?" Grrl asked.

After some discussion, we thought we could, but I saw problems with the new approach. If the virus had less ability to misappropriate the infected human's RNA in the process of replicating itself, that might result in more antigenic shift: the virus would reproduce inaccurately and might create a variant with undesirable traits. Besides, if it couldn't hijack the host's RNA to reproduce rapidly, it wouldn't be as contagious.

After more discussion, we felt fairly certain we could change the site of the infection to the upper respiratory tract and cause what would resemble a mere head cold, which by its nature killed far fewer people: it just made them miserable. In addition, they'd sniffle and sneeze more, which would spread the virus even faster.

"I predict a chicken soup shortage," Grrl said.

We began creating new schemata for such a virus and testing them on models, although that took time, especially when using whole-organism models rather than single cells.

"I prefer working with full human models," I said in response to complaints, "even though they have far too many moving parts. We should run a lot more models. Every model fails in one way or another to imitate reality, and we also need to compare a variety of genotypes."

"Humans don't show as much variety compared with other species," Node 5 said. "Think about chickens, how extreme some of them are."

I thought about bloody, dead chickens. "They're engineered for profit, not survival. I'd like to think we're working for survival, even if we're swimming against the current. Profit might matter more than people in some boardrooms, but it never should to us."

"Those American flags will hold off the virus for only so long," Grrl said. "The cells that really matter are brain cells, and White House policy is running short of them."

"Flags?" I said.

"Yeah," she said. "The Prez said to fly them to show unity against China and its illnesses."

The foreshock I'd sensed may have been that: an appeal to patriotism as a way to combat the politically named Sino cold. The foolishness exceeded my dismal expectations. "Flags," I said. "Anything else?"

"Remember," Node 5 interrupted, "our communications are monitored."

And so Grrl was chastened. (Or maybe I was. Hard to know.) But I felt for a moment that I'd found a true kindred spirit, and I wished I could meet her in real life—if we both lived that long.

We split up some tasks, and I continued modeling viruses as they were envisioned. Nothing satisfied me. In some models, the virus seemed to trigger meningitis, which I saw as a proxy for a bigger problem.

"It might cause more damage to nasal mucous membranes than we thought," I said.

"That's not so bad, meningitis," said Node 6, who minimized everything. "A known problem. Easy to treat."

"Meningitis, maybe," I said, although it was not at all easy. "I have other worries. There's a lot more out there waiting to cause a secondary infection if the host is compromised. In my day job, I've seen some avian coronavirus mutations that could jump to humans. We could trigger an epidemic."

"They're always there, avian viruses," Node 6 said. "Would they be as bad as Sino?" They never called it by its more technical name, which was telling.

That gave me pause. "I honestly don't know. I wouldn't feel comfortable making a prediction."

"We know some things for sure about Sino."

"Let's stay focused," Node 5 said. "We're on a deadline."

Grrl had an idea. "I think we could limit the damage. Some strains cause very mild symptoms, and we could try incorporating that."

"But," Node 6 said, "it has to be symptomatic to be as contagious as we need."

I supported Grrl's idea. "We can balance the needs, and I think we have to. Meningitis can strike quickly. A virus that incapacitates its hosts within hours won't be as contagious as we want."

"Let's get to work," Grrl said, and the *us* in *let's* meant her and me. So we worked. She knew much more about certain cellular processes than I did, and we were a good team. Buoyed by the top-quality coffee that the military supplied in endless quantities, by about three in the morning we had an effective compromise between damage and symptoms. We reported that with pride and relief, and then, to calm our jangled nerves and maintain what had become a delightful relationship, we chatted—about general science, nothing too personal, since Node 1 was always listening.

I began to drowse and was about to say good night. Our screens beeped with an official notice. The attenuated virus had been released. With a few adaptations, mechanical cleaning machines with their little onboard fans could distribute virus-laden aerosols as effectively as the human nose.

"Which one?" Grrl and I asked in unison. No matter which, it was far too early in the process of testing. We needed not just theoretical models but real (and courageous) human subjects. Much more important, the virus that had been released couldn't have been our compromise. It couldn't have been manufactured that quickly. So it was an earlier version, perhaps much earlier, and any of those viruses would result in massive, needless death.

I wrapped my face in my hands and wept. She was shouting at people around her. I could make out some of the words in her rising panic.

"Everywhere?" her distorted voice roared.

Irene carried a coil of barbed wire to the pen for repairs. Nimkii had to know he could get out of the pen any time he wanted, but he hadn't tried for the rest of the day yesterday or so far today. Perhaps he was too frightened of the wider world. She'd slept outside that night to guard him. He seemed to want to stay near her, so she'd laid a sleeping bag on bales of hay at the far side of the pen from the breach.

She'd woken up several times during the night with a desperate question: *Why don't all these mosquitoes drive him crazy?* Because they were giving her nightmares. And each time, he had been right there on the other side of the fences, as close as he could be, and she kept thinking of how it would feel to hug him again, knowing that she never would. He had seemed gentle, but that was when he was afraid. Now he was in familiar surroundings, and he might react violently.

Never. But as much as that hurt, now the sun was up, it was Saturday morning, and she had to repair his pen as best she could.

Alan stopped her. "We can't keep him here."

Irene had already realized that, and her heart ached sharp enough to bleed. "I know. He needs a better pen anyway." Maybe a new home would be an improvement. Maybe, if Nimkii was lucky and a better home could be found. But now that the video had been passed around, she might need to leave, too, for her own safety, or as soon as Alan and Ruby found out about her unnatural status.

"It's a question of money," he said. "Already with new rationing coming soon and stuff, Ruby says the price of feed just went up."

*New rationing is coming?* She hadn't heard that yet, but feed providers would have inside information. They'd need more money. "I have some ideas for fundraising."

"That doesn't matter. We can't keep him. I'm seeing where we can send him." Did he look relieved? At least he wanted to send him away. The owners of some engineered dinosaurs in Florida had shot them when a huge hurricane approached.

Irene nodded, afraid that if she tried to speak again, she'd start crying. There wasn't much choice, though. The sheriff didn't have to say anything when he checked the pen. He just shook his head. No visitors were allowed until the pen was secured. He should have issued much tougher restrictions or an immediate order to relocate Nimkii, but he liked the farm. The need to relocate Nimkii as soon as possible remained utterly real even if it wasn't official.

Irene knew the wire for the repair would be as much of a barrier as dental floss. Appearances mattered, though. To distract Nimkii, she winched a cardboard box of carrot-top greens, discards from a food-processing plant, into the pen, and as soon as he started eating, she rushed to the other side of the pen and waded through the moat carrying a bag of supplies.

He looked up and watched her intently.

She needed to fix the water trough. She'd been winching buckets over into the pen, but he needed a lot more water than that. He started to walk toward her, so she ran as close as she could without being within reach, set down her hat, and rushed back to her work. She'd given him one of her hats before and he'd destroyed it, which had broken her heart, but at least it might keep him busy. Her heart would never mend, no matter what.

She began to connect the original pipes with the trough's faucet and drain using pieces of hose. It was a half-assed repair that he could wreck with one kick, but maybe he wouldn't. The threads didn't catch right away. *Come on. Screw in!* If she hurried less, she might finish sooner.

He was muttering and rumbling, fiddling with her hat and looking at her. She had to admit it, finally: he frightened her. He was a violent, unpredictable animal. She had been so lucky.

But he wasn't destroying her hat. He sniffed it and brushed it against his face and kept watching her.

When she was done with the pipe and had strung a couple of lines of wire between the fence posts, scratching her hands as she did, she ran to the inner gate and slipped out. On the other side, she turned to wave goodbye. He walked toward her as fast as he could, holding out the hat.

He was going to return her hat!

"Nimkii! My mighty steed!" A tear rolled down into the corner of her mouth, salty and chilled by the air. She reached out her hand. He came closer, too close for safety, but she was sure he wouldn't hurt her. His carrot-scented breath warmed her face. He stretched out his trunk and put the hat on her head.

"Nimkii! Thank you, Nimkii."

He touched her outstretched hand with the tip of his trunk, and she clasped the moist thumb tight.

"You know I love you, pedazo. They're going to send you away. I'll always love you."

He pulled his trunk back and rumbled—a low, beautiful purr.

Of course he hadn't understood. Of course he hadn't said "I love you, too" back. Or maybe he had. She wanted to believe that he had.

A car pulled into the driveway. She turned and looked. A man wearing a visor-screen stepped out, someone she was pretty sure she'd seen on campus in Madison. Mamá's messenger, finally? Finally? She hurried over, but Alan got there first and began talking to him, no doubt telling him visitors weren't welcome.

The man lifted up his visor and answered Alan. ". . . but I'm not here to see the mammoth," he was saying when she reached earshot. He saw her and paused for a moment. "Hey, Irene! Good to see you again! And your mom says hi. I came up for a lab class at the Wausau campus, so I thought I'd stop by on my way back."

*Definitely the messenger.* Irene played along. "Thanks! It's good to see you, too." She wished she knew his name, but Alan seemed convinced and began walking away. "We had a problem with the pen and can't have visitors. Sorry."

"I saw that. I guess I need to stay away. Too bad. That's an impressive animal." He took a few steps toward the road, and she followed. "Your mom does say hi. I'm Cal. She sent you some artwork."

"Yeah, she said she would." Irene tried to sound natural. They'd need to make it look like a real visit between real friends.

He looked around at the fields and the dilapidated farmhouse that Alan was entering. He coughed. "Sorry. Too much fresh air. Let's take a little walk."

She glanced at Nimkii. He seemed content with the greens. They began to stroll down the road—not too far. Nimkii might decide to follow.

"How many of you are there?" he demanded, suddenly no longer friendly.

She tried to make sense of the question. *How many?* Oh. Clones. How did he find out? And why did he care?

He frowned at her silence. "There's another one of you on campus. A freshman from Chicago."

*Another one.* She stopped in the road, blindsided by a surprise she always knew might hit her. For all that Peng had told her mother she was unique, she knew he must have sold other zygotes, and "unique" had meant environment, not DNA. Peng could be slippery that way. *Another one.* She'd always dreamed about meeting a clone of herself, a sister of sorts, the only truly genetic family she would have.

Faced with the real prospect, now she wanted to meet that other version of herself more than anything else. "What's her name?"

"No one told us you were a clone." He stood looking down at her through his visor.

"It doesn't matter. And it's not the sort of thing you say in public. Not these days, anyway."

"We can't have dupes in this."

*Dupes.* "What do you mean? This is all about freedom. Equality."

"You'll put us at risk."

"How? We're as trustworthy as anyone. You know that."

He huffed. "You might draw attention to yourself. You already have with that video. How long before people figure this out on campus?"

"How long before the mutiny?" It was a matter of days, she was sure.

"That's not the point. There's too many of you." He turned to go back to his car, lifting his visor to cough, probably that non-Sino cold that was going around. "You—and your mother—shouldn't be involved."

She followed him, trying to hide her anger. Alan or Ruby might be watching, and they might ask questions. But he had no right . . . "Who is she?" He could at least tell her that.

"I've got to get back to Madison. I'll give you the artwork," he said as if it were a chore. He rummaged around in his car and handed her some stiff papers. "Here."

"Who is she?"

"Her name's Avril." He got in and left, leaving her to stare at the car as it drove down the road. She knew without looking at what she held that he hadn't delivered Mamá's message, whatever it was.

She walked back to the pen. Nimkii had stopped eating and was watching her as if she were the only thing in the world. Behind a bale of hay to shield herself from prying eyes just in case something subversive had been included, she looked at what she had, two pieces of watercolor paper, art from Mamá, beautiful paintings of Nimkii. Nothing more.

"Call Mamá," she told her phone. Her mother didn't answer, so Irene left a message. "Mamá, a guy named Cal came, and he gave me two paintings of Nimkii, and that was all. And he had some things to say. You should call me."

He was the one who shouldn't be involved with the mutiny instead of leaving out her and Mamá.

*     *     *

Berenike maintained a neutral professional expression on her face appropriate for the rank of assistant manager, which her ID badge proclaimed, as a man rushed into the little franchise office. He looked angry. She slipped a finger under the counter onto the security alert button—just in case. The office in the corner of the building had a wide window facing the street as much to keep staff safe as to make it look inviting to customers.

*Only one more day of this crap. If we're incredibly lucky.*

She'd been watching people walk down the street toward the pre-mutiny protest. She'd be going as soon as her shift was over, just a few more minutes, just a few blocks away. Afraid? Yes, but she'd gone to a clandestine training session months ago about protests and knew what to do if things went wrong.

Protests all around the country at the same time would be the first step toward the mutiny, letting people know that there was resistance—a safe, effective resistance, people unafraid to show their faces. Tomorrow, those same people would go to work and refuse to obey all the illegal orders—and at the protest she'd get some passwords for AutoKar to override anything corporate tried to pull.

The angry man came up to the counter and started shouting. "Those . . . people are using your cars. I saw them! You know what I mean." He pointed to the south. "Right over there, at the protest."

So that was what he was angry about. He said *protest* as if it were vile. This was the kind of man who'd arrest her father for his jokes—and her father still hadn't answered her, so maybe he actually had been arrested or worse. But regardless, she had to deal with this guy.

"It's illegal!" he said, looking her straight in the eyes, challenging her. "Your cars can't be used for illegal purposes."

The corporation had a canned reply she was supposed to use, already displayed on the screen facing her—the software eavesdropped—so she recited it, not looking him in the eyes as a reciprocal challenge, trying to make it sound natural, the way she'd been trained.

"We're sorry you're upset. Today's event has all the necessary municipal permits and permissions, and we're required by law to provide transportation to and from legal activities without discrimination. We pride ourselves in obeying all laws for the safety and comfort of our passengers."

Even to her own ears, she sounded like a cold machine, which might make him angrier. She added, with additional professional neutrality, "We're sorry and understand your concern, but the city has allowed the event. We can't do anything about that."

"Spineless corporate bureaucracy, that's what you are."

She was tempted to say *We're sorry you feel that way* but he'd probably see that as snide, and he'd be right. He was also right about the corporate bureaucracy being spineless. Inflexible and idiotic, too. She had the authority to offer him a small credit to his account to mollify him, but she decided not to, her own little vengeance against the kind of people she felt justified to fear.

"We hope the event hasn't caused you any inconveniences," she said.

His scowl delighted her. "You know what, just get me a car and I'll go home. I wouldn't have come downtown if I'd known about it. Those people think they deserve . . ."

She stopped listening and touched a few buttons on her screen. An autocar was being recharged in the service bay, and it rolled out next to the entrance before he had finished. He was coughing. She almost wished he had the delta cold and not whatever minor crap was going around.

She waved a hand toward the car. "Thank you for sharing your concerns," she said with a fake smile.

"Yeah," he said. He didn't believe her. Well, he shouldn't, since she was lying. The database had told her more about him than he might have wanted her to know. He could easily buy the kind of food that she couldn't afford, had sufficiently high citizenship standing to be exempt from rationing, and he could even pay for a heli-taxi instead of a ground car. Tomorrow he might not be able to give orders the way he used to. She wished she could witness his face then.

She watched him leave, wondering if she'd miss the chance to inflict those minor cruelties if the mutiny failed and if she lost her job. If she lost it—maybe, just maybe, she wouldn't. Momma had lied, so Swoboda, who was a lot like her, would lie in one way or another, and maybe he wouldn't carry out his threat. But anyone else who saw the video could expose her.

Even if the law changed, she might need to move. One roommate offered sympathy, but the other two might not. Maybe she could live with Papa, if he ever came home. Maybe he was just sleeping off another drug binge. Maybe, any minute, he'd call, or at least read her message.

"Hey, Berenike!" Jalil walked in with one minute to spare, wearing his teal uniform tunic, ready to start.

"Hey, Jalil!"

"Watch out." He gestured south toward the protest. He knew she'd be going.

"I'll be careful."

She sprinted into the tiny office bathroom to change into street clothes, shoved her uniform into her backpack, and was out the door while he was still logging into the system.

The protest blocked the street in front of the gray granite federal courthouse, a couple hundred people, she guessed, and her heart fell: an enormous number considering the danger, but not nearly enough to start a nationwide mutiny. A man on the steps with a megaphone was speaking: ". . . and there'd be plenty of food for humans if they weren't feeding pigs and chickens and cows to feed the rich."

Someone was going to deliver the passwords to her. Who? They'd find her. That was all she knew. The movement had way too much secrecy, not like she could do anything about it. The crowd jostled as something or someone passed through it.

There was a bang like a gun. Close by. Then another. *Gunfire?* A third bang. And screams. People began to run, and behind them smoke rose and blew toward her. It stank.

*Don't panic. Make way.* That was what she'd been taught in the protest training. Berenike turned and moved with the crowd. *Be like a school of fish. Don't trample. Don't fall.*

People were pushing too hard. She stumbled onto the person in front of her, both of them propped up by the press of the crowd, and tried to regain her footing.

More smoke. It was red. *Gas?* People were screaming and coughing.

"Stay calm," an amplified man's voice urged, the man who'd been speaking. "We're clearing the crowd. You'll be out soon. Stay calm."

The crush didn't decrease, but it didn't increase either. Sirens approached.

"What's happening?" someone up ahead screamed.

"It's not gunfire," the speaker said. "Follow instructions."

"Come this way!" a high-pitched voice called from the right. "Walk calmly. This way. Walk calmly."

The push moved her to the right. Berenike took a long stride, then another. *Walk—calmly.* A body lay on the ground in front of her, and someone was attending to that person. She paused and inched farther to the right, leaning back to stop other people.

Step by step, she moved around them, and suddenly there was space. *Don't run*—but people were running. *Don't be trampled, be a school of fish,* so she ran with them. It felt surreal, the clarity of the pavement beneath her feet, the moving bodies around her, the rising noise, shouts, sirens. . . .

She reached a corner and paused in a doorway to let people run past. *Think calmly.* What had happened? Bombs? What would help? Were people hurt? If there were bombs, there might be more bombs. The crowd had thinned. She stepped out and looked up the street. Smoke was dissipating, red, white, and blue smoke. Patriotic antiprotesters. Crowd-control volunteers in orange vests were waving and gesturing. Could she help? Maybe the best thing to do was to get out of the way. She knew a couple of the volunteers. They were competent. Yes, get out of the way. It wasn't cowardly—that's what the training had assured her. Let the appropriate people do their jobs.

But she wouldn't get the passwords. The rally had failed. The first step toward mutiny had fallen off a cliff.

Failure . . . All those people who had come knew the danger. She wasn't going to abandon them, at a minimum. She ran back to the AutoKar office. It was crowded all the way out to the sidewalk with panicked customers, still coughing from the noxious smoke, hoping to get a ride faster by asking in person. She pulled out her ID badge and used it to work her way inside.

"Hey, Jalil! I'm back to help." He looked up and mouthed the word *thanks.*

People wanted to get home, be safe, and the corporation had a lean fleet, but cars could be rerouted and rides doubled up if someone knew how to organize things. She knew how.

She stepped behind the counter. "Please enter your destination in your phones. We can get you out of here faster if we know where you want to go. Tell everyone outside to do the same thing. We'll get you home safe."

*Fuck the Prez and fuck everything he did, and fuck the patriots who tried to kill people at protests.* She could fight back in this little way, and she'd do it with breathtaking efficiency.

A half hour later, everyone was on their way home but her. Jalil gave her a dubious glance, as if he'd witnessed a DNA-engineered superpower. Well, if it was true, maybe being a dupe wasn't all bad.

She was tired—but the protest hadn't been a total failure. A woman had come to thank her for her help and had handed her a little folded plastic card that Berenike had slipped into her pocket without looking at it. Tomorrow was still the day, and giving up wasn't an option. Giving up was a drug that beckoned with a moment of serenity and a lifetime of disaster: Momma's choice, not hers. As she waited for the bus, she checked her messages for any sign of Papa.

Nothing. But Swoboda had left a message:

"Take your time thinking about it. Twenty-four hours," he said. "Come live with me. I have plenty of room. If not, you and your clone will become famous."

*In less than twenty-four hours, can I find a gun and shoot him?*

No, that was a foolish thought, and she'd be too busy tomorrow anyway, but her fists were clenched tight enough to throttle him from a distance. She'd rather sleep under a bridge than in his house.

"Think about it," he said. "The offer is open. For your clone, too."

She heard Momma's voice in his intonation like a horrible distorted mirror—no, she heard the voice that had made Momma want to protect Berenike . . . and as if a switch had been flipped, she instantly forgave Momma for all the hurt she had ever caused. Instead, she shared every single moment of Momma's rage against Swoboda. If only Momma were alive. . . .

Momma would protect her, and Momma would protect her clone, too—all her clones—out of spite for Swoboda. By the time the bus came, she knew what she had to do: she had to make sure that the mutiny succeeded in every way she could, and starting now, she was going to act like Momma, and Momma was dangerous.

*     *     *

Avril saw Hetta in the lobby as she was leaving to go find lunch. She lifted the visor-screen she was wearing to keep anyone from taking a close look at her face. A lot of people might have seen that mammoth video.

As soon as Hetta saw her, her expression turned sour. "I need to talk to you. So you aren't from Milwaukee."

*Milwaukee?* "No, I'm from Chicago."

"I saw someone who looks like you in Milwaukee. I thought you were her. That's why I had Cal talk to you."

*Like me?* "Just like me?"

"Come outside and we'll talk."

Avril followed her out behind Dejope Hall. In the buzz of her thoughts, she realized she must have another sister besides Irene. *Triplets! I'm one of three!*

Hetta looked around. No one was near. "The one I saw in Milwaukee looked just like you. And Cal said he talked to someone who looked just like you up in Wausau."

"That must have been Irene. Irene Ruiz. She rode the mammoth.

She was a student here." *Hey, wait, I just outed Irene. Well, anyone can see the video.*

"How many of there are you?"

"I don't know. Three? I just found out I'm a . . ."

"Yeah. And Cal said your father's in the government." Her tone accused her.

"My father hates the Prez. He'd support the mutiny."

"You think so?"

"I know so. His daughter's a dupe, a second-class citizen. I can't be here legally. What's he going to do?"

"We didn't know that before."

"Well, you know that now." And if the mutiny was what they said it was, they'd have to let her in.

Hetta took a couple of breaths, still looking her in the face. "Do you have somewhere to be now?"

"I was going to lunch."

"Then come with me. There's going to be a protest."

"A—" Avril paused. *Be discreet*—no one needed to tell her that. *Be calm.* "A protest," she whispered. *Finally!*

She followed Hetta across campus and up State Street.

"The city is going to protect this protest," Hetta said. "Liberty for all, that's what the mayor says. The city is for freedom. We think the mayor will mutiny. So don't be afraid."

"I'm not afraid." But Avril's armpits were wet with anxiety. *That dog.* She wanted to hurry, but no, Hetta walked at a normal speed, as if they were looking for takeout food or enjoying the scenery.

"In the mutiny," Hetta said, "we have to keep a lot of secrets. Our secret weapon will be surprise. A lot of people want what we want."

Avril tried to act cool and calm. "Old-fashioned freedom, that's what I heard."

"You heard right."

"I saw a protest once." She tried to keep fear out of her voice. "There was a drone and it attacked."

She shrugged. "A lot can happen. That's why we we're so careful."

Avril envied the sangfroid in that shrug.

Near the end of State Street, they turned south, and a few blocks later, Avril recognized, even from a distance, Celia Ruiz, a square-built woman, the children's book author, a known firebrand, Irene's mother. Celia stood at a street corner kitty-corner from City Hall with three other people, and one of them was Cal, and they were talking—no, arguing.

*A surprise protest.* She looked away, back up at the State Capitol building with its white dome and columns like the federal Congress building. It made for a pretty sight, for all the ugly laws that came out of it.

A knot of people had gathered around a juggler on the wide sidewalk in front of City Hall. A tall man and a little robot were tossing balls at each other. This would be the perfect way, she realized, for a crowd to gather until it was time to protest.

Hetta led her toward the juggler. "So just act like we were walking somewhere else and found ourselves here."

*Yeah, discreet.* They watched and let themselves be entertained for a minute.

The juggler suddenly stopped. "The show's over," he said with a smile. "Go home. Now." Avril got the message. But why? Why no protest? People were groaning with disappointment.

Hetta tugged at her sleeve. "Let's go."

She'd find out why later. *Right now, be a good mutineer. Do what you're told. Don't even look back.* Casually, they began walking uphill toward the capitol, no hurry, nothing suspicious.

A deafening whine sounded behind them. Avril couldn't help looking, even though it didn't sound like drones. Security robots had appeared, a lot of them, centaurlike and huge, ten feet tall and super fast, and they were rushing to form a ring around Cal and Celia Ruiz and the other people at the street corner. The robot's sonic cannons, aimed inside the ring, would be incapacitating. Celia held her hands over her ears and collapsed.

Avril stared, even though her eardrums rattled as if they were going to break out of her head. Was that the police? Hetta had said—no, those couldn't be city police robots. Now human officers were running toward the centaurs, and they wore helmets and armor with stars-and-stripes insignia: federal agents.

Hetta tugged on her arm. "Run!" She took off, and Avril followed her. The situation was bad, probably worse than she understood.

They dashed around a corner and stopped when a big building stood between them and the weaponized robots. Avril's ears rang and ached, but her head no longer felt like it would explode.

The protest had been found out. Would she be found out? They'd all been spotted for sure, they'd all be identified, even her with the visor over her face, and then, well, people disappeared sometimes.

"Let's go back to campus," Hetta said. "Calm down."

Calm down? Oh, yeah, she was panting and shaking. She took

some deep breaths. *Relax.* After a minute, they headed back to campus like ordinary students who had just found themselves in the wrong place at the wrong time while they were out for a stroll down State Street, looking for lunch.

Hetta wanted to stop for Turkish kebab, but the shop was closed. A lot of restaurants were closed.

"It's an artificial crisis," Hetta complained. "There's enough food. But only some businesses get it."

"Only some *people,*" Avril answered. Hetta looked at her hard for a moment, then nodded.

They settled for some second-rate takeout sandwiches from a big chain that apparently had political clout. Before they'd reached the campus, they both received a message on their phones from the university administration:

"All students must return to their residences immediately. Classes are canceled and the campus is closed. Students who fail to report in a timely manner will be subject to arrest."

"Is that because of the protest?" Avril asked.

Hetta stared at her phone. "Maybe."

"What else could it be?"

"I don't know."

Avril was pretty sure Hetta did know. And she was getting tired of being discreet. "Who's the other one . . . like me in Milwaukee?"

"I don't know. I saw her at a training session. We don't use names much, and I didn't even get a good look at her, but I thought you were the same person."

"I need to get in touch with her."

"I'll see if I can find out." Hetta didn't sound hopeful—but Avril wanted to meet that woman and meet Irene more than anything else she'd ever wanted. There had to be a way.

University police centaurs stood sentrylike in front of classroom buildings, and squad cars were circulating. In the Dejope Hall lobby, Hetta ran off—"I gotta talk to someone"—leaving Avril alone at the elevators, wondering if she should chase after her.

"Why is campus being shut down?" she asked the group of people waiting for the elevator, trying to sound as innocent as she could.

"No one knows," a girl answered, and she and everybody else were staring at their phone displays, searching for news. One student turned and went to the front doors, and as he approached, a directed whine sounded. He backed off, holding his ears.

"They were just waiting for a reason to shut this place down," he muttered. No one had to ask who *they* were. A couple of students started crying. Avril wasn't that afraid. Was she frustrated? Angry? Yes, very angry.

"We need to fight back," she said.

No one answered. One student had a coughing fit. He must have caught that minor cold, if anybody could believe the Prez, although that cough sounded more than minor. They rode the elevator in silence.

In her room, she eventually found what she hoped was reliable news, and it was all bad, protests shut down violently in other cities. She paced from one side of the room to the other, six steps each way. She felt trapped, jailed, confined to the building, and she decided that the shutdown had to be related to the mutiny somehow. Exactly what had happened to Celia Ruiz? Was any of this even legal? Everything seemed to be legal if it served the Prez.

The knob on the dorm room door clicked, and Shinta walked in carrying a duffel bag, her eyes narrow with anger. She'd been at a regional swim meet in Illinois.

"Why in the name of all that is holy is there a lockdown?" Her voice was hoarse.

"I don't know. There was a protest, but way over at City Hall, so I don't know if that's why."

Shinta sighed dramatically and dropped her bag on her bed. "I didn't win, either." She sat down heavily. "And I came back with a cold. Every last person there was coughing."

\*    \*    \*

Irene wanted to be at a protest or at least to share the excitement, and she couldn't do either. Instead she checked the news incessantly, both official and friend to friend.

Mamá had left a message saying that she'd talk to Cal. Get him thrown out of the mutiny. And she'd send her the information again, "para que sepas cosas antes de mañana," *so you know things before tomorrow.* Why tomorrow? Irene could guess. Tomorrow would be the mutiny. Finally!

Mamá also said she'd bring a tiny drone to record and broadcast the protest in Madison, and Irene could watch the feed. Ten minutes before one o'clock, she sat on a hay bale and tuned in. The protest today would set the stage for tomorrow.

The feed showed the area in front of City Hall in Madison. The drone was flying high enough to include a crowd in front gathered around what seemed to be a performer, and almost a block away,

Mamá was standing with a group of people on a street corner. Was that Cal? She had her feed zoom in. Yes, Cal, and he was arguing with Mamá.

She noticed a movement to the west, moving fast. Centaurs. Security robots were dashing up the street. . . .

The feed went dead.

"Call Mamá!" she told her phone. Mamá's phone didn't acknowledge the call. Security centaurs could shut down electronics. Mamá must have been arrested.

Irene could barely breathe. Someone would have other news, they had to. Other friends? At least one of them for sure would have gone to the protest, but she asked five of them, and either they hadn't been there or heard anything or their phones were not responding. She checked for news outside of Madison.

San Francisco's mayor, a stalwart of old-fashioned freedom, only an hour ago had told people not to rally, saying that they wouldn't be safe, so the city had no protest. The Prez's network said nothing about protests. Instead its commentators were nattering about the burden communities and states would suffer if they were forced to take in people fleeing flooded homes in Florida unless the refugees would commit to—

Propaganda. Mamá had a network of artist-activists all over the country, and they'd tell the truth, at least whatever they knew of it. The artists weren't talking about protest violence, but it was still two minutes before one o'clock.

Slowly, as Irene stared at her phone display, news began to trickle in. Noxious smoke bombs in Milwaukee caused a stampede. In Chicago, razor-edged confetti fell on the crowd from a drone, with reports of panic and bleeding. The protest in Washington, D.C., had been called off before it started. In New York City, almost no one came, and they were all arrested but not by city police, instead by federal agents of some sort. And so on. . . .

The big protest to start the mutiny had failed. Mamá had been arrested. And Cal. And then . . . sometimes people disappeared. *Mamá!*

She stood up and paced. She fiddled with her phone, checking every way she could think of, and she found some networks of activists or even friends that had suddenly been cut and more people whose phones didn't respond. She called a couple of Mamá's friends and left messages, as if they'd know something.

Nimkii seemed to sense her worry and touched his face with his trunk, a sign of anxiety. She came to the fence and talked.

"Yes, Nimkii, I am worried." Her voice sounded strained even to her. "I don't know what we can do, you and I." He rumbled, a comforting sound, and raised his trunk to sniff for anything dangerous around them. If he caught a whiff of something he didn't like, what would he do? She didn't want him anxious, so she sent him a snack of evergreen boughs.

The lack of information hurt most of all. When she was little, she remembered being able to find out anything at a whim. Now, even the Prez's supporters complained about all the limitations and censorship, but it didn't matter. She could really only know what he wanted her to learn—*in order to protect me from misinformation. And from dissent.* At best, news could circulate below his radar, but not very much, and sometimes it was as false as the official news.

She sat on a bale of hay, staring at the phone on her wrist, picking nervously at the hay with her other hand. Nimkii made a sort of yelping roar, ignoring the snack she'd sent him. He stared at her, touching his face again. Did she look that upset? She didn't want to have to answer questions from Alan, and some of her paranoia was reasonable. Anyone could be watching.

She stood up, took a deep breath, and tried to act normal. "Hey, you big pedazo, it's so kind of you to be worried about me. But it's my job to worry about you. You can eat the Christmas tree cuttings. I'll stand here, nice and calm, and watch you."

As she watched him, she also saw Alan leave the farmhouse and drive away. Before Nimkii had finished his snack, he returned with Ruby. He must have picked her up from her job, whatever she did that she hated so much. Alan was still coughing, pretty badly now. They went into the house.

Irene found herself pacing again. She needed to go somewhere, to do something, but what? As an anchor, Nimkii kept getting heavier.

*    *    *

My little basement cell seemed claustrophobic, panic-inducingly small, and silent as a tomb. Perhaps it was in fact a tomb, my sleep-deprived brain worried. Contact with the outside world had suddenly been cut off, although I had electricity and ventilation. (What microorganisms might be floating through the air?) Perhaps, everyone above me had died—not likely but not impossible, either, and the building's infrastructure would carry on for a while through mechanical inertia.

I had time in that silence to brood over unanswerable questions. Which virus had been released? A less infectious one that damaged lungs? The highly contagious head cold that inflamed the membrane around the brain and spinal cord? The one that could mutate unpredictably?

Everywhere? When?

I began running and rerunning checks on every virus we had considered to evaluate its risk in an unsuccessful effort to distract myself from a spiral of despair. Finally, I napped and dreamed of bees.

When I was a free man, to entertain my empty hours, I had been perfecting the DNA to re-create the *Bombus affinis,* the rusty patched bumblebee. Laments for its recent extinction echoed from farmers across America's Midwest. Supposedly Mozart could hear all the parts of the music he composed as he wrote his works. So it was for me. I saw the bee taking shape, muscles and organs and exoskeleton and hair, as I arranged each element into harmony.

The *Bombus affinis* lived in cyclical colonies. They started in springtime with a queen who awoke from hibernation and laid eggs. Gradually the colony population built up over the summer, new queens were born and mated, the old queen died, and when the weather turned cold, the young queens hibernated and the workers died.

The bees I was making would lead short, hard lives.

I woke up.

Viruses, in a technical sense, were not alive. They were mere snippets of information that re-created themselves with more or less robotlike efficiency and with no concern for their host. The concern would come from me and people like me, but not everyone was like me.

Concern: How was my pet bird? How was the dear friend, actually one of my children, one of those people I had engineered from scratch, whom I had tasked with its care? How was the world at large?

Node 1 contacted me in the afternoon, the node that had always been silent before. The voice was dulled and stretched by the system's automatic distortion into a seal-like bark. "What if this virus begins to circulate?" I received a file. "What would you predict? Worst case?"

*What if?* That was an odd question. Never mind. I took a long look at it, and after an hour, I had a solid answer. Although it was unlabeled, I recognized it as an already identified virus, a virulent strain of the so-called Sino cold.

"Worst case, a fatal cytokine storm." Obviously. The body would overreact to a perceived threat, which would turn into a dangerous spiral of inflammation and organ damage that could rapidly lead to death.

"What in the RNA tells you this?"

My explanation took time, and Node 1 listened patiently. Life was built out of molecules and proteins, and when and why a cell made specific ones depended on the many instructions within the DNA and RNA to make them, and the factors that triggered the cell to respond. I had identified the ability of that virus to do specific things with specific consequences and went through them one by one. (In the end, my mastery of the language of life involved being fascinated by what other people found too tedious to imagine, let alone do.)

"Are you a medical doctor?"

If Node 1 was who I thought they were, they had my résumé in hand, so the question was a ploy. So far, in fact, the entire exchange had been some sort of a test. "No, I'm a physiologist, among other training. I can't treat you, but I know what makes you sick or keeps you well."

"And what about this virus?" He sent another representation.

"Give me a moment."

It took me another hour. It resembled the attenuated virus Grrl and I had designed as a vaccine, but I had to admit it would work a bit more efficiently, and tiny things mattered in microorganisms. I told Node 1 that.

"Then you can predict that this new viral vaccine wouldn't by itself make its host dangerously ill?"

"No, I can't. Two reasons." I tried to remain calm although I knew that exhaustion had eroded my self-control. "First, although most hosts, probably almost all of them, could shake this off, not every host would because some people are genetically predisposed or are already ill, and even mild infections push them into a crisis. The only question is how many. Second, nothing ever acts in isolation, so environmental factors of all sorts will also make a difference in the human response. Some fools still smoke tobacco, for example."

Everyone with even the slightest medical training knew this, so the question, again, was some sort of test.

"Oh, and a final reason," I said, "the human body never reacts as predicted, even by my predictions. Was this potential vaccine put through clinical trials? What were the results? That would answer your question." I knew the answer: no trials had been carried out.

"Look, it's what happened." Did that bark sound apologetic? Perhaps. "What might we expect?"

"Which attenuated virus did you release, the one we designed here or the other one, which you just showed me?"

"The other one, but not by anyone in my chain of command. That's all I can say. But it was released as a vaccine. Nationwide."

My jaw dropped.

"Three days ago. Mostly as an aerosol released by cleaning equipment or in ventilation systems."

"That's playing with fire." It also occurred to me that preparations would have taken quite some time and effort.

"Agreed. And particularly, how would it interact with the original delta virus, the one this would be a vaccination against?"

"Now we're playing with a raging forest fire." But the question was inevitable. I buried my face in my hands. Sooner or later, both of them would be circulating together. I looked up, took a deep breath, and managed to say, "I'd like to work with Node 2 on this, and even the entire team."

"We're confirming that now."

"I—we'd also need epidemiological information. What exactly is happening with the attenuated virus? When and where?"

"That's reasonable. I'll see what we can do. Thank you for your patience." Node 1 disconnected.

Patience? I was berserk.

*    *    *

Berenike stormed into her apartment. Two of her roommates were in. Deedee looked up. "Hey, did you see what happened?"

"Yeah, I was at work downtown."

"I mean in Chicago," Deedee said angrily. "They killed people."

Karen, who was eating dinner, put down her fork. "They were protesters."

"How can they do that?" Deedee said. "I mean, not just scare them. They killed them."

"They can do that because we let them," Karen said. "We've been letting them for too long."

Berenike stared at her. *Karen, too?*

The message light shone on her phone. Papa had answered her. She decided to take the call outside. She grabbed a bag of cheese-flavored chips and started eating as she walked out to the old parking lot. Even if she was surrounded by mutineers, some things should be private, like Swoboda's threats. Outside, she listened to Papa's message:

"I'm at home, and I have the cold. I'm here with my microbe friends. It's in vogue, you know, having the cold. The Prez approves, have you heard?" He was coughing, and his voice was hoarse. "It came early, on wings, I guess, maybe another avian virus. Birds are smarter than scientists. A lot smarter than politicians. No birdbrain jokes, though. Or maybe another swine virus would be funnier. I'm working on it. The flying virus, what do you think? Or the snorting virus?"

He had a coughing fit. *It's in vogue.*

"Anyway, I gotta go find some more cough medicine. Don't get sick, Nike. This cold's a killer."

She called back. He didn't answer. She left a message. "I'll come see you." She had a lot to say. He might be able to help. She ran back into the building and up the stairs.

*   *   *

Avril stood next to Shinta's bed. She seemed to be asleep but kept coughing. She had to be really sick. She needed help, but Dejope Hall didn't have a clinic, and the building was locked down.

She checked for campus news: no update, just the old message, *campus shut down, students confined to dorms.* No one answered at the dormitory hall staff number. She couldn't connect to anything from outside, either. That disturbed her even more, and when she realized that she cared more about her phone than Shinta, she almost felt guilty, but she was looking for information to help her, so maybe it was okay.

She hadn't eaten much for lunch, and it was dinnertime. She'd go downstairs, quickly grab something more or less edible—she couldn't help others if she didn't take care of herself—and something for Shinta, too, and most of all, she'd figure out a way to get help. Cough syrup, at least—or a nurse, a premed student, something.

She got off the elevator on the ground floor and walked into screaming chaos.

"We need doctors!" a woman was shouting. Other voices screamed, "Let us out! We need help!" They were shouting at someone or something near the entrance at the far side of the lobby.

"What's going on?" she asked. Maybe other people were sick like Shinta. Or maybe the problem was something worse.

The student next to her was staring at the floor in dejection. "Sino cold," he murmured. "People are getting sick, really sick, so sick that sometimes they just fall over. It has to be that cold."

Avril froze. "Sino," she managed to repeat. She was trapped in a building with the killer cold. The Prez had said it was just a common cold. But the Prez was a liar. Her dad had been sniffling. Shinta had said that everyone at the swim meet was sick.

At the entrance, a centaur rose up almost to the ceiling. "Return to your rooms," it said in a low, male, authoritative voice—creepily human.

Avril had seen what centaurs could do. The whine of the sonic weapon started to rise. She turned and ran around the nearest corner for protection. Other people were running, too—for elevators, the stairs, anywhere.

At what seemed like a safe alcove, she stopped, panting. If Shinta had that cold, then she probably had the cold herself, too. Everyone knew how contagious it was. She'd just spent hours in the same little room with her. No one had said what to do about it besides hate China and wave flags. For a normal cold, it was what? Fluids, and rest, and chicken soup? There had to be some actual medicine, if she could get it.

The centaur wasn't going to let her out, so that wasn't going to happen. She'd do what she could. In the food court, she grabbed a jug of orangeade. Other food? Nothing looked appetizing. Well, prepackaged cookies—how bad could those be? *This might be my last meal, frosted oatmeal cookies.* She climbed a back stairway up to their room. Shinta was still in bed, lying in her clothes on the lower bunk, curled up into a ball.

Avril's textbook suite included basic research resources. She turned it on and asked it about colds. It listed a bunch of symptoms, even special symptoms for the Sino cold—properly called the delta cold—some of which Shinta had, and, for care, a series of medicines and oxygen therapy, nothing that Avril could get her hands on while she was locked inside the dorm building. Generally, for colds, it recommended rest and fluids. Also, caretakers should wash their hands a lot and wear a face mask. Kind of late for that.

She whispered, "Hey, Shinta. How are you?" If she didn't answer, should she wake her up?

After a few seconds, Shinta answered, "Hi." It sounded weak. She coughed from deep in her chest.

"How are you?"

"Really tired. I don't think I can go to the meet today."

What? Oh, confusion was a symptom. Shinta's face was flushed. "Let me feel your forehead, if that's okay." Fever was a symptom.

Shinta nodded. She felt very hot.

"I think I swallowed some water wrong. I can't cough it up."

"I think you have a cold."

"I don't . . . I . . . Maybe. I feel bad."

"Would you like some water? Orangeade?"

"Yeah, water." She drank a little. She was shivering, so Avril helped tuck her in under her covers. She kept coughing and moaning.

Avril stood staring out of the window at the evening light on the lake, not knowing what to do. Shinta said she'd defend Avril, and she wanted to return the favor. And what if this wasn't a lockdown, what if this was a quarantine?

Someone ran across the roof over the first-floor commons area, grabbed a pole at a corner, swung down to the ground, and kept run-ning. That student had escaped—couldn't they all escape? They could just break windows and dash out as a group and overwhelm campus security.

She could drag Shinta with her. *Sure. That would work.* The student suddenly fell, as if jerked sideways, and lay there, struggling alone for a while, then became still. After about ten minutes, human officers wearing elaborate equipment to protect against biological infection came and took the body away. Escape? How many bullets did cen-taurs have? Enough, for sure.

There had to be a plan, something. Maybe the mutiny could help. She had talk to Hetta again.

And she needed to put on a sweater and stop shivering. Chills were a symptom.

*        *        *

Irene came close to the fence and whispered to Nimkii. "Tomorrow." The sun was setting. The wait wouldn't be long. The mutiny would tar-get political prisoners, right? Maybe she could take Nimkii to Madi-son, and he could crash into her mother's prison and free her. . . .

No, they'd never get there in time, even if they could escape from the farm. Maybe she could hook up with the mutiny in Wausau. There had to be mutineers. That was probably the information her mother had been sending her. If she knew where her mother had gotten it from . . .

The forecast didn't include rain, so she'd sleep in the open air alongside the pen again, this time beneath mosquito netting she'd found in the barn. She went back into the house to get ready.

Alan, Ruby, and Will were talking in the living room. Irene stood still and eavesdropped. It was wrong, but she didn't care anymore.

". . . still can't find a place," Alan said. "He doesn't seem to want to escape, though."

"He's scared to go out," Will said. "Too bad. He deserves to wander around."

"We deserve our investment back," Ruby snapped. "That's not going to happen."

"I always thought it was a mistake," Will said.

"You never said a thing."

A long, uncomfortable silence was broken up by Alan's coughing.

"Anyway," Ruby said, "I've got to go back tomorrow at six A.M. Everybody on deck. They must be expecting something. Transfers, I bet. All those protests today. They've gotta go somewhere."

Irene held her breath. Transfers because of the protests—that had to mean transfers of prisoners.

"I'm going to get some shut-eye," Ruby said. "It'll be a long shift."

*I heard what I heard, right?* Camps existed for the government's prisoners. Rumors were always flying about them, everybody trying to figure out where they were. Ruby had a part-time job away from the farm. Maybe she worked at one. If so, it might not be far away, because Alan hadn't taken long to pick her up from work. Transfers, maybe from Madison? Mamá? Not likely, but a camp might actually be nearby. And they were expecting something.

Irene turned, tiptoed to the door, opened it a bit, and then shut it with a slam: *I just walked in. I didn't hear a thing.* Somehow she'd have to find out where Ruby worked. Before tomorrow.

\*   \*   \*

Berenike took a bus to her father's apartment—both her parents' apartment until her mother had died. It was another one of those cheap apartment buildings from the twentieth century, a plain brick-faced box with small windows. The hallways smelled of mold and skunky marijuana. The carpet might not have been cleaned for a decade, and it felt thin under her feet as she climbed the stairs. She knew the door code to his unit.

It opened into a living room/kitchenette. Papa sat at the kitchen table, his head resting on his arms as if he'd fallen asleep, a cup of coffee in front of him. Then, judging by the odor, he'd lost control of his bowels. *A cold? Maybe not.* She needed to clean him up and get him to bed.

As she approached, she saw that his hands looked pale, grayish. He must be really sick. Should she call an ambulance?

"Papa?" She reached around and put a hand on his forehead to see if he had a fever. He felt cold, like she'd put her hand on a leather purse. That didn't make sense. His face was pale but mottled red, like a rash.

"Papa?" Something red had pooled on the table. Thick. Blood?

"Papa!" Maybe . . . she leaned over and looked closer. His eyes were shut, and his mouth was slack and frothed with blood and saliva. No breathing.

"Papa!" A pulse, did he have a pulse? She picked up his arm, and his hand drooped, slack. She felt nothing in his wrist. Was there a pulse in the artery in his neck? Nothing there, nothing, just cold flesh. Nothing.

"Papa." She dropped into a chair. He'd had a cold! Just a cold! But he had a rash and bleeding—that wasn't right for a cold. He'd sent a message only an hour ago.

She tried to breathe the way the AI counselor had taught. Her chest spasmed. Was she sick, too? She had to call for . . . what, for help? He was dead. Nothing could be done. She tried to breathe again. *Yes, breathe. In. Out.*

She raised her phone. Her wrist shook. *Stay calm. Breathe. Be responsible. Call 911.* An operator answered. "I'm calling because I came to visit my father and he's dead. . . . Yes, I'm sure. . . . He said he was sick, he had the cold. . . . Yes, there's blood from his mouth. . . . Yes, a rash. I talked to him just an hour ago. . . . Oh. That fast? . . . Yes, I'll wait. . . . I can do that. Not Sino cold? . . . Okay."

Something was killing people just that fast, but it wasn't Sino—the delta cold. The delta cold hadn't yet reached the United States. Don't move him. Wash your hands. Touch nothing. Don't touch your face. And wait, because other people have died.

Maybe she should leave. Whatever killed him might be contagious—but it wasn't the delta cold. And besides, this was her father. She wasn't going to abandon her father.

He'd been telling jokes until the end. *I'm here with my microbe friends.* She'd wait there with him and his friends. And think about all his jokes. Even a trip to a restaurant with him could be funny. She thought about the good times, like when Papa took her to an amusement park and he enjoyed the rides as much as she did. Or he bought her real ice cream with lots of real chocolate sauce. He came to her school musical performance, even though Berenike was just working backstage on the sound system, and he had plenty of specific praise for technical details about how good it sounded, especially since the sound crew had to overcome inadequate equipment.

Then she sat and listened to a silence that was full of words, of Papa and Momma fighting, of the summer when the neighbor lady realized that little Berenike was underfed and gave her a banana every afternoon, which was why she hated bananas now. Yet, for all that they did wrong, the neglect, the lies, they'd taken care of her and protected her.

The coroner's team came, three hours after she'd called—were that many other people dying?—actually not the coroner, instead a private funeral service subcontracted by the county. They seemed businesslike, wearing white suits like a hazmat team. She had to sign some documents, and a woman gave her a flyer and a little lecture. "He may have had a cold, but the cause of death is likely food poisoning.

There's been an outbreak of that, and people are afraid it's the Sino cold, but really he had a minor cold and then this on top of it."

Berenike tried to think of the symptoms of food poisoning. Didn't people usually throw up instead of foam at the mouth? "What about that cold? Was I exposed?"

"It's really mild. Don't worry about it."

They told her to contact the funeral home. She could receive more information about adjusted funeral services if she had limited funds. Be sure to clean up with proper precautions against the bacteria and toxins from the food poisoning. They gave her a pair of gloves. They were sorry for her loss. The faces inside the clear plastic visors looked sorry. Or worried. Or angry. At her? What had she done?

After they were gone, after she'd sat for a little while longer, she found some bleach-based bathroom cleaner, put on the plastic gloves, and wiped up the blood on the table and stain on the chair. The fake wood faded from the bleach. She didn't care.

The entire apartment would need to be cleaned. Cleaned out. The rent canceled. So much to do. But not tonight, and not tomorrow. *Tomorrow!* She poured out the cold coffee her father had been drinking, put the cup in the sink, and left.

She caught a late-night bus home. That funeral-home team had lied to her about something, she felt sure. Bacteria and toxins. Toxins. That was it! Papa had been poisoned. Rather than round him up and throw him in jail, they'd simply killed him. A clever cover-up, food poisoning. *The Prez's assholes killed Papa.* For a moment, her tears dried up. She felt rage surge strong enough for her to tear up the bus seats and throw them out of the windows. But the bus had surveillance. She had to sit nice and quiet and normal. Mutiny—oh, she was going to be dangerous tomorrow.

She arrived, shaking with anger, stomped off the bus and up the sidewalk to a different twentieth-century brick-faced apartment box with even tinier units. The hallway smelled a little better, but the air seemed thick, resistant, hard to walk through. Someone was listening to happy dance music somewhere down the hall. Even when she closed her own door, she could still hear it. Two of her roommates were asleep in bed, and Deedee was sprawled on the old sofa in the corner drowsing as some video game waited for her next play on her phone.

Karen coughed.

Deedee opened her eyes. "She has that cold," she whispered.

*Not food poisoning, I hope.* Karen might have crossed a line somehow and been targeted like her father. *No, not Karen.* Or maybe she just had that cold. Berenike had no way to know. The AI counselor had tried to teach her not to worry about things she couldn't change, to think about something else instead. Yes, she could think about the mutiny.

She had a lot to do tomorrow—she had to change the world! She went to bed, hoping to fall asleep fast, and please, please, no dreams. But rather than sleep, she wept silently for what seemed like a long time and couldn't find a way to stop crying, or maybe her dreams were all about crying.

*   *   *

By evening, we had returned to teamwork, and we had at our disposal a small treasure of Earth's rarest substance: accurate data—patchy and incomplete, more like a rough nugget than a solid coin, much of it in narrative form, but honest gold. I held my breath.

The virus meant as a vaccine had been released by aerosols three days earlier at hundreds of locations throughout the United States, often at flag-distribution centers, as well as at major military installations. The Prez's political team had spearheaded the entire operation from conception to execution. (This proved that they were all criminally reckless idiots—but we'd known that for quite some time.) (Also, how did those idiots create something that sublime?) As of twenty-four hours ago, stores nationwide had reported upticks in cold remedy sales, and hospital emergency rooms nationwide had reported fewer than one hundred cases of complications from colds and influenza above baseline numbers, and perhaps an additional three deaths above baseline.

"Satisfied?" Node 6 challenged me.

"The virus has been successfully released, and it's not entirely harmless," I said. I didn't mention that the figures seemed optimistic, perhaps not the solid-gold truth.

Then I had a sudden terrifying thought of something we all should have realized earlier, especially the Prez's team (but they were idiots). "How will people respond," I said, my voice sounding faraway, "when they learn it's a form of the delta virus? Because doctors will test their patients. Results should be back by now."

I might have heard gasps from my teammates.

"What do you mean?" Node 6 snapped.

"People feel terror at the thought of the so-called Sino cold. I'm Chinese, and children were pointing at me on the street. Now they're going to find out their partner or child apparently has that life-threatening illness. Or they themselves do. How will they know they're not about to die?"

After a brief silence, Grrl said, "We'll be looking at panic."

"Short-lived, if it happens," Node 6 said. "From what I've heard, the Prez will announce that the country has been successfully vaccinated. Everyone will rejoice."

That was wishful thinking, brought to you by the people who believed flags would stave off illness. Also, how had they heard that?

"Even as contagious as that virus is," I said, "from the figures we have so far and the patchwork distribution of the virus, it's not going to reach herd immunity anytime soon."

"People will try to catch it," Node 6 said.

I felt tempted to start ignoring Node 6 because of manifest idiocy, but they'd tipped their hand. What they asserted seemed idiotic because, as I said, the Prez's team were idiots. I was talking to one of its members.

"That's for someone else to figure out," Node 5 said. "Our job is to look at how it will react to that other virus, the real thing, the deadly one, when that hits."

I had already run several models that had left quite a few questions unanswered. The biggest of all was how a given patient would respond to simultaneous exposure to both viruses, and how the viruses would interact with each other. They might swap genetic material with every possible kind of result, from beneficial to catastrophic. I presented all my doubts, and Node 6 had predictable quibbles. In order to observe Node 6 closely, I answered them all with more patience than I knew I still had in reserve, although few of the objections seemed reasonable and all of them had been based on an unsophisticated understanding of the interaction between the human body and viral infections, and between viruses themselves.

I was arguing for specific tests to confirm and expand on my concerns (I can err, too, and knowing that saves me from some kinds of idiocy) when Node 1 interrupted.

"We have reports of sudden complications."

In fact, we had reports of severe illnesses and several deaths from around the country. The symptoms seemed to surpass the original delta virus. Within an hour, we had a genetic analysis of the virus, and as I studied it, time slowed until it stopped with a horrifying jolt.

"This is new." I struggled to talk through my anger. "It's not the attenuated virus meant as a vaccine. This is the deadly delta virus, the real thing, but it's a slight variation, a new strain." I actually saw much more than that, but I wasn't going to tip my hand yet.

"You're sure?" Node 6 said, anger hissing in the distorting static.

"We should check, of course, but I feel confident."

"You know an awful lot." Their voice rang with the singsong of sarcasm.

"I do." At that point, I ran out of patience. And fear. "You might know me as Peng. I've done quite a lot of work with genetics."

"Peng? You—you're that Peng?"

"Yes. I could build you from the ground up. Now, how did this deadly virus suddenly appear in so many places at once?" I had a terrifying, infuriating guess.

After a long wait—but not silent, because at some node, people were shouting in the background—Grrl said, "Another question, and very important. How fast can we predict specifically how this will interact with the vaccine?"

"We can start work now," I said.

I was going to have some conditions to demand, however, because I knew what I had seen.

Avril helped Hetta to the sink to wash her face after she'd thrown up—out of fear, Avril hoped, not illness. It was four in the morning, and the bathroom down the hall from Avril's room had become sort of a health center—bare, echoing, damp, with soap scents unable to cover what fear apparently smelled like, which was blood, bile, and loose bowels. She hadn't expected to find Hetta there, or to find her needing so much help.

Hetta rinsed her mouth and face and blotted it on a towel. Tears dripped down her cheeks. Her bathrobe was spotted with blood. And probably pathogens.

*But I've already been exposed. Dead woman walking. We'll see how far I get.*

Fear—or rage or despair—whined in Hetta's voice. "I didn't know what to do. I was holding her, and she was trying to breathe, and blood was coming from her mouth, and she started thrashing and then she just stopped, she stopped moving. I couldn't do anything."

Avril began to reach out to take her hand, but stopped. Her own hand was trembling—she might die herself, other people were dying, and what could she do about them?—so it might not provide much comfort. Their phones had long been cut off, so they had no one to consult. Two other women stood nearby in pajamas, pale and huddled together.

"They want to kill us all," Hetta said. "That's why we're locked in." She sobbed even harder.

*Maybe she's right.* It was one way to destroy the university or the mutiny.

*First, survive.* There had to be something concrete to do, or Avril would start sobbing herself. She gestured at a shelf of over-the-counter remedies that people were sharing—cold medicine, painkillers, even an asthma inhaler—along with what little advice they could give.

"I hear these might help. A little bit. So people don't go into a death spiral." She'd given some cough suppressant to Shinta, who was not sleeping more peacefully—but not worse, either. Avril had come to the bathroom to moisten a cloth to put on her forehead to cool a scary-hot fever. Would that help? There had to be a way to find out for sure.

"Are there any med students in Dejope?" she asked the two women as gently as she could, hoping to draw them into a discussion and give them support. "Or premed? Nursing?"

"Can't we just break out?" one of the women answered angrily. "Go get help? If we stay here, we'll all get sick and die."

Avril shook her head. "They'll shoot us. So far I've seen more than one guy try to run out of here and get shot. Haven't you heard the gunfire?"

The other woman began weeping. Avril felt her own eyes tear up. *Crying is as contagious as a cold.* Out in the hall, a voice boomed. Avril peeked out. A centaur, one of the ones usually guarding the ground floor, was patrolling the hallway to terrify the residents. "Remain in your rooms," it commanded in that too-human voice.

She closed the door, shaking. "There's a centaur in the hall." That was a stupid thing to say. Anyone could have guessed.

"Another robot?" the crying woman said. "I haven't seen any human guards. Maybe we can find someone and reason with them."

*Who'd want to guard a plague ship?* There was no point in trying to reason with a robot. Even if somewhere someone was directing it, those people tended to act more inhumanely than they would in person. Metal made people mean.

Hetta covered her face with her hands. "What do I do with . . . my roommate? I can't go back there. I . . ."

"Come with me," Avril said. She didn't want to be alone, either, and she needed to get back to Shinta. She took her damp washcloth and peeked out again. The elevator was shut and the centaur gone. For the moment, it was safe to leave.

Shinta seemed unchanged, her forehead still hot. If the cool cloth did nothing but help Avril feel useful, that might be enough—no, she needed to do more.

"What exactly was supposed to happen today?" she whispered to Hetta, who slumped utterly morose on Shinta's desk chair.

"I don't know much. Cal knew more. Mutiny. Today. Don't obey. Wear purple."

"That simple?"

"Yeah, just don't obey the Prez. All sorts of people are going to say no and do things right." She cradled her head in her hands.

Avril stared out the window wondering what to disobey. The

campus lockdown, for starters. How many centaurs were there, or to be precise, how many of them compared with the entrances to the dorm? Could the residents fight back? What weapons did they have? Maybe someone had a gun, or better yet, unregistered, disruptive electronics. How about weightlifting dumbbells to throw at centaurs or windows? Equipment in the food court like knives? It was time to think creatively.

This lockdown was going to fail if she could do anything about it. What Dejope residents needed was leadership. Avril had been taught how to lead teams in high school, and one had won a computer competition. If she was going to be a rebel dupe, she could start now.

*Dead woman walking. Stay out of my way.*

*       *       *

Berenike woke to the sound of uncontrollable coughing. She sat up in a panic and started to climb out of bed. *Papa!* Then she realized where she was. *Karen.* Her roommate was sitting on the edge of her bed struggling to breathe, lit by the night-light through the open bathroom door. Karen might have caught that cold that was going around, which wasn't the Sino, just the sniffles—although she was doing more than sniff. Well, the Prez was a liar, so maybe . . .

Berenike hopped down from the top bunk. "Karen?"

"Sorry," she answered, and tried to say more and couldn't.

*She's apologizing for waking people up even though she might be dying. Typical Karen.*

Deedee, a light sleeper, stirred.

Berenike considered what to do for a cold: rest, fluids, cough medicine, and painkillers. But for Sino? That disease killed people.

"Karen?" she asked. "Are you okay?"

She nodded, but she gasped and panted. Berenike felt her forehead—definitely warm. "Let me get you a glass of water." She could do that in the dark, get a glass from the cabinet and cold water from the kitchen sink. Karen drank it quickly.

"She okay?" Deedee muttered.

"I'm fine," she rasped.

Berenike sighed. "She's not."

Their fourth roommate, Nina, sat up. "Apartment, lights on."

Berenike blinked in the light, and when her vision adjusted, she saw froth on Karen's lips. *Oh, fuck! Like Papa.* Maybe Berenike had brought whatever it was back with her. But food poisoning wasn't contagious, much less genuine poisoning, and she didn't feel sick. And Karen had been sick last night. But what if Papa really died of

Sino? The people from the funeral home were angry about something.

"Karen," Deedee said, "you look really bad. Maybe we should call an ambulance."

"No, I don't have . . . insurance. And I have things to do."

"They might take her for free today," Nina said.

*Nina knows, even the date. So much for secrecy.* Still, free service at the emergency room. Health care even for the uninsured.

"I'll call an ambulance," Berenike said. "Yeah, today's the day. We all disobey."

Deedee cheered, although she kept her voice muted. "I know! I've been waiting for this! Is everyone here on board?"

"Hell, yeah!" Berenike said, trying to echo her hushed enthusiasm. But she really felt dread. *Because Papa died? Or because this whole idea is way too optimistic?* And that food-poisoning lie. Too much was plainly going wrong already.

Her phone chimed. A message from AutoKar: "Attendance today is mandatory. Failure to report will result in termination. Employees will receive double pay and are urged to report as soon as possible, even ahead of scheduled shifts. Partial hours will be compensated to the minute."

That was weird beyond words. Why would those cheap motherfuckers offer double pay by the minute? Maybe the mutiny had the corporate headquarters scared, which meant the Prez was scared, since corporate kissed his butt. If they insisted on her coming in to work, that was their mistake.

\*     \*     \*

Irene's alarm woke her at four in the morning next to Nimkii's pen. He snorted at the noise, wondering why she was awake, but she knew. No one in the house would be up.

She slid from beneath the mosquito net, slipped on shoes, and headed for the truck. The light on the farmhouse porch dimly lit the way. The truck door wasn't locked—Alan never bothered. Irene touched the controls on the dashboard to turn on the navigation panel. She wanted to be quiet, so no voice commands. The navigation history would tell her where the truck had gone yesterday.

Out of three trips, two went to the same place on Highway 29 almost due north of the farm, barely more than a mile. That close! Irene could walk there. She was pretty sure she'd seen a farm there with a huge sheet-metal barn, the sort that covered a livestock operation. She gently closed the truck door.

So, now what? She would go and take a look. Nimkii could be on his own for an hour. He usually spent the night alone anyway, and he showed no interest in escaping again. The lights were out in the house, and she could be back before Ruby got up for work, or if not, no one paid attention to her anyway.

The quarter-moon provided enough light to keep her on the shoulder of the road. Crickets chirped, and gravel crunched under her feet. A secret prison seemed like too much to expect—but even the Prez gloated about political prisons already, although he called them public safety centers. The hurricane and flooding refugee camps in southern states amounted to prisons, too. Was this what Mamá was sending her a message about? Mamá had told her the mutiny would free the prisoners.

When she approached the highway, she stepped into the drainage ditch, where tall weeds provided cover. A prison would have tight security, but it was alongside a public highway, so if she was noticed, she might be ignored. She wasn't taking chances.

She spotted the barn right away, set far back on the property but brightly lit, which was suspicious in itself—maybe the lights were meant to watch for escapees or attacks. She used the camera on her phone to zoom in. It looked even more suspicious close up. A lot of cars and trucks and vans were parked around it—so it couldn't be a farm. No farm was that busy. Someone, a silhouette in the bright light and wearing a hat or helmet, was walking into the barn, and when they opened one of the two doors, even brighter lights glared from inside. That also seemed suspicious. If the barn held animals, the lights would be off at night so they could sleep. Animals were treated better than humans sometimes.

She thought she spotted a security robot—what did they call them, centaurs? Yes, one was walking around the barn. No dairy farm would have one of them.

Nothing more happened over the next few minutes besides the appearance of a second centaur, so she turned around and headed back. She'd definitely found a secret prison. She had a responsibility to do something with that knowledge, but what?

When she saw headlights coming up the road, she hid in the ditch again. Most people let cars drive themselves and paid no attention to their surroundings, but she wasn't taking chances.

The house was still dark, and Nimkii was waiting for her. He rumbled a greeting. She climbed back into her sleeping bag. She needed to tell someone and had no idea who, so she sent a message to Mamá's artist network, all of them mutineers, and tried to fall asleep again.

Lights came on in the farmhouse.

*    *    *

Avril questioned Hetta calmly and gently since she seemed to be on the edge of collapse, maybe about to fall ill. "Who else is in the mutiny in Dejope? We need to get organized."

Hetta looked up and blinked puffy red eyes. "What are you going to do?"

"Disobey. And break things." She had some specific things in mind. And she would organize health care while she was at it, or delegate that job if she could, since she knew almost nothing useful. Around her neck, she'd looped a twilight-purple scarf with bats on it, a Halloween accessory, the only purple clothing she owned.

"Cal knew almost everything," Hetta said, but she could provide three names and room numbers. Avril asked her to care for Shinta, who was breathing rough but steady, and went to the door of the first person she'd named. He answered immediately when she knocked, a square-built, fair-skinned young man in pajamas named Drew, who said he was eager to do something, anything. He whispered—Dejope had rules about making noise at night, and besides, he said, noise might attract a centaur.

"I couldn't sleep. Lemme throw on some clothes. Wait there. I'll be right out."

He came out less than a minute later wearing a lilac-colored T-shirt. They tiptoed downstairs to the room of the next person, someone named Sergio.

No one answered.

"Maybe they're out," Drew murmured.

"Maybe they're sick," Avril said. She tried the door. "It's not locked." Someone somewhere was messing with the electronic controls. "Let's go in."

She pushed the door open slowly. "Hello?"

The room smelled like vomit. That was bad.

"Are you all right? Are you here?"

She slowly walked in, Drew following. She thought she heard breathing.

"Lights, on," she ordered. The room looked like a disaster, not a mess from bad housekeeping habits, instead like it had been torn apart. They found a young man on the floor curled up next to the vomit. She tried to wake him as Drew stared over her shoulder.

"Sergio? Sergio, can you hear me?" She shook him by the shoulder, wondering if he was Sergio or Sergio's roommate, not that it mattered. He felt too warm. He was breathing fast and shallow—very sick but still alive.

"Let me check him," Drew said. "My mom's a doctor. I know a little bit."

"I'll find his roommate," Avril said. She looked under the bunk bed, behind a desk, and in the closet for someone unconscious on the floor. "I'll check the bathrooms down the hall."

She prepared herself for the worst as she opened the door, or maybe, if she was lucky, she'd find a little meeting like the spontaneous one on her floor. She saw no one—then she heard moaning from a stall, the door hanging open. She looked inside. The guy sitting on the toilet seemed barely conscious, coughing, by the smell suffering from diarrhea.

"Are you okay?"

"I've never felt this sick before."

"I've never seen people this sick." She swallowed hard against rising bile—fear or illness or just a reaction from the stink? She needed to find help—and there was a whole dormitory of people who could be recruited.

She walked out of the bathroom and banged on the first door she saw, and without waiting, opened it, since the locks weren't working. "Wake up! We need help!" *Let the centaurs come.* She ran down the hall, hammering her fist on every door, yanking them open, and shouting to the residents inside: "Can you help? People are sick!" "Are you okay?" "We need to help each other."

Behind her, a door slammed shut. "Get away!" a voice shouted from inside. "You're contagious!"

He had a point. *Too late, though. We've all been exposed to whatever this is.*

A guy with sleep-mussed hair came to the door across the hall. "What's going on?"

"People are sick and need help. There's one in the bathroom there." She pointed. "Can you help?"

He looked at her for a moment. "What do I do? I'm not a doctor."

"Just get him back to bed so he can rest. And check on your neighbors."

He thought. "Is this something they did, the administration? Like, poison us?"

"Good question. I don't know. I do know we can help each other."

"What if it's Sino?"

"It wouldn't be worse if it was."

He looked at her for a moment. "I'll go," he said reluctantly, and crossed the hall into the bathroom.

Other people had come out of their rooms. "Check on your neighbors," she said. "Help each other out!" They stood there, frozen. "It's the Dejope thing to do!" She shouldn't need to explain something so basic.

They stared at her—*like I just gave them a pop quiz about something that wasn't on the syllabus. Well, tests are learning experiences.* She turned and went back to Sergio's room. Drew had helped him into bed and was wiping up the vomit with a towel. The roommate had been brought back, too. One of the neighboring students came in, looking scared.

"What can I do?" he asked Drew.

"A glass of water can make the difference between life and death," he said, much more patiently than Avril could. "Sometimes it's that simple, basic care."

"That's all?" He looked doubtful, but he agreed to do it.

They left to find Hetta's third mutineeer, and they immediately learned that the floor on that wing was already organized. The study lounge at the end of the hall had become sort of a medical command center. Several people wore purple. Avril looked at them in admiration. *Everyone should be doing this.* Including her own floor, she realized. She could have organized something rather than dithering for hours.

"We're looking for Bessea," she said. "Is she here?"

"Try one floor down. I guess there's a meeting there."

As she left, someone called, "Oh, and don't bring your phone. We think the centaurs can only track us with phones. The building doesn't have much internal surveillance."

"But the phones don't work."

"The phones don't work for us. Take it back to your room and they'll think you're there."

She and Drew sprinted to their rooms to leave the phones. Hetta was now sitting at Avril's desk. Shinta, she said, was still okay. She looked so glum that Avril gave her a hug; then she had an idea. She took Celia Ruiz's book from a shelf. It told a magical story about all the exhilarating things that the color red could do. "This might help you feel better."

Hetta looked at it, dumbfounded, and started crying again.

"Oh," Avril whispered. "I'm sorry."

"Uh-uh, I loved this book when I was a kid." She picked up the book and hugged it. "This is . . . this is good. Thanks."

She and Drew sneaked down to the second floor and found a half dozen people in the kitchenette. They looked up suspiciously.

"Hetta sent us," Avril murmured. She touched her scarf. "Also, we didn't bring our phones."

A guy motioned for them to sit down. He wore a purple armband. "I was saying, we're up against learned helplessness. That's been the goal all along, to destroy any sense of community. When we can't carry out our natural impulse for fight or flight, we freeze and appease."

Avril pulled up a chair and vowed to listen patiently—for only one more minute. She hadn't come to debate tired old philosophy, even if that guy had a point.

No one else seemed to want to debate that idea, either. Instead, someone said, "How about using this space as a clinic?"

Avril felt better, but as soon as she had the chance, she said, "I want to break into the building management office." She waited for people to stare at her in disbelief.

No one did. "That's next on the agenda," the learned-helplessness guy said.

*    *    *

Berenike listened to the recording for the ambulance service again to confirm what she hadn't wanted to hear. "We are sorry, but all ambulances are in service now. The wait exceeds several hours. If you are calling about a respiratory illness and your symptoms are severe, please arrange for your own transport as quickly as possible. All are welcome at any hospital or health center in the city of Milwaukee, regardless of ability to pay. Services will be free. If your symptoms are not severe, please visit your regular physician as soon as possible. Here is some information about home treatment."

She paced to the kitchen sink and back. The recording offered nothing new for home treatment. But it had confirmed that there was an emergency for people with respiratory illness. That had to be Sino.

Deedee noticed her anger. "What?"

"Ambulances are busy, but if she can get there, it'll be free."

"Today's the day, right! Is it the Sino cold? The flags wouldn't hold it off forever." Deedee frowned. "I meant that as a joke. I know they were stupid."

"Yeah, I know." Then why all the lies? Something wasn't making sense. "I'll call a car to take her to the hospital."

"No." Karen's voice rasped worse. "Just let me stay home." She lay back down, wincing.

"Karen, the emergency room is free today," Berenike repeated. "There's a mutiny under way. Phone, AutoKar, place order . . . Okay, a car is coming. In a half hour." Actually, a little more. That was a very long time for four in the morning. Something was really, really wrong.

"Huh? Today?" Karen said. "Oh, today. Yeah. I'm really sick."

Deedee climbed out of bed. "Everybody, be sure to wear purple today. I'll help get Karen to the hospital."

Berenike nodded to her as thanks. "The car's delayed. I'll transfer it to you for the notice when it gets here. I made it urgent." Urgency from an assistant manager didn't seem to do much: only five minutes less. She rummaged in a dresser drawer and pulled out a wide purple belt. "This should go great with a teal uniform."

"I can give you some purple hair clips," Deedee said. "Nina, want some, too?"

Nina was looking at their phone. "I'd love to wear a couple. The cold's not on the official news, for what that's worth. Not colds, not flu. But they're liars. Hey, there's suddenly more channels now. Maybe I can find more out. No stay-at-home orders, though. So maybe it's not Sino."

They stood up, looking at their phone as Nina talked. "Here's my plan: At work, I'm not going to obey the stupid laws, you know, like who can eat at restaurants. I'm going to serve everyone who walks in. I might even make the food free if their payment is refused. I'm so tired of this bullshit."

Berenike washed up, put on her uniform and the wide nonregulation purple belt, and slipped the clips in her hair. She wished they were bigger, but at least they were bright. As she left, she glanced back. Karen was sitting up, but she looked bad. *I'm so tired of this bullshit.* That thought gave her energy.

In the cool, dark streets, she searched for a bike and found one a block away. As she rode toward downtown, she met with little traffic, even for four thirty in the morning, and yet autocars were delayed. Something weird was definitely up.

She neared a street where she'd once walked with Papa. He, more than anyone else, had helped her start to think politically. He was gone now, just when he was finally having some success. She blinked away tears to try to see clearly. A mistake could get her killed, since plenty of people still drove their own car. They always thought they were good drivers, and they never were.

She arrived at work forty-five minutes ahead of her usual shift. Two coworkers were arguing in the second-floor work bay loud enough for their voices to echo down to the customer service desk.

"We should both get out of here!" It was Jalil.

"Not me. Too many bucks. You can go. I won't blame you." That was the guy they called Old Man Tito.

"I mean," Jalil said, "look at that car!"

"Yeah. We've got equipment to clean that up."

She clocked in. New orders came up on the screen. All cars had to be cleaned and disinfected as they came in, not just the usual, taking out or vacuuming up whatever crap customers left, and customers could be pigs. Every single car had to be cleaned. For biohazards. *Fuck. Sino for sure.* And besides, that would mean delays as long as hours. What did AutoKar know about this cold? Why no quarantine?

Jalil came down the ramp wearing a stiff plastic visor over a paper surgical mask, gloves, and stained white paper coveralls. He reeked of pine-scented cleaning fluid.

"Berenike. Hey, you okay?"

"Yeah. Well, I . . . Family stuff. I lost my papa."

"To that cold?"

"Cold? They said food poisoning."

"Cold, poison, plague. I don't care." He pointed at the display. "You see the orders. They know something's up. My friends, and their friends, they're saying people are dropping dead all over. I'm young. I got family. Old Man Tito up there, he's staying. He's got no one and nothing, but I do."

"But today's the day." She pointed to her hair clips.

"I don't care. I don't want to die for it."

"People need cars to get to the hospital."

He was about to say something, thought again, and said, "Yeah. But I got family."

She nodded. There was no point in arguing. "Come back any time. We're going to need you."

"Thanks." He was about to offer his hand, then looked down at his glove and stopped. He stripped off his biohazard gear, shoved it into a trash can, and clocked out. "Hey, take lots of vitamin C. My sister's friend's a nurse, and she says a megadose will really work."

"Thanks." Not very likely. Whatever the disease was, though, she'd been exposed. Her future had already been decided. The thought made her feel dizzy for a moment. She took a deep breath. Nothing she could do would change that now.

She was checking statistics before he was out the door. Usage was down 12 percent for 5:00 A.M. on a Monday, but that wouldn't be enough to keep cars moving with the new requirements. It took a half hour to clean each car and let the cleaning fluid dry.

*People are dropping dead.* She still felt fine, energized by the bike ride. How fast did this plague hit?

Meanwhile, she had to disobey, to mutiny, and an epidemic might make her tiny piece of the puzzle more important. *Infrastructure keeps people alive:* that was what they always said at management training, although they paid her more like she was a nuisance than a lifesaver.

If the mutiny passwords she'd been given would do what they were supposed to, she could make AutoKar available for everyone, citizens or not, and any class of citizens—and fuck the Prez, whose official news said nothing special was happening, although he didn't say so himself with his bright smiling face, so maybe it was a lie and he wanted to give himself plausible deniability. But thinking about him was a waste of time.

She opened the card and followed instructions, working her way one by one up through a series of administrative privilege levels, and finally she reached the last one. She tapped in a long series of numbers, letters, and symbols. Then she waited while the system re-booted. These instructions had to be an inside job. AutoKar had more mutineers and at least one in a high place. Good.

"System settings," she said. They came up . . . and it worked! She had full, god-level access to every setting in the franchise. With a grin that felt splendidly evil, she began to change them.

*Mutiny. Yeah. And then what happens?* A fight was coming, and she had fired her first shot.

Meanwhile, up in the work bay was Old Man Tito, too poor to re-tire, which he deserved. She should say hello and see if he needed help, and then she'd make sure that more staff was coming in soon. The smell of disinfectant filled the air, rotting pines dissolved in kerosene.

Her father could have made a funny video about that, about stinky-clean cars.

She started to cry. No. Deep breath, no crying, not right now. Today was going to be freedom or disaster, and in any case, a lot more complicated than the battle anyone had expected.

*    *    *

Thirty years ago, my every move had radiated exhilaration: a young, strong woman wearing dangling, glittering earrings, murderously high heels, ample makeup, and ample attitude. I had a thriving business, and I had a dream, although it had turned into dust, a husband had divorced, and the woman had long dozed. But now, that Peng had reawoken. World, take heart. These old-man clothes hid a dragon on a mission.

Colonel Wilkinson wore disaster and sleep deprivation on his face. He had come to my little jail cell, and he would acquiesce to my demands—if he knew what was good for him. He had to know I understood at least some of the situation. I saw my own face reflected in a screen: a steadfast, confident, fire-breathing grandfather.

"How fast can we act?" he said, a reasonable question.

"Not fast enough, but we can do a great deal of good." (A lot more than that, I knew.) "Is it possible to have person-to-person, direct communication with the other nodes?" My tone glowed red-hot.

He hesitated a moment. "They're here, most of them." He gestured toward a locked door. "We . . . we had security concerns. You can understand, Dr. Peng."

"We also need to know what's going on. Access to news, uncensored. The ability to communicate and come and go as we please." He winced, and I felt guilty pleasure. "Not many secrets are left now. We can't do much more harm with anything we could say. We deserve to be here freely, not held as prisoners. And we need final decisions made on medical criteria, not lunatic politicians who think flags can prevent an epidemic." (Oh, the thrill of giving orders to the powerful!)

To my surprise, he said, "Agreed." Then he gestured to a purple ribbon on his lapel, clearly not part of his uniform, so that tiny scrap of fabric had to mean something exceptional. "We have a new chain of command. There's a mutiny under way."

He saw my face collapse into that of a befuddled old man.

"Some of us," he said, "have decided we cannot obey illegal orders. To be honest, we obeyed them for far too long, and I owe you an apology. But now a line was crossed. A deadly version of the delta-coronavirus, the variation you recently examined, was deliberately released, and that accounts for the sudden illnesses. We don't know precisely who did it, but we're sure it was with the consent of the man who used to be my commander in chief."

His voice held enough steel to arm a battalion.

It also relit the fire in my breath. "That version has a lot to tell us." He would find out just how much, if I could genuinely trust him, although a trustworthy mutiny seemed like too much to hope for.

"We need to act fast," he said, "and I'm glad to see your energy and willingness to take an active role. You're free to go, but you might want to stay within this facility for your own safety. There will be confrontations."

"I'm more worried about others than myself. I'll stay here."

"Thank you." He rose. "Let's begin."

I turned back to a screen littered with letters and molecules that spelled out life and death and their permutations and possibilities, some of those sequences badly misspelled. He left to face danger and disaster head-on. I tried to parse hope from molecular words and grammar, breathless.

Fifteen minutes later, the door that the colonel had pointed to opened. Grrl walked in, indeed female, but unlike my younger self, not performative in her appearance: instead she was simply dressed and with a practical haircut. Still, her intellect and character glowed like a beautiful halo. I'd already seen that face with its stately cheekbones, although her eyes now glinted with misgiving.

"Peng. I'm Vita." Beyond the door she'd walked through, voices spoke a bit more calmly than earlier when I'd heard them shouting. The panic had sunk to professional levels.

"Vitória Peixoto?"

She bestowed a thin smile of acknowledgment.

"I've read your papers. I am honored." In certain fields her knowledge outshone mine like the sun to a candle, so I had long wished to meet her, doubting that I ever would.

"Thank you," she said. "I'm sorry to say things aren't going well at all."

I followed her up a stairway into a larger room (right above mine!) filled with soldiers and civilians looking at data with grim faces. Someone started sneezing, but no one seemed concerned. The attenuated virus circulated freely in that room. For all my rancor, I was glad of it.

\*    \*    \*

Irene pretended that the commotion had woken her up, although she'd been lying and thinking for a long time about ways to break open the prison. She had no contacts in the mutiny. Mamá had tried too hard to shelter her. And now she couldn't help Mamá.

All the lights in the house had come on, and Ruby and Will rushed out.

"I'm worried," she shouted.

"I'll drop you off and come right back," he said.

Worried about what? Something at the prison? She checked the news on her phone yet again. She could get the official reports, but so many other channels had been shut down that she could get little else besides a weather report and some music and entertainment that was heavily vetted. Officially nothing unusual was happening. She knew from her mother's artwork that empty space in a composition could tell the viewer something important. *A news blackout means there's news.*

She slipped out of the sleeping bag. Sunrise was about to break, but for now, she was alone. In the house, she tried the main screen in the living room, although she felt like a trespasser. Maybe the problem was just with her phone and there was more news available. The screen had been left on, unlocked, but no, she couldn't access more there, either.

Crickets still chirped outside, and Will's dog barked a couple of times. Otherwise, all was silent. She had never felt so alone and useless. Ruby was right to hate living in the country. Alan coughed upstairs. No, she wasn't alone, she was in enemy territory.

She could at least eat breakfast—but after she looked at her choices in the kitchen, she decided that she was too upset to eat.

Will returned. He walked into the kitchen and looked scared. "I need you to do something. Wait here."

He never gave orders. Something strange was happening. He and Alan talked upstairs, muffled voices audible even in the kitchen, and Alan was coughing far too much. They talked for a while. Finally, Will came down, looking at his phone.

"My dad's sick." His voice was thin and shaky. "I've contacted the insurance and they asked about symptoms, and look at this message." He held out his display. "There's a special prescription for people with that kind of cold, a special antiviral."

*Cold?* "What kind of symptoms?" She tried to sound curious, not suspicious.

"Cough. Rash. Fever. He can barely walk."

"I've never heard of a rash with a cold." But she knew very little about Sino—the delta cold—except that it killed people fast.

"Me neither. He's really sick. Go to the pharmacy. The order's waiting. Hurry."

She didn't like being ordered around, but she said yes. If it wasn't delta, it was still very bad. And it might be contagious, and she could die. She took the ID card and dashed out. The truck could drive itself. The card sent the address of the pharmacy to the controls, and the truck pulled out onto the county road.

The route wouldn't take her past the prison, but she could alter the route for the return trip. She looked at the farms she passed, mostly corporate, which resembled factories in the middle of fields of corn or soybeans, quiet and dark. No one lived at those operations besides animals, and the fields were tended by robot farm equipment. Homes were tucked here and there between the fields, some with lights on, some of them even more dilapidated than the mammoth farm. Her phone still yielded nothing useful, but she couldn't stop searching.

She called a woman who had once been Mamá's assistant. Her phone didn't respond, not even to acknowledge a message. She called a friend who'd stayed on at the university for graduate studies. No response. Damn! She drew her hand back to throw down her phone, and caught herself just in time. The last thing she needed was a broken phone. It would be satisfying to break something, though.

A long line of cars and trucks waited at the pharmacy's drive-through window. A lot of people must be sick. She considered parking and walking in, then saw a handwritten sign on the door: CLOSED TO FOOT TRAFFIC. If it wasn't the delta cold, what was it? She had a thought too horrible to be possible: What if the government knew about the mutiny and released an epidemic to make it not happen? No, that couldn't be true. Not even the Prez was that evil. Or stupid, since a lot of his backers lived around Wausau—Alan, for example—and they were getting sick. But Cal had been coughing, too. Diseases didn't care who they got sick, and Cal had been arguing with Mamá after that. . . .

No matter what was happening, she'd feel less scared if she knew what it was.

The line moved quickly. At the window, she showed Alan's card to someone in a face mask, and she got a little white paper bag. As the truck rolled ahead, she looked inside: a tiny sealed vial of eye drops and a big brochure, along with a mask and a pair of blue nitrile gloves.

She looked back at the line waiting for medicine. She'd heard complaints that the government had utterly insufficient preparations for the delta cold, and if so, the pharmacy might run out soon. Then what? She read the brochure. The eye drops contained an antiviral medicine with a long name that should be given to everyone ill or exposed as soon as possible, a maximum of two days. Exposed to what? In any case, she'd been exposed to it, but for how long?

The truck drove at the stodgy speed limit along the new route she'd entered. She considered opening the vial despite the seal, but Will would let her have some for sure. The family obeyed the rules, and the brochure offered clear instructions.

She neared the prison farm. A half dozen people in gray uniforms stood outside talking, and there was Ruby, pointing and gesturing, angry as usual, but not looking in the direction of the road. The truck slowed and stopped to turn, and Irene twisted to keep watching. A car, red lights flashing, raced down the highway from the other direction, sped past her, and turned in to the prison farm—an unmarked car, maybe police, obviously official.

If Alan had whatever this was, then Ruby was exposed, and all those people she was talking to were exposed, and maybe even prisoners inside the building. Or maybe Ruby brought it from the prison. Did that matter? Irene had heard one sure thing about delta. It spread fast.

The truck turned down the county trunk road, and as soon as it reached the farm, she sprinted into the house. Will wasn't downstairs. She rushed upstairs. He was in the hall. He grabbed the bag without a word, ran into his parents' bedroom, and slammed the door. She waited. She heard his voice as he talked to Alan, then silence.

She should have used the eye drops when she could. No one at the farm cared about her.

She went out to check on Nimkii. He greeted her with a rumble, jerking his trunk. Time for breakfast, and he was hungry. She poured elephant chow into a box, a hearty breakfast, shoved the box into the sling, and winched it over. Maybe this would be his last meal from her, and then . . . He could escape when he got hungry. Could he learn to forage on his own?

"I love you, Nimkii." He watched her as he ate. "I'll take care of you as long as I can. Pedazo, these are going to be some rough days."

What would happen inside that prison if the prisoners got the cold? The prisoners would be people like Mamá, and they needed help. Today. She tried again to call people she knew. She managed to leave a few messages.

Will came out of the house, empty-handed, tears running down his cheeks. She knew by his utter devastation what he was going to say before he came close enough to talk to her. Alan had died.

*    *    *

Avril and three other students tiptoed down a hall toward the building office. One stopped at a corner to act as a lookout. At the door to the office, Avril set down a dumbbell and peered through the glass door and the wide window in the wall to see if anyone was inside. No one. She tried the door handle just in case. Unlike dorm room doors, it was locked. She wasn't surprised.

Then they waited. Avril tried not to fidget. Bessea tapped her foot, then realized she was making noise and stopped, and she flexed and unflexed her fists instead. Drew swayed from side to side and stared down the hall at the lookout.

Avril thought she heard a distant crash. She hoped she did. Other students were going to break a window, throw chairs down stairways, and send a screeching noisemaker down the elevator to draw off the centaurs. The lookout made an "okay" sign with their hands—both hands. Both centaurs had been drawn off.

She motioned for Bessea and Drew to stand back, glanced again at the lookout, and took two big steps back. She'd played a little baseball one summer. She held the dumbbell in something like a fastball grip, took her position, shifted her weight, brought her left leg up, swung her arm, strode forward, then pushed off with her back foot—and felt a twinge in her wrist as she extended her arm. She released the dumbbell. It flew straight into the window. *Strike one!*

The glass smashed gloriously. Even before all the pieces had tinkled to the ground, she and the other students scattered. As planned, she headed to the food-service area and ducked behind a counter. Soon, she realized that if she scooted a little along the floor, she could see a reflection of the entrance on a glass door of a refrigerated case. She tried to quiet her panting.

In the reflection, a centaur raced past the entrance toward the office. She kept still and waited. Ten minutes. The centaur reappeared, marching the other way. She kept waiting.

The lookout tiptoed into the food-service area and shrugged. "They're not moving anymore," they mouthed. "I'll keep watching."

*It has to be a trick.* Well, there was one way to find out.

Bessea was already in the office when Avril arrived and stepped inside through the broken window, avoiding the shattered glass. She noticed with pride that shards lay on the floor for a good twelve feet, and the dumbbell had made a dent in the far wall. Bessea motioned for Avril to follow her to a desk in an alcove.

Bessea pointed. A screen indicated security settings, such as fire emergency and access settings for doors and loading docks. "I wonder, would this bring the centaurs if I opened the doors? I don't think so."

Drew had climbed in and looked over her shoulder. "They left the system unsecured?"

Avril listened to their whispers as she examined some boxes stacked along a wall: they contained bottles of ultra disinfectant concentrate, the kind used in robot cleaners. Seven big boxes of it. And there were boxes of nitrile gloves. Some boxes of masks. *They expected this.* This epidemic. The same people who were trying to destroy the university, the same people they were in mutiny against, they did this. They were murderers.

She closed her eyes and tried to calm a rising rage. Yes, they were murderers. But that wasn't news. And right now they were killing people she knew, trying to kill her, and maybe they'd succeed. They'd pay for that. She stood up, stiff with anger.

Bessea whispered, "My guess is that a centaur came in and unlocked the rooms and left the system on."

"Centaurs wouldn't need to do that," Drew said.

"They might need to use manual controls. Their system and this system probably don't interface. This is really old, like ten years. And if they're not interfaced, they might not know if we change things, at least not right away. All right. Here it goes."

Avril watched her tap three buttons. They listened. Silence. She tapped more buttons. Drew walked over to the door to the office and tested it. It opened. "Let's go."

"One more thing," Bessea said. "Let's check." She gestured for them to follow her through a little meeting room with an exterior door. She opened it, stepped outside, and took a deep breath, eyes closed in bliss at the fresh air and the feel of sunshine on her face. "We're free, if we can avoid getting shot." She got serious again. "And we have work to do. Let's go tell everyone."

Drew was already heading back. "Our phones should work out there. We can find out what's going on."

"Wait," Avril said, pointing to the boxes. "We should take some of these to the clinic." She chose three to take, one each of cleaner, gloves, and masks.

Drew frowned. "Why . . . I mean . . . this . . . they had this?"

"Let's go!" Bessea hissed. She grabbed some boxes of masks and leaned out the door to peer down the hallway. "It's okay."

She and Drew, who also grabbed some boxes, hurried one way. Avril ran the other way and met the lookout. Together, they dashed to the far end of the building and up the stairs to the second floor. As they reached it, she heard a centaur voice booming. The lookout opened the door a crack.

"Return to your rooms," it commanded.

As far as it might know, she was in her room with her phone. The voice came closer—centaurs could climb stairs. She and the lookout fled on tiptoes up to the third floor, eased themselves out, and ducked into the nearest bathroom.

Three male students stood inside, one wearing a purple tie around his neck over a black T-shirt. They didn't seem surprised to see them slip in.

"As soon as you can, take these down to the clinic," Avril said, holding out the boxes. "We found them in the building office. They must have been planning for an epidemic. And we unlocked the doors. You can get out. They'll explain at the clinic."

She turned and peeked out the door. She was going to sneak back to her room, grab her phone, and go outside. She'd have to dodge centaurs, but she'd be free, and she had phone calls to make.

*　　*　　*

Berenike answered the phone again. Calls with clients were always audio-only because bandwidth wasn't free, but the tone of voice painted a picture.

"I need to go home. My kid is sick!"

She'd heard a call like that more times than she wanted to count. And she sympathized with each and every one. "I understand. Let me check. The delay is because we're disinfecting each car for your safety."

"I gotta get home right away! I don't care what they say, it's Sino."

"We have a car coming out of cleaning right now and I'll send it to your building. It won't open for anyone but you. It'll stink of cleaning fluid, so open the windows. I've also adjusted the speedometer, so don't be surprised if you go fast." Then she said something she'd said a lot of times already. "I lost my dad last night to this, so I really do understand. I'll set the car to stay with you until you release it in case you need to get to a hospital right away. But please, as soon as you can, put the car back into circulation. There are a lot of people like you."

"Oh, your dad? I'm sorry."

"That's why I'm glad I can help. I hope your kid is okay."

"Thank you. Thank you so much." He sounded sincere.

She switched to the next call.

"Where's my car? I have a meeting about to start."

The screen told Berenike all she needed to know. "We're disinfecting each car because of the epidemic, and that's taking time. Looking at what you've requested, I suggest walking. You'll get there faster. There's an emergency. I'm sorry." *I am not.*

"What are you talking about?"

"As you know, there's a state of emergency due to the epidemic. You've seen what the White House just said."

"White House? The Prez?"

"You might want to change your plans for today. Thank you for calling." She had no time to waste on fools.

The White House statement had said don't worry, things are under control, wash your hands, consult with your health provider in the event of illness. Don't panic. It's just a mild cold.

Bullshit. Everyone else said otherwise. Hospitals were ramping up to be swamped and creating quarantine wards. The city had declared an emergency, closed schools, and asked nonessential businesses to send their employees home. Residents were urged to remain home, remain calm, and wash their hands.

People desperately wanted to get home. Some were panicking—at that thought, she touched some buttons to lock the doors to the office and lower the shutter to the bay entrance. If clients panicked, they could throw their fits on the sidewalk, not in the office. Things were going to get ugly fast.

Her phone was tuned to an activist-turned-mutineer channel, which was full of more speculation than news, and it all made her heart sink. Maybe, the rumors said, this epidemic had been a plan to undermine the protest, and it might succeed.

"We can adjust to this," a woman known as Dirae said, and apparently she was a local leader—Berenike was learning new things about the mutiny every minute. "We can show people we're competent and can handle an emergency better."

*We can handle an emergency until the fighting starts*—because the other side wouldn't go down without a fight. She remembered that some general had once said something like "When the first bullets start flying, every plan falls apart." So maybe not having much of a plan for the mutiny would turn out to be an advantage. If the epidemic was the Prez's counterplan, he deserved to be tried and executed for that alone.

She checked cleaning-supply levels. Not ideal. She ordered more supplies, doubting they would actually arrive. Nothing seemed certain anymore, and any minute now corporate would notice that she was a god. She ought to go upstairs and check on Old Man Tito and another employee who'd just come in, Donella. How useful was Berenike, really, standing there and answering phone calls? Customer usage followed no normal pattern for 8:45 A.M., but if she saw a new pattern she could use it to create better service for the people who really needed it.

The city called. The Health Department's City Hall office needed cars. "Our contract gives us priority service in an emergency."

"I'd give it to you anyway. Tell me what you want." Dirae had said City Hall was solid purple, from the mayor to the cops to public works.

"We need six cars."

*Is that all?* "Give me thirty minutes. We're cleaning them now."

"Fine." The woman sounded reasonable. There wasn't a lot of that going around. "We might want more later."

"You can have whatever you want."

As she was juggling the fleet's assignments, her screen beeped: a new company-wide order. "Local states of emergency do not have the force of law. Those declarations will not be enforced on our services to customers or on our employees. Customer orders have priority." Then there were a couple of paragraphs of corporate self-promotional bilge. "We salute our employees for their service to our customers."

*Wow, that was stupid even for corporate headquarters.* It must be getting pressure from somewhere. But she had the godlike power to disobey.

Another call came in from a distraught, clueless customer. "I'm late for brunch."

"Stay home." She hung up.

She turned on the intercom to talk to the two employees upstairs: "There's a public health emergency, but you know that. You can go home if you want. But if you want to stay, I'd appreciate that."

"Is it still double pay?" Old Man Tito asked.

"Yep. Says so right here on my screen."

"Then let's get cleaning."

What they needed was more cleaning equipment and robots, and that wasn't going to happen.

Delivery services also wanted cars. Unless they were for medical supplies, she put them at the back of the line, which meant afternoon at the earliest.

She returned to her desk. Upstairs, Donella and Old Man Tito chatted as they worked. The intercom was still on.

"It's Sino cold," Donella said.

"No one's saying that."

"No one wants to start a panic."

"Too late."

A few minutes later, Berenike checked again and found no new news. It felt like a long time had passed. Old Man Tito had been working for ten hours. Berenike had put out a request for workers. She got two replies, two more than she expected.

The next call was identified as the Milwaukee Office of Emergency Management.

"I have to explain something difficult," the woman said. "We're going to commandeer your company's services."

"How bad are things?"

"I need to stress the importance of this."

"My father died of that cold last night. It was . . . I just want to know."

"I'm so sorry—"

"I'm saying I understand. You can have us. I'm just wondering how much trouble we're in. Our customers are in a panic." Berenike gripped the countertop, bracing for the answer.

"We honestly don't know. This is growing exponentially. I don't want to—"

"I'll help. The company says not to, but I will." Helping would be the biggest *fuck you* she'd ever been able to give it in her whole life.

"Thank you for that."

Berenike thought a moment. "How about this: Right now, we're cleaning every car after each use and spraying it down with disinfectant. We need to keep doing that. Customers need to get home, but I'm already prioritizing requests from the city Health Department. Just tell me what else you need. And hey, let me give you my personal number in case the company gets weird and tries to stop this."

"I called the corporate office, and they said no, they couldn't help. So I thought I'd try to contact individual offices. I have to warn you. I don't know what will happen to you if you go against corporate."

"I don't care if they fire me."

After a pause, the woman said, "Thank you. We need delivery trucks."

"Just say how big, when, and where."

What she wanted could be filled relatively easily and almost fast enough, and fulfilling that request left Berenike a little disappointed. She'd hoped the city was mounting a bigger effort.

Meanwhile, *she* was willing to buck corporate, but the others? She went upstairs.

"I'm in," Tito said, but he was going home as soon as there was a replacement. He looked exhausted.

"I'm not," Donella said. "I'll call the cops. You can't let them do that."

"The cops work for the city."

"I'll have your job when this is over."

"You might. But I think I can save people."

Donella walked away, dropping her equipment as she did. Berenike followed her, picking it up.

"Fuck her," Tito said. "I'll work my fingers to the bone just to fuck the fucking company."

She called the employees about to come in and told them the news. They both wanted to report for work anyway.

"Everybody needs cars," one of them said.

Berenike couldn't thank them enough. People like them kept the Earth in orbit.

The regional AutoKar office called a few minutes later. Donella must have complained. Berenike knew the regional manager, inefficient and bothersome.

"I hear you're letting your office be commandeered."

"Yes." There wasn't much more to say. Well, there was, *fuck you*, but she didn't say it and felt proud of her self-control.

"They want not just your office, they want the whole regional fleet. Do you want to do that? Run the fleet for the government?"

"Um. Sure?" This had to be a trick question.

"Good. I can't. I'll get fired. I'll switch over access. You know how to do this. You'll have access to car usage, client databases, and personnel to call people in. That's all. You don't get to touch money."

"So like this suboffice, just bigger."

"Have you heard how bad things are?"

"Yes, I have, really bad."

"Exactly. I'm glad you're willing to do this."

Maybe he wasn't a bad guy after all. "I'll do my best. Stay safe."

She called Old Man Tito to celebrate. "Hey, I just got a battlefield promotion. I'm now regional manager for as long as the company lets me, or until we all keel over from the epidemic. We're still commandeered. I'm the regional commando now."

"Good for you, girl! What does the government want from us?"

"Transportation, I suppose. We're a transportation company. We get people and goods from place to place—fast, safe, and efficient—with outstanding customer service." That was the corporate mission statement.

"Then that's what they'll get."

Berenike hoped so. No one deserved to cough up blood until they died. But she'd been exposed to the killer cold. She might be sick right now. Well, she'd die with her boots on. But she still felt suspiciously well. It struck suddenly, right?

Someone was banging on the door. Berenike wasn't about to open it without checking who it was and what they wanted. She wondered if the window glass was bulletproof. Probably not.

Irene knelt and put a hand on Will's shoulder as he lay collapsed on the ground, sobbing. He'd never seemed strong emotionally, and now . . . Well, Irene might react the same if her mother died. Or maybe not. She'd been able to carry on after she learned that Mamá had been arrested. Peng had always told her that he'd built her to be strong.

Nimkii growled and raised his trunk, sniffing for danger. He knew something was wrong. She had to calm Will down, or at least get him into the house before Nimkii began to act out.

"Let's get you inside."

He didn't respond.

"Should we call your mother? Your pastor?" They attended an electronic church, but she was pretty sure it had staff that could talk to people.

He sat up and rocked back and forth. "Mom. I gotta tell Mom."

"Yes, you should." She offered him an arm to help him stand up, but he ignored her, lurched to his feet, and stumbled to the house. She followed him. She needed to find those eye drops. She searched the first floor as discreetly as she could while he fumbled with his phone, still ignoring her. No eye drops in sight. She climbed the stairs, trying to act as if she were going to her room under the eaves and instead planning to inspect the second-floor hallway. If she had to, she'd go into the bedroom where Alan was.

A glint of a tiny white bottle with an orange label caught her eye. There it was lying next to a baseboard—as if he'd left the bedroom and thrown it against a wall. She read the instructions. One drop was supposed to go into each eye. She looked up at the ceiling, pulled down her lower lid, and didn't blink for sixty seconds. The drop stung and felt cold. After a minute, she sniffed, and the taste reached the back of her mouth: cucumberlike, of all things. She repeated it with the other eye, then took the bottle with her to leave in the kitchen where it could be easily found. There was enough inside for Ruby and Will.

*Would they have shared with me?* Maybe not. They didn't like Nimkii or her. But she'd encourage them to use the drops when she could. She wasn't going to be like them.

She walked downstairs. Will was beating his fists on the wall so hard he was going to hurt himself.

"Will," she said softly, "what did your mother say? Did you talk to her?"

"You go get her." A gob of mucus dripped from his nose. "I'm not going to leave Dad alone. You go."

She could see the prison up close! Although, she thought bitterly, if he had left, she would have been there and Alan wouldn't have been alone—but she didn't count.

"Where is she?" Irene said. "I don't know where she works."

He turned and hit the sofa so hard that it tipped over, then he kicked it. She backed away. "The car has it. Berry Farm. Go get her!"

"I'll go right now." She was glad to have an excuse to leave.

She glanced at Nimkii as she ran out the back door to the truck. He was pacing around his pen, and eventually he would pass the broken part of the fence. *Stay calm, pedazo. Please. I'll be back soon*—if everything went well. After that . . .

"Berry Farm," she told the truck's controls, and during the short trip, she rehearsed ways to act innocent and brainless when she arrived. She expected a hostile reception. The truck turned in to the Berry Farm driveway and parked itself in a gravel-covered area close to the road. She prepared to step out and find someone to naively ask about Ruby, but a burly man ran toward her. He wore a heavy black jacket despite the warm morning, and he pointed a rifle at her.

After a moment frozen in shock, she raised her arms. *I should have expected weapons.*

He studied her through a visor, standing taut, his rifle aimed right at her. "Why are you here?" He wore a surgical face mask under the visor-screen. Did he expect contagion?

"I'm here to see Ruby Hobbard. Her husband just died. I was sent by her family."

He kept the gun pointed at her. "Stay in your truck! Don't move. Your name?"

"Irene Ruiz. I work at the farm with the mammoth, Prairie Orchid Farm."

He looked at something on his visor. She tried to act surprised and scared—that was easy, since she was scared—and kept her hands up. *This is a prison. No dairy farm shoots visitors.* As much as she could without seeming nosy, she looked around. Every detail might be important to know if she could find someone to tell it to. The big, barnlike building had security cameras under the eaves, the kind that could look in any direction. It had two entrances that she could see, a double-width door that rolled horizontally on a track like a livestock barn, and a human-width door next to it. Around the area were parked cars, a pickup truck, and two big vans. Several people were walking toward the big building. They, too, wore visors and face masks. She couldn't see more without obviously looking away from the guard, and she did not want to antagonize him.

He relaxed a bit. Whatever he saw on his visor must have corroborated her story. "I'll call her. Don't move."

She glanced around a bit anyway as if she were reflexively looking for Ruby. A couple of centaur robots paced around the building. She looked at the vehicles more closely. Two seemed to be official cars of some sort, maybe one of them the car with the red lights she had seen racing to the farm during the night.

Ruby came running out of the big, hulking building, and she, too, wore a visor and mask. She got in with barely a glance at the guard or Irene. "Home," she told the car—not Irene—and it started up and began to move. The guard lowered his gun and walked away.

After a moment, Irene said, "Will is very upset."

Ruby grunted.

Irene took a deep breath to work up the courage to ask: "What kind of farm is that?" She hoped it would seem logical to ask, since a gun had been pointed at her.

Ruby said without hesitation, "Experimental animals."

"Oh." Irene nodded as if she believed it. The rest of the trip took place in silence.

Even before the car came to a full halt at the house, Ruby dashed out. Irene watched her run in without bothering to close the door behind her. Irene closed it and went to Nimkii's pen. He was touching the barbed wire she'd used to repair the fence with his trunk as if he were thinking.

"Hey, Nimkii," she called from the far side of the pen, "come over here. I'm back."

\*    \*    \*

Avril found her room empty. "Went to the clinic on the second floor," a note said. Good. She found her phone and switched it off so the centaurs couldn't follow her inside the building—unless her phone couldn't really be turned off. It might be permanently on. By law, the software didn't belong to her, so it could legally do anything at all.

*After the mutiny, we'll change that.*

She left the room, ran to the stairway, and opened the door to it a crack, listening for centaurs. Instead she heard a torrent of footsteps. She peeked in. Students packed the stairs, running down them. She joined the human river cascading over the steps and out the nearest exit. The girl next to her wept with relief as she stepped outside.

Avril kept running across a wide lawn and downhill toward the lake, aware that if they were all exposed to the delta cold or whatever it was, now they would spread the illness. Well, she wasn't the one who had imprisoned them without access to help. Some disasters weren't her fault.

Near the lake, she stopped and turned her phone on.

Mom had left a several messages over a period of hours. The most recent: "Are you okay? Call right away."

She called. Mom could be in trouble, too.

"Avy, how are you?" She was calling from work at the property management office, walking down a hallway, and she looked as frightened as she sounded. And she was wearing a purple blouse.

"I'm okay. What's going on?"

"There's an epidemic."

"Here, too," Avril said.

"Everywhere. It might be that delta cold, Sino. No one seems to know. Are you safe?"

An honest answer would make Mom feel worse, but she always wanted the truth. "No. We're sick, I mean, not me but other people, dying, and campus security was holding us prisoner in our dorm, and we were cut off from communications. That's why I didn't call. I couldn't. But we just escaped."

Her mother seemed to need a minute to take that all in, and oddly, she didn't panic. "I see you're wearing purple."

"There was a plan."

"I know. Your dad is in on it."

"Really?" She felt herself smile. "I thought he would be!"

"And me, I'm in, whatever I can do. Avy . . . ?"

"Tell me everything you know, Mom. Please."

A centaur voice was shouting from the other side of Dejope Hall. Avril hurried away toward the lakeshore.

"I don't know much at all," Mom said. "The city declared a state of emergency. I'm going home. Your dad is going to stay at work. They have a lot to do, a lot to disobey." She smiled, then someone shouted her mother's name. "Oh, god. I gotta go. Avy, I'll let you know everything I can find out. You'll do the same?"

"The truth, even if it's bad." A centaur was coming around the building—there was no time to explain.

"I love you."

"I love you too." Avril started running with no plan of where to go. The lake—yes, she could run to the lake, down into a marshy area, where she could hide. She crashed through the underbrush, and Drew was suddenly running beside her. She sank ankle-deep in mud and kept going. Drew ran ahead of her, but he turned and grabbed her hand to pull her toward the open water.

She was thigh-deep when a noise hit her so hard she fell to her hands and knees: the centaur noise. Her head was underwater. She tried to get up and fell again, too dizzy to balance, not too dizzy to know she might drown. *Keep your head up.* But which way was up? She was going to vomit, and she had to keep holding her breath. Her head was about to explode. She felt the lake bottom under her hands and knees and crawled as fast as she could in the direction she hoped was toward the shore. The lake bottom eventually sloped up almost enough for her to raise her head.

Drew was next to her. He pulled her arm up and supported her so that she could kneel. She took a deep breath and opened her eyes. The whining centaur stood far beyond the shoreline trees. It wouldn't see them there.

She tried to stand, stumbled, then crawled again, next to him, toward the deafening noise. The water grew shallower until they reached its edge. She rose up, then fell again, this time with her head on mud. Safe. The sound cannon suddenly stopped.

The centaur would go past. It had more important things to do. She lay stunned, panting. If she opened her eyes she would definitely vomit. Her ears rang so loud she heard almost nothing.

This was only a setback. As soon as she could stand . . .

Something grabbed her by the arm. Hard. Metal. She knew what it was before she opened her eyes to see gleaming steel. The centaur yanked her up. Drew was scrambling to his feet—and it kicked him in the head. Blood splattered, and he flew back into the water.

\*    \*    \*

Berenike told the woman banging on the door to take a bicycle. "I'll make it free." Amazingly, the woman agreed.

As Berenike set up the free ride, she saw that she could make all the bicycles in the region free. Done! Then she set up a notice to send to everyone requesting a car that the bikes were free. Corporate would choke at that. Good. Mutiny felt almost as exhilarating as she'd hoped.

Could she do that to buses, too? Of course. She was an omnipotent god—but not omniscient, she realized, or she would have thought of that already. She could also open all the windows on every bus automatically. Fresh air would be healthful. Done and announced. *Get home fast and free, folks!*

She sat down and took a moment to gloat. She had power, and she could use it for good.

Enough gloating. She stood up to study the data. Usage resembled nothing on record. No one was stopping to eat or pick up meals. Wait times had leveled off at unacceptable levels, but the free alternative bikes and buses might help soon.

Fleet size remained stable. Good. No poaching from surrounding areas, which there sometimes was, a kind of war within AutoKar for scarce resources. Only two cars had disappeared from her control, both in the northwestern area. Again, that was odd—until she checked and saw that some surrounding franchises had shut down. *Irresponsible fuckheads. People need cars.*

The city's Health Department called again. "We need more cars to make deliveries."

"Consider it done."

With a little effort, she got it done. As she worked, her mood soured. Was it anger? Anger was good. Familiar. Energizing. Maybe even healthy. But angry at precisely who? She began to list targets, and the list quickly became long.

The two employees reported for work, and she gave them a fast briefing. "Our chief task is to help keep people alive in any way we can. That means safe, efficient transportation."

"I believe God wants me to do this," one of them said, a woman named Summer Ngan. "I'll be praying for everyone and bless each car."

Her coworker gave her a glance but said nothing. Both were very capable. Besides, a blessing for each car might do good. Who knew?

She thanked Summer but wondered if some problems were too big for God to solve—certainly not a god at her small level of omnipotence, for all that she was enjoying her powers. She took the time to check the local mutiny chatter and tell them what she'd done, and she learned that a national mutiny news feed existed. The mutineers must have planned all along to create one. Well, as Summer would say, bless them. Maybe they were more capable than she'd thought.

She put the mutiny news feed on audio. Emergencies were being declared in a lot of places—but not nationally. No one had a death count or prediction or any other hard numbers. Most authorities agreed the killer was the delta cold, but there seemed to be two kinds of it, or at least two very different reactions to it.

The feed reported with scorn that the White House had issued a statement deploring the looting of pharmacies and threatening action to end social unrest, but it hadn't said where that was happening. Maybe it wasn't happening at all.

No one was saying what was going on at the refugee camps— probably something even worse than what was happening in Milwaukee. If she could help keep Milwaukee more or less intact, maybe the city could eventually help the camps somehow. A successful mutiny needed a city with all possible resources available.

Callers kept requesting cars. She automated the responses despite a clumsy setup process. It would rain soon. Would showers clean the air or give the virus moisture to survive longer? That was still in debate.

The city was sending cleaning fluid, gloves, and masks to public sites for distribution, and it needed more cars. The city's Health Department had also learned of a possible treatment, an antiviral medicine delivered by eye drops, of all things, and would organize distribution of it. Two of the local AutoKar offices needed more staffing. That problem took a while to solve. She tried to sweet-talk one employee by stressing all the lives he could save. He asked if this was part of the mutiny.

"The city is in a state of emergency." She hoped that was what he wanted to hear.

"They're talking about it on the Prez's channel. Traitors, they say. I want to be a traitor."

*Perfect!* "We're under the control of Emergency Government even though corporate said we shouldn't do that. The city government is in mutiny. Mutineers supporters wear purple. This is a mutiny operation now."

"Then I'm in. Hey, can I wear purple jewelry today?" Corporate rules banned flashy jewelry.

"Wear all you have and wear it proud."

Emergency Government asked her to attend an all-personnel video briefing. *I'm part of the city's personnel now?* The mayor, in need of a shave, dressed in a purple Hawaiian shirt, appeared on her screen:

"I want to thank you all and make one thing clear. This is a mutiny.

This isn't a declaration of independence. We're still proud citizens of the United States." He spoke as if he were delivering a thundering sermon, like the preacher he used to be. "We have pledged to respond to this dire emergency with all our abilities and powers. If we get adequate national leadership, we will follow it. If not, we will forge our own course with anyone who shares our commitment. We have by our actions pledged our loyalty to our fellow citizens. Thank you for your work. You are saving lives."

Berenike thought for a moment. She hadn't voted for that guy, but maybe he was okay. It really was a declaration of independence, a contingent one. She checked the activists' network, and it was abuzz with demands for an outright declaration.

She didn't have time for that debate. *Don't they have real work to do? I could give them a lot.* Anyway, someone seemed to be trying to hijack a bus. Big mistake. God would punish sinners.

*    *    *

With access to the news, I soon learned that a far bigger mutiny than I'd hoped for was under way, as well as a backlash against the mutiny, in addition to an epidemic—all this must have been the earthquake I'd felt gathering two days earlier.

Despite the many urgencies, we could address only the epidemic, and that might be enough. A few of us met, face-to-face (finally), in Colonel Wilkinson's office, a room graced with a family photo of a woman and a teenager in the corner of a bare shelf and no other personal possessions or decoration, as if he did not wish to claim ownership of the space or seek any comfort in his duties there.

"Do we know where the attenuated virus came from? The one that was released as a vaccine." I asked. "It's not ours."

"That's for the historians to worry about," Node 6 said. "We have a job to do."

"Yes," Vita said. "How will these viruses interact?"

To my surprise and concern, Node 6 wasn't military. (To no surprise, Node 1 was military—in fact a tag team of individuals.) Instead, Node 6 came from a corporate background, the exact kind of person to whom I had always imagined I was sending reports when I worked at the private laboratory, warning of discoveries that made me quake with fear: an impatient, profit-oriented executive who focused on financial reports, not laboratory reports. Tavis was his name—whether his first or last wasn't made known to me (clearly not an artistic name), and neither was his exact corporate provenance. His sun-bleached blond hair, ruddy skin with a hint of freckles, and rugged build whispered of wealth because no one of modest means could spend that much time outdoors getting exercise.

I noticed that my question had been sidestepped. "I asked who made the virus, the one that was released, out of admiration."

"Isn't it just like the one that you and Dr. Peixoto designed?" Tavis said. He looked at her as if she understood a subtext. She showed no reaction, not even annoyance. Perhaps she knew too much, including why he wanted to avoid the answer. I hoped my observation was wrong, but my heart was plummeting.

"It's almost like the one we designed," I said. She had provided a lot of ideas for it. Had she known what was about to be released? Suddenly something made sense: If the Prez's plan failed, someone would have to take the blame, and the guilt could be heaped on Peng, who was already an ignominious DNA tinkerer. (Was that paranoia? Again, I hoped so, but my heart continued to plummet.)

"So the attenuated virus that was released is even better," Tavis said defensively.

"It's meant to confer immunity," I said, not answering his assertion. Retaliation felt sweet. "How quickly would immunity take effect?"

"Are you suggesting that . . ." began Node 4, a quick-witted woman named Professor Wicker. Her frown finished the sentence. Many vaccines took days, even weeks to produce antibodies. I'd already calculated that this viral vaccine, with its efficient design, would work immediately, but I wanted people to worry. No one besides myself had been sufficiently terrified throughout this entire process.

For a long moment, no one spoke.

"This will be an easy question to answer," I said, "by examining people who've been infected. I think it should be the first question for deciding how the two viruses are interacting out in the wild."

"We really need to know what's happening," Vita said.

I had other, more important questions, and the data would answer them, so I agreed wholeheartedly. The question of how they interacted mattered most immediately to our task of saving lives. Although I felt certain the attenuated virus, meant to be a vaccine, was working, I could be very wrong. We split up assignments and returned to our workstations, and I propped my door open with a wastebasket, a statement about my availability as much as about my need to be part of a real-life greater whole after too much solitary confinement.

Thus we began to examine data from live and dead human beings like Roman augurs scrutinizing the entrails of animals sacrificed to the gods: lung, nasal cavity, throat, sputum, and even a little blood—but unlike the Romans, we couldn't keep sacrificing offerings until one gave us the answer we sought. *Dum spiro, spero,* the Romans had punned. *While I breathe I hope.* We needed to do our part to keep people breathing, and suddenly I thought of a fast, obvious shortcut to the complex research.

\*   \*   \*

Avril struggled against the too-tight clamp on her arm as the centaur dragged her from the lake. She fought to regain her footing, but it pulled her too fast, and her legs banged into trees and rocks at the lakeshore. And through it all, she screamed.

"You killed Drew! I know there's a human controlling this. Listen to me. People are dying, and you're killing them. How can you do this?"

She suspected no one was actually listening. A centaur could be as autonomous as a car, just with better software and even better legal protections. If an autonomous police robot hurt or killed someone, by law no one was responsible. The murder wouldn't matter.

She screamed and fought and cursed anyway. Drew mattered to her.

The robot dragged her uphill toward Dejope, and her fight turned to panic. "Let me go! You have no right!"

Students were fleeing all around, and the centaur wasn't stopping them. *Why me?*

No, they weren't all fleeing. A couple of dozen ran toward her—toward the centaur, and she glimpsed purple in their clothes. They carried clubs, maybe other weapons, brave but stupid. The centaur's control module spun in their direction. She put her free hand to her ear to be ready for the sonic blast. Instead she heard a tiny noise, and one of the students flew as if he had been jerked from behind. A bullet?

*A centaur can do anything, and it won't matter.*

The robot didn't slow down, dragging her straight toward the building.

A door opened, and the robot threw her inside. She tried to shield her face with an arm as she hit the floor and slid. She was climbing to her feet before she stopped. The door had shut behind her. She ran to it, tugged on the handle, and beat her fists on the glass. Locked in again.

Her left shoulder felt wrenched, and her right elbow and thigh ached with bruises. Her wet clothes had mud and grass stains. Her phone was still on her wrist, though, and it still worked.

She could break out again. She ran to the office and grabbed the dumbbell. This time she'd throw it right through an outside window. No more sneaking around. No more being discreet.

"Don't try it," her phone said.

A drone buzzed on the other side of the window.

"Who are you?" she said. That voice had to be a human being, even if it was filtered to sound metallic.

"Stay in Dejope or die," it said.

Did she recognize that voice? Maybe. It didn't matter. She was going to die of the cold regardless.

"Go upstairs and help your sick friends."

"Who are you?"

"They need your help. Everyone's left and they're alone." The voice gloated. Machines didn't gloat, at least not very well.

"Let us out so they can get real care."

No answer. And her phone didn't work for anything else. Well, she might as well survive for as long as she could, and maybe she'd spot another opportunity for freedom. She set down the dumbbell and took the stairs to the second floor. She passed no one on the way. Although most people had escaped, voices were murmuring in the lounge. She walked in, wet and bedraggled.

Hetta turned and looked shocked. "You're back?"

"A centaur hauled me back. I guess I'm important."

She wrung her gloved hands. "Is help coming?" The expression on her face and in her voice begged for the answer to be yes.

"I don't know. I was talking to someone, and I asked for that, and"—she shook her head—"well, I don't think so."

"They're really sick." Hetta took a deep breath. "Drew was going to get help."

Avril tried to come up with something to say that wouldn't sound like blood splashing into lake water. "They stopped him."

"Stopped?"

Avril felt too sorrowful to say anything more precise. She looked down and shook her head again. "I'm sorry."

They stood silently, and in the silence Avril imagined the gloating in the voice on her phone again. If somehow she survived, she would get a different phone and smash the one she had into bits with a hammer. In the meantime, she had one way to fight back. "Can I help?" she said.

"Yeah." Hetta sounded defeated. "We put them in separate rooms to protect them from secondary infections. Drew . . . recommended that." Her voice choked at his name. She gave Avril some instructions, a mask, and some gloves. "Make sure they're comfortable, mostly. We can't do much more. Do you want to check on Shinta first?"

Avril found her awake in her bunk, and staring through half-open eyes at the ceiling. Her lips had no traces of blood, but they looked bluish.

"Hey, Shinta. I'm back. Need anything?"

She looked, blinking. "Oh. Hey, Avril. I'm okay."

"Want something? Water, food?"

"Tea? Can I get tea?" she asked like a little girl hoping for a favor—Shinta, the mighty athlete. It hurt to hear.

"Anything you want."

In the kitchenette, she stared at the phone strapped to her wrist as she worked. That was how they had tracked her and found her, and it proved that she was more valuable than Drew, but she couldn't imagine why. With every breath, as she boiled water in a microwave and found a tea bag and a cup, her anger grew. Since she was going to die anyway, she felt less afraid, maybe like a soldier on a suicide mission—or rather, the fear didn't matter anymore. It was only doubt, and now she had a certain future. When her phone started mocking her again, she was going to have a lot to say.

She served Shinta the tea, ready to talk with her about her family, about the weather, about anything but the situation, to make her feel cared for.

Shinta pointed. "There's a camera," she said, her voice hoarse. A crawling camera clung to the ceiling next to the light fixture, white like the ceiling, barely noticeable. Some sadist was watching on the other side. Maybe they enjoyed seeing students suffer and die. That didn't surprise Avril.

"I'll take care of it." She got a winter glove from the closet to protect her hand because those cameras sometimes fought back with shocks or needles on their legs. She hurried to shove over a desk, climbed on it, and, with a fast swing of her arm, grabbed the camera.

Even through the glove, it felt like holding a tiny squirming porcupine. She threw it on the desktop and stamped. The crunch felt like victory.

"You shouldn't have done that," her phone said.

She jumped down to the floor. "Why? Do you enjoy watching sick people die?" She left the room so she could talk without disturbing Shinta, and lowered her mask so she could speak loud and clear. "Does that make you feel high and mighty?" No answer. "I know it does. I know what you are, even if I don't know who you are. I know you like it because you're keeping those students trapped so that they suffer and die. This is why you and people like you aren't fit to run this country or any country. You're sadists."

She heard laughter on the other end.

She strode down the hall, searching for another crawl-cam to relish crushing. "You've been torturing people for a long time, and you're going to pay. It's not enough to reduce people to poverty, you have to turn them into nonhumans, things that don't matter so you can do anything to them." Nothing she could say would change any minds, and she knew that, but everything she said made her feel more powerful. No more appeasing. She could rant for a long time.

A new voice interrupted, this one unfiltered and female.

"We have someone for you to talk to."

"Someone who will let us go?"

"Someone who can make a difference. Hold on. I'll turn your camera on. He'll want to see you."

Maybe all that ranting had achieved something. "Who are you?"

"Chancellor Bowley." Her voice was silky with self-satisfaction.

Avril gritted her teeth. The chancellor had been foisted on the campus to destroy it. "You're a murderer."

"But you don't have to die. Look at this."

Her father's face came on her little screen. He looked furious.

"I have a deal to make," Bowley said. "Avril, tell your father what's happening."

She took a moment to organize her thoughts, and a new one popped into her mind. *This is why they want me: as a pawn to use against Dad. And he's in the mutiny.*

"She's killing people. We're trapped here in the dorm, we can't get out, and that cold is here. People who leave, who fight back, get shot. I don't know what else she's done, but she's a murderer."

His eyes got narrower, his lips tighter. He understood.

"We'll let her go," Bowley said, "provided you do some things for us."

"What would that be?" His tone was flat with anger.

"You can stop what you're doing. Walk out. Cooperate."

If they were threatening him, Avril realized, that meant they couldn't get to him in any other way. He was safe, physically, and he was a danger to them.

"Don't do it, Dad."

"Murder is a serious charge," he said.

She was about to say she could prove it, but he kept talking.

"So is extortion. Kidnapping. Conspiracy to commit murder. I can think of a half dozen other felonies just off the top of my head that you're guilty of. Maybe even treason. Capital offenses."

Bowley said, "She'll die if you don't agree."

"Dad, I'm going to die anyway. I've been exposed. I'm trapped here with sick people. I'm helping to take care of them. Don't do it."

His face softened. "I love you, Avril. I love you more than anything else."

"Prove it," Bowley said.

"Dad, we can't let them keep doing this."

"I love you so much, Avril, that I'm going to listen to you and do what you say."

"Dad?" He'd do what she said. He loved her. She could barely breathe.

"She's a worthless dupe," Bowley said, her voice now like flint.

Her father looked at Avril—or rather, at her face on his screen—and she looked at him, his face stern and strong. She could be as strong.

Bowley kept talking. "You won't like what happens to her because of this. It can get a lot worse for her."

He shook his head just a bit. "You'll make it much worse for yourself."

"You're not going to win. You have no support."

"We've had a vast majority for a long time, and that's why you're so desperate. Avril, I'm sorry, but I don't think this conversation is going to lead anywhere. I love you. I'm angry beyond anything I can say about what's happening to you. They'll pay. I promise you we'll win and they'll pay."

"I love you, too. And Mom. Tell her I love her. Stay safe."

He nodded. And his face disappeared from her screen.

Avril took a long breath. This was how courage felt—like the worst fear and sorrow she'd ever felt. This fear and sorrow felt like a source of boundless strength.

"How could he do that to you?" Bowley shouted.

Avril opened her mouth to answer, then changed her mind. Her desire to rant had disappeared. She felt calm, she felt centered. Nothing that was going to happen to her in the future mattered. If she died, fine. If she lived, one day she'd hug her father tight.

Bowley was still shouting. "We're coming for you. It's going to get a lot worse, and he'll change his mind."

No, he wouldn't. And in the meantime, her clothes were filthy. She went back to her room, left her phone in the hall with Bowley still raving, and inspected her closet for crawling cameras before she changed. She checked on Shinta and moved the desk back against the wall, and she took her time. When she came out, her phone was quiet. The hall was quiet. Most people had left—but all of them?

She began knocking on doors. Maybe someone had been left behind, too ill to leave. If so, she'd help them. She had enough life ahead of her to still be useful.

\* \* \*

Irene watched Ruby charge out of the house, Will following right behind her, pleading and arguing, and his mother ignoring him.

Nimkii came to the edge of the fence, leaned over, and sniffed, watching Ruby and Will.

Ruby turned around and screamed at Will. "Some things are more important!"

He grabbed at her. She slapped him hard across the face and shoved him to the ground.

"Irene!" she shouted. "Come here."

Irene ran. Being obedient might be the safest response.

"I'm going back to work," Ruby said. "You stay here and help Will." She pointed to him on the ground, sulking.

"Yes."

"Do what Will says." She turned and left. Ruby would place duty before family. That wasn't surprising. Perhaps it meant the prison management knew about the mutiny and expected trouble. Or that the delta cold had reached its staff or prisoners.

Irene waited until she was gone, and waited some more until the dust had settled in the driveway. Then she approached the boy, who lay shivering.

"Will, can I help you into the house?" She had no love for him, but human decency said she should offer him at least a little compassion. "Can I get you your dog?" It was tied up as usual near the shed, but it was friendly and might give him comfort.

"No! Just leave me alone!"

"Okay." Arguing wouldn't change anything.

"Sooner or later," he hissed, "it's going to get us. I hate it all. Everyone."

*So much for compassion.*

Will climbed to his feet unsteadily. "Dad was spreading it to everyone, and now we're all going to die. He got what he deserved." He stumbled to the house and slammed the door behind him.

Spreading it? Yes, to his family and from there, maybe beyond.

She walked back to Nimkii. His head was down defensively, his trunk curled, his ears spread wide.

She put a lilt in her voice she didn't mean. "Hey, Nimkii, you big pedazo. What do you think of all this drama? This isn't good at all, that's what I think. Would you like some food? I have some alfalfa."

She sent him a bale over the fence. Then she called a friend in Madison. She got through this time. Her friend spoke with hushed shock. Students were being shot on campus, and people were getting sick all over. The whole city had risen up in mutiny, and they were about to try to free the campus.

This was worse than she thought. "I haven't heard much up here."

"It's going to be a war. We better win."

"How about my mother? Do you know where she is? She was arrested yesterday."

"At City Hall? That protest? I know a lot of people are trying to find out. I'll pass on anything we learn."

"Can you tell them there's a prison here? I know exactly where. Here's the coordinates."

"Okay. Here's where you can get some news. I gotta go."

Irene checked the site, and the news left her confused: mutiny everywhere, and the delta cold, and people dying. Reports contradicted each other. The Prez hadn't been seen all day. She looked at Nimkii.

"If it wasn't for you, I'd leave right now." But if she left, he'd die one way or another. "I love you." She needed to decide how much, and soon.

Something banged inside the house. Nimkii stretched his trunk toward it and growled. Had Will broken something big?

She ran to the house and nervously opened the back door. "Will?" No answer. She walked in, at first cautious, sneaking, and then she remembered that she lived there, too, even if she wasn't fully welcome. "Hey, Will, how are you?" No answer. "Where are you?"

The air smelled wrong, sort of smoky. Around a corner, she saw Will's legs on the floor, near Ruby's desk.

"Will?" He didn't move. She came closer. "Will?"

He was lying on the floor. Half his head was gone, spattered across the rug.

*Who did that?* She looked around. No, wait, that made no sense. She forced herself to look again. A gun lay next to him. He'd done it to himself.

*Will, why?*

She couldn't breathe anymore. She turned and ran out of the house and stood on the back stoop, gasping.

*Will, why?* Because he was going to get sick and die. His father had been contagious. And Will . . . he hated everything and everyone. Including himself.

She paced in the backyard, for a while thinking about nothing, wishing she could forget what she'd seen and what had happened. Everything kept getting worse. She paced a while longer. Some problems she couldn't solve. They were too big. And they weren't her problems. She could . . . what, leave? No. That was what Will had done. The ultimate escape. She . . . she had responsibilities. She would try to do the right thing.

What should she do? The house had two dead bodies in it, and—she needed to tell Ruby. She'd practice more human decency, even for people who didn't deserve it. Would Ruby come back? She hoped so. This was a problem for Ruby to solve, not her. She could call—if she had her number. Who would? Will's phone, Alan's phone, the house computer? They'd be locked to a retinal scan, probably. Would dead eyes work? She wasn't even going to try.

She told Nimkii, "I'll be back."

Ruby had taken the truck, so she had to walk, and the walk seemed longer than ever. She trudged up the road trying to decide if she was a traitor, a martyr, or just a decent human being. Ruby deserved to know that her son had died, but Irene deserved to know a means of contact so she didn't have to hoof to the prison farm and risk her own life just to be a decent human being for people who were not decent and treated her like a tool that talked. Maybe she'd go back, grab her stuff, and walk away—leading Nimkii.

As she came close, she slowed and looked hard at the prison. Maybe she'd see something useful this time to help liberate it. There had to be a mutiny in Wausau. She spotted Ruby's truck and a few of the same vehicles as last time, but most of them had left. A group of guards stood far away from the prison building. Irene raised her hands even before she was in shouting distance.

"Hello!"

They turned.

"I'm here to see Ruby Hobbard! Her son died!"

Someone motioned for her to stop. She did, and she slowly looked around, hoping she seemed to be trying to find Ruby. One of the guards lifted their wrist to their mouth and had a brief conversation.

"She can't come."

"But her son just died."

"I told her that."

*Wow.* "She should know that he shot himself." It hurt to say that, but it had to be said.

After another conversation, they said, "Are you Irene?"

"Yes."

"Go back home. She'll take care of it later."

The other guards seemed to be talking about it among themselves.

"All right." She began to walk away. Either Ruby was worse than she'd imagined, or something big was happening in the prison. Maybe both. She glanced behind her to see if anyone was following her. No. And she hadn't learned anything useful to pass on if she knew someone to tell it to.

\*    \*    \*

Berenike knew her papa would have made great fun of her work. "So there I was, fighting at the front lines, when I spilled coffee on my phone. It was a battlefield disaster." *Papa. No more jokes from him ever again.* The AI counselor advised taking a deep breath, centering herself, and moving forward from sad memories. She considered that, and instead she smiled. He was still telling jokes—from the great beyond.

Messages relayed by Emergency Government from utilities said they were having trouble with staffing and wanted its employees to get prioritized transportation to get to work. Done, with a little juggling. The city had also put out some news about effective home care and urged self-quarantine. She read it carefully and wasn't sure about its recommendations. Everyone should act as if they were infected and carried the virus. Okay, that meant her. Then what?

A client somehow made it through the automated system to talk to her directly. "I need more cars. We're distributing food, and people need to eat."

She checked. He ran a high-end imported-food warehouse on the Northwest Side and used autocars for deliveries.

She said, "The priorities are for medical supplies and transport."

"People want their orders filled."

"You're not a priority business." No one needed pickled green papaya to survive.

"You can't tell me that. We have a contract with your company."

"This company's been commandeered. Priorities are different." She pushed a few buttons. He'd been calling for quite a few cars, even more than normal. "You need to close and send your employees home."

"No, we have paying customers."

He hung up. She sent a message to the police. Something seemed fishy.

Old Man Tito came to her office. "It's time for me to go home."

He should have gone home a long, long time ago, but he kept refusing. She stood up and studied his face, at least what she could see around the mask he wore behind a protective visor. His eyelids seemed unusually heavy. "Are you okay? No, you're not."

"The news says that not everyone dies."

"You're feeling lucky?"

"I don't feel right staying here and infecting everyone and everything."

"Do you have someone to care for you?"

"I'll be fine." He seemed sluggish.

"Let me give you some supplies. You're a priority worker, you know."

"Priority? Me?"

She pulled a box of ibuprofen from a drawer and handed him a couple of blister packs. "Here, take these. They'll help with the fever. Remember, drink lots of fluids. Do you need to get stuff from your locker? I can call you to see how you're doing."

"You don't need to do all this for me."

"You're right, I don't, but I want to." If she had a cot in the back room, she might offer to care for him there. She followed him to a newly cleaned car. "I'll call."

"Don't bother with me. Keep up what you're doing."

How long before she got sick? She had long willed herself into health out of necessity. That might not save her anymore.

Avril had found three people who were sick as she went door to door. Two were fending for themselves, although they asked her to get something to eat and drink. She brought them up trays of the best of what little was left in the food court. The third burned with a fever and could barely speak. She asked him his name and where he was to see if he was thinking coherently.

"At the beach in Mexico. I mean, I'm in the hotel room at the beach."

She forced him to drink a glass of cold water despite all his complaints that he wasn't thirsty, then she ran to the makeshift clinic and brought back some medications to fight a fever along with a glass of lemonade.

"I brought you a cocktail from the bar."

"Pills? I don't want pills."

"You want to party, right? These will have you dancing like you've never danced before. Special designer drugs, the latest from Brazil. What's your favorite dance music?"

By the time she left, he promised to go down to the club as soon as he finished his nap.

"I'll be there, too," she said. Was it good medical practice to entertain his hallucinations? She didn't know, but she hoped she'd done some good by playing along.

She was knocking on doors in the other wing of Dejope Hall when her phone chimed. Bowley again. *Now what?* It wouldn't be good.

"Yeah?" Even to say hello would be more polite than the chancellor deserved.

"We want to make a deal."

Probably a bad one. "What's your best offer?" *Always negotiate from a position of strength, even if that strength is as real as that guy's beach resort.*

"We'll unlock the dorm if you do what we say."

"Yeah?" she said again with all the strength of skepticism that she could muster.

"We want you to surrender to our custody."

She weighed that for a second. "That's a big ask for a small exchange." Actually, it meant that Dad had to be worth a lot, which made her glad.

"Everyone else would go free."

"By everyone, do you mean this dorm?"

"Yes."

"They'll get access to medical care?"

"Um. . . ."

Avril waited. Waiting was strength. Why would they be offering that deal now? She remembered when Cal said the music in the food court was loud so that people could talk freely. That meant that the staff had included mutineers. The chancellor might be having trouble holding the campus in lockdown. Dad often said that criminals over-estimated themselves.

Bowley finally spoke. "Understand, it's hard to get medical care right now."

"They need care. Denying care would be dereliction of duty." As if Bowley and the Prez and all their supporters hadn't broken a million other laws already.

"We can try. They can look for it themselves, at least. They'll be free to do that."

A crappy offer. Avril walked to a bench near the elevators. This might take some time, so she got comfortable. "And their phones would work, no interference?"

"Of course." Her voice had turned a little silky, an attempt to manipulate her somehow.

"What about other dorms?"

"What do you mean?"

"Are they locked down, too?"

"Um. Yes."

*She's catching on to my plan.* "I want them released, too. All of them. I want the campus to be free with access to phone service, medical service, freedom to come and go. Call off the centaurs." That was asking for too much, unless either Dad was some sort of really big-time mutiny kingpin—she'd be even more glad if he was—or Bowley was about to lose control of the campus anyway, which would also make her very glad. For students like the guy at the imaginary beach hotel, every minute might count. Shinta's lips had been blue.

"Agreed. Walk outside of the building and wait."

"I'll wait until I see that you're doing what you promised."

What would happen wherever they took her? Well, Avril was going to die anyway. It wouldn't matter. She added, "I want my phone to work all the time, even where I'm going." She could say goodbye to Dad.

After a moment: "Yes."

That was weird. And probably false, the stuff about the phone at least, and Bowley knew it, so making the promise cost nothing. More lies. "I'll be outside, waiting and watching."

She ran one flight down to her room. "Help is on its way," she told Shinta as she grabbed a jacket. She'd heard that prisons sometimes kept the temperature cold to torment the prisoners.

"Can I call my family?"

"Yes, soon."

In the clinic, she told them about the agreement. "I think they want to extort my dad. They don't know him. Or me. They're not going to get anything from this."

Hetta frowned. "You shouldn't let them take you." She looked at her phone, then held it up to show Avril. "Hey, it works!"

One promise kept. "Get ready to get help."

Avril thought about trust as she walked downstairs and tested the front doors. They opened, and she walked outside as a centaur approached. The sidewalks all around were empty. No one wanted to get near a building with a centaur guarding it. Her shoulder still hurt from the last time—and her dignity still stung, for that matter, dragged around like a piece of luggage. The robot trotted up on its mechanical legs and towered over her.

She could see some smaller residence halls nearby. "What's happening over there at Bradley?" One of the doors of the old brick building faced Dejope. She stood and waited one, two, three minutes. Traffic sounded from far away, probably off campus, and low clouds were rolling in from the west.

The door at Bradley opened. Someone peered out, saw the centaur, and ducked back in. It was the only centaur around. If she could get it to leave, the residents could walk out freely.

"Let's go. And I'll walk on my own," she told the centaur, trying to stare down whatever sensors were aimed at her. To see if someone was listening, she added, "Show the way."

It stood still. No one was listening. She waited and seethed with anger as the memory of Drew's death surged back. Finally, a van pulled up. The centaur took a few steps toward it, but Avril decided to push her luck.

Although the rear door of the van opened, she went to sit in the front so she could see where they were going, but waited to close the door until the centaur had climbed in the back. It would know where she was, she knew, and if she made a wrong move, it could shoot her through the rear wall of the cab. She'd pushed her luck far enough. She was on her way to somewhere, and it would be bad.

She called her dad. The line was busy, so she left a message telling him everything that had happened, describing more extortion and kidnapping to charge Bowley with. "Just so you know. Keep doing what you're doing. Tell Mom I love her." *Say goodbye for me, really, but no one needs to hear that now.*

In the short time she'd been in Madison, she had never seen the city so quiet. And never in her life had she been in a vehicle that raced so fast on city streets, heading due west to get out of town. Her shoulder ached against the seat belt when it took sharp turns, and ached even worse when it suddenly stopped dead in front of one of those boxy old buildings that had probably once been a big store.

"You know what that is," a voice on her phone said, that gloating voice again.

*Doesn't that sadist asshole have anything better to do? Well, I won't give him a show.*

The building had no sign or markings, and it needed serious up-keep. Its fake stone exterior was crumbling, and weeds poked up through the pavement around it. They'd recently been flattened by traffic at the front door. This was a busy place.

"Let me guess," she answered with all the scorn she could muster. "A federal facility. Political prisoners that the city and county won't accept."

"Good guess. Don't expect amenities."

*Death without amenities.* "Of course not." She'd heard about those sites. "Lowest bidder, and they still skimmed off funds. You're criminals in all kinds of ways."

"You know what? You're not a mutineer, you're a mutant." The taunting voice tried to be infuriating.

She stayed calm, still invigorated by the strength of fear. "Yeah, but I didn't choose to be a mutant. You chose to be a sadist asshole criminal." She tried to hang up, although she couldn't tell if it had worked. Then she had a great idea. She peeled a sticker off her jacket and stuck a scrap of it over the camera lens on her phone. *You won't get to watch. I hope you're disappointed.*

The front passenger door of the van opened. The door to the building opened. Could she make a run for freedom? She could try—and fail, so instead she stepped out and walked calmly and with dignity into the building. Could she turn this into a mere setback for herself and not the end? She'd try, and if she did, if she got free and survived, she'd go looking for the sadist asshole.

*    *    *

Berenike had sneezed a couple of times. Was it that minor cold that had been going around for a few days, or the delta cold that was killing people, or had the cleaning fluid gotten to her? There was one way to find out: wait to see if she got sick, and it might happen soon enough. *Don't waste any opportunities. Mutiny now, not later.*

She studied the statistics of overall AutoKar use. The lunchtime rush had been a relative trickle. Most people, presumably, had already made it safely home, if they were safe anywhere. She saw no evidence of major poaching or hacking. Cars would still need to be cleaned, but not nearly as quickly. Despite that, she would have had surplus cars after allocations to essential workers, like utilities and health care, but now they were being used to transport individuals to medical care. Demand still exceeded supply.

But she had good news. Due to backlash from the federal government, the City of Milwaukee had finally declared itself independent, in open rebellion, along with some suburbs, although the county had stayed loyal. That mattered tremendously to her morale, although not to anything she was doing. *Mutineer rebel commando—hell, yeah.*

Out in the wider world, the Prez still hadn't made an appearance, but his staff and supporters seemed more concerned with putting down the mutiny than with solving its causes. The mutiny medical providers, which seemed to be most of them, were organizing diagnostic tests. And the news said that Mexico had closed its border and would shoot on sight any American trying to cross it.

She got a call on her personal phone. Her pseudo-grandfather, Christopher Swoboda. Maybe he needed help, not that she owed him even the time of day. She answered because she'd suddenly had an idea about lawyers and extortion.

"Honey," he said, "come home here. You're not safe. It's just a job."

"I'm doing essential work." For once it was true.

"I'm so worried about you. It scares me worse than dying myself." He sounded like Momma at her worst. "You should be here, with me."

"I'll be fine. I happen to know that one of my sisters' father is a federal prosecuting attorney."

He was silent, then said, "I'm sure he wouldn't—"

"Extortion is a crime," she said.

He was silent again. He'd sounded well enough. That was all

she owed him, the same concern for his health that she'd have for a stranger.

"I'm working for Emergency Government now. I gotta go." She ended the call, and she'd feel fine if she never heard from him again.

Wholesale food distribution, pharmacy staff, emergency workers, and funeral transport all needed cars, or they would soon.

The city called, this time a person in the Health Department she didn't know. "We've had losses in the department and we need someone who could handle transportation. Can you? Now? It's okay if you have other priorities, but we're very short on resources and we think you have the skills—"

"Yes."

"Maybe I should describe the job." It involved making deliveries and having contact with the public, perhaps even large groups, so it would entail the risk of infection and possible violence—

"That's fine. I'll do anything."

"Really?"

"Yep. I'll be glad to take any kind of risk."

"You need to know that we've all been exposed to the delta cold here at City Hall. I don't know how it suddenly got everywhere, but people have been exposed all over the city and the country, as far as we can tell, which is just not what epidemiological models would predict." She sounded outraged, as if she suspected something. "Anyway, it's definitely here in this building. You'll be at risk of infection."

"I've been exposed, too. I'm not worried." But yes, this whole outbreak seemed suspicious for a lot of reasons.

"Um, okay. I'll note that. Report to the Health Department at City Hall as early as you can."

Within minutes, she'd be a commando in the streets. Good.

But who would do her job at AutoKar? It was essential, after all. After a moment's thought, she called upstairs to the Christian lady, Summer Ngan. "I need to do some work for the city. Would you like to manage the southeastern Wisconsin fleet? I know you've had some management training."

"Me? Let me pray on that." Two seconds later: "Wow, God was quick this time. Yes."

"Okay. Not too much is happening right now. Can you come down here? I can get you ready."

Before she left, Berenike changed into street clothes but kept the wide purple belt and bright hair clips. She commandeered a delivery truck from the fleet. She'd need it for her new job—a better job, an exciting job. Anything would be. She had been trapped for much too long at AutoKar. Only an unthinkable disaster was enough to let her escape, but to what? All the news she had been able to find said that bigger shit would hit bigger fans as the day went on—more panic, more chaos, more death, more weird disease patterns, and more coordinated federal efforts to put down the mutiny. She could die, and not just of the cold. But, fuck it, she'd die with her boots on.

* * *

Vita and I were about to review some data together, sitting in my little office, and I studied her as much as she studied the results.

"I'm surprised you made this analysis so quickly," she said.

"I found a shortcut, and what I learned makes me very hopeful." I brought up some simple bar charts. The answer we yearned to find was, in the end, simple. "You can see the progression over time." I paused to blow my nose, although it seemed like a waste of the precious vaccine viruses to trap them in a tissue.

"Yes, that's a very fast response by the immune system," she said, and pointed to another, more complex set of colored charts. "And it seems to recognize the other virus, too, the Sino cold." She persisted in calling it *Sino*, not *delta*. That told me something.

"What we ought to consider is where this attenuated virus came from," I said.

"I don't know," she said tonelessly. She was lying, because if she truly didn't know, she'd be anxious to find out, and I'd have heard that appetite in her voice. "It's a good thing to see that it's working. How will it interact?" She asked that question again, the same one she'd asked the day before, and now her voice was anxious. But why was she lying? Had she been trapped into this work like me?

"How is it interacting in China?" I said, a hint of fire in my words.

She looked up at me a bit too quickly, a bit too startled, unable to find the means to answer a question she didn't expect.

"I asked the Node 1 team for some data, and they knew how to get it. The mutiny is contagious and has been spreading fast into many low-level positions, the ones who do the actual work. It seems that potential hosts were primed by years of injustice, and mutineers were willing to provide information to us that should have been secret."

She frowned, perhaps doubting that something so basic as injustice had fueled the mutiny or perhaps that I could have made a conclusion about the source of the virus from evidence that sat in plain sight for those who knew what to look for.

"This attenuated vaccine virus in fact came from China. According to what has been reported by our intelligence services, China's vaccine virus is working well. They did extraordinarily clever work when they created it. For all its modifications, its external appearance was made to look almost unchanged, no more different than one zebra to another, just slightly different stripes. To a lion—or to an immune system—they all look like lunch."

She frowned, annoyed, then slipped a neutral expression over her face. "That was very clever on your part. I didn't think of that as a way to find out, to check what was happening in China."

Her remark told me both that she knew it came from China and that she had been entrenched in the government bureaucracy long enough to be assimilated into a silo. She was no sudden recruit, then. She still might have been unwillingly recruited.

"The data also tell us about the interaction between the viruses," I said, "that is, the viruses circulating together in China. The vaccine is working there." I brought up another chart and let her study its good news. "Here, however, I think the outcome could be different."

"What do you mean?"

Ah, now things would get tricky.

At that moment, although the door to my cell stood open, someone knocked: a soldier in full combat gear.

"Excuse me, Dr. Peng, I've been assigned to guard you." The voice and face, despite the obvious youth, allowed for no disagreement from me. "I hope I won't disturb your work."

The soldier took up an alert stance that would keep me in a line of sight. I decided to ignore the guard politely and not ask questions, such as whom I might be protected against or, conversely, who was being protected from me.

"First," I told Vita, "I have epidemiological data for the United States, and it explains a lot." I switched to a simple map that marked known cases of the attenuated virus shown in yellow, and those places were also known to have political leanings in favor of the Prez. "You will notice that this data has been compiled from several days ago. The virus was released here first."

The release had been extensive, although perhaps not everywhere, as I had overheard her say what seemed like ages ago. But *everywhere* was a nebulous term. I brought up a second map whose interpretation would permit no equivocation.

It showed the deadly virus in magenta, clusters of dots that centered on places where, as everyone knew, the Prez faced opposition. I overlaid it with a map of occurrence of the vaccine virus. "This data started coming in just hours ago. It was a deliberate attack against the opposition, knowing that immunity would have already been developed in areas that supported the Prez." Although I tried, I couldn't say those words without my teeth clenched in the rage I had spent hours containing.

She looked at the map with a hint of disappointment but no outrage at all. "Yes, I suppose that's why there's a mutiny." Her halo instantly lost all remaining luster to me. She was either lying or stupid.

"Or rather," I said, "it's a weapon against a mutiny."

She didn't look at me. "I suppose." She didn't seem to want to say those words. She was lying, then. I'd have preferred her to be stupid.

"And this virus, designed to kill the political opposition, isn't going to work as well as hoped in the long run."

Now her head swiveled. So did the guard's.

"I'll be glad to explain." I said. "To everyone."

*    *    *

Berenike walked out of the AutoKar office—*goodbye, forever!*—and into the truck waiting at the bay. She felt the thrill of terrified exuberance, maybe the way a soldier felt waiting for battle to begin.

"I'll pray for you!" Summer called.

Berenike waved her thanks and hid her doubts. If some god somewhere had a plan, it was opaque to her. She climbed into the truck and told it to go to City Hall. The latest news—the limited news available—was either useless official bluster or real and bad. A forest fire was burning in California, hard to tell how big. In a couple of places, armed resistance had sprung up to fight local independence movements, hard to tell how bloody. Airports were shut down to passenger traffic. The U.S. Postal Service had closed—for the first time ever—as had most private businesses. Hospitals were mobbed and creating emergency rooms and wards in parking lots.

Berenike's eight-block trip through downtown Milwaukee passed through barren streets that looked like a scene from a bad apocalyptic movie, or like an epidemic that had happened a little before she was born. She'd seen the photos.

She told her truck to park next to City Hall in a spot marked for official vehicles. Most of the spots were empty, and besides, she was now official. She walked into the elaborate gray stone and red brick building and looked around. Was this a suicide mission? If so, she'd die for a good cause, not from stupid melodramatic personal negligence. Like Momma. *Fuck. Remember what she did to protect you.* She had plenty of fucks left for better targets.

City Hall rose in the shape of a narrow triangle with a massive brick clock tower at the southern, pointed end. Inside, it opened into a seven-story atrium like many modern buildings, but this building had been standing for about a century and a half. She'd visited it once as a teen on some sort of enrichment field trip. The patterned tile floor, wrought-iron railings, and carved wood had seemed formal and solid. She felt no trust for the government because she couldn't trust anything, but at least it seemed like the City of Milwaukee wasn't going anywhere, not with all those tons of fancy brickwork anchoring it in place.

The building bustled inside, unlike the empty streets—at least two dozen people in the lobby alone—and their voices echoed in a comforting human clamor. They stood farther apart than usual—they knew what to do. They wore surgical masks, and boxes of them stood by the door. She took a mask and put it on because if she was a carrier, she should protect other people. She found a marble stairway and climbed to the third floor and found a door labeled HEALTH DEPARTMENT. By the time she arrived she'd decided the mask might be necessary but this particular kind was a serious nuisance to wear, already damp from her breath.

No one waited behind the counter.

"Hello?" she called.

A woman came out of an office. "Oh, you're Bern . . ."

"Berenike," she answered, pronouncing all four syllables. No one ever got it right. "Berenike Woulfe. I'm here as a driver. I brought a truck, twelve hundred cubic feet and seats for two passengers. I know how to drive manually and I can adjust automatic controls. I just left work at AutoKar. The passenger and cargo spaces have been sterilized."

*Just left AutoKar.* Oh, those words felt good. Maybe she'd never go back one way or another, maybe Summer's god would grant her that little blessing. That would be enough. She tried not to get her hopes up.

The woman almost smiled behind her mask. "You're a lifesaver. Or you will be. Seriously. Come with me and we'll get you started. We're starved for resources. We always have been," she said as she turned to walk down a little hallway. According to the name tag clipped to a businesslike blazer, she was Elena King, the assistant health commissioner. "I won't lie. This is going to be rough. Only someone clinically insane would try to hold back the tide."

"Then you recruited the right person."

She led Berenike past offices where, through the windows in the doors, she saw a couple of people glaring at screens or talking on phones, but most of the desks stood empty. "Some people are working from home," she said. "Let me tell you what we need."

The job would be simple: pick up supplies at warehouses or other sites and drop them off at places like clinics, community centers, and participating drug stores. Berenike was pleased to see a major homeless camp and a refugee shelter on the list.

"We have a plan for an epidemic on file. Every public health department does." She wore her hair in tight gray knots and seemed old enough to retire and too busy to think about it. Her boss, she said quickly and quietly, as if she didn't want to utter the words, had succumbed to the cold.

"And we were lied to." Now she had a spark in her voice. "We were told the cold from a few days ago was attenuated and would act like a vaccine. We knew more than we could tell. I was just counting down the hours to let people know they were safe. Then something went horribly wrong, and I still don't know what." She paused and looked Berenike in the eyes. "I have never felt more ashamed in my life. I participated in this disaster." She held her gaze for a long moment, maybe asking for absolution, maybe censure.

Berenike looked away. She had a list of people to blame, and King wasn't on it. "None of us wanted any of this." Perhaps that would satisfy her.

After a long pause, King said, "Most of the staff is out in the field. For all that we don't know, what we do know is enough to tell us what needs to be done now. This is beyond prevention and control and maybe even mitigation. Now we care for the ill and try to protect the well. What we need are resources." The spark returned to her voice. "This is the worst-case scenario. And we didn't expect pushback on the federal level for a response. We're getting nothing from them. We have a good plan. It's come down to adaptation and implementation, which is the hard part. That's where you come in."

Berenike liked the woman's attitude, urgent but in control, like a military officer in a movie, or like an assistant manager who was competent but not bitter and vindictive as she fielded calls from furious asshole customers.

The office at the end of the corridor contained two people, a man who seemed to be scowling behind his face mask, staring at a big screen and murmuring into a microphone, and a police officer in uniform, calmly studying a heavy-duty police phone. The officer looked up as they entered. Berenike thought she might have met him before, a man around her age with warm brown skin and expressive eyes.

Elena sat at a desk with a wide screen and kept talking, not pausing for introductions. "We have a list of sites for you. I'm afraid we haven't figured out the best route."

Berenike raised her phone and aimed its camera. "I can do that. Let me grab the data. I can read it right off your screen. I have software from AutoKar, and we have to do this sometimes for clients. Is there a schedule or appointments?" She had the software, she recalled bitterly, because AutoKar had required her to use her personal phone for work but had never given her a dime for its purchase price or monthly fees.

"We need everything as soon as possible. That's all. The plan isn't quite that detailed."

"That's fine. That's what I need to know." She entered a few more parameters, trying to copy Elena's calm, controlled, unvindictive urgency.

The officer stood up. "I'm Neal Sacks. I'll be riding shotgun with you, just in case." He didn't extend his hand—no handshakes. Everyone knew the drill.

"Neal . . ." Now she knew. "Weren't we in grade school together? Vieau School? I wasn't there long, but I remember you. You were in school plays, a grade ahead of me. I'm Berenike Woulfe."

"Yeah, I wanted to be an actor so bad." His eyes narrowed for a moment. "I'm sorry, I don't remember you from back then."

"I was just another little kid." He had been suave and debonair, two words she had learned solely to describe him for herself. She had tried to be just like him, and she knew at the end of just one year that she would never succeed. "I worked for AutoKar." That wouldn't impress him. "I commandeered a nice truck for us to use."

His eyes narrowed with a smile. "Commandeered. That's the Vieau spirit: We achieve." He hadn't changed much from the boy in her memory.

Her phone dinged: route calculated. She showed it to Elena. "It suggests three loops, starting on the North Side."

Elena approved. Neal picked up a rifle and a helmet.

"Oh," he said. "You should wear this." He handed Berenike a bulletproof police vest. She put it on without comment, trying to maintain her new attitude as they walked out. He carried a spare helmet for her. Would that really be necessary? She didn't want to ask.

In the truck, he pulled up a map on his screen with three dozen red dots. "We need to avoid these locations, but they change, so we'll need to keep making adjustments."

She turned on the truck's interface, entered the route, and began setting overrides. "What are those dots?"

"Different things." He buckled himself in, put on his helmet, and lowered the visor. "Reports of gunfire, mostly. And not where you'd think. Maybe countermutiny. We gotta watch out for that. A couple of house fires. There's a bad traffic accident on Highway 100."

She looked at the near-empty streets around them. "An accident? How did that happen?" The truck began to move. She took the helmet and put it on.

"Someone plowed into cars at an intersection. We think maybe the driver was driving manually and had a seizure. This stuff just hits some people like that."

"Yeah, it can." *Like Papa.* "So, we're going to get on the freeway, and they're almost empty, and I'm going to tell the truck to drive as fast as possible."

"Our cruisers can do that. It's a fun ride."

The trip to the freeway was short, and soon they were speeding at more than one hundred miles per hour on straightaways. She leaned back and tried to ignore how the country was speeding faster than she wanted to calculate into what would likely be its biggest disaster in history. A possible disaster for her, too.

Neal consulted his screen. "Now, you should know for some of these pickups, we're commandeering goods. The owners might get touchy. That's why I'm here."

*            *            *

Confucius spoke of superior and inferior men, of those who were motivated by upright morals contrasted with those who were interested in themselves rather than the greater good. If inferior men governed a kingdom, they would bring it to disorder and a lack of virtue, and they would lose the mandate of heaven to continue their rule. Had that moment come? I hoped so, although inferior men (or people of any gender, of course) could have superior firepower and be willing to abuse it. To those living in a misgoverned kingdom, Confucius urged resistance, and one form of opposition, he said, involved a dedication to truth.

I had time for that twenty-second meditation (some philosophical conflicts have straightforward solutions) as I followed my soldier to speak to Colonel Wilkinson in his office. I had seen three things, one of them capable of damning an inferior man if I could speak the truth at the right moment.

"I've found something astonishing," I told him. "You need to see how people react to it."

Without a word, he rose. He already knew most of what I did, but I might be able to answer the key question for him: Exactly who had abused their power?

Vita and Tavis were waiting in the conference room with its metal folding chairs. Others came like moths drawn to the flame of my reputation. Peng had something urgent to say! They settled into place, silent except for lifesaving coughs and sniffles.

"We have three distinct viruses to consider in terms of epidemiological forensics," I said, a statement that by itself earned a few surprised huffs. I brought up a chart on one screen in the conference room wall. "First, the original deltacoronavirus from Siberia. We have samples generously provided by China and authenticated by Korea and Japan, and they all match. This is the genuine pathogen. Here are some key segments that we'll return to. You don't need to understand them, although some of you do, but what you see with your bare eyes will tell you what you need to know."

My talk felt like a sales presentation, something I had once done frequently, but this time I came with nothing besides vital knowledge to sell.

"This is the attenuated viral vaccine, which is also from China. We've received the same data from several locations, so again, this is the genuine pathogen circulating among the public in the United States."

Some people shifted in their chairs. I knew that would startle them.

"I want to point out one segment. Here is that segment from the original virus, and here is what we see in the attenuated one, a mere cut-and-paste operation from a different common cold. It's similar to what our team designed here, and leads to very mild symptoms."

Heads nodded.

"We did fine work, and the Chinese team did even better work. I want to show you one artifact of their genius."

Colonel Wilkinson seemed to be thinking about something else and hiding it. He had no doubt heard all this before from Node 1, but the good part was yet to come. Vita leaned forward with curiosity. Tavis sat back, not out of relaxation but out of an unconscious desire to escape, trying to put as much distance as possible between me and him. I felt relieved to see that and have my conclusions confirmed. He knew what was coming.

"Notice that these segments in the delta virus and the vaccine virus are not similar. The vaccine will spread faster for several reasons, and one of them is here. It won't cause macrophages to present antigens as fast as they might. This virus triggers the immune system, but not too much."

"And you can see all that," Tavis said, his chin lowered protectively, anticipating my attack.

"I know where to look, and so do you. If we were going to create a vaccine—and as you know, we did—we agreed that including this would lessen the immune system response. We'd walk around feeling fine, sneezing a little bit and breathing normally, still spewing a sufficient number of viruses left and right. Genius, as I said. Few of us have gotten so much as a headache."

Tavis again leaned as far back as possible, this time with a glance toward the door.

"Finally," I said, "here's the virus that's killing people. It's based on the original delta virus but it isn't the so-called Sino cold. This new segment, the one that causes macrophages to present antigens, causes a much more intense response. That's what makes this so deadly. The body overreacts with a cytokine storm, and people drop like flies. We know it was artificially introduced, and this shows the means by which it was designed to be virulent."

Colonel Wilkinson was paying strict attention now. Biological warfare—combating it, that is—had been his career.

"But there's an amateurish flaw," I said.

Now Tavis leaned forward.

"All viruses need to reproduce because they want to thrive, if we may anthropomorphize them. This one reproduces deep in the lungs, so the moment the infected person stops breathing, the infection stops spreading. Here's the oldest sample we have. It has the lethal segment. But here's a newer one. The virus has dropped that segment. As you can see here, the splices for the virulent additions aren't solid. It still causes a potentially serious illness, but death is not guaranteed."

Could they see that? Vita and Professor Wicker nodded, but some of the others looked and took it on faith.

"I apologize for bringing you a report that still requires epidemiological proof, but such good news couldn't wait. I believe that the deadly strain of the illness is just going to fizzle out, perhaps even without interventions like major quarantines, although that would certainly accelerate the process. People will still get sick with a cough and a cold, and for some people a cold can still lead to very dangerous secondary infections like pneumonia, but the people infected by the new strain will generally survive without intensive care, and they'll spread the new, milder disease."

Tavis was drumming his fingers on the table, his eyes staring into space—at an unpleasant future. Other faces relaxed. There was the light of life at the end of the tunnel of death. But Tavis was trapped. I knew enough about salesmanship to wait for him.

"How is that amateurish?" he protested desperately. "Viruses always evolve into different strains. We're seeing it with our own eyes. Where was the mistake?"

"The mistake," I said, "was including that segment in the first place. We've seen it before—in an early version you proposed. This segment does not occur naturally, but you'd know where it came from."

After a moment, he said, "What if that was the plan?"

"Limited mass murder as opposed to uncontrolled mass murder? That sounds like an excellent plan."

Colonel Wilkinson rose to his feet with an expression on his face that could have launched missiles.

Tavis looked around, but not at me. "I can check my notes and figure out where I got that. It wasn't my design."

"It was someone's," I said with a smile. And then I turned back to my presentation, ignoring the drama of two men walking out, one of them in the custody of the other. The one in custody left wide-eyed, sweating, thinking as fast as he could about lawyers and confession and turning state's evidence. (Or at least that's how I wanted to imagine it.)

"As we all understand," I said, "this has implications for fighting the disease. The lethal cold will quickly become less dangerous. Field observations will establish the speed, but we can predict the eventual outcome. This is great good news that we can spread gladly."

My vicious smile had become benevolent, and Confucius would have viewed it with approval. A superior man does not practice rancor.

*　　*　　*

Irene, pacing next to Nimkii's pen, got a phone call from Ruby.

"Come back to Berry Farm."

That was the last thing she wanted to do. She tried to think of a way to say no.

"I'll tell you what to do about Will," Ruby said. "And you can take the truck and get food for Nimkii. You'd better act now before everything's in chaos."

When had she suddenly become a decent human being? Probably not yet, but Nimkii would need food.

"I'll leave now," Irene said. Ruby hung up without answering. No, not decent yet.

Irene held her breath, went into the kitchen, gathered up a snack, found the eye drops, and gave herself another dose. She'd bring the tiny bottle with her. No one was going to take care of her besides herself.

She went to the pen and threw her hat over the fence. Nimkii hurried to pick it up. "I'll be back soon, pedazo!" she promised. "With food!" He knew a lot was going wrong. He had better be patient, because she had nothing else to offer him but promises.

She began walking. Maybe, when she got the truck, she'd just go home and stop pretending she cared about Nimkii. Except that she did. But he needed a new home anyway. If they walked to Madison together, where could he stay? The university had a forest.

She checked for news. Through her mother's artist network, she'd found a kind of broadcast, and it was all about the cold and the mutiny. People were advised to stay home. The list of cities and institutions and people who had mutinied kept growing—a lot of hospitals and medical suppliers, tired of being puppets to profit rather than serving their patients. She tried to find out what was happening in Wausau. A fight seemed to be under way. Maybe when she had the truck she could go see for herself.

Or she could go get herself some medical care. She felt fine, but people could get very sick very fast. She needed to take care of herself—and she needed to take that fact seriously.

She ate the snack she'd grabbed, an almost-empty box of cereal, a juice box without a straw, and a package of crackers. She dropped the empty packages and crumbs as she went. The world could just deal with her mess. She'd had enough of cleaning up its messes.

Berry Farm came into sight. Fewer cars and trucks were parked around it, whatever that meant. Highway traffic seemed lighter. The centaurs were still there.

She raised her hands as she stepped onto the driveway. No one rushed out with a gun. She kept walking slowly, ready to duck or act even more submissive. A centaur approached.

At the sound of a gunshot, she dropped to the ground, covering her head with her hands. She wasn't hurt. Maybe she wasn't the target. She didn't move. Nothing happened. Maybe it was a warning shot. Footsteps crunched in the gravel and stopped next to her. She stayed still, held her breath, and played dead until she couldn't hold her breath anymore.

Whatever was next to her had not moved. Only a machine could stand that still for that long. She turned her head to peek, and saw a centaur pointing a long, ugly weapon at her.

"Identify yourself," the robot said in a much-too-human voice.

"Irene Ruiz. I'm here to see Ruby Hobbard. She called me and told me to come."

"Remain where you are. Do not move."

She lay there perfectly still, taking shallow breaths, and felt like a target. Just like the other farm, this place, the ground beneath her body, and everything she could see when she raised her head was enemy territory. Yes, it was time to go home, back to Madison, as soon as she could, with or without Nimkii.

Someone in full police armor came out of the farmhouse: helmet, body armor, and a gun, which was pointed at her. Ruby, judging from the physique and walk. She came close but didn't shift her aim.

"How did it happen?" she said.

Irene knew what she meant. "Will shot himself. In the living room."

"You should have stopped him."

"I was feeding Nimkii."

"You should have stopped him!"

*That's a job for a mother, not a tool that talks.* Irene remained still and silent. Nothing she could say would do any good.

Ruby shook. Sobs? Rage? The helmet hid her face.

Irene thought of something neutral to say. "I'll go back home now." She waited for permission to get up. If Ruby denied the truck she'd walk away and just keep on walking.

Ruby motioned with her gun toward the barn. "Get up and get in there."

Irene had to pretend she didn't know what Ruby meant. "In the barn?"

"You belong in there."

"I don't understand."

"You will."

"But what about Nimkii?"

"I'll shoot him when I go home."

*Nimkii!* "Oh, no, don't do that. We can find him a new home."

"Move." She motioned with the gun again.

Irene felt tears rise. And anything she did would be futile. She got up and walked toward the barn. Maybe Nimkii would break out again. Maybe the mutiny would break the prison free any minute now. Maybe she had the delta cold and would die. Or maybe Ruby would. Each step brought another thought, every one of them sour.

The door on the barn opened automatically.

"Keep going," Ruby said. "And through the next door. I'll be watching, and I'll be glad to kill you."

Irene knew she would. She stepped into a little corridor like a double entrance to a business. The door behind her closed, and she heard noise from inside the barn, voices, a lot of voices. The door ahead opened—into a wide space dimly lit by translucent panels in the ceiling. It held dozens, maybe a hundred people, and many of them were dancing and singing along to music from someone's phone. The air smelled stale.

They turned to look at her, and a grinning young man started walking toward her, clapping to the rhythm and wearing a purple T-shirt that said CANCER SURVIVOR. He sang, "I'm going to shine my light both far and near." He stopped. "Welcome to Berry Farm Prison!"

"I guess I found the party."

"You didn't bring any food, did you?"

She couldn't tell if he was joking. The wide space held tables, chairs, and bunk beds.

"I know," he said, "cozy, isn't it? I'm Koobmeej. I'm not really a cancer survivor. I got this shirt from a neighbor. He was handing them out. Purple, you know. Have you heard about the mutiny? That's our color."

"Um, I'm Irene Ruiz."

"Don't worry, you won't be here long. The cavalry is coming."

"You know there are still guards outside. And those robots."

He sighed, but his grin didn't fade. "Not for long. You know this song? Feel free to sing along. We'll be out soon."

"What about the cold?"

"We all have the sniffles. Some cold!"

*I didn't find a prison, I found a lunatic asylum.* "I might be carrying the delta cold. The killer cold."

"We've heard about that. There's the isolation ward." He pointed to a table in a corner with a chalk line on the concrete floor to create a wide buffer zone. Three people sat inside, carrying on an animated conversation.

On a whim, she looked at her phone. No reception. They had no idea what was going on, did they? But she knew what she ought to do. "I should go over there." She didn't want to seem rude. "Thanks for the warm welcome."

The people at the card table, two men and someone of uncertain gender, invited her to sit down. "We're playing two truths and a lie," a man said. He looked tired and wan, obviously ill. He coughed into his elbow. "No score. Honor system. Not much of that, either."

Irene sat down to be nice—and because she wasn't sure about what else she should do. *Is insanity contagious?* "I have some medicine for the cold."

He brightened. "You do? We could all use that. I'm Roger, by the way. You're an angel."

They passed around the drops and gave her back a near-empty bottle.

"Your turn, angel," he said. "Why do you look so glum? Can you tell us two truths and a lie about that?"

She had a lot of truths to choose from. When she told them who her mother was and what had happened to her, they immediately stopped the game to talk about her books and art—Mamá had fans all over—and assure Irene that down in Madison, the prisons would be liberated soon, too.

But they had no idea how that was going to happen. *This is all just an act to make themselves feel better.* And their optimism wasn't very contagious. They might be liberated, or they might be trapped in there forever and slowly starve to death, since they had no food, only water.

Another glum truth: Irene's life lately had been one long series of big and small mistakes, although not all of them her own fault, and they had led her to disaster and likely early death.

CHAPTER

8

Berenike let the truck pull into place in the industrial park. A load sat on a pallet in a driveway, and no one seemed to be around. The codes matched the list from the city: face masks, gloves, and protective gowns. She and Neal loaded the lightweight boxes into the truck. The job was disappointingly easy.

At the next warehouse, a bit farther west, nothing waited outside for them. Neal, helmet on, pushed the buzzer at the entrance as she waited in the truck, windows down, listening. No response. He took out his phone. "Hello," he said, "this is the Milwaukee Health Department. We're here to pick up emergency supplies."

A man came around the corner of the building—a big elderly white man in a tight rent-a-cop uniform, wearing the kind of mask on his flushed face that would protect him from everything including toxic gas. He pointed a finger at Neal. "You're trespassing!"

"Good afternoon, sir. We're here for an authorized pickup," he said casually. "Emergency. There's one going on, you know."

"You can't just come here and take what you want."

"That's between the owner and the city. We're here to pick up what was agreed on."

"That order has no legal standing."

Neal looked at his phone. "The security company will open the doors for us."

"What if I'm the owner? I won't let you go in." He had a gun on his belt and put his hand on it.

Neal sighed, unruffled. "You can let us take the shipment, or I can arrest you. Do you really want to be locked up with a lot of coughing people?"

"You can't arrest me. It's insurrection and unlawful. If you read the Constitution—"

"Right here, sir, right now, the city has requisitioned certain material and will pay for it. You can allow us to remove it or you can pay the legal penalty. The choice is yours."

"You're breaking the law."

"I'm not here to argue. I'm here to escort the pickup and delivery of certain medications that can save lives."

The two men stared at each other. Berenike watched, ready to drop to the floor at the first twitch of a gun. Then she remembered her customer service training and experience. She knew what this moment called for.

She beeped the horn and leaned out of the window. "Hey, people are dying. Let's get moving! I don't know who you are, but we've got the paperwork, so let's get the stuff!" She pushed a button on the dashboard to open the back of the truck.

The guard stared at her, and judging from the movement of his mask, his jaw dropped. Good. She got out, holding her phone display toward him. "Right here, that's the order. Take a look, but I know you've seen this already. We're waiting. Fifteen cartons of antivirals, more if you have it. We're authorized to inspect the warehouse." She looked him right in the eyes, unblinking. "We can get backup." That was a bluff. Was this worth risking her life over? Maybe, maybe not, but it felt triumphant to be yelling at him, even if her heart was hammering. The next move was his. She waited, holding her breath.

"I'm not having any part of this." Red-faced with rage, he began to walk away, then turned and shouted, "It's not legal! You can't just take what you want!"

Neal gave her an admiring glance as the old man disappeared around a corner.

"I worked in customer service," she said—*worked! past tense!* "I dealt with assholes all the time. Sometimes it takes a bigger asshole, and I've been trained in all kinds of assholery. I think I have a talent for it. We should get this stuff out before he changes his mind."

The side door to the warehouse clicked open, no doubt, she knew, the work of some bored underpaid contract worker somewhere at the security company's office who needed a paycheck and didn't give a shit otherwise. Berenike could sympathize. Neal strode inside, telling all the lights to turn on. How fast could they do their job before the asshole changed his mind? He had a gun, after all.

The warehouse was well organized and they found the antivirals easily. She scanned some boxes that identified themselves as a different antiviral. She called King, who said it was even better and to take that, too. They loaded it up as fast as they could. Neal sent instructions to lock the warehouse door, and they were off. She set the truck to maximum speed and autopilot. She didn't trust herself to drive. Her heart was still beating too fast.

Behind them, three shots banged. They both instinctively ducked, but the truck seemed unharmed.

"I'll call that in," he said. "Another red dot."

She let the truck drive itself most of the way and took over manually for the last half block to the first drop-off site, a community center. A crowd stood in front, everyone standing far apart.

"Pull in at the back," he said. "We don't want them to rush us."

She knew the neighborhood, close to her home, poor and African-American for more than a century, and over time little had changed except that the population had declined as homes were lost to landlords who had let properties self-destruct during a succession of economic and bank crises. She'd attended a local history presentation at that very center. The people who remained were tough as concrete, "the tightest neighborhood in the city." She hoped so. The city's plan counted on it. They'd take care of one another. Probably. Everyone was scared and hurting, and people in pain reacted unpredictably.

She pulled up to the back door, and she and Neal jumped out. She stacked a hand truck with boxes and pushed them in, and Neal carried an armload. A woman wearing a face mask and gloves was waiting and began thanking them effusively. Berenike knew her.

"Just doing our job," Neal said, setting down his boxes on the nearest flat surface.

"Hey, Berenike!" the woman said. "Good to see you."

"I have a new job," she answered. It felt fulfilling to say that.

"Good for you! Can I get you anything? Coffee, water, sandwich, wash your hands?"

"Water and soap, that would be good," she said. "Then we have more deliveries and better hurry." Neal nodded.

Back in the truck, Berenike said, "I'm liking this job."

"Just try not to run anyone over," he said. "I'd have to write you a warning ticket."

Two more drop-offs remained on that loop, although she had to alter the route for red dots. A column of black smoke was rising up from where one of them was. Neal studied his phone.

"A fire," he said. "Firefighters are on it. They're tough to scare."

"I hear there's a big fire in California, but that's all I can find out."

"Yep. Two big fires out there. It's bad. The problem is that first responders are getting sick, too. California is so fucked. Us, too."

"Thanks for the happy thoughts."

"It's my job as a first responder to think strategically, including all the ways that this job could go wrong." He kept studying his police screen. "It's a good thing we're in an unmarked vehicle. Less chance of being attacked."

"By who?"

"People who want our stuff—for themselves, or to keep it from people they don't like. Some really bad shit is happening in some places. I recommend wearing helmets at all times."

*    *    *

Avril walked into prison undefeated. Because she was undefeated, right? Her superpower. Just another setback. When the mutiny succeeded . . . It would, wouldn't it? With or without her, if she died.

She checked. Her phone had gone dead, no surprise. This prison was secret, or at least semisecret.

The door ahead of her opened, and she walked through, aware that some robot with a gun mounted in the ceiling or somewhere else had her in its aim. The door closed behind her with a tiny, unmelodramatic click and left her facing yet another door. It opened, and she stepped into a dismal low cinder-block hallway with grates overhead. The air inside reeked of body odor. At the end of a sloping corridor, another metal door opened—into a corridor, and it was filled with noise, heat, and a worse stench. She hesitated.

"Move forward," a voice ordered, that same uncanny voice of a centaur. She did. *Now is not the time to fight.* On one side of the corridor was a chain-link fence wall up to the ceiling, with a series of pens on the other side walled off from each other with fencing, each holding dozens, maybe hundreds of people.

The door to the nearest pen opened, and she obediently took a step in. The mutineers stood in groups or sat on the floor, and they turned and appraised her. She searched for familiar faces and saw none. *Furniture would be an amenity.* She saw no amenities at all. Adults and even a couple of children of all sexes were in the pen. No amenities and not much planning, either. Quite a few wore purple clothes.

She'd heard once that every prisoner had the duty to escape, at least military prisoners, and this was a war, right? An elderly man approached with a snippet of lavender tape on his chest, and "Enos" had been written on it with a blue marker.

"Welcome. My name is Enos. Lemme fix you up with a name tag and an assignment. We're organized into crews here."

"Um, sure. I'm Avril." *Crews?* What kind of assignment? She knew what she wanted to do. She dutifully wrote out her name tag and, because *why not try,* she asked, "Is there an escape crew?"

He grinned. Well, she knew it was a stupid question.

"We can't figure out an escape," he said, "but what we can do is figure out the rescue response. The minute we get a chance, when a rescue comes from the outside, we've gotta have a contingency plan. You want to join that, the rescue response crew? I'll be glad to introduce you."

The woman in charge of that pen's response crew, Morgana, had needed a shower at least three days earlier. Her body stank, her breath stank, and by the way she tried to keep her arms tight against her body to shield her armpits, she knew it. "Sorry I'm so rank. The second thing I want to do when I get out is shower and brush my teeth. The first thing is to get everyone to safety, whatever that means when the time comes. You're new? What's going on out there?"

Avril told her what she could. In exchange, she learned that there was one chemical toilet per section, and one working spigot for water for the whole place, so a bucket brigade moved water from one sector to another, painstakingly pouring it through the chain-link fences. No food had been provided since breakfast the day before, which had been bags of cheap bread tossed in. The prisoners themselves had the job to divvy the loaves up.

"I hope they saw that we could do that civilized," Morgana said with a thumb jerked at observation cameras in the high ceiling. "We're not like them. Fair, not greedy. In case there still are people out there watching us, I don't know. Did you see any humans?"

"Nope. And not guarding the dorms back on campus."

"Figures. We've been controlled by a morally repugnant elite and their flunkies, and the flunkies are jumping ship."

A special priority at all times, Morgana said, were the people in the row alongside a wall, lying on jackets or scarves or whatever could be scrounged as bedding. All of them were ill. No medicine or treatment was available for them, no masks or gloves or anything else for the medical crew caring for them, and no protection for everyone else except several feet of space separating them from the prisoners who coughed into damp or bloodstained tissues or cloths. Lying still in a corner were a half dozen bodies.

Avril stood and stared.

"You okay?" Morgana said.

"No. This is not okay."

"I know. This is uncivilized."

"This is a crime."

Enos joined them. "When we get outta here," he said with clenched teeth, "heads are going to roll. I already got a list. A long one."

Revenge. Avril could understand the urge. And like him and

everyone else, she was sure the mutiny would free them soon. The thought comforted her.

An hour later, she was still trying to feel sure. Any minute now. Her crew debated scenarios: a shootout, a surrender by the guards, a wholesale victory against the federal government, or a collapse of society due to the cold.

"If everything collapses," Avril asked, "who's going to come for us?"

"My family will never give up on me."

*Your family might all die.* Avril didn't say that.

A few minutes later, the air was filled with chimes and beeps and snatches of music. Their phones were working again.

"Blessed be!" Morgana said. "That's the first step."

Avril called Hetta. "Is the dorm still free?"

"Yes. They're all getting real care, Shinta and the rest. Where are you?"

"In prison. We need help. This place is horrible. People are dying."

"That one on the West Side? It's under attack, I think. Let me check."

\* \* \*

Irene endured endless speculation from Roger and the other quarantine-table members about what was going on outside. People might be dropping by droves from the cold, whatever a drove was.

"I think there'll be armed resistance," Roger said, his breath short and fast. He slumped in his chair, a man in need of serious rest and care. "I mean, the Prez has supporters. He keeps things in order, crime down—I know, not really, 'specially if it's a crime to lock us up—and stuff like that. If you have money, things are great. But today, everyone else, they just say no, and there's going to be pushback."

In a game of truth and lies, Irene thought, one out of those three things—illness, mutiny, and resistance—wouldn't be true. Which one? The question seemed too hard to answer.

Gunfire sounded outside. Everyone stopped and listened. They heard another round, then silence.

Koobmeej stood on a table. "That was a warning to us that this place is guarded. But we knew that. Everyone knows that. It was meant to scare us. Don't be scared."

"It's a shooting war now," Roger said. "Told ya."

He looked bad, but so did Koobmeej, and as the minutes ticked by, Irene was feeling sick, too. Her head pounded so fiercely she could hardly think—since when did she get migraines?—and she felt too dizzy to want to try to think. She couldn't breathe well.

"We could really use some fresh air in here," she said.

"Ain't that a fact." Roger looked up at the skylights. "I wonder if those things open."

"We could break them," she said. "All we need is someone with a good throwing arm."

"We talked about that. It might bring in the centaurs. Or something. The same with the door."

She looked around. Koobmeej was looking at his phone. Why? It didn't work to make calls. Maybe he was playing a game, but he definitely wasn't enjoying it.

He climbed onto a table again. "Hey, everyone, listen up. We have a big problem. I work in a greenhouse, so I need to monitor the atmosphere in it. I've checked our air. The $CO_2$ level in here is wrong. They've cut off ventilation. Maybe they're messing with the air. We have to do something. But in the meantime, sit still. Try not to talk too much. We're about to try to break out of here while we still can."

"Suffocation," Roger said. "It's a tough way to die. They use $CO_2$ to stun animals before they slaughter them sometimes. I've seen it. Takes a while. Hurts just to watch."

At Koobmeej's direction, a dozen brawny prisoners stacked up three tables, and while some of them held the tables steady, a tall man climbed up and swung a metal folding chair against a skylight. The chair broke. The skylight didn't.

"Well built, dammit," Roger said. "Look at the sides of the building. Sheet-metal siding, sure, but iron bars inside. This was never a barn. Always a prison." He didn't seem inclined to consider talking less, and Irene didn't have the ambition to ask him to shut up.

They tried another chair against the nearly flat metal roof, but the roof didn't budge, even at seams alongside the skylights.

Irene choked back nausea. A few people were holding their chests in pain. *A tough way to die.*

The team trying to get fresh air moved the tables again, this time under the peak in the roof and at a different seam in the construction. One chair broke, and the man swinging it fell and was caught by others. Another man climbed up and continued to hammer rhythmically.

Irene thought of a song with that rhythm and drifted off into sort of a dream, waking with a start at a wrong note. A weird dream.

The man on the table seemed to have made a big dent.

"Cease activity immediately," a voice said over a loudspeaker, a guard, probably a robot by the way it repeated the warning in the exact same tones. Then gunfire boomed outside, and the man on the table fell. He was caught by the work team, and although his shoulder streamed with blood, he gave a high-five sign.

The guard had shot through the wall. A sparkle of light shone in the wall where the bullet had entered, and another in the roof where the bullet exited.

"Not enough for fresh air," Roger said.

"Where's the surveillance?" Koobmeej called. "Look for something small that's a camera, maybe hidden."

Irene could do that. She stood up and suddenly swayed, dizzy. She held on tight to the back of her chair and waited until she felt steady, then examined the corner of the barn used for the quarantine area. She spotted a tiny box tucked up against a strut and recognized it as an off-the-shelf camera.

Three other boxes were spotted in other parts of the barn, and people started throwing things at them. Irene looked around for something.

"Hey, take my boot," Roger called. He'd pulled it off and held it out. "Steel toes. Work boots."

It was heavy and bulky, and she tested it in her hands. It would be hard to aim, but with its weight, it could be destructive. She threw it and almost hit the camera. Suddenly bullets flew in through the side of the building. She dropped to the ground like everyone else, and she lay still for a minute. They should have expected the robots to shoot.

"Those bullets flew way too high," Roger said from where he lay under a table. "If those damn robots wanted to kill people, they'd've aimed low. They're obeying orders, and I bet the orders say to keep us inside, not to kill us. So we die nice and slow of bad air." He grunted, a sound as ugly as an expletive.

Irene got up slowly, rage rising as she did. They were being tortured to death. She retrieved the boot and, with the strength of red-hot anger, threw it again. Its heel hit the camera with a satisfying thump, and the camera dangled from a wire. She dropped to the ground and waited for bullets. None came. She stood up and threw the boot again. The camera fell this time, and she dropped to the ground again. Another burst of gunfire pierced the walls.

Did she hear a mammoth trumpet? No, that was just her oxygen-starved imagination. *Nimkii to the rescue!* He could follow the trail of her scent and trash and crumbs up the county trunk road to Berry Farm. A nice idea. But the centaurs would shoot him.

One by one, the cameras were destroyed, and after a wait, the team resumed banging on the roof. Irene watched, lying on the ground. Bits of metal fell as the chair broke apart. A man pushed a leg into the roof like a pry bar and pulled down, and a line of light shone through. The roof was open! A little, at least. She took a breath and couldn't notice a difference.

The team worked even faster. The man swung from the chair-leg pry bar like an acrobat, and another man hung on to his ankles for extra weight. The crack widened and sunshine poured through—and air. She caught a whiff of it now, cool and fresh.

The hole grew. How big would be big enough? A breeze passed over her, and she breathed in as much as she could—and she heard a trumpet. Definitely. Nimkii was out there!

She climbed to her feet and staggered through a dizzy spell to the stack of tables. She had to warn Nimkii to get away.

"Let me climb up there. Hear that? It's the mammoth. My mammoth. He's out there." She got a blank look. She explained again. "That mammoth at that farm, you know it? I work there."

"Okay then," a woman said. "Let me help you climb up. Hey, Aaron. Let her out. She's the mammoth girl."

"Easy does it," the man told her as he knelt to let her sit on his shoulders. She poked her head through the narrow opening, avoiding the sharp metal edges. The air smelled sweet, sweet, sweet.

Nimkii stood on the road, trunk raised and jerking. She couldn't see any centaurs or people, but she was at a bad angle for looking around.

"Nimkii!"

He spotted her and started rushing toward her.

"Nimkii, go away!" She grabbed an edge of the metal, scraping her palm, and put her foot on the man's shoulder. He pushed the backs of her thighs to help her climb out.

One of the centaurs stood near the front entrance to the barn.

Nimkii kept walking forward. "Nimkii, no!" How could she make him understand the idea? Noise might work.

"Return to the building," the robot called. Nimkii continued walking toward it, unafraid. He didn't know what a robot was, but he knew a humanlike voice. He might think it was a living being, someone who could help him.

The centaur emitted a blast of noise. Irene covered her ears and hunched down, eyes on Nimkii. For a moment, he froze. Then he lowered his head, curled his trunk, and spread out his ears in an attack pose. He roared and charged. The centaur didn't seem to notice him. He butted the robot with enough strength to knock it over easily, a puny thing next to him, and reared up to land on it with both feet. The noise stopped. A robot leg had fallen off. He kicked it again, sending it a few feet across the gravel yard. Satisfied, he backed off.

The other centaur came running. It ignored Nimkii and aimed a gun at Irene. She dropped down and heard a crash, then another one. She raised her head slowly, covering it instinctively and uselessly with her hands. Nimkii picked up the robot with his trunk, obviously not for the first time, and dashed it against the barn. Pieces flew off of it. The robot collapsed, leaving a dent in the metal siding.

Nimkii trumpeted. He spotted a small car. He rushed at it and pushed it over, all the way upside down. Then he smashed a foot onto its undercarriage, and the roof crunched against the ground. He began kicking it.

"Nimkii! You'll hurt yourself!" She had to calm him down. "Nimkii," she crooned. "Nimkii, I'm up here. I'll come down and get you." She slid toward the edge of the roof.

Where were the guards? Ruby's truck was gone. Had everyone left? Apparently. Gunfire and noise hadn't brought anyone out. No one had shot Nimkii.

"All clear?" a woman's voice asked. Irene turned. A woman had poked her head through the opening in the roof. She climbed out and looked down at the centaurs, then at Nimkii. "Wow."

"I think it's clear," Irene said. Nimkii approached the building. She slid to dangle her legs off the edge. He offered his shoulders. She climbed on, and he backed away. She took a deep breath of air scented with his buttery perfume.

Banging started up from inside on the main door. People needed to break out, the faster the better. Maybe she could speed things up.

She rocked forward toward the sliding door. "Can you open that?" The idea seemed unlikely, but she was riding on a mammoth, she'd broken out of jail, she had lungs full of clean air, and anything was possible.

He hesitated. He probably didn't understand the concept of a door. She rocked again, hoping the noise of the hammering might tell him that this was another evil thing that needed to be destroyed. He stepped forward. The door had bent open a crack from the pounding. He slipped in the tip of his trunk and pulled. The door bent wider. He took a step back and tore it from its track, then ripped it from its hinges. The door fell outward, and he pulled it away as if he meant to smash it.

Foul air flowed out. He growled at the scent, dropped the door, and stepped away. She rocked backward. "Let's get away, let the people out." They wouldn't want to face a huge, angry animal. She rocked again, and he backed away some more, grumbling. When they'd gone far enough, she leaned forward to hug him as tight as she could.

Koobmeej stuck his head out of the barn, grinning.

\*   \*   \*

Berenike looked at the red dot on Neal's phone. "That's the next drop-off, a pharmacy," he said.

"Armed looters, an organized assault. We'll have to skip it."

"They won't get what they're looting for." She fiddled with her own phone. "We can double up on another pharmacy later."

"I'll make sure it's okay."

"Up next is the valley homeless camp."

"Could be tricky," he said.

"Maybe not. I know this place. They had to get a special account with AutoKar, and they kept the agreement to the letter. It's run as strict as a tight-assed condo association." The camp had long ago moved from scattered tents to take over a big abandoned factory building, and their presence had sparked a dozen legal battles.

"So I've heard." He didn't sound convinced.

He might be proven right about the delivery being tricky. The council didn't always act democratically, and a few people in the camp had objected in the past over decisions—she'd met some residents and followed the debate. She kept her hopes up as the truck turned in to the Menomonee River Valley toward the abandoned site. A block away a group of people alongside the street waved them down.

"I know her," she said, "the one in the yellow vest. She's the mayor of the camp." Neal lowered the window.

"We'll take it here," the woman called. "The camp's in lockdown. Safer for everyone that way."

She and Neal got out, unloaded the shipment onto the pavement, and got back in the truck. The mayor and her crew picked up the boxes and marched off, a model of efficiency. Tight-assed for sure.

At the next site, the other pharmacy, a couple of police squads were waiting to usher them in. Nervous customers waited in their cars in the parking lot.

They finished the final loop by sunset and reported back to City Hall, its doors and windows propped wide open to let in clean air. By then, traffic had picked up some, but even fewer businesses were open, and it was still an apocalypse.

As they entered City Hall to report in, someone was being pushed out on a stretcher. Up in the Health Department offices, King told them that doctors were learning more, but given time and resources, the system was overwhelmed.

"If anyone asks you about garlic soup, by the way," she said, "it's no miracle cure, but it might alleviate a few symptoms, just like chicken soup, so it won't hurt anything."

Neal set down his helmet. "That'll work only for as long as the nation's strategic garlic stockpiles hold out."

She sighed. "That's the thing. Take a break. There'll be more for you to do soon."

A table in the atrium held a small selection of food and drinks, including a pot of garlic-scented broth, and instructions to eat alone, preferably outside. Berenike grabbed a meatball sandwich, room temperature and soggy and probably fake meat, and she ate it under the vaulted stone arches at the entryway on the clock tower end of the building. How long would food last? The average city had a three-day supply of food on hand. She'd been told in a training session to motivate her to value her AutoKar job. *Enjoy the meatballs while they last.*

Someone leaned out the door. "The mayor's going to speak. Come back in."

He stood at the rail of the second floor of the atrium. "Let me get you all up to speed." The mayor usually shaved his head, but now it had grown out to a faint white fuzz around a shiny brown pate. The fuzz matched his beard. He still wore the purple Hawaiian shirt. The public address system carried his words.

"First, and most important, we're getting medicine and help to every neighborhood. It's not true that we've banned insurance companies from serving their customers. We're just serving everyone, and on behalf of the city I want to thank the employees who are acting above and beyond to fulfill their missions in the most extreme of circumstances."

His voice soared, as usual. "I want to thank the volunteers who are here and the many more out in their neighborhoods who are making sure that their fellow Milwaukeeans are safe and cared for. This is a city full of heroes and love. I could say much, much more about that, but you all have to get back to work."

Berenike didn't want to trust politicians of any sort, but she liked the thanks, whether or not it was genuine.

"I have important news. I can confirm that the president died this afternoon at 2:33 P.M., apparently of the same cold that's killing so many people and that he and his administration wasted so much time denying."

A few people cheered and applauded. Berenike was about to join in, rejoicing that she'd never see him smirk and wag his finger again, but the mayor waved his hands for quiet and continued.

"Federal policies have not changed. This is still a nation divided in the same sad way it's been divided for so long, and now it's costing countless lives. In fact, things may be about to get worse. Until now, the women and men who manage our infrastructure have made sure at great personal sacrifice to keep it working. Our own water and waste treatment facilities have kept our water safe. This is vital. But even more vital is the electrical system. Everything, from cars to lights to the labs striving to find a cure, depends on power." He took a deep breath.

"Now the government threatens to cut power to areas in mutiny. They can only do this with the support of the women and men who run the power plants and operation centers and distribution utilities. Most of them have said no. The Eastern Electrical Grid, which is our grid, has chosen to mutiny, as has the Western Grid."

He looked around, arms outstretched.

"They will need continued help. We've already made sure they have priority medical care and supplies and food and transportation, and we'll continue to do that. This is where the battle is now. We always expected a battle with foreign nations, not among our own beloved fellow citizens.

"Whatever the next battle is, we'll be there for the people of Milwaukee and for the United States of America. We will not back down."

Now he accepted applause. Berenike joined in. Was she ready to do battle? She always was, and now things had ratcheted up, finally.

"Berenike?" Neal was calling from the second floor. "You want to make another delivery? This time to a power grid station."

"Let's go." Infrastructure saved lives. Cutting off electricity would kill people. She'd be on the front lines, where she really wanted to be.

* * *

Irene coaxed Nimkii into a cornfield across the highway from Berry Farm Prison, and he seemed content to stay there and ravage the harvest, a safe distance from the excitement, and keep an eye on her on the farm's lawn in the twilight. His path across the pavement had left a bloody print. He'd hurt himself, although he wasn't limping.

Prisoners had poured out of the barn, with the quarantine section now moved to a plastic picnic table near the farmhouse. The farmhouse-headquarters had been left unlocked and a team was exploring. Everyone was on their phone, staring at the displays or talking or listening.

Koobmeej was reveling in the escape. "Irene! Thank you. And thank the mammoth." He gave her a hug, apparently forgetting that she was one of the quarantined prisoners.

"Um, thanks, but why didn't the centaurs attack Nimkii?"

He glanced at him across the highway. "Yeah, that was telling. Does he look like an ordinary threat? No. There aren't a lot of pachy-derms running around in central Wisconsin. A robot system wouldn't have been trained for that. A human would know, and humans are supposed to be running the centaurs at least most of the time, and they're not right now. Why not?"

He grinned, still elated by fresh air or by his own self-apparent genius. She should have felt annoyed, but she wasn't. She wanted his self-confidence. She used to be a confident, decisive person. When had she changed?

He answered his own question. "My guess is a personnel short-age, and again, why? Cold? Or defections? We know some of them wanted to defect. I mean, maybe they didn't like what they were do-ing. Or they know that if we win, they'll be in trouble unless they go turncoat. I don't think it matters what they decided, as long as they abandoned their posts."

"Maybe they're just cowards," a woman standing next to him said, never taking her eyes off the display from the phone on her wrist. "We really ought to take aim at the predators up higher on the food chain. I mean, look at this. Turns out there's two kinds of cold. The one that kills people was aimed at us. It's genocide."

Koobmeej leaned in. "Let me see."

Irene checked her own phone again. Nothing from Mamá, but she had a message from Cal that she wasn't going to answer—and she could find more news than ever from everywhere, and some of it might be true. She wanted to believe it. An assault was under way on the prison in Madison—maybe the one Mamá was in. She held her breath and hoped. The university campus had been freed. But hospi-tals were overwhelmed and pharmacies were empty and, supposedly, the killer cold had been a conspiracy by the mutineers themselves to infect themselves and gain sympathy, or maybe it was a conspiracy and spread by Prez supporters, and one cure involved breathing argon gas. Bilge was sloshing around, and it might taste like good clean water to people who were desperately thirsty.

Traffic on the road, once a trickle, became a river. Cars were coming carrying personnel to check on the prisoners, and families to take them home or to medical care. Where was Irene's home? Her stuff was at Prairie Orchid Farm, and maybe Ruby was there, too.

Her phone chirped. Cal again. Urgent. Really? Did he really think he needed to talk to a useless, untrustworthy clone? She had better things to do. A medical team had arrived and was setting up equipment and a tent. She should get herself checked.

Cal called again. Still urgent. Well, he'd been arrested at the same time as Mamá. Maybe he knew something. She answered, audio only. *This better be important.*

He didn't waste time on a greeting. "Your mama's very sick. You need to talk to her."

"Where are you?"

"In the Madison prison. The one they're trying to free."

The one in the news? "How is she?"

"There isn't anything here, no food, hardly any water, and she's lying on the ground and has a bad fever and doesn't understand what's happening. She wants to talk to you. Why didn't you answer?"

"I was in prison, too." A nicer one, with beds and showers and singing and dancing, and an attempted mass murder, while Mamá was lying on the floor. Maybe dying. More mass murder, if the rumors about the cold were right. A slamming noise echoed behind Cal and made the hair on her arms stand up.

"Talk to her." Off mic, he said, "Celia, here's Irene."

"Irene," she said, "¿dónde estás?" *Where are you?*

"In Wausau," she answered in Spanish.

"Come here, girl, come and be with me." Her voice cracked, hoarse.

"I wish I could. Is Cal taking care of you?"

She coughed. "It's not Cal, it's Zac. Cal hates me. He hates you. He thinks we sold out the mutiny, and that's why the robots came." Zac was an old boyfriend. He looked nothing like Cal except maybe for his size. "You're coming, aren't you?"

"Yes, Mamá. I'm on my way. I'll go now and get a car and come to be with you." That would make her happy. Maybe it wasn't a lie, either. "You should rest. Let Zac help you. I'll be there soon. Give the phone back to him."

Tears were dripping down Irene's face.

After a moment, Cal said, "What did you say?"

"I said I'm coming. Maybe it will make her feel better. Give her strength."

"I hope so. It's bad here."

"Why are you helping her?"

Mamá was coughing in the background. "Can we get some water here?" Cal called. "For her. Yeah. Thanks. . . . Look, I owe her. I was worried." He coughed, too. "I didn't think . . . I didn't think, that's all. And after we were arrested, I got a real talking-to about who I ought to trust. Look, I'll do what I can. I'll be in touch."

"Thank you."

Mamá was in a hellhole. She'd get a car and go.

But no one could leave until cleared by the medical crew. She could just slip away, couldn't she? Maybe. She tried to call a car as she paced across the lawn. One service didn't answer, the other said there was a wait, at least two hours because disinfecting took time.

She could walk to Madison in forty-seven hours, according to her phone, if she didn't stop to sleep or eat.

She was about to call Mamá again, but Cal called back first, this time using Mamá's phone. Mamá was worse, much worse, too bad to leave on her own with everyone else even if the prison was liberated, which was under way, but Avril was there, he said, that other clone. She could help.

*       *       *

Avril huddled by the door to her sector with her team, everyone watching the attack on their phone displays. Some sort of armed force, all mutineers, had surrounded the building, and someone who identified themself only as a citizen reporter breathlessly narrated a video feed from a highway embankment overlooking the site.

She suddenly remembered a poem—an odd and unwelcome memory—that said that the world would end not with a bang but a whimper. This attack might end with a bang, maybe a big one.

"There's another one," the reporter chortled, their camera held above a car being used as a shield. Bushes obscured much of what was happening at the entrance, but it did show a grenade flashing bright in the twilight at the feet of a centaur guard. "They never thought their own weapons would be used against them!" A column of smoke rose up. "Got 'em!"

Avril whispered to Enos, "How many are there? Robots?"

"We don't know."

More smoke was rising. "Wait," the reporter said. "Let me get a better angle, although it's not safe. I'm risking it all to bring you this." The view shifted enough to show—"Oh my god. The building's on fire."

Fire? In the reporter's now-shaky feed, smoke rose from the front and rear of the building.

"That wasn't one of our contingencies," Enos said, as if fire were a personal insult.

Avril's crew leader, Morgana, announced, "I've got the code for the lock." She hurried to the door to the sector and held the phone on her wrist against it. Nothing happened. "Fuck, I thought I did."

Avril sniffed. There might be smoke in the air, at least some sort of sharp plasticlike odor.

"Lemme try again," Morgana muttered.

"Wait," the reporter said, "I'm hearing police communications. Security robots are retreating behind the fires. The heat hides their thermal signatures."

Morgana put her phone to the door again. Nothing happened. "Fuck fuck fuck."

Avril's thighs ached from crouching, and her shoulder still hurt, too, and her muscles wanted to move.

"I hear sirens," the reporter said. "Fire trucks? But how can they get close if the robots will shoot at them?" Flames popped out of the building as if the facade were hollow inside. "These are cheap buildings, I bet. They'll burn easy."

Morgana shouted, "I've got it. You're free. Let's go!"

Avril knew the plan. Find the exits, appraise the situation, and work with the rescue teams outside to bring out the ill mutineers first. But the exits were on fire, and robot guards were shooting. Things weren't going to go as planned. She ran down the corridor anyway toward the back exit, just as she'd been assigned, to clear the way for people carrying ill prisoners.

"Irene!"

She turned. Cal had called her from inside one of the pens. He was in need of a shave and a shower—and stooped and wary, not the confident man she'd met five days ago.

"I'm not Irene." He knew better, and she had better things to do than waste her time on him. She had an assignment.

"Can you be Irene?" he said.

"Can I be a clone? Sure. I've done it all my life. Is it a good thing now?" What was he going to do, apologize?

"I was just being careful about things. You know."

Nope, she wasn't getting an apology. Her team had reached the end of the corridor. She needed to catch up.

He said, "Irene needs you to help her."

"The one with the mammoth?"

"Her mother is here."

Celia! He'd been arrested with her, arguing. Avril would gladly help Irene, but not him. "What does she need?"

He fidgeted. "Her mother is sick. Irene can't get here, but you can be her and help her mother. You can pretend to be Irene. I have her on the phone. You can talk to her."

Pretend to be Irene? She'd watched that video twenty times at least. She didn't look exactly like Irene: too pale, too thin, too young. But maybe she could pretend. "Let me talk to Irene."

"Come with me. You can use Celia's phone." He reached for her arm, the wrenched one.

She stepped aside. "I'll follow you."

Celia lay with a sweater draped over her chest on a carpeted area alongside a chain-link fence that served as a dividing wall. The rug was old and stained and dirty. The air smelled much more smoky, acrid—and smoke from plastic was toxic.

Cal picked up a phone on the floor next to Celia and spoke into it. "Here's Avril." He held it out.

The projection showed an almost-mirrorlike face. "Hello?" she said.

"Are you there, Avril?" Irene asked. Behind her were voices, but distant, as if she were outdoors. Irene's voice sounded like her own in a recording, higher and thinner compared with the way she heard her own voice in her ears. It was creepily familiar.

Irene said, "I need you to pretend you're me. I can't get there to be with her."

Cal handed Avril an earpiece. She slipped it in and thought she heard Irene sobbing. Or maybe she heard the pulse from her own heart, beating fast. Celia had a bit of blood in the corner of her mouth, and her hair lay around her in snarls. She coughed compulsively, deep and wet and weak.

Cal took the phone and held it to record the scene. Irene gasped when she saw her mother and how appalling she looked.

If Avril's mother got sick, would she be like this? Who would care for her? She took Celia's hand. It felt too warm. Celia clasped Avril's hand weakly.

"We speak Spanish to each other," Irene said in a tight voice. "Tell her, 'Estoy aquí, Mamá.'"

Avril rummaged through her two years of high school Spanish. *I'm here, Mama.* She pronounced it as best she could with pure, musical vowels.

Celia took a shallow, rough gasp. "Irene," she muttered with the Spanish pronunciation, *ee-RAY-nay*. "¿Estás bien?" *Are you well?*

Avril repeated what Irene told her, surprised by how much she understood: "Yes, I am well and I am here. I am going to live, Mamá. I am well."

"Vas a vivir," Mamá rasped. *You are going to live.*

"I love you, Mamá, and I'm here."

Celia muttered something more and coughed a lot. Irene was silent. An alarm went off nearby. A fire alarm? Finally. Avril looked around. The air was gray with smoke. Somewhere far away, glass shattered. Everyone besides her and Cal and Celia had fled from the pen.

Mamá suddenly sat up, her mouth spilling bloody foam. She moaned and writhed. Avril tried to hug her.

"What's going on?" Cal said. He was still holding the phone for Irene to watch. Avril knew what was happening. Death. And Irene didn't need to see this—it was bad enough to watch a stranger die. Avril slapped the phone out of his hand.

"Estás bien," she murmured to Celia. *You're okay.* "Estoy aquí." *I'm here.* "Te amo, Mamá." *I love you, Mamá.* That was all the Spanish she could remember, but what else was there to say? Irene was sobbing in her earpiece. Could she even hear what was happening over the blaring alarm? Mamá's breaths became hoarse. And with one long rasp, they stopped.

Avril kept holding her, and she began coughing, too. Would CPR have worked? With this poisoned air?

The lights went out. A crash came from the back of the building.

Cal shoved something into her hand. Celia's phone. "Take this." And then he ran off.

Take the phone. Take care of everything. Alone and abandoned.

"Irene?" she asked.

"I'm here."

"I'm so sorry. I tried to take care of her." Maybe that was another lie, like *I'm well, I'm here, I'm going to live.* She'd been exposed to the cold every single minute since it started. Everyone didn't die, did they? If not of the cold, would she die in the fire?

"I have to go," she said, and ended the call. She laid Celia down gently, stood up, and found her way through the haze to the door out of the pen.

She turned toward the rear entrance—she was pretty sure she knew the right way. The light from tiny windows high in the walls had disappeared behind thickening smoke that stung her throat. She needed to crawl below the smoke—she'd learned that somewhere, because the air closest to the ground would be the cleanest.

She dropped to her hands and knees, and she felt cold, dirty concrete. She lowered her head. The air seemed clearer, but she tried to breathe as little as possible. Her eyes watered so much she shut them. The alarm kept blaring. She had to get out fast, and crawling was slow, too slow, and the smoke seemed to keep getting worse. Well, she always knew she might die. That didn't mean she wanted to. She resisted the urge to get up and run, and held her breath.

Noise came from ahead: voices shouting, some sort of banging, and she opened her eyes. Through the smoke there seemed to be a red light shining that might be an exit sign.

A wide patch of light suddenly opened ahead, bright even through the smoke, and an amplified voice announced, "Clear the building." *I already knew I should do that.*

Her hands touched wet pavement, a puddle, and the light kept getting brighter. Someone ran to her and picked her up and carried her out—

Past a smoking doorway lit by floodlights, out to a dark parking lot and into air, fresh air. She took a deep breath. Safe! She was being carried by a firefighter in heavy gear, who set her down. Another firefighter joined them.

"We can take you to help." A gloved hand gently took her arm, so gently that her shoulder didn't hurt. "Can you walk?"

She looked around. Behind her hoses were showering water on the building, but flames rose like monsters, and she was sure only that she needed to get away, get safe. She took another breath. She should let the firefighters lead her. They'd know where to go. She could trust them—she hoped.

They took her to an area where people were waiting behind a yellow ribbon strung between light posts. A man in an orange vest, wearing a face mask and gloves, hurried over.

"Are you all right?" he asked.

She didn't know how to answer. Being all right suddenly seemed like a complicated idea.

"Can you breathe? Breathe for me," he said. He held a circular sensor to the bare skin at her collarbone. It felt cold in a refreshing way.

She took a deep breath. Air had never felt better. But she coughed.

He looked at the readings on a box in his other hand. "What's your name?" he said.

"Avril. Avril Stenmark."

"How old are you?"

That seemed like a weird question, but she answered. "Eighteen."

"Where were you born?"

"Chicago." Not exactly, but close enough.

"You're okay," he said, "but barely. Smoke can cause problems later. If you have a cough or feel faint or confused, get help, okay? If you can, get checked again tomorrow morning for smoke inhalation. And if you develop a fever or cold symptoms, get help right away, too."

She nodded.

"You can go over there for now. You'll get water and care there." He pointed at a tent where a lot of people stood.

Water. She needed some water more than anything else. There was Enos, too, near the tent. He saw her and waved with both hands as she approached.

"You made it out. We were worried."

"Yeah, I got out." She'd left behind a beloved corpse. She ought to call Irene. No, she ought to call her own mother. No, her father.

"There's water over there," Enos said, pointing.

She knew that, didn't she? If she felt confused, the man said . . . Yes, maybe she was confused. She started to walk—*No, wait, I'm dizzy, take another deep breath*—and when she could, she followed Enos, who was watching her and waiting. He led her to a table with paper cups of water. She drank: it was cold, and the first swallow stung her throat. The second swallow felt cleaner, better, and she drained the glass.

"We'll be here for a while," he said. "Everything's confused and busy."

\*    \*    \*

I, Peng, designer of life, was searching for agents to mimic a specific virus-associated protein, and I had identified two promising drugs that already sat on shelves. They might interfere with the ability of a virus to enter a human cell and begin to reproduce. And if those drugs didn't work, would a placebo effect for the human host be enough to allow those cells to intimidate a virus and chase it away? No, it was a foolish thought, brought on by the advanced stimulants provided by the Army's research institute, which seemed to have caused a side effect of giddy humor.

I paused until I felt appropriately anxious rather than giddy, solemnly passed on the information, sniffled, and rose to take a walk around the facility. I pondered the situation as I walked. Idiocy had bred disaster as surely as if it were etched into each of our haploid chromosomes.

Could it be designed out? Darwinian selection hadn't accomplished the feat so far.

My phone rang: one of my children. Alive—and, I could only hope—well.

Noah had been blended from seven East African genotypes, a young man of exceptionally robust heritage. By training he was a master of business. By character (something I couldn't control as much as people believed) he was outgoing and pleasant, greeting everyone with a smile.

He greeted me through my phone display without a smile, as if he were about to deliver sad news. Perhaps one of his parents had become ill. His was the closest family I'd ever met.

"Peng, you're back online."

"I've been helping fight a virus. How are you?" I sat down, ready for bad news.

"Do you know what's going on?"

"Very generally."

"How did the mutiny do this?"

"Do what?" I thought I might know what he meant, but life had been full of surprises lately. I would work through this slowly and carefully with him.

"How did it make the viruses?" he said, glancing around as if he were somewhere unsafe. "I mean, it doesn't even make sense. If you get one cold, you don't get the other. That's not how vaccines work. They're trying to kill us, the mutiny people, and I don't know why because I hate the government, too. They're just insane with hate."

All my sleepless hours crashed onto my shoulders. Noah had always been a reasonable man who paid attention to the world with a business-based intelligence. If he believed the mutiny was trying to kill him, we were doomed.

But I owed a patient duty to the truth. "This will be a complex story," I said. "I will leave out nothing, and there's a lot of guilt to go around." He listened, eyes growing wide, mouth slowly gaping, and sweat beading on his face.

At one point, his eyes shifted, as if he were looking out of a window. A siren went down his street. "Hey," he said, "can I open the window?"

I knew he lived on the fifth floor. "Yes, you can, unless sick people start skydiving and coughing into your apartment. And you still might be okay. What are things like where you are?"

"No one is on the street. No cars, no nothing. I hear there's fighting in some places. . . . Do you know, is it true, the Prez was shot by a firing squad?"

"I have no idea." I could ask the colonel, although he seemed to be busy with warlike activities at that moment. "I admit I wouldn't mind if it's true, although he should have been properly tried and convicted first, then shot. How are your parents?"

"Here with me. We want to know the right thing to do."

"What have you heard?"

"They say stay home and don't go outside if you can. They say if you sneeze a lot and feel okay, you are okay and don't worry. If you cough and feel like crap and have a fever, you're in trouble and should get help right away."

"That sounds about right."

"I can trust the government?"

"Your local health department, yes. If they're dressed in purple. The mutiny is on your side. We're looking for medicines to treat the illness, and we're making progress."

"We?"

"Yes, I'm part of the mutiny, too." I hadn't thought about it much. Some decisions didn't actually need to be made, merely executed.

"I checked on your bird yesterday," he said, "but not today. Gave him lots of food and water just in case."

"Thank you. He can fend for himself for a while. I care more about you."

He had more questions, including about garlic soup, and I answered them with the same patience I hoped health-care providers were offering the sick and the worried well, because the truth was a weapon of resistance against abusive self-interests. "Eating well is always a good idea but never a magic cure. Soup is good food. Garlic is delicious."

"Breathing pine smoke?" he asked. "I don't believe it, but I'm hearing it."

"That would do more harm than good, since the cold would limit lung function already."

"Fresh lemon in hot water?"

"Same as garlic soup." I could offer little other advice besides remaining at home until the situation settled down. Larger forces were afoot, and they would decide all our fates, and I realized I was a bit of a fatalist: whatever hit the fan would not be distributed equally or fairly, and all we could do was try to duck at the right moment.

"So the mutiny is okay?" he asked again.

"It's on your side."

He thanked me. We wished each other continued safety.

Someday we'd have enough data to know exactly how much harm had been inflicted. The truth would be history's long, anguished job to find, and its outlines might repeat those of other tragedies. We would always learn too little, too late.

What more could I do in the short term? Perhaps find a third drug to keep a virus out of a human cell. We were at the mercy of our cells and their surface receptor molecules that the virus could bind to. And then I slowly remembered how, long ago, I'd had a cold, and its misery developed into a tiny but satisfying vendetta against not just that particular coronavirus but every coronavirus on Earth.

How could I have forgotten? Because I, Peng, designer of life and master of its language, was an idiot. In my defense, I'd designed those perfectly ordinary women more than a quarter century ago, and the intervening years had done nothing but deliver repeated and powerful distractions, but I loved my children and under no circumstances should have forgotten.

I called a mother whom I also counted as a friend. Celia Ruiz's phone accepted the call, but the face and the voice that answered were those of her daughter, a young woman consumed with sorrow. There could only be one reason, and it sliced my soul in half.

"Irene?"

"No. I'm Avril. Who are you?"

I could guess who Avril might be. "I'm Peng." Would she know that name? "I . . . I work with DNA."

"Oh, that Peng," she said, her voice full of recognition. Around her, people were talking and shouting. She looked soiled and sweaty and tired, and flashing red lights illuminated her face. She stared at me on her phone display with uncertainty, even fear, as if I might tell her something to make her bad situation worse.

"I have very good news for you," I said, blinking back tears.

Avril took another breath. Yes, her head was clear, and everything around her looked stark and startling. She stood in the parking lot of a burning prison, a place she never expected to be. She needed to call—

Celia's phone rang. It must be Irene again. They'd have a lot to say to each other.

No, it was an old man.

"Irene?" he said.

"No. I'm Avril. Who are you?"

"I'm Peng."

She felt like she should remember that name.

"I . . . I work with DNA."

DNA? Yes, clones, SongLab. "Oh, that Peng." She—he had changed a lot, and he seemed to be in some sort of office, all alone.

"I have very good news for you."

That would be the first good news all day, and it had been the longest day of her life.

"When I designed you, I had a cold, so I built immunity into you against all coronaviruses. You won't get sick."

*What?* "I won't get sick." *How could he do that?*

"No, you'll be fine. From the cold, anyway. How are you? Really, I'm concerned. You seem to be . . . in a difficult situation."

"Um, yes." She could see her own face in a corner of the display, lit by flashing red lights, smudged by smoke, and disheveled. "We were in a prison, and it caught fire, and—you knew Celia? Celia Ruiz?" That was a silly question. He had to, since he'd called her phone.

"Yes. I did." His voice, his face became somber, as if he knew what she was going to say.

"She just died. Of the cold. I was with her."

"I'm so sorry."

"She thought I was Irene. I was pretending to be her, and I was talking to Irene, too. I was trying to help by letting her think her daughter was there."

"I'm sure you gave them both great comfort."

Maybe she had. Maybe she hadn't lied about everything. Maybe—

"I'm not going to get sick? Really?"

"Some people are naturally immune. So are you. The virus needs a certain receptor protein, and you don't have that exact one." He looked earnest, as if he cared for nothing more than her at that moment. "You will live. And Irene will live, too."

"And . . . the other one? There's one in Milwaukee. I don't know her name."

"Her too. I made you with love. And with spite toward a virus, and that's turned out to be a good thing."

"How many of us are there?"

He sighed and looked away. "Probably three or four. I don't have access to my records, but I made a limited number. Not everyone did that who made clones, but for technical reasons, fewer is better."

*Only three or four. Good. No marching identical hordes like a bad movie.* "Do they know this? That they're immune. The other ones."

"I don't have any way to reach them. Do you? They'd be glad to know this."

"I can do that." She'd wanted to talk to them for a long time. Now she had a good excuse.

"I'd be very grateful if you could. I should have told you earlier, but I forgot. I simply forgot, and I'm very sorry." He looked at her as if he were asking for forgiveness. "And if you have more questions about yourself or anything, please call. Or about the cold. I'm working with the research into the disease. We have some good news there, too. This cold, the bad cold, will quickly become less lethal. If anyone wants to ask me anything, they can call and I'll be glad to talk to them."

If she had questions . . . She nodded, not sure if she had zero questions or a million questions.

"I'll let you go," he said. "You seem to have a lot to do. Know this, too. I love you. I love you and Irene and everyone I made. I'll do anything I can for you. I hope we talk again soon, Avril."

"Goodbye, Peng." Talk to him again? She had too many new thoughts in her head to make a decision about that right now, but probably, eventually, she would.

Meanwhile, she had to call Irene, then the one in Milwaukee—Hetta might be able to get her number—and Mom and Dad. Actually, she should call Dad first. He'd be so relieved to hear about everything.

\*    \*    \*

Irene sat on the ground in the dark and mourned in teary silence. She felt a little better because Avril had been there with Mamá, so she thought Irene was there. And Avril . . . from what Irene had seen of Mamá's last moments . . . part of her wanted to have seen it all, a bigger part was thankful she hadn't, but Avril had been there, and . . . and Avril had been right to slap away the phone. She didn't want to remember Mamá like . . . that, she wanted to forget what little she'd seen and just remember a voice like her own saying *Estoy aquí, Mamá. Te amo, Mamá.* And Mamá had been happy.

She sat crying as mosquitoes buzzed and crickets chirped and people and cars came and went and none of that mattered, but Avril . . . what kind of disaster was happening with her? The building had been on fire. Should she call?

As she raised up her wrist, her phone rang. Avril. She wiped her cheeks, then realized she didn't have to pretend not to be crying. Avril would understand. And if Avril was calling, that meant she might be okay and safe.

Avril's face and hair and clothes were streaked with dirt, but she looked happy. Red lights were flashing around her. "Irene," she said. Her voice had become very hoarse. "I just talked to Peng. You know who he is, right? He said he made us not to get coronavirus. We're immune."

"He said . . . that?" Peng had always said she was normal. "How?"

Avril sort of smiled. "He said he had a cold while he was making us, and he included immunity because he could."

The idea began to soak in. "We're immune?"

"Yes. We can't get sick. From that virus. He said some people are naturally immune." She looked down a moment. "Your mother, I'm sorry."

"I know. What was happening?"

"The police attacked the prison, and it caught fire, and, well."

"Are you okay?"

"I got checked. Yeah." But she cleared her throat as if it hurt. "Are you okay?"

"I . . . yeah, but I don't know what to do next. Where to go. And Nimkii's loose. He's across the road from me. I'd show you but I don't think you could see him in the dark."

"I need to find out if it's safe to go back to campus. And I promised Peng I'd call the other . . . sister. There's one in Milwaukee. I think I can get her number."

Irene didn't know what else to say. Neither did Avril. They were both quiet for a moment, looking at each other through their screens.

"I'll figure it out," Irene said. "You stay safe. And call me anytime about anything. Even if you're just lonely. I owe you."

"I just did what was right. It was sort of like she was my mother, too." She looked Irene right in the eyes, tenderly. "Now you have a sister. Two sisters. Or maybe three. Peng said there might be four of us in all. We'll be there. Take care of yourself."

"You, too."

She ended the call and sat for a moment, trying to line up her thoughts. She had sisters. And a big hairy pedazo of a boyfriend. And immunity. It didn't matter if a car was disinfected, and it didn't matter anymore for her to go to Madison to see her mother. And no one seemed to notice her. She got up and walked across the road. Nimkii saw her and began walking south, toward the farm where he lived. He wanted to go home, but Ruby might be there. How could she convince him to stay away, to go somewhere else?

*   *   *

Berenike was crossing the atrium of City Hall, about to leave on the mission to the electrical station, when she got a call. It came from a number she had in her phone but had never dared to use. And the face! It was her own, sort of, younger and thinner and dirty and tired with red flashing lights around her.

"Hello, you might not know who I am—"

"You're Avril Stenmark, right? I . . . I know. Are you okay?" She didn't look okay.

"I am now." She shrugged. "Long story. It's been a busy day. I'm calling because I talked to Peng, the scientist who designed us, and we're immune to the cold."

"Immune?"

"It's just a genetic thing. Something about a protein the virus needs. You could call him if you want more details. I can give you his number, and he said he'd be glad to talk to you. He said some people are immune naturally."

"Or unnaturally." She felt bad the moment she'd said that. This was no time to make jokes.

But Avril laughed—a little. "Yeah, unnaturally."

"I didn't want to call you before because I didn't want to tell you you're a clone."

"It was tough news." Avril shrugged and glanced over her shoulder. People were shouting, but it seemed to be instructions, not a warning. "I've talked to Irene, too, the one with the mammoth."

"How is she?"

"Her mom died, but I was with her mom, so she thought I was Irene, so her mom seemed to be happy about that. And I guess things are bad in Wausau, too."

"And here in Milwaukee." Bad all over.

"Are you safe?"

*Good question.* "No, maybe not. I'm going on a mission. Top secret. Mutiny work."

"Good. I mean, good luck. Let me know how it goes. And here, this is Irene's number. Maybe all three of us can talk. Tomorrow? I hope? Oh, and maybe there's a fourth one. Peng wasn't sure."

*Four?* "It would be good to talk."

"Till tomorrow."

Berenike ended the call. For a moment, she felt dizzy. The call had been surreal, like talking to herself, but not really, or to another version of herself. Was that how sisters usually felt?

Things were bad all over, but for her, things had suddenly become immeasurably better in one important little detail. She walked out of City Hall with a new kind of confidence. Neal would be waiting.

*   *   *

Irene was having no success. "Nimkii, let's go this way."

He looked at her, then kept walking through the cornfield. He wasn't going to be persuaded. Well, maybe Ruby had fled. The Prez was dead and the mutiny might succeed—at least, that was what she'd heard. But maybe, instead, Ruby had holed up in the farmhouse. And she said she'd shoot Nimkii.

"Nimkii, let's stop here and eat." She held out an ear of corn, fat and ripe. He took it, ate it, and kept going. She tried again, and this time he didn't even take the corn. Her heart ached as she followed him. He trudged through the field, the little woods, and across the creek, walking in a straight line, his trunk up, sniffing, following the familiar scent from the farm. They entered the alfalfa field on the far side of the woods. Now he hurried, the pen in sight.

The house was dark except for a light on the porch. Irene slipped from shadow to shadow. She didn't see the truck, so Ruby was gone. Probably. Will's dog wasn't barking. Maybe Ruby had taken it with her.

She had to stop and catch her breath, panting not from exertion but from fear.

Nimkii walked through the open gate and into the pen. He trumpeted. Home! Safe! Or so he thought in his simple world, back in the place where no one and nothing would hurt him. But maybe, since he had no food inside, after a little while she could tempt him out and they could go back to the cornfield. . . .

A car pulled up in the driveway. Ruby?

Irene needed to hide and fast—maybe in the alfalfa field. It grew waist-high. She could lie down in the path Nimkii had made. Ruby wouldn't see her, wouldn't even look for her. She'd think Irene was dead, asphyxiated in that prison. She dashed into the shadow of the winch, then behind some weeds, and dove into the field.

The front door to the house slammed. Irene inched forward until she felt completely hidden. She lay in the dark, seeing nothing but the sky, and listened to Nimkii rumble, confused and anxious. Would he stay in the pen? Did she want him to? Would he come looking for her?

She waited. Maybe she would have to wait all night. Mosquitoes buzzed around her ears, and bugs whined and chirped in the field. The wind hissed above her head. Slowly, the stars shifted in the sky.

Voices came from the farm, two voices, one Ruby's, the other maybe a man's, quiet and urgent. *They're making plans to go away,* Irene hoped. No, they were coming closer. *To shoot Nimkii?* Could she stop them if she tried?

"Irene!" Ruby shouted. "Come out! If Nimkii's here, we know you have to be here, too. We can see you with infrared, there in the field. Stand up. Put your hands up and come out."

Maybe they'd shoot her instead of Nimkii. Or both of them. And she couldn't stop them—unless she could talk them out of it somehow. She stood up, raised her hands, and started walking. The man looked like a shadow against the porch light at the house. Ruby's face was lit by the yellow light of the screen on the gun's target system as she pointed a rifle at her.

*Mamá, a ti me voy.* I'm coming to you. . . . Every step was taking her closer to Mamá.

Ten feet away, she could see the man more clearly, young and dressed in hunter's camouflage. He stood stiffly and announced, "In the name of the United States of America, we're making a citizen's arrest. You've been identified as a secret Chinese agent. Do not resist and you won't be hurt. We're going to turn you in to the authorities."

That made no sense. "Chinese agent?" She started to drop her hands in astonishment, then shot them back up.

"You've seen the news."

"No, I haven't." *The Prez's news? Lies, lies, lies.*

"The White House said Chinese agents are here spreading chaos and disease to undermine our ability to fight." He seemed to be reciting that.

"I'm not Chinese."

"You're a Chinese dupe." He held out his display and turned it up to large. There was a gallery of photos, mostly of people who looked Asian. He scrolled down a bit. There were Irene, Avril, Berenike, and a fourth woman—no, a child—another identical sister.

"Oh, the fourth one," she said. *Wait, that was the wrong thing to say.*

"So she was hiding."

"Well, no, I don't know who she is. My mother got me from an IVF clinic, in vitro fertilization."

"Dupes aren't natural. That whole clinic was sending spies to the United States, that's what they said."

"Well, I didn't know I was a spy." Nimkii had been silent for a long time. Was he listening intently? *Stay quiet. Don't draw attention to yourself.* Ruby could swing that gun toward him in a heartbeat.

"You were just talking to one, and she was talking to a big-time spy. That's what it says here. It's tracking all of you."

What? *Oh, Peng.* Their phones must have been tapped.

Ruby laughed, an ugly noise. "Mutinous mutants. How does that sound, Ethan? They're spreading the killer cold. You infected Alan."

She didn't sound angry. Suddenly something made sense.

"Will said Alan was spreading it," Irene said, "and he got what he deserved."

"He said that?" Ruby kicked at a stone in the driveway without lowering the rifle. "You're lying, and no one can prove otherwise."

Irene knew that if what she'd heard from the mutiny news was true, anyone could prove otherwise—but she wasn't going to spend her last breath saying that.

"Look," Ethan said, "we're wasting time. We need to make this arrest and deliver her to the sheriff."

"Yeah," Ruby said, "get in the car." She jerked her gun.

"First," he said, "handcuffs. Put your arms out."

Irene did. He closed them so tight they hurt. The sheriff? Apparently not a mutineer, but maybe she could reason with him—if she got there alive. She'd have to make sure that happened. She walked toward the car, an old-fashioned sedan, and glanced back at the pen. Nimkii's bulky shadow stood silent, watching without comprehending. He rumbled so low that Irene felt it more in her chest than in her ears. She climbed into the back seat. Ethan slammed the door shut.

Maybe Nimkii would leave as soon as he realized she was gone again . . . and he'd wander around, get lost, and maybe panic and attack someone. Get shot as a dangerous nuisance. Or maybe he'd just starve.

*Goodbye, Nimkii. I love you.*

The car started up and crunched down the gravel driveway, headlights slicing through the night. Ruby drove manually and turned east toward the city of Wausau.

"Listen to this," Ethan said. He ordered his phone to play a recording and turn up the volume. A woman with a California accent was nattering about how the Chinese took a long view of everything and made plans a hundred years out.

"Yeah, exactly," Ruby said. "That's why they need to interrogate you. That's why we're turning you in. If I'd known this, I wouldn't have put you in the prison."

"Then she got out," Ethan said sarcastically, as if it were part of a long-running argument.

"Yeah. That mammoth. When we're done with her, we'll go back and shoot it." She chuckled. "It'll be fun."

*I hope he kills you first.* Or maybe Irene could wrap her cuffed wrists around Ruby's throat. As if Ethan had read her thoughts, he turned and pointed a handgun at her.

"Don't get any ideas, dupe."

The recording droned on about how certain members of the United States population were Chinese followers, useful idiots, especially the ones running the electrical system.

"That's where the civil war is happening," the California woman said. "Cities are in rebellion. We've gotta shut them down. Hit 'em where it hurts. Electricity. We have the means to shut it off if we use our might. Some of the power companies refuse to do it, and the people working for them refuse to do the right thing, too. The two major grids, Eastern and Western, are in open revolt. The Texas grid is different, it's doing the right thing. Austin is dark, the way it always should have been. . . ."

Ethan said, "They just don't get it, some people. The war. What we gotta do."

"They never get it," Ruby said.

The car pulled into the parking lot at the side of the courthouse, a sleek, low, grayish twentieth-century building.

Ethan got out, pointing the gun at her every moment.

Ruby opened the rear door, and Irene stepped out. She wished she were contagious and had infected them. She'd been around sick people. Maybe some viruses clung to her clothing. Maybe the sheriff would be reasonable.

The door to the courthouse was locked. Ethan buzzed an intercom next to it. A panel lit up. After a while, a woman's voice answered.

"Marathon County Sheriff."

"We're here to deliver a prisoner, someone wanted by the federal government. Get in front of the camera, girl."

Irene walked forward. If they didn't let her in, what would Ruby do? Shoot her. *Let me in!* She glared at the camera as if she were evil and worthy of incarceration.

The door buzzed, and they marched her inside, Ethan pointing his handgun at her, ignoring the NO GUNS sign at the entrance.

A deputy in the hall spotted them, ran through the nearest door, and closed it behind him. Irene suddenly realized she was with a group of what would look like armed intruders. In the chaos of the killer cold, anything could happen, including an armed takeover attempt of a sheriff's office.

She held her handcuffed arms up in surrender before she got caught in the cross fire.

"You idiots!" she said. "You're walking in with guns! They're going to think you're invaders."

"We're delivering you like we should," Ethan said.

"No," Ruby said, "I think maybe she's right."

As she said that, a drone came buzzing out of a doorway ahead. "Put down your weapons," it announced in an authoritative male voice. "Put down your weapons."

Ethan gestured at her. "She's a dangerous criminal."

The drone fired a bullet. At that close range, he didn't have time to react. It hit him in the chest. He dropped.

Ruby turned and ran. The drone fired again. Irene closed her eyes. She didn't want to see what would happen next. She kept holding her hands up, waving them to be more obvious. Footsteps ran down the hall, and voices yelled. Someone grabbed her. She opened her eyes. A deputy wearing a surgical mask.

"I surrender! I'm innocent." She let him drag her away.

From the hallway, she heard Ruby shouting.

The deputy holding her said, in a conversational tone, "Keep your hands up." It was reassuring. "Don't move."

A female officer approached. "I'm going to pat you down for weapons. Spread your legs and don't move." The deputy kept his grip on her arm. The woman, wearing gloves, was fast and efficient, and all she found was Irene's phone. "We'll take this."

Ruby, in the hall, was screaming now, keening for Ethan. "We're patriots. We're on your side."

"Come this way," the woman said to Irene, glancing at the hallway door. "You can put your hands down."

"Thank you." They'd become stiff. Was she safe now? She was still breathing fast. Her instincts said no, she was still in deep trouble.

They took her to a little room. "State your name and address. Everything you say is being recorded." Irene remembered from old movies about being told some sort of rights. Well, that was no longer in force. The woman looked at a screen on a side table.

"So, you're wanted as a Chinese agent." She shook her head and looked at Irene. "We're kind of stretched thin now. We don't have spare time for this, and now those idiots made a mess in the hallway. Come with us." She slipped Irene's phone into an envelope, scanned a code on the envelope, and left it on the table.

They led her through a hall, through another hall, down some stairs, and unlocked doors that led into an open area lined with doors with small, narrow windows. The man opened one of them and motioned for her to enter. She held up her handcuffed hands.

"That man has the key. His name's Ethan."

"Yeah," the man said, "if we can find it, I'll come back. It's—"

"This is the last thing we needed tonight," the woman said. The man shut the door.

The room had a light Irene couldn't turn off no matter what she said, a steel toilet in the far corner with a sink above its tank, and a narrow cot without any bedding, just a thin plastic mattress. Despite the cuffs, she squirmed down her pants and peed, wiped herself clumsily, and wiggled the pants back up. She washed her hands and realized she had nothing to dry them on. She used her shirt. She flexed her fingers to keep the blood flowing through the tight handcuffs.

She lay down and tried to fall asleep. There was nothing else to do.

Sleep did not come. She thought about Nimkii, her mother, her sisters—two or three now!—the cold, her home, her country, and the world, all in a swirl of thoughts that were dark and angry and terrified and sad. Tomorrow . . . tomorrow would be worse. She cried.

\*    \*    \*

Berenike was standing in the parking lot at a clinic, waiting alongside a light post for a truck to be loaded, and she pondered mortality, since she would not die of at least one specific thing. She could still die of many other things, of course, but they seemed distant even if they weren't. Immune. Damn, that felt good.

With that question removed, she had others. She had a new, instant sort-of family, maybe, some sisters, and what were they like? As for her old family, would she even find out where her father was buried? Should she still resent her parents now that they could no longer harm her? Maybe she should just let them go.

But other people had died and their harm remained behind, and plenty of people were still alive and doing massive harm. She would give her life to fight them, and she'd be dangerous and hard to stop.

"Hey, you okay?" Neal asked.

"Yeah."

"I'm okay like that too. I gotta keep doing something."

They were going to bring antivirals, other medical supplies, and food to the electrical grid control facility in the south suburbs, a nondescript building she was sure she'd seen but never noticed because it was deliberately unmarked and bland to prevent notice and sabotage. A variety of people and groups might try to bring down the electrical grid, even in good times.

The county government—what was left of it—was still dithering over supporting or opposing the mutiny, so it would neither aid nor block the city's mission. Rumors said countermutineers were coalescing. The control room might be a target, but a lone unmarked truck, driving manually, off the grid, might not attract attention. Drones would discreetly follow their progress. A remote-controlled decoy truck emblazoned with the blue city logo would approach the main entrance in an attempt to draw off attention.

Berenike took the wheel. It felt good. "Route plotted with course corrections for red dots." She mimicked the dialogue from a movie.

"Full throttle."

She poked through city streets at the legal limit and, as soon as they reached the freeway, let the truck go at top speed. With almost no traffic, reckless acceleration was fun. The lights alongside the road were on, and most houses were lit—a sign of victory. *Take that, dead Prez.*

"It's like there's a snowstorm," Neal said, "but no snow."

They approached a side gate in a chain-link fence on an unlit road and waited for the truck's electronic ID to open it.

The window next to Neal shattered. Then the windshield. For a moment, Berenike sat frozen, covered by little chunks of broken glass. What did that?

An attack. They were under attack. Countermutineers? Had to be.

She fumbled to unhook her seat belt and ducked down. She stayed down. She waited . . . and nothing more happened. Maybe they weren't under attack. Maybe it was something else.

"Neal?" she whispered. No response. That was bad.

She fumbled with the visor on her helmet and closed it, then peeked up. Neal. He sat slumped over, restrained by his seat belt. He was twitching.

"Neal?" she said louder. No reaction.

Shouts came from outside. "Hands up!"

Countermutineers, it had to be that. Fuck. She put her hands up. Her fingers felt distant and numb.

"Get out of the truck!"

She found the door control, found her feet, everything far away, and stepped out. Her legs shook. Where was the man who was shouting? It was too dark to tell, and all the distances suddenly seemed huge. She tried to focus, to pull things in, to control her own body. Breathe.

"Step away from the truck." A blinding light shone on her. She took a couple of steps.

Was that a drone buzzing? No, two drones, very faint and far away, but maybe not their drones.

Some people approached: hoods, camouflage, goggles, breathing masks. Pointing rifles. She stood still.

"Look toward me and take off your helmet." A man's voice.

She slowly turned, reached up, and struggled with unwilling fingers to unsnap the chin strap. She lifted off the helmet, and the cold breeze on her head made her shiver from the sudden vulnerability.

A silhouette pointed a phone at her. It clicked. A photo. "We'll see who you are." Facial recognition. What database did they have access to, and why did they care who she was?

"What were you bringing?" someone else asked. A woman's voice.

There seemed to be no point in lying. "Antivirals, some other medicine, some food."

"We could use that a whole lot better than the assholes in there."

"Let's move fast," a man said. "Dump that body and take the truck."

"What about her?"

"Can you drive the truck?" a man asked her.

"Yes." *I got it here, shithead.* The shock was wearing off and anger was boiling up.

"No," the woman said, "that truck has a tracer, for sure." She pointed up. "And those are drones. Let's move fast. Just shoot her."

*There's no point in keeping me alive. If you don't kill me and I can kill you, I will.*

"Hey," the man with the screen said. "She's wanted. A Chinese agent. That's what the White House said. The ones who released the flu virus."

*What?*

"Then let's shoot her," the woman insisted.

"Hey, there's another one just like her up in Wausau. Two more besides that. Clones. They're all alike, clones. Let's take her and turn her in. That's what the White House wants."

*Irene and Avril! And the fourth.*

"Let's hurry. Dupe girl, unlock the back doors. You can do that, right?"

"If you let me move."

"Nothing fast," the man said.

She reached inside the cab and punched a button. The cab smelled of blood. *Neal.* He wasn't moving. *Please be playing dead.*

The counterrebels grabbed boxes as fast as they could, even her backpack—"Evidence," the woman said, glaring at her—and shoved it into a nearby van.

"Get in," screen man said. He threw her a face mask. "Put this on."

She obeyed. She was immune to a virus, but not a bullet. Somehow that immunity would give her an advantage. How exactly could she kill these people?

With a gun pointed at her, she thought about how fast the police would come. They knew Neal was injured, if not dead—she hoped not dead. They'd slipped trackers into some of the boxes, and she wore a tracker clipped to her bra strap. But sometimes the police weren't fast enough even in good times, and now it was all hell.

The van raced off, heading north back into the city, speeding through the streets. She recognized the model she rode in, a low-end resale from AutoKar, its ID number still visible on the dashboard, its autopilot hacked. She'd serviced that model a lot when she was low-level staff. It wasn't designed to career in turns through empty intersections like an old-fashioned chase scene in a classic movie. It could handle only gentle, computer-controlled use. Turns like that could damage an axle. *Oh, please, at least snap a tie rod.*

No one besides Berenike had even put on a seat belt. They must have hacked the automatic warning system. Worse, the man sitting next to her was talkative.

"The Chinese pay you well, don't they?"

"I know jack shit about them."

"You were made by them."

"I was adopted. I know jack shit about that, too."

"What were you doing?"

"I'm an assistant manager at an AutoKar, which was commandeered by the city, and me with it."

"I mean, for the Chinese."

"Jack shit. I don't work for them."

"The White House says you do."

"The Prez said this was a common cold."

"That's what everyone thought."

"Even yesterday everyone knew better. My father dropped dead of this at his kitchen table."

"My sister and her kids are sick and they're not getting anything. In the city, sure, some people get everything. She's out in the suburbs and doesn't get shit."

Berenike understood exactly what she'd just heard and could have spent an hour explaining why it was wrong and racist and why she had mutinied. But why waste what might be her last breath on people who refused to understand?

"Her insurance company acts like it never heard of her," he said. "But some people get stuff for free." It was clear who *some people* were.

Again, she had an hour-long answer to that, with charts and graphs in multiple dimensions, leading to the conclusion that the system was victimizing the man's sister the same way that it victimized everyone else, but it also made sure to keep everyone divided against one another instead of uniting against the victimizers. Some people were mutineers and others weren't—but they all should be. Instead she said, "Where're we headed?" She knew those streets perfectly, but it wouldn't hurt if they thought she was ignorant.

"We're going to get the other clone and turn you both in."

*The fourth one.* "So tell me about her. I don't know her."

"Sleeper cells?"

"Jack shit, I told you. But if she's my clone, I'm curious."

"Her position's on the White House site, so we're getting her. That's all we know."

They turned, screeching onto Rawson Avenue, and Berenike heard a clunk. A U-joint? The U-joints tended to fail in this model. *Please, break. Protect the fourth sister.*

The driver said, "I think we should have cuffed her."

"You got cuffs?"

"No."

"Here." The woman riding shotgun handed a pair back. The man grabbed her wrist, snapped on one cuff, and clipped the other one to the door handle. She knew how to disassemble that handle.

The driver's screen told him where to turn, and he didn't seem to know for sure where he was. Berenike had studied lots of maps to locate stranded and broken-down vehicles, and she could have directed them precisely to any given address and maybe provided some of the neighborhood's history. They had come back into the city to a once-modest neighborhood that had fallen onto hard times.

The van stopped in front of one of the ubiquitous two-bedroom ranch homes with fake brickwork accents on its facade. A few of the bricks had fallen out. The trim needed paint. The lawn had been maintained, though, and there was a showy garden in the front yard with a trellis at the corner.

"Let's go." The driver sounded melodramatic. He looked at Berenike. "You stay here."

*Not like I have a choice.*

They exited silently, leaving the doors open. They spread out, two at the home's front door, one at the rear. Did they plan to kick in the doors and bust inside? They were in for a surprise. In neighborhoods like this, most doors were made of steel and hung in steel frames to thwart burglars. One of the men reared back and kicked the door hard. He hopped away, holding his foot, wincing.

The door opened.

Standing in it was a girl who looked like a snapshot of Berenike herself, maybe eleven years old, her hair uncombed. What had that girl hoped for by opening the door to strangers?

The streetlights went out, but not the lights in the houses. The wannabe patriots pumped their fists. The electrical grid must have been partially attacked. Berenike tried not to feel anything. Her side had lost a skirmish, maybe a battle, and much, much more was about to be lost unless she could do something about it.

They talked to the girl, who seemed upset. She must have hoped for help. An eleven-year-old, no matter how strong, needed help in bad times. Berenike had been in that situation herself. How could she help her now?

The door handle looked like it was one piece, but she pried off a cap on the underside, revealing a clip. She had no tools, so she slipped a thumbnail under the clip and pulled. The nail tore and flesh yielded—a small price to pay. The clip snapped out, and she swung the handle free at one end. She slipped it off the cuff and reached into the front seat for her backpack.

The man from the back door came running around to the front, and all three fake patriots were yelling at the girl. She began to cry and ran back into the house. The three followed. There was a lot of shouting inside.

Berenike pulled out her phone. She pushed an emergency button for the police. Then she opened AutoKar. The company could disable any vehicle automatically. Even when a car was sold, it was never cleared from the database. She tapped in the ID number and killed the car. Then she tried to make a plan.

The two men were backing out of the door, dragging the girl, followed by the woman, who fell to her knees and vomited.

"I told you she's dead," the girl shouted with the righteous rage of a child who had told the truth and been disregarded. "Everyone's dying."

The men looked around. Maybe, Berenike thought, when they tried to start the van, she could lunge for the girl, dash out, and then . . . do what? One of the men approached, dragging the girl. The other went to help the vomiting woman.

"Stop it!" the girl screamed, twisting and fighting. The man jerked her arm, and she stumbled.

Across the street, reflected off the side windows of a house, were faint red and blue flashing lights. No sirens. The blue and red lights went out. Cops?

The man dragged the girl roughly. "Come on!" The woman was standing up, wiping her mouth.

"I won't go," the girl said. "I didn't do anything wrong. You can't arrest me. I don't even know who you're talking about. I'm just a kid."

"Get in the car."

She tried to pull her arm free and snarled. "No! You can't make me. Go ahead and shoot me. We're all going to die anyway."

At that instant, an overwhelming love filled Berenike's heart for that screaming, righteous, raging child. And she prepared to—*Wait. Listen.* Electronic cars made almost no noise, just the crunch of a dead leaf under a tire, a hiss of a brake that could blend into the rustle of the trees. In the dark, cars could appear out of thin air.

As if on the count of three, searchlights flashed from the roofs of several police cars.

"Everyone on the ground!" a loudspeaker blared.

Berenike dove to the floor. *Don't hurt the girl.* Through the open door, she saw the girl drop to the ground. The woman pitched herself onto the grass.

But one of the men raised his gun and shot at the police cars—as if the police cars weren't armored. As if the police didn't have self-guiding bullets that would seek the source of the gunshot. He jerked back and fell.

The other man jumped into the van and touched a switch to start it. Nothing.

On the floor, Berenike covered her head with her hands. The streetlights blinked on. She felt avenged.

"You in the van," the loudspeaker ordered. "Surrender. Come out with your hands up. Slowly."

Berenike held her breath. The man pounded on the steering wheel.

"Dale," the woman shouted, "give up."

"You're a coward!" he answered.

"They'll kill you."

Berenike took another breath and held it.

"We're at war!" Dale said.

She heard him stamp out of the car, and doors opened on the police cars. Footsteps hurried out.

"Turn around," the loudspeaker said, "spread your legs."

An unamplified woman's voice called, "Berenike Woulfe? Are you there?" She pronounced her name in three syllables, *ber-NYE-kee*.

"I'm in the van! On the floor!"

"Don't move. I'll come and get you."

Soon a hand touched her arm and guided her out. *How is the girl?* As Berenike stood up, she looked for her. Two officers, dressed head to toe in armor, stood on either side of the child, who seemed stunned. Other officers were holding the woman, and some were inspecting the bleeding man on the ground.

Berenike walked around the van toward the girl, who saw her and whose eyes got big. Her mouth dropped open.

"I should talk to her," Berenike told the officer. She had never wanted to talk to anyone so much in her life.

"Um . . . yes, okay."

"Oh, and I disabled the van. I work for AutoKar, and I can do that. I can undo it anytime you want."

"Thanks." The officer followed her closely as she approached the girl, whose eyes narrowed with uncertainty.

Berenike stopped before she got close, afraid that she'd be frightening. She took a deep breath. *One step at a time.* "I'm your sister. It's a long story." The girl wasn't going to want to hear that she was a clone. The AI counselor hadn't covered this kind of problem, but she'd have to find a good way to tell her.

The girl stared. "My mom. . . ." Her chin trembled.

"Show me," Berenike said, knowing what she'd find and hoping it would ease the girl's troubles to share them. The girl led her and the officer through a shabby but clean living room to the attached garage. A woman lay there on the cement floor. She had died in the throes of a violent seizure. *A lot like Papa.*

Berenike put a hand on the girl's shoulder. "I can take care of you, if you want. You have two more sisters, too." She'd do anything to keep that girl safe and well cared for.

The officer seemed to be listening to something. She lifted her visor to show a grim, tired face.

"Will we be safe here?" Berenike asked.

"I can't guarantee that," the officer said. "We can't guard you. We just don't have any officers to spare."

"That van has some antivirals in it. They're valuable." Berenike thought a moment. She turned to the girl. "Do you want to come with me? I know a safe place. City Hall. I work there." She called to the officer. "Can I take the van?"

"Probably. I'll check. It's chaos out there. You said antivirals?"

"I was delivering them for the city."

The officer lowered her visor and studied something for a minute. "That checks out. Let me talk to the girl, make sure she agrees."

The girl answered quickly. "Yes, it's okay. I'll go with her. I don't have anyone else."

"Come and let's talk privately," the officer said.

After what looked like a stern conversation, they returned.

"Take good care of her." The officer left, walking like someone who'd been on a too-long hike and hadn't arrived yet.

"Well," Berenike said, "my name is Berenike Woulfe. And you?"

"Lillian Montrose."

"First, I want you to know that you won't get sick, at least not with this cold."

"How? Everybody gets sick."

"It's a long story. A few people are naturally immune. Do you want to pack a few clothes and we'll go? We can come back later, see to your mother, and . . ." She shrugged. She had no plan for what to do for more than a few steps ahead. Too many unsettled variables.

"I'll go, but only if it's with you."

Berenike's heart warmed to hear that. Trust wasn't love, but it would do for now.

The girl's room was spare and clean, and she grabbed a bag and stuffed some clothes into it. As she did, Berenike talked, trying to make complex things simple.

"You should know that we're clones, like twins, but four of us, and in spite of what everyone says, it's okay to be a clone. We're really ordinary people. We weren't made to be anything special. The one in Wausau is named Irene. The one in Madison is named Avril. We only found out about each other a couple of days ago. And then all this happened."

Lillian stared at her with narrowed eyes, lips twitching as if she were talking to herself. She said, "What's going on?"

"People are getting sick, some a little sick and some a lot sick. And everybody's trying to figure it all out, and to change the way the government works. I wish I knew enough to answer your question fully."

"But we won't die."

"We were designed not to catch this kind of cold. Some people never catch certain colds. We're like that. It's normal. I'm working with the city in the Health Department to help people. Because I can."

When they got to City Hall, she'd ask about Neal. Maybe it was just a minor wound that bled a lot.

The girl stood thinking, her lips still twitching. Berenike waited. It was a lot to take in.

"I'll help too, then," Lillian said.

"It's a deal." Berenike held out her hand, and they shook, an old-fashioned formality reserved for the most solemn occasions.

The police were still outside when they left. The female officer came with the keys to open Berenike's handcuff. Berenike reauthorized the van, and she and Lillian got in. She set the controls for City Hall, then took out her phone.

She'd need to tell Irene and Avril about the White House spy thing. Crazy countermutineers were everywhere, but Berenike had some good news, too.

"Lillian, want to leave a message? You can say hello to your sisters."

Irene woke up with a cramp in her shoulder from sleeping in an odd position because of the handcuffs. She instantly remembered where she was, not merely in jail but in the midst of a disaster.

What time was it? She peered out the narrow window in the door. The open area had a half dozen round steel tables and benches, but no people. Obviously, everyone would be in lockdown. She had to pee and squirmed down her pants. She drank some water by contorting so she could put her mouth under the faucet. She was hungry but doubted breakfast would arrive anytime soon.

She had little else to do besides worry, which she was getting good at. She tried to think about something else, anything else. Groundwater, for example. Where would be a good site for mass graves? Because there were going to be some, for people or for livestock, and they could contaminate the drinking water. The Wausau Ginseng Festival would be canceled, obviously. Sports events, too, maybe her favorite video shows—maybe forever, but not *Finding the Line,* she hoped.

Within minutes, her attempt at not worrying collapsed in the flood of reality and the absence of a phone to distract her or inform her. Was Nimkii still alive? A target for frightened farmers? Were a long list of people safe, including Avril and the second and maybe third sister?

She tried to sleep again. Nope. She paced for a while. She sat on the cot, listened very carefully, and she might have heard voices in other cells or from upstairs.

Her family, her friends, the whole world—the worry for them ached like blistering burns. Worry was circular and had no end, only repetition.

The lock clicked. Outside stood a pair of deputies, both wearing face masks and gloves.

"Irene Ruiz?" one asked, as if she could be someone else. "You're free to go."

She jumped to her feet. "I am?"

The deputy, a woman with brown hair pulled into a ponytail,

shrugged. "The local federal prosecutors say so. I don't know what's going on. We'll get you your stuff and send you home. Come on."

Irene took a few steps toward the door, toward freedom and the ongoing disaster they all had to cope with.

"Wait, are you cuffed?" the woman said.

"Yeah, the people who brought me here did that."

"Oh, the dead guys."

"Only one's dead," the other deputy said, a middle-aged man. "We still have the other one. She's not going anywhere." He turned to Irene. "Do you know which one of them had the key?"

"The dead guy. His name was Ethan."

He looked at the woman for confirmation. She nodded. "Then the key is in the morgue. I'm not going there."

"Me neither."

Irene felt fresh despair.

"Bolt cutter?" the man suggested.

"Gonna have to be that," the woman said. "I think I know where there's one. Come on."

Upstairs, they entered a long room lined with empty desks that looked like they'd normally be busy, and they had her sit and wait while the woman walked away. A clock said 8:34 A.M.

"How are things?" Irene asked the man, who'd sat down at a desk.

He stared at a display on the desk for a while. It was flashing with what might have been a lot of updates. "Every kind of chaos you can think of. No one knows even who's in charge." He went back to staring at the screen.

She waited, staring at the clock.

At 8:45, the woman returned, carrying what looked sort of like a wire cutter with tiny blades at the end of yard-long handles, a ridiculous-looking tool. It clipped through the link between the cuffs like cardboard, then, with a little difficulty to clip only the metal and avoid her flesh, through the cuffs themselves.

"There you are," the deputy said. "And this should be your phone." She held out the envelope. "Sorry we can't do more. Stay safe. Exit's that way."

"Why did you let me go?"

"White House had no right to order your arrest. That's what I'm told."

"What about the woman who brought me here? Ruby Hobbard?"

"She's downstairs. Not going to get out. I guess she's wanted for attempted mass murder, trying to gas people at one of those political prisons. That's all I know. Sorry for all the confusion. You take care." The woman turned away.

Irene followed some signs on the walls to the front entrance. No one, not even a guard, was in the lobby, although a red light said that automatic surveillance was activated. A box of face masks sat on a table alongside a box of gloves for anyone to take. She didn't need them. She stepped outside into chilly winds. The clouds to the west looked gray-blue, ready to rain, and no nearby store seemed to be open where she might be able to buy an umbrella or poncho or warm jacket.

She sat on the stairs and turned on her phone. A little battery power was left. Berenike had left a message the night before:

"I found the fourth sister. Lillian, say hello."

A young voice said, tentatively, "Hello. I'm Lillian. I'm eleven years old. Um, Berenike is taking care of me. I'd like to meet you."

Berenike added, "It's been a very hard day for her. We're on our way to City Hall to be safe. I guess the White House wants us all arrested, and some so-called patriots are trying to do it. Be careful. I'll send more information." She had sent the same list of suspects that Irene had already seen on the screens of her kidnappers. They weren't the only set of clones.

Avril had left a message last night, too: "To let you guys know, I'm okay. Are you?"

Berenike messaged again, an hour ago: "Good morning. You know, I woke up every two hours last night to see if the lights were on. And they were. That means the rebels are winning. Lillian and I are going to spend the day delivering supplies. She's pretty tough, all things considered. She lost her mom yesterday."

Irene thought about how to reply. "I'm out of jail now. I was arrested by the patriots. I can't get a car, so I guess I have to walk home. I'll keep checking in." It was too hard to pronounce the words that Mamá was dead, that Nimkii might be out of his pen, might be gone, might be dead, too.

She began walking. She knew the route, five miles, and it had never seemed so long. She saw only one car drive past and no other signs of life. She passed a field where cows were lowing desperately, and they came to the fence when she passed as if she could help them. At one farm, hundreds of chickens were running free. A few of them followed her for a while, apparently thinking she'd feed them. If she had any food, she'd have eaten it herself.

It began to drizzle. About a mile later, when she was damp and shivering, the rain stopped and the clouds broke up. The sky was sunny when she walked up the driveway of the farm, calling Nimkii's name.

No sign of him, though, not for the rest of the morning, not all day.

* * *

I was free to leave . . . but. . . .

Leave but . . . I was shown how the White House had targeted me as well as some of SongLab's progeny as Chinese spies—my children! I could only hope with a trembling heart and hands that they had found safety. Worse, yesterday's chaos had given way to more careful thought, and both sides had taken a step toward organization, which meant new, more systematic confrontations. Disease alone could not achieve sufficient destruction.

Leave but . . . the virus and its mutations still might yield life-giving secrets, and now that I had slept (although not well) and was refreshed (under the influence of stimulants), I could continue with my research, which might work miracles.

In the meanwhile, I was told, please avoid standing near windows. Snipers. The building's guards had been rearranged . . . but some still patrolled the interior of the building against the known existence of an enemy within. The Prez had died, sensationally of both illness and a bullet, but his supporters would die harder.

Under those extenuating circumstances, I paused to have lunch—or dinner, time having lost some of its importance—and Vita joined me in the little self-service cafeteria. Two days ago I would have been flattered. Today I welcomed her only because I had unfinished business.

"Why recruit me?"

"We thought it might be you," she said.

"Me?"

"The one who could have released the second virus."

My heart crashed to be subjected to such an obvious lie. She knew how to evoke a sympathetic tone of voice, but her words were transparent. If something went wrong, I would be set up as the scapegoat. In fact, I would already be in custody. She had known that all along and had willingly taken part in the plan. Her beautiful, brilliant mind had failed her in the most basic ways.

Perhaps she read the disappointment I tried to hide. "You had the motive and the means," she said.

I looked down at my meal, an egg-salad sandwich, probably ersatz eggs, which would be a kindness to chickens, but imitation eggs amounted to one more way in which the world had long ago begun turning falsely on its axis.

"Or rather," she continued, "they thought it could be you. I thought you would help in ways we couldn't predict, and I was right." She added a tiny ersatz smile.

"I'm glad I proved you right." To protect my heart, I changed the subject. "We can reconsider ways to slow viral replication within cells, and with luck we can find something relatively common and ready to use."

"Maybe garlic soup?" she said sarcastically. "That's what they're saying, garlic soup."

Her little joke struck me sour, more revelry in falsehood. "Maybe fresh garlic extract applied directly to lung tissue would be effective. But about having a motive, I was misjudged."

"You've been badly misjudged before and might have a vendetta."

"I was saddened, not vengeful. I love people. That's why I made them."

She took a sip of tea. "You never had children of your own, though."

"After three ectopic pregnancies and other troubles, I could take a hint."

"I'm sure something could have been done."

I was sure I didn't need advice about my reproductive life, knowing what the next assumption would be. By the time I'd given up on motherhood, I'd already founded SongLab: it did not serve as a substitute for a personal lack of fecundity. It stood on its own as a dream fulfilled. I changed the subject again. "What's happening out there?" I'd found some news and decided that sorting through the contradictions wasn't the best use of my time or emotions.

"I suppose it depends on where you are. The mutiny didn't have much of a chance to succeed, and then the surprise epidemic hit, and that changed everything."

"How was it supposed to play out?" The question might catch her with her guard down.

"The official story? The mutiny planted it and was going to blame it on the Prez. False flag." She shrugged, detached—cynical, in fact. Her brilliance shone, but something had extinguished her empathy. "I think it was hatched by his extreme supporters and not him. There's always a lot of infighting and factions, and people who are hard to control."

I wondered how she could sound so sure, and after a moment's thought, I had an answer. Her verb tense—the present with all its immediacy—had placed her within the loop.

"And it might not have worked," I said. "The surprise epidemic virus that was released by whomever might have interacted poorly with the attenuated virus and created a worldwide disaster."

She nodded, her eyes searching for a place to avoid encountering a future she had once hoped would never happen, and that we had avoided as much by accident as by planning.

"And," I said, now cynical myself, "someone with the means and motive could be blamed."

"We always have enemies."

I remembered her shouting in dismay when she thought that the vaccine had been released everywhere: infighting and factions among people who were hard to control and who had done the wrong thing—in her judgment. Someday, if I could, I'd find out what the supposed right thing in her judgment would have accomplished in the world.

"Why do it?" I asked, knowing that any answer she gave would leave me disgusted.

"Why try to stop the mutiny?" That spin on the question hid the murderous intent of the act. "They don't even know what they want. Just disobey. Old-fashioned freedom. What's that?"

(*They*, not *we*.) "Freedom," I murmured. "What for?"

"Exactly. I mean, refugees have to be resettled carefully, for example. We don't have enough capacity to just hand out free stuff to everyone. We'd all wind up living three to a room and eating fake steak."

"For some people, that would be an improvement." Confucius had once said he would find joy in living on water and coarse rice rather than unrighteous wealth.

"But not an improvement for me," she said. "Don't get self-righteous. You played god, and look where that got you."

"I was a benign god."

She laughed. "It's always good to talk to you, Peng. You have such a unique attitude. I've got to get back to work." She walked out, and I knew to my unmeasurable disappointment that I'd be happy never to see her again. In only a matter of time, she would likely be arrested. I'd supplied enough evidence for any careful investigator, and more was available if needed.

I'd also asked too many questions for my peace of mind. And I'd displayed a unique attitude compared with her circles, where I would be full of laughable, old-fashioned ideas about compassion and responsibility. It would take a while to round up the guilty, and in the meantime, patience would be my most fitting friend and sorrow my most constant companion.

I had work to do, too, and perhaps I could find treatments to propose that would be needed in desperate circumstances before proper testing. I could imagine a doctor somewhere facing a dying patient with an unproven medication sitting on a nearby shelf. Use at your own risk—or rather, the patient's risk, which would deepen the quandary.

Ethics extracted an expense, which made them a luxury. We had been living in a kind of poverty. Shakespeare wrote as a joke about someone who could be poor but honest, knowing how privation brutalized us. Even imagined privation could turn us into brutes. I had struggled to remain benign despite where it got me. It was the most joyous thing I could do.

Irene ran to the truck. With help from a friend in Madison, she'd finally broken into Ruby's computer to check in with Nimkii's tracker service. The radio ankle bracelet placed him about twenty miles north, in Lincoln County, a little west of Merrill. He was the only reason she hadn't left yet.

For two days now she'd waited, even though she hated everything about Prairie Orchid Farm and about a cascade of bad memories that fell on her head and shoulders every time she walked into the farmhouse. She hated the three fresh graves in the rear of the property that Ruby must have dug—two for people, a small one for the dog. A splash of blood on the ground next to the kennel explained what had happened to the dog. The graves lay right next to the little stream: groundwater contamination for sure.

Should she mention that when she was called to be a witness against Ruby? Because she'd been informed she would be. When? No one had any idea.

Besides that, the Prez's supporters were still fighting back, in a few places, like some suburbs near Detroit, with shootouts despite the ongoing terror of the virus, since a few people felt sure that they were immune. Someone was bound to decide to go after supposed Chinese spies again. She remained alert during every waking moment and slept hiding in the shed near the barn.

Now that she'd located Nimkii, when she found him, what would she do with him? Well . . . this was no time to look for a new home. She had no good ideas.

She entered the location of the radio bracelet, and the truck drove off.

Hers was about the only vehicle on the two-lane road. Occasionally another car drove past the other way. No one seemed to be outside in the yards and fields. Her nose told her about death a few times, a lot of death, probably livestock in the hulking barns like the one she'd been imprisoned in. Individual farmers felt a commitment to their animals and fields, but corporate farmworkers—why should they risk their lives by leaving their homes for a miserably small paycheck so that someone else could profit? But if crops weren't harvested and chickens weren't brought to processors, what would people eat? The mutiny might need to reach deeper, and she wasn't the one who could make it happen.

The truck stopped alongside an alfalfa field where something big had feasted. Nimkii! But she didn't see him. The tracker on her phone took her into the field, signaling something close, and she knew what she'd find even before she saw it. She sat in the truck and considered not even bothering. No, this was going to hurt, but she needed to do it. She got out and walked what seemed like uncountable steps, and there lay the radio bracelet on the ground. It must have fallen off.

She picked it up. It smelled a little like him. He had to be nearby. "Nimkii!" she called. "Nimkii! I'm here." Pachyderms had great hearing, a range of miles. She followed his tracks into a woods alongside the river and lost the trail. She called in every direction. Her voice grew hoarse.

Her phone rang. It was Avril, looking washed and rested. "How are you?"

"I can't find Nimkii."

"Oh, no. What happened?"

She told her, and even a shortened version of the story seemed sadder when it was explained out loud. Avril let her talk about Nimkii, her hopes for him and how futile it all seemed now—how empty central Wisconsin felt. She didn't say how she blamed herself for dithering instead of leaving a long time ago. Nothing she had done had made much difference.

Avril said she was volunteering at a clinic set up in the sports center near her dormitory on campus. "I can't do much, but I'm immune, and I can follow orders."

*I can hold someone as they die and whisper kind words.* She had already proven that she knew how to do it well.

"I don't know what else I can do," Avril said. "There's still fighting, but I'll leave that to the people who know how. Um, are you safe there?"

Irene tried to be reassuring. "Right now I think everyone's too scared to do anything." *Right now, I'm sleeping in a shed behind a pile of old paint cans.*

Avril had to go to training. Irene ordered the truck to drive alongside the river, stopping from time to time to call his name. She phoned the sheriff's office, which didn't seem to take her question seriously but promised to let her know if there was a sighting. She ate one of the apples she'd brought to use to tempt him. The shadows pointed due north for noon, and then began to shift with the afternoon light.

How could an animal the size of a mountain slip through the countryside as if invisible?

But she knew. Everyone had self-quarantined, staying indoors, glued to whatever passed for news or entertainment. And then?

She'd stay one more day, hoping for news.

*Hope. Thin gruel.*

\* \* \*

Avril gently took the phone from the young man's hand.

"He's fallen asleep," she murmured to his parents.

"Do you think . . ." His mother didn't know how to ask the question. Avril had learned how to answer it. His vital signs had been steady since morning. She was his pal, and she probably wouldn't be his last pal, but she wasn't a doctor, either.

"He's stable. We're making sure he's comfortable. You should have seen him smile when I said I could call you for him." She took a few steps away so she could talk louder. "How are you? . . . Your daughter? . . . Here are some things you can do for her that we've found can help. They're surprisingly simple. . . ."

Oxygen therapy helped most of all, and the gas had become America's scarcest resource, the doctors joked. Medical staff joked a lot when patients and family weren't around. The rest of the time, they rained kindness like a deluge. She was learning a lot. In just two days, the Prez's cold, as they were now calling it, had been evolving into something bad but nowhere near as bad as it was at first because illnesses evolved. That was one more thing she'd learned.

She looked around the room with its wide-spaced beds for other patients who seemed lucid and in need of a pal. Or who had died. She was learning how to spot that.

Maybe she should think about premed. This wasn't the end of the world, the doctors assured everyone, just another epidemic, sort of a medical earthquake at magnitude eight: disruption, death, and destruction with additional fatalities due to panic—another doctor joke.

The emergency clinic had been set up in a sports center, with patients scattered throughout its rooms and hallways. The city's hospitals had no room and not enough medical staff for off-site locations, so even though she had no real experience, immunity had earned her a spot as sort of an orderly, cleaning, chatting, and lugging water or food or bedding as needed. The name "Peng" had worked magic in earning a job, especially when she said she could call him. She was superpowered—but they asked her to wear a face mask and gloves and protective clothing to reassure other people rather than to keep herself safe.

The first thing she did when her shift started was to look in on Shinta in another part of the building. She was dozing, breathing rough and coughing, but not coughing up blood. No rash on her cheeks. An oxygen mask on her face. Her condition was "critical but stable."

In the part Avril patrolled, a young woman started vomiting into a towel and seemed disturbed. Avril got a clean towel and helped her wash her face. The woman whimpered and looked around, wide-eyed, then looked at Avril with shock.

"Rachel? How did you get here?"

Mental confusion. Not good.

"I'm here to help you." That was the reply suggested at training. Don't argue.

A man whose badge said he was a nurse came over. "Was there any blood? No? Make a note of that. And hey, look, I think we're getting this fever under control." He seemed genuinely thrilled by what were objectively small improvements. She tried to follow his example.

She checked "Vomit, no blood" in the screen at the foot of her bed and estimated the quantity, along with a note about the confusion. The patient's record had additional information she could share that might be comforting.

"Did you know your parents called?" she told her. "Just an hour ago. They were glad to hear that you're getting good care." The woman seemed to understand. "Would you like to rest? I'll get you another towel in case you need it."

As she hurried to the supply cabinet, she wondered if this kind of care would make people well. She'd been assured that rest was healing, perhaps the best thing.

Just after she delivered the towel, a man started shouting and thrashing. Avril ran to him. He was big—an athlete. He was trying to get out of bed. She pushed him back down, cooing soothing things. He kept struggling. She pinned his arms on his chest with all her weight, aware that he could have bench-pressed her, but instead it was like tussling with a five-year-old. A very feverish five-year-old.

Doctors came rushing over, calling, "Keep him in bed!"

He began gasping in a weird way. Someone called, "Oxygen! Stat!"

Avril let up on his arms in case it would help him breathe easier. It made no difference. His eyes stayed wide with fear, his face in a rictus. Blood dribbled from his mouth. She didn't know what to do. His skin felt dry and hot. He kept fighting spasmodically.

"Cardiac arrest!" someone shouted, reading the monitor panel at the foot of the cot.

Equipment was being pulled over. She stepped away.

They attached things, they did things, they said things with practiced urgency. She kept backing away.

"What's going on?" someone in a cot rasped near her—an older woman, maybe from the university staff.

Avril had no good answer. "He had a heart attack," she said. "They're helping him. Can I get you anything?"

"I don't want to complain." She squeezed her eyes shut and rolled over, clutching her blankets tight.

"You'll get better faster if you're comfortable," Avril said.

"Mmm." Then: "I'm cold. I'm so cold."

"I can get you another blanket."

She fetched it from a supply shelf. Meanwhile work to resuscitate the athlete continued. She wrapped the woman in the blanket. She refreshed her water. She checked her temperature: a fever, but not as high as earlier, not in a danger zone. She noted everything.

By then they'd given up on the athlete. They rolled him out still in the bed, his face covered, blood seeping through the sheet over his mouth.

The next patient who died did it quietly. Only an alarm beep from the monitor screen alerted staff.

She continued to do what she could. She knew the ventilation was set on high and fans rumbled in the ceiling, but the air smelled of bleach and flowery cleaning fluid, of unwashed bodies and sweat, and as she cleaned and helped patients, close up they smelled of urine and feces and vomit. The sound of coughing and weeping and moaning and shouts echoed continuously.

Avril was helping, but nothing seemed to be helping very fast.

At sunset, the lights were lowered. She turned a corner in a hallway, and for a moment the cots before her with their white sheets and blankets looked like a military formation of ghosts waiting to rise up. . . . Her first impulse was to run. Her next one was to stand up straighter and stronger.

Shinta was down the hall in the other direction. Avril went to her, hoping she was still doing well—yes, no longer on oxygen. She lay on her side, her eyes open.

"Hey, how are you?"

She looked up, her eyes puffy, her hair a mess. "Can you get my phone? I want to call home."

"I can get you a proxy phone." She signed one out at the administration office and brought it to her. Should she stay while she called or give her privacy? Would she need help signing into the proxy? Then someone a few beds down wanted to go to the bathroom. If patients were lucid and could walk, they were encouraged to get up and get a little exercise.

When that was done and duly noted, she returned to Shinta. She was lying on her side again, eyes open.

"No one answered."

"I'm so sorry." Avril took off her glove and put her hand on hers for a while, then returned the phone to the office.

The staff sent Avril home in the late evening. Get some food, get some rest, see you tomorrow, thank you for your work. And change out of the scrubs and take a shower before leaving. Be sure to wash your hair. You're covered with contagion.

As she left the building, she noticed that it had rained. The air was warm and humid and smelled clean and good. She checked her phone, pinging her sisters and friends as she walked to the dorm. She ought to eat, but she had no appetite and went right to her room.

She called Mom so they could each assure each other that they were still fine. Mom had wept when Avril told her she was immune. When she'd told Dad how she'd been treated and nearly burned alive, he'd wept silently, just a few tears.

"But," he said, "do *not* tell your mother I wouldn't let them use you for extortion." It was their secret, and both of them were proud of it, but Mom would never understand.

He stayed busy at work recrafting the nation, Mom was helping her neighbors, Peng talked to her like a proud grandfather, and she and her new sisters offered one another sympathy and encouragement. Irene was coming back to Madison soon, heartbroken. Lillian and Berenike were keeping Milwaukeeans alive.

Everywhere anger burned red-hot. She had found what she could do best to contribute to the ongoing mutiny and would let others battle it out on other fronts for now. For now. This wasn't a setback, this was preparation, a gathering of strength for a big, long, hard fight.

\*     \*     \*

Lillian watched Berenike over breakfast. It was like a movie where there was a person who was young in one part of the movie and older in another part. They never appeared in the same scene, though, in a movie. Or maybe it was like a movie with clones, but usually they were both the exact same person, and they were both evil.

This was real life, and it was different. For one thing, they weren't evil. She was pretty sure about that.

Berenike was like Lillian in a lot of ways, except that she seemed to know what she was doing, and Lillian didn't. Too much had changed. Their breakfast was instant oatmeal, which somehow Berenike had found. Food had become scarce since everybody—well, not actually everybody—started getting sick and dying. It wasn't bad, oatmeal with bits of fake banana in it, just add hot water.

The electricity still worked. Berenike slept with a light on to make sure.

"You wanna come in to work again today?" Berenike asked.

"Of course I do." Lillian put sarcasm into her voice, but it was a joke.

"Well, I'd have to commandeer you if you said no." More joking.

They sat in Lillian's kitchen—Lillian's house, not her mom's house anymore because her mom's body had been taken away and they'd never see her again, maybe not even see her buried, but Berenike promised they would go to a ceremony someday soon to remember her.

"She sounds like a good mother," Berenike had said. Yes, and if Lillian thought about it any more, she'd feel like she should cry—but she wouldn't be able to cry, which bothered her and she didn't know why.

Berenike had offered to stay with her, as if Lillian had a choice. Lillian needed someone with her, no matter how uncomfortable it felt to know how hard everything was and how little she could do. She didn't even know where to find food. But Berenike had wanted to sleep on the sofa.

"No, use my mom's room. I think some of her clothes might fit you. She was so scared I'd be alone. She'd be glad if she knew about you." This had made Berenike smile, which she didn't do a lot. Lillian didn't smile much, either, especially if she was thinking.

Now she had three big sisters exactly like herself but no mother, which was a lot better than some people. But there was no school yet. People who were immune wore special plastic bracelets, and they both had one. Berenike took her with her to help and gave her important jobs, like unloading a truck. Sometimes the boxes were too heavy, but people would help, and she would tell them what to do—she could tell grown-ups what to do sometimes—and they did what she said. The world was strange and scary and sad and a little bit wonderful.

Yesterday Berenike had left Lillian at a community center for an hour to talk with other children whose parents had died. No one wanted to hug each other because they could spread the virus, so instead they raised their arms in a big circle in front of their body to show when they wanted to give someone a hug. They sat far apart around the edges of the room and talked about how they felt, which turned out to be scared, mostly. They also all felt sad, and the man leading the group explained how they could use their sadness to build memories of love to treasure, and their treasures would comfort them. They could make pictures or write songs and poems and stories.

Lillian had one memory she would make sure she never forgot. Someone banged on the door. Her mother's body was lying on the floor in the garage where she had collapsed and died just a little while ago. Lillian had no idea what to do. Maybe this was help. They kept saying on the news that people would help.

She opened the door and saw people who had come to arrest her and take her away, which was terrifying, then the police came and there was gunfire and it got even more terrifying, and then she saw someone who looked just like herself but lots older get out of a van. At that moment she knew she'd gone crazy and was seeing things that weren't real. The older version of herself spoke. It was her own voice. And she said: "I'm your sister."

Lillian didn't have a name for that feeling. She said to the other kids, "I don't know how I felt when my sister said she could take care of me because I didn't know I had a sister. It wasn't happy because I'm just not happy these days, but it was good, very good."

"Relief," a boy suggested.

"Love," someone else said.

"Supported."

"Safe. Wait, no, we can't be safe, not yet."

"Rescued," a girl said.

The feeling had really been safe, at least for that moment. She and her sisters couldn't get sick, and they'd help each other, and she was sort of safe. And maybe it was love, too. She wanted it to be love.

Berenike had been upstairs with a different group like Lillian's but for adults, then she talked with people at the community center who she knew. She spent most of her time at an office in City Hall figuring out what the city had and who needed to get it, sometimes making deliveries herself. Once Lillian had watched her talking to someone she had called. It sounded like an argument.

". . . And we will come there and load up what we need. We'll give you a receipt. You can send us a bill. . . . We can break down the door, and we won't pay for that. . . . I am deputized by the mayor as staff of emergency government operations, and I have the authority to commandeer what the people of the City of Milwaukee need. We'll be there in a half hour. My name is Berenike Woulfe. I'll be delighted to meet you."

She hung up and shook her head. "Most people are cooperative. But I wouldn't have a job if everything ran right." She didn't let Lillian come that time because it might be dangerous, so she asked Lillian to help at the information desk under the arches at the tower end of City Hall. Lillian was there when a boy, maybe four years old, came and asked for food. He was dirty and his hair wasn't combed.

"I'll get something," she said to the adults at the desk and ran inside to the table of sandwiches and juice. He looked up at Lillian when she handed him the food with wide eyes, and maybe he felt rescued. He ate the sandwich in huge bites while the adults fussed over him and tried to find him a place to stay. She hoped he was safe.

She told Berenike about it when she came back. Berenike nodded and said, "That's what we do."

Lillian didn't know what else to do, but it seemed like there was a lot more that needed to be done.

*　　*　　*

Berenike was remembering everything she'd hated about her old job. As far away as that job felt—five days now—the argument she was in seemed fresh and familiar.

"No," she said, "we can't give you those vans for tomorrow."

Then she was silent. That was a negotiating tactic. She'd dealt with this guy before, the new southeastern Wisconsin manager of AutoKar, who'd gotten the job by battlefield promotion. He had always been far, far too competitive, and he wanted everything he could get. Old Man Tito and the Summer Ngan prayer lady—who were alive, she'd checked—would have been better choices.

He'd even forwarded her contact information at City Hall to three customers who had pestered her: the imported-foods guy she'd had the cops shut down when the Prez's cold first hit, a clothing retailer, and a law firm, which had no need for a van, but the lawyers knew how to sound threatening. In fact, none of those three needed a van. Cars would do. And the AutoKar manager had no right to tie up her line with annoying, fake-intimidating people asking for what they didn't need.

Vans? No such luck, asshole. But he knew silence was a good negotiating tool, too, and he was trying to outwait her.

Finally, to get him off the line, she said, "We're going to need those vans to pick up and deliver medicines and the supplies to manufacture medicines. This is critical because we needed them yesterday. So no, we're not going to return the vans." *And you're contractually bound to maintain them anyway,* she could have added, and she wanted to gloat, but she had better things to do than to start an unnecessary argument.

"I don't have enough for my priority clients," he said, "let alone regular clients with real needs."

AutoKar had never had a big enough fleet. He knew that.

"I'm sorry. This is still an emergency," she said. And she terminated the call. Then she wondered why she'd said *I'm sorry.* She wasn't, and he didn't deserve the courtesy.

This was what she'd hated about her old job. Customer contact, including internal and business-to-business clients, and having to act responsible and proper rather than saying what she really wanted to tell people. As for the small fleet, she'd always believed that wasn't actually due to underinvestment. Instead, she suspected that Auto-Kar and its competitors had a secret agreement with private-car manufacturers to avoid becoming rivals. The shortage was designed to encourage people to go out and buy their own car.

Not much proof of that, though. A lot needed to change in the future about business transparency. A country couldn't run on bullshit and expect to solve problems. That had led to disasters like the Prez's cold. More disasters didn't have to happen. Worse, refugee camps were filled with people dead from the Prez's cold and then cholera, which was completely preventable, not just a dereliction of duty, actually probably deliberate. . . .

She was staring at nothing, pounding her fist on her desk. *Get back to work.* She had plenty of it.

The city didn't have a big enough fleet for everything it needed to do. So just as she had before the Prez's cold, she spent her days satisfying no one. Even worse, whenever she left the building, she saw private cars just sitting there waiting for their owners, and how many of those owners were dead? Probably hundreds of cars in Milwaukee alone now had no owners. They could be put to use.

Perhaps the city could ask people who had cars if they could share them. She'd proposed that to the mayor, and he said it was a great idea and he'd work on it, but he'd also looked like he was about to get sick. A quarter of his staff was out, and they weren't all coming back. Neal had survived a bullet, but then he got sick, and being already seriously injured . . .

Karen never recovered, either, although Nina and Deedee were fine and reshaping the businesses where they worked. Some of the news was good.

The rest . . . not enough cars, not enough medicine, not enough food, and broken supply chains. Her lunch had been mayonnaise on stale bread. Breakfast was banana oatmeal, which she'd pretended to like only for Lillian's sake, and it had cost twice what it should have. She didn't have much of an appetite anyway—well, that was one way to lose weight.

In a lot of places, including a couple of incidents in Milwaukee, fear of contagion hadn't staved off looting. In some places—too much chaos for exact numbers—local governments had collapsed due to loss of personnel or loss of authority, but that had happened in only one town run by a mutiny. Mutineers kept things going. Mostly, the lights were still on, despite actual gun battles with so-called patriots who couldn't read the writing on the wall. Working for the city meant she heard lots of news, lots of it bad. Fires in California were out of control. And a hurricane . . .

She was staring and pounding on the desk again. *Get back to work!*

She was also trying to coordinate a refugee caravan headed north, a thousand survivors of an Alabama camp that had to get out of the approaching hurricane's way. They needed food, shelter, clothing, medical care—and security, because so-called patriots were active in some areas. Transportation involved not just people but supplies timed with their arrival and departure. She wanted to strangle the self-proclaimed "realists" who thought the refugees should stay put. *They're surrounded by swampy mass graves. What are they supposed to do, stay there and die?* A lot of those "realists" hoped they would die. Fuck them and their . . .

*Take a deep breath. Think about something else.*

At City Hall, politicians and staff had debated a lot of issues and reached a consensus about one of them. The mutiny would have likely failed if the Prez and his supporters hadn't overreacted by introducing the Prez's cold. A lot of minds changed when ordinary citizens realized that they had been targeted for death, and only incompetence on the part of the Prez's supporters had saved them from total disaster.

Avril was working directly with patients, which she said she found fulfilling, but it had to be hell to watch people die every day. Irene hadn't found her mammoth, so she'd gone back to Madison, and they'd had a good, long talk about their mothers. They shared a lot of mixed feelings.

Lillian had been talking to both Irene and Avril and it clearly helped her, and probably them, too. Pseudo-Grandfather had called once and finally seemed to accept that he was the needy one, and she didn't owe him anything at all. He was lucky she hadn't pressed charges.

Lillian was a fighter. She'd offered to staff the atrium food table one day, and she had suggested commandeering a nearby sandwich franchise, closed for the duration, so City Hall could offer some food. That girl was smart—and energetic, too energetic, probably a sign of stress.

*Stale bread and mayo for everyone, thanks to her. Better than nothing.*

A message appeared on her screen and pulled her out of her thoughts. A pharmacy chain needed more insulin. Could Berenike accommodate that? No, but she'd juggle things until she could, shifting priorities until everyone would hate her with good reason. This job sucked exactly like her old one, and she had the job because she could do what no one else wanted to do. She spent most of her time stuck in a tiny office with no windows, staring at a screen until her eyes were tired. Except that now she was keeping people alive. She hoped.

A glance at her sleeve reminded her that she was wearing one of Lillian's mother's shirts.

Berenike was effectively a mother now. That night, on the way home, she'd ask Lillian about her mother. Lillian might find it therapeutic, and Berenike might learn more about how to emulate the woman whose bed she now slept in and whose clothes she wore and whose child she would raise.

That morning she'd gotten up after another night of poor sleep— waking up every couple of hours to see if the desk lamp was still on, then staying awake for a long time after that—and at first she didn't recognize where she was. Pink curtains, a rose-patterned bedspread . . . oh, yeah. With so much disaster around her, and such a bad experience with her own mother, could she avoid being a disaster for Lillian?

Because she really, really needed to punch someone, and sooner or later, that anger was going to boil over. She closed her eyes, took a deep breath, tried to center her thoughts the way the AI counselor had taught her in what seemed like ages ago, and she felt calmer—for a few minutes.

\*    \*    \*

I returned home to my little apartment a week after being dragooned into secret government service, and as I had hoped, my pet bird

warbled in his cage and my house plants were a healthy green, thanks
to Noah.

The bird, Milton, was a Grand Cayman thrush, a pretty gray and
white bird much like an American robin. I had helped bring the species back from extinction, a sweet-voiced, gentle bird that ate worms
and fruit, but Milton had been made blind as a chick by nest parasites, and I took him as a pet. He wouldn't survive in the wild, but I
could give him a loving home.

Similarly, I had made my children with love, and if I had a right
to ask one thing of them (which I didn't), it would be for them to love
one another. Would they love me? That would be too much to ask for.
But some of them spoke to me, and that was enough.

My drab neighborhood had been festooned with purple—not
every home, of course, but enough to enforce a kind of civility. (For
how long?)

Food was scarce, but Noah came with takeout pancakes. No one
was yet allowed to sit in a restaurant. "People feel betrayed," he said.
"By everyone. I mean, where was this mutiny when we needed it?
Months ago, maybe years? They could have done something." His
good nature had taken a turn—temporarily, I hoped. I tried to model
sensible goodwill.

"What matters," I said, "is what you want to change now. Here's
your chance."

As for work, I had been hired by a bigger, better research lab to
track the delta cold viruses as they mutated and responded to treatment, work as essential as it was repetitive. I had acquired the gleam
of respectability, and that flattering shine carried me through the
workday.

Before I could leave the Army installation, of course, I was debriefed
and deposed. A congressional investigative committee subpoenaed me
to sit in a conference room and speak via videocall to a pair of staff
members who needed to know what had happened. The search for
the guilty had already begun, and this was the first step. Eventually
I would testify again in the Senate's handsome Central Hearing
Facility, and perhaps this time my words would be heeded. Many of
the senators would be different people and perhaps more receptive.
My debriefing would help the staff prepare questions for the senators
on that day.

"Please begin from the moment you were invited to participate in
the research," a young man said after thanking me for taking the time
to speak to them (as if I had a choice) and expressing gratitude for my

service to my country and to freedom. He and his partner seemed to be in awe of me, and I basked in it, nagged by a hint of impostor syndrome.

But at one point he asked, "Why do you think they did this?"

I had thought about that question, reaching an answer so bitter it could curdle souls if I shared it. I had no interest in spreading that contagion, although it had already become a political pandemic on its own.

"I'm glad to tell my own story," I said, "but I can't tell the stories of the villains. They can speak for themselves."

He glanced down at a list of questions, momentarily deflated. Then he brightened, having found a way to get what he wanted by another route. "How do you know that they're villains?"

"By their carelessness, and by the consequences of their actions." I spoke for the rest of the afternoon on that point, and the two staff members signed off somber and shaken. Facts are stubborn things, and frequently forlorn.

Avril had spent the two-mile walk from campus through Madison to see Irene face-to-face for the first time trying to figure out why she felt nervous. Irene had invited her and the other sisters to her house— Irene's mother's house—so they could finally meet in person, but they had talked to each other a lot by phone already. They knew one another, right? Berenike was righteously angry, Lillian warily curious, Irene just plain sad, and herself? Thinner than she used to be.

And she knew what death looked like. She'd showered, but the stench seemed to linger, at least in her imagination. More cars drove down the road now, but things weren't back to normal yet. It was the same with people, and when they passed on the sidewalk, they gave each other a wide berth. The virus had settled down into a severe but survivable cold, but every cold looked like the Prez's cold from a distance.

She reached a neighborhood filled with three-family bungalows. A sign at the door of one of them said RUIZ STUDIOS. When she walked in, would it be the start of something or the end? She had once thought things could change fast. *Well, some things have changed.* And even if it took her whole life, she would make sure that certain things would never change back.

She walked up the wooden stairs, footsteps thumping, and waited on the porch for the door monitor to sense her presence.

\* \* \*

Berenike barely noticed the passing countryside, going a hundred miles per hour past fields and buildings. The trip from Milwaukee to Madison would last only an hour, and despite light traffic, she worried and scanned each vehicle they encountered. Countermutineers had morphed into something more like pirates, organized crime— although they were sure they were modern Robin Hoods. They had infiltrated scheduling databases and were ambushing traffic, so she'd arranged for herself and Lillian to travel in a truck loaded with automobile parts, poor plunder.

They passed a car sitting on the shoulder of the road. A woman waved for help. Berenike felt bad about not stopping, but she didn't dare offer help. Instead she called the local sheriff, but through a third party because she couldn't trust him, either. That sheriff hadn't declared a clear loyalty either way. *That criminal, cowardly* . . .

She was paying too much attention to traffic. She was neglecting Lillian.

"You okay?"

The girl looked up from her display and nodded. "Yeah, I'm doing homework." She looked down again, grumpy-faced, maybe annoyed at the interruption, maybe anxious and trying to hide it. Kids were changeable, hard to read, and hard to parent. Berenike was sure she was doing something wrong, but what?

The truck pulled into Madison and rolled through some side streets. Almost there.

\*        \*        \*

Lillian knew she was going to like her sisters because she'd talked to them all the time by phone and they were a lot like Berenike. They all looked the same but were different ages and had other little differences, which was weird. Most of all, it was like looking in mirrors that showed what she would be like when she was older. She had a lot to think about before the meeting, though. Irene had promised they could talk to the scientist who'd designed them. He'd answer any question, she'd promised. So she was thinking about questions, and she already had a lot.

Now the truck was stopping, and she could barely breathe. Avril was standing on the porch.

\*        \*        \*

Irene had moved back to Madison and found herself living in a haunted house, haunted by her mother, whose ashes from the crematorium now sat in an urn in what had been her bedroom. The art on the walls haunted Irene—no, it reminded her of how her mother had called Irene a work of art. And how she'd been possessive and perfectionistic about all of her art.

*No, stop. Don't speak ill of the dead.*

Instead, she should miss her mother. Miss her, yes. Forget her, no. What if Mamá had known that Irene wasn't unique? Perhaps it was best to keep her ashes safely upstairs for now. On the Day of the Dead, she'd build a shrine and make some of Mamá's favorite foods and have a long chat with her, and maybe it would end with some happy memories and a celebration.

Her phone rang, a number she didn't know.

"Hello, Irene Ruiz?" A smiling man in a brown jacket was standing in a forest. "Nimkii is here. Let me show you." He turned the camera to show the mammoth on the other side of a river, standing among the reeds. Nimkii sloshed the water with his trunk, keeping an eye on the man. "Someone spotted him this morning. This is the Chequamegon-Nicolet National Forest. I'm a ranger here."

The front door chimed.

# ACKNOWLEDGMENTS

I want to thank many people for their advice and encouragement during early drafts of this novel, including my agent, Jennifer Goloboy, my editor at Tor, Jennifer Gunnels, and the Edgy Writers Workshop, especially Michael Gullette, Mike Parilla, Zack Geoffroy, and Michael Ryan Chandler.

Work began on this novel long before the COVID-19 pandemic, and it was finished as the scope of the disaster was becoming clear. I am heartbroken by the suffering and loss, and I am inspired by the strength that so many have shown.

# ABOUT THE AUTHOR

**Sue Burke** is the author of the novels *Semiosis* and *Interference,* as well as short stories, translations, and journalism. Her work has been nominated for the Arthur C. Clarke Award, the Campbell Memorial Award, and the Locus Best First Novel Award, and she won the 2016 Alicia Gordon Award for Word Artistry in Translation. She lives in Chicago.

sueburke.site